An immortal Egyptian Prince, a monstrous shapeshifter, an impossible romance . . . blends magical realism, horror, and romance.

"Thrilling fantasy... gripping story... mythical fantasy blending Egyptian history throughout the alluring narrative."
Literary Titan Golden Book Award

In this contemporary supernatural fantasy, the horror element starts in the beginning and continues to loom just over the horizon as the story progresses. The engaging narrative switches swiftly between the present day and ancient Egypt - a gripping supernatural tale that combines two different timelines, capturing the past and present through eternal devotion between two soulmates.
Lit Amri for Readers' Favorite
Silver Medal Award

"Intrigue and supernatural horror . . .a complex series of involvements that test Krista's courage and her ability to love and trust another. Add an

engrossing Egyptian back-story for a mystery/
fantasy exploration that will leave readers guessing
to the end."
Midwest Book Review

'This book was so good I could not put it down, it
held me from first word to last, an exciting tale of
ancient Egypt with a beautiful love story woven into
modern day."
Jeangoony

"Page turner to the end.'
Mike Midthun

From The

PAINTED TOMB

Something Ancient is on its Way

Brenda Hill

ISBN 978-0-578-87953-6

BrendaHill.com

LCP

USA

Cover by BrendaH
Formatted by Polgarus Studio

OTHER TITLES by BRENDA HILL

Paranormal:

The House on Serpent Lake

Mystery/Suspense:

With Full Malice
Ten Times Guilty
Beyond the Quiet

For A Complete List:

www.amazon.com/Brenda-Hill/e/B002BODTK6/

BONUS EXCERPT:
The House on Serpent Lake: A Haunting Story of Timeless Love

MY THANKS TO:

M. Jean Pike, fellow writer and dear friend, whose literary writing and beautiful stories never fail to inspire me, and who always listens when I need to bounce ideas. Thanks, friend.

Janis Patterson: thanks for your time and sharing some of your vast knowledge about

Egypt, a fascinating country, both past and present.

Cindy Finkelstein, spot-on Beta-reader. Thanks for your helpful comments. They certainly improved my story.

To Linda Monson Powell. Loved your contribution. Thanks!

Linda Campbell, life-long friend who, years ago changed my life.

Maxine Piotrowski, sister in heart.

Mary Littleton, friend and supporter.

Joanna Lattery, Crosby, MN former mayor.

Mike Midthun, Retired MN Crosby, MN Police Dispatch/Records Mgr/Evidence Tech.

Mary Bowman, whose response to my stories encourages me to write yet another one.

And always, my love and thanks to Roger & Michelle, who continue to drop everything and respond to my SOS calls.

To Mae and Kyle, the lights in my life.

From The

PAINTED TOMB

FROM THE PAINTED TOMB

ONE

The first howl pierced the night and echoed through the deserted state park. Birds took flight. Frogs and crickets went silent. Krista Hawthorne stiffened on the bench overlooking Lune River.

"What was that?" She scanned the frost-covered grounds around her and peered through the heavily-wooded Appalachian forest. What was out there?

Beside her, Todd Mitchell chuckled. "Coyotes. They won't hurt you. They're just as afraid of us as we are of them."

He didn't seem alarmed, so maybe it was just a coyote, although that howl was unlike anything she'd ever heard: deeper, stronger, and aggressive, as if from a maddened animal. Krista listened intently for another sound, but water splashing over river boulders was all she could hear in the black night. She tried to relax and enjoy the rest of the October evening, her first night out since her transfer.

But something felt wrong. The forest creatures were too quiet.

"There. Now take a look." Todd directed her attention back to the water. Over the far bank, the rising full moon cleared the trees and cast an iridescent reflection on the river, its silver streaks rippling with the current.

"Oh, how beautiful. Just like you said."

After growing up with sagebrush and cactus in the Sonoran Desert region of Arizona, Krista loved the lush forests and rivers in the West Virginia mountains. But in the month since her move, she had been too busy settling into her job and apartment to see much of her new state. Or to socialize.

And she had been so lonely.

Still, when Todd, the newspaper's senior reporter, suggested an evening out, she'd hesitated. She had no interest in another relationship—not this soon, maybe never again. But after another weekend alone in her small apartment, she'd caved, agreeing to go only if they went as friends and she paid her own way.

"You'll have to see what this town is famous for," Todd had said over dinner. "When the full moon rises over the river, it's a beautiful sight, one you shouldn't miss. It's a town requirement, you know, for all new residents." He grinned, looking so nice with his blond hair freshly trimmed and a pullover covering his large frame that she smiled in return. "And I promise," he added, "you won't forget it."

She should have realized that with the park

closed, there would be no facilities. And no lighting. While the scent of pine from the surrounding forest lingered in the air, she could distinguish only vague outlines of the trees and brush.

She wouldn't be able to see if anything was creeping up on them.

A cold breeze blew off the water and ruffled her penny-colored curls. She caught a slight fishy scent along with a hint of musk. Canine? Were wolves in the area? Ice prickled her spine and she shivered, suddenly reminded they were the only people in the park.

Todd moved closer and for a moment, she felt grateful for the warmth.

The moon hovered over the river, its radiance bright against the indigo sky. Cast in its brilliance, the trees and bushes took shape. Krista should have felt relieved, but something was off. Unnatural.

Why were the frogs still silent?

She scanned the woods around her and peered into the brush. Nothing moved, but her heart raced with a primal urge to run.

She took a deep, calming breath. She didn't want Todd to think she was easily frightened. As the lead reporter, he could recommend fluff pieces instead of actual news, and she wanted to write things important to her new community, things of which she could be proud.

And she desperately needed a reason for pride. Her ego had been so severely wounded she didn't know if she'd ever recover.

A soft rustle sounded a few feet beyond the pines. Without moving, barely breathing, she whispered, "Something's out there."

Todd glanced up. "Just an owl taking flight."

"Shhh. Don't talk so loud. Something might hear you."

"There's nothing out here except that owl." He laughed and pointed to the bird fleeing the area, its wings brushing stark tree limbs. "See? That's what you're hearing. Don't worry, I'm big and strong. I'll protect you." He tried to draw her into his arms, but she pulled away.

So far he'd respected her wishes to spend the evening as friends, but now she wondered. He'd been a gentleman and she had enjoyed the evening — until the howl and the uneasy feeling something was out there, watching them.

"Let's leave." She kept her voice to a whisper.

"Relax. The evening's young. We should get to know each other." He slipped an arm around her shoulder and dropped his hand to her right breast. All of her senses, already on alert, went into overdrive. Before she could react, he pulled her toward him and eased his other hand under her jacket. She wrestled free and sprang from the bench.

"I told you I wasn't interested in anything more than friendship."

"Aw, come on." Smiling, he tried to pull her back down. "Why'd you think I brought you out here? With all that red hair, there has to be fire underneath that ice, and I'm the man to ignite it."

"I'm leaving." She spun around and headed for his truck.

He jumped to his feet and trailed after her. "Hey, what's the harm? I just wanted to get friendly."

"Your idea of friendly isn't the same as mine." She knew nothing about him, only that he had been courteous at the office, taking the time to show her around and making sure she knew the routine.

He caught her, grabbed her arm and pulled her to a stop.

"What's the big deal? You're not some shy virgin."

That stung. At thirty-two, with only her former fiancé as a lover, she felt like one. She yanked her arm free.

"Look. We obviously expected different things from tonight, so this isn't going to work. Please take me home and we'll forget this ever happened."

What was she thinking, agreeing to go out with him? Weren't the wounds she carried from the last time she'd trusted raw enough? Never again, she swore, heading for his red Tacoma. Once home, she'd make some hot tea and try to forget this evening. No more dates, no matter how lonely she felt, no more failed expectations. She'd live for her new job with no romantic attachments and no traumas.

Dried leaves encrusted with ice crunched under her feet. His truck stood about ten feet ahead. She didn't want to ride back with him, but the state park was miles from their small mountain town.

He strode past her, turned and blocked her way.

He stood too close, his bulk outweighing her petite frame by a hundred pounds. She took a step back.

"Todd . . ." Was he drunk? But no, they'd each had only one mixed drink at dinner, then coffee afterward. Drugs? That would account for his ruddy complexion, but wouldn't she have noticed if he'd been high?

Eyes narrowed, he stepped closer.

"Just stay where you are." She backed up another step and kept her voice firm, as if she were speaking to a hostile animal. It broke in a tremor. How could this be happening? Keeping an eye on him, she checked the grounds for a stick, a rock, anything she could use as a weapon.

"You think I'm going to force you or something? Don't worry, sis. I've never had to strong-arm any woman. But I put out for a nice meal, and I'd think you'd be willing to put out too."

"I tried to pay for my dinner, but you —"

Dried vegetation crunched behind Krista as someone or some thing trampled through the leaves. She whirled around and scanned the underbrush, a hundred wild thoughts racing through her mind. Who was there? What was moving out there?

Todd peered into the brush. "What the hell . . ."

"Shhh . . ." Slowly, cautiously, she stepped around him and toward his truck. If they kept quiet, maybe whatever it was would go away. It had been insane to visit a deserted campground this time of year, especially one in a state park that bordered the national forest. Wild animals could easily invade the site since it had closed for the season.

A deep rumbling growl, soft and menacing, sounded from the foliage. Every nerve in Krista's body reacted. Her frantic gaze met Todd's, and they ran for his pickup. Behind them, a twig snapped, then another. Deep thuds pounded toward them.

Todd reached the truck just ahead of Krista. He jumped in and started the engine. Krista grappled for the passenger door handle. It was locked. She pounded on the door.

"Let me in!" Looking wildly behind her, she expected to see a bear or a pack of wolves breaking from the trees.

"You wanted to be Miss Independence, now's your chance." Todd flipped her the finger and gunned the engine. His truck shot down the blacktop road.

"Todd!" She ran after him, but his truck didn't slow. Stunned, she stared incredulously at the red taillights receding in the night.

"God . . ." He left her, actually left her alone. She whipped around, scanning the area for a bush large enough to hide behind, or a tree with heavy branches.

A second howl ripped the night wide open, a lingering, inhuman wail that reverberated through her mouth, her eyes, her skull, penetrating every sense with terror.

What in God's name was it? She'd never heard such a sound, not even in the movies. Her heart pounded in her throat. She dashed across the road and ducked behind a thick oak.

Did it see her? Afraid to look, terrified if she rose and peered around the tree she'd come face to face with some ungodly creature, she stayed hidden. And still as death.

Thumping noises from something massive pounded away from her. Krista didn't realize she'd been holding her breath until she gasped for air.

Did that creature know she'd hidden? Would it come back to look for her?

She had to get out of there, had to let the authorities know something dangerous was loose in the forest. Something terrifying.

She reached for her handbag and her phone. And went cold. Her phone was in her handbag, and her bag was in Todd's truck.

What was she going to do? She had nothing—no car, no credit cards, no cash, no phone to call for help.

Would she make it through the night?

TWO

Krista crouched low, her senses alert for any sound, but the forest was so still she could only hear her own breathing. If she moved and stepped on a dry pinecone, would the animal hear the crunch?

She had to try. She had to find the highway and get home.

If only she knew what kind of creature was out there. Had it left the area? She rose and risked a quick glance around, but the tall firs and pines blocked most of the moonlight, and she could barely see the road.

She took a few hesitant steps away from her hiding place, stopping and listening for footsteps, a growl. After a few seconds of silence, she used the cover of underbrush and crept to the side of the road.

A tension hung in the air, the atmosphere heavy. Charged. The fine hairs stiffened on her arms and the back of her scalp. She found herself breathing heavily, nearly panting, ready to flee at the first sign of the beast. She glanced uneasily around her, peering through the dense forest bordering both sides of the road.

An animal's enraged roar split the night. Krista froze and peered ahead, her heart thumping crazily in her throat. The squeal of heavy brakes followed. Todd's truck? Had he heard that terrible roar and realized he couldn't leave her? *Please, oh please . . . .* Keeping to the shoulder, Krista hurried toward the pickup.

The truck's brake lights flashed several times. Todd had stopped, thank God. *Thank you, thank you.* She'd be safe, and they could get out of there.

The moon hung over the trees, but drifting clouds threw veiled shadows and she could barely see the road ahead. Only the red taillights stood as beacons in the night. She hurried on.

Sudden screams nearly stopped her heart, frantic, hysterical screams. Todd. That animal must have seen his taillights too.

Against every instinct urging Krista to hide, she moved forward in measured steps, trying to see through the haze of patchy light. His truck appeared about fifteen feet ahead. The driver's door lay on the ground, and something . . . something taller than the truck was reaching into the cab.

Todd screamed again and again.

In the dappled light from the veiled moon, Krista caught flashes of movement, as if a video were rhythmically playing and pausing, images of something huge, standing upright, grabbing Todd, hauling him out . . . massive paws, claws ripping, slicing his flesh. A bear? She tried to make sense of what she was seeing.

Todd screamed again. She had to help him. She scanned the edge of the forest for a tree limb, a stick, anything to distract the enraged creature. But nothing took shape in the blackness.

Barely moving, praying to avoid the bear's notice, she took a hesitant step on the graveled shoulder and put her foot down slowly, toes first, as silently as she could. Her heart pounded so loudly she feared the creature could hear it.

Her foot slid on a rock. She stumbled. She clamped a hand over her sharp intake of breath. Too late. The beast turned its head to her, red eyes burning with fury, mouth open in a snarl. At least seven feet tall, it was covered in dark fur. No snout.

That was no bear!

In that instant, the moon slid from behind the clouds, throwing full light on the beast. A humanoid face, the skin dark, almost black to match its fur. Pieces of clothing clung to its body. Tattered human clothing. From around its neck, she caught a brief shimmer of some sort of medallion. Fangs several inches long dripped saliva.

But the eyes, narrowed in rage, were nearly human as the beast glared at her.

What in God's name was that thing?

Holding its prey in razor claws, it stared at her.

She rose slowly, unable to look away. Todd's panic-stricken eyes found hers. He tried to speak. Blood flooded his mouth and ran down his chin.

Krista desperately wanted to help, but she stood helplessly frozen. Nausea rose like a solid menace, burning, threatening to spew. She forced it down. She couldn't be sick; she had to do something, anything, or Todd was going to die.

He moaned her name, a soft plea. A swipe of claws silenced him. He screamed, the sound ending in a gurgle. Jagged wounds gushed red.

The ground swayed under Krista's feet.

Fangs bared, the beast pulled its prey close.

Todd frantically struggled against the powerful claws.

With a frenzied snarl, the creature leaned in and ripped out his throat. Blood splattered. Bits of muscle and sinew dangled from its mouth. Todd's struggling body stilled. Only a ragged tendon held his head on his lifeless body.

Eyes wide, Krista couldn't breathe.

The creature threw the corpse aside as if it were weightless. Mouth dripping red, gore hanging from bloodied fangs, it turned its gaze on her.

Panic surged through her body, releasing her frozen limbs. She raced across the road, through the bushes, stumbling blindly over branches and twigs, knowing she couldn't outrun that thing.

Her toe caught a half-buried tree limb. She floundered, then hit the ground so hard she lay paralyzed. She gasped for air.

The creature loped toward her. The ground thumped.

Krista struggled to get to her feet, but the ground swayed dangerously. She fell to her knees.

The creature burst through the bushes.

She was going to die.

She closed her eyes. Waited for the sharp claws to rip her flesh. Would it hurt beyond all reason? Would she feel each tear? Or would she mercifully black out and feel nothing?

A second. Two seconds. Three. Nothing moved. She heard nothing but the swish of blood rushing to her head.

She opened her eyes. The creature was staring at her, blood- red eyes locked onto hers. From around its neck a silver ankh medallion glistened, an icon similar to the pendant she always wore. Why was this nightmarish monster wearing an Egyptian symbol?

The beast huffed.

Krista didn't want to die on her knees, so slowly, laboriously, she rose to her feet. The image of her mother's grief-stricken face flashed before her.

"I'm sorry, Mom," she whispered.

One long moment of waiting, then two. And more. Why didn't the creature get it over with? She couldn't stand this unbearable agony.

"What are you waiting for? Dammit, do something!"

A rumbling growl started low in its belly, a sound so horrific that a tear formed and rolled down Krista's cheek.

Staring at her, the beast remained motionless, then huffed again and slowly backed away. After one lingering look at her, it turned and crashed through the forest.

Krista stood motionless, not believing what had happened.

Why was she still alive? Would it be back?

Her moment of bravado gave way. Bursting into tears, she sank to the ground, giving in to all the anguish and terror she had endured. She tried to keep quiet, but the sobs came uncontrollably, and she wept until she was too weak to shed another tear.

Finally, wiping her face on her sleeve like a child, she sat quietly. What was she going to do?

Somehow, she had to survive and let the authorities know what happened. That creature had to be stopped.

A cold breeze swayed barren oak branches. Dry leaves swirled. She'd heard a snowstorm was moving into the area, and already the temperature was dropping. With only a jacket over jeans and a pullover sweater, she didn't have much of a chance. If that thing, whatever it was, didn't come back for her, she could die of exposure. She had to keep moving, keep her body temperature up.

She should check on Todd, but she could do nothing for him. He was dead. His truck was her way out of the park, but that would mean she'd have to leave his body here, get the authorities, and come back for it. Or, she'd have to try to get him into the truck.

Could she do it? If she could bear to look at his mangled bloody body, could she manage to get him into the truck?

She had to try.

Just as she reached the road, she hesitated. The beast could be with Todd's body, feasting. Her stomach curled. She doubled over and lost her dinner. After wiping her mouth, she sat back.

Did she really want to go back to the truck? Not only did she not want to see what might be occurring, but she didn't want to risk another encounter with the beast. For some unfathomable reason, it let her live, but should she chance it again? Better to keep to the woods. She could parallel the road back to the highway and flag down someone with a phone.

Creeping through the brush, she kept the road in sight. When she spotted the pickup just ahead, she curved deeper into the forest and moved as quietly as she could.

A rustling sound came from her left. She swallowed and peered through the trees. Nothing moved. Judging from the slight sound, she thought it had to be a small animal.

After a few moments of silence, she continued her hike. *Don't look to either side, just straight ahead, left foot, right foot.* That would get her to the highway.

A frigid gust of wind sent chills from her legs to her neck. She shivered, wishing she had worn a heavier jacket. Damn Todd! If she froze to death, he could be brought up on charges for abandoning her.

Of course, she realized, almost hysterically. He had been damned. The beast had seen to that. But she wouldn't be its next victim. She would push on, survive. Her brother's death in a skirmish in the Middle East had left her as an only child, and she doubted her widowed mother would recover from her loss as well. Krista had planned to move her to the area as soon as she felt settled so they could both start over, but now, everything had changed. No way would she live anywhere near that beast. And she certainly couldn't bring her mother here.

Her heart hammering, she took another step, but she felt so exhausted she could barely draw a breath. Her wobbly legs wouldn't hold her. Desperately needing to rest, she found a large pine and ducked underneath. With her back against the trunk, she scanned the area around her. If the creature found her, she wanted to see it coming.

Her teeth chattered. She raised the collar of her jacket and rubbed her arms for warmth. Her toes were numb. She should be safe at home under her warm comforter instead of freezing in an isolated park, keeping watch for some kind of fiend from Hell. Worse, she had watched a man die. Horribly. All because she'd been lonely.

She should have kept to the vow she'd made before her move: no more commitments or emotional involvements, no more allowing herself to trust. Having faith in someone only led to heartbreak. Tonight she'd learned she couldn't even trust a friend, or someone she thought was a friend. Her judgment was totally skewed, and because of that, she wound up at the mercy of a horrendous creature. If she got out of this alive, she'd never again allow weakness to put her in a vulnerable position.

Her eyelids felt heavy. She leaned against the trunk. She'd rest . . . for only a moment. Her thoughts faded. Her eyes drifted shut.

No! She jerked awake. She must not sleep. She had to keep watch.

But no matter how she fought, her eyes kept closing.

Before sleep overtook her, she saw again the bloody fangs, the nearly human face and eyes.

What was that thing?

And why hadn't it killed her?

THREE

Memphis, Egypt
Prince Rahmor Lupaster 3rd son of Thutmose III
1479 BC to 1425 BC
18th Dynasty

Prince Rahmor shifted in his ebony chair, third from Pharaoh's throne, and tried to summon interest in the parade of ambassadors, petitioners, and bounty from his father's latest military conquest. He couldn't wait to escape the confines of the palace, the stink of bodies the perfumed braziers failed to mask, and taste the rushing wind from his new chariot.

On the king's right sat Rahmor's older brother Amenemhat, firstborn and heir to the throne. As one of Pharaoh's generals, he'd led the king's division during the invasion of upper Canaan and Syria.

The battle had gone well.

As third in line to the throne, the bounty had little interest for Rahmor, but he loved and honored his father, so he curbed his impatience as well as he could.

The procession inched toward the throne, slowing even more as the people stared at the grandeur surrounding them.

Three rows of colossal limestone columns the color of the great sands lined each side of the hall, each meticulously painted with scenes from Pharaoh's military campaigns. Statues of polished granite bearing the king's likeness soared toward the ceiling, and from a side corridor, the music of lyres, harps, and flutes filled the air. Dancers, nude except for dyed feathers and jewelry, swayed and pranced before the seated musicians. Every few feet along the ceremonial hallway, incense of pine resin, cinnamon, and Frankincense burned in copper braziers, their dancing flames gleaming on the golden figures of the gods.

Nothing so grand stood in their homeland, Rahmor knew. As pharaoh's son, he'd joined his brothers in battle and had witnessed the scarcity of riches and simple luxuries in the lands of upper Canaan. While he understood the people's awe, he wished the lines would move more rapidly.

The procession slowed before the towering figure of Sekhmet, a goddess with the head of a lioness, her lustrous headdress flowing over her shoulders. Jabbed from behind, the people inched forward again, staring openly at the figure of Amun-Ra, King of the Gods, who wore the headdress of two tall plumes. They slowed to a crawl before Osiris. Rahmor smiled. He had to admit the icon was impressive. The artisans had crafted the god beautifully, painstakingly mixing their paints to get the exact shade of green for the face.

At a nod from Pharaoh, palace guards prodded the lagging procession into moving forward at a faster pace.

One by one the Canaanites and Syrians approached the king, prostrating the customary seven times before speaking. Tributes of sheep and goats were given, favors asked and were granted according to how the deed might affect the Egyptian people's welfare.

Pharaoh wore his blue military headdress and held the crook and flail with quiet dignity. A leopard skin lay across his shoulders signifying fearlessness and strength.

While not as elaborately dressed as his father, Rahmor, like his brothers, wore a wrapped kilt secured by a golden belt, and on his feet, braided leather sandals. His wig, face paint, golden collar, and arm bands completed his dress.

His sisters wore their customary light-weight sheath dresses of sindon muslin from the flax plant, but their pleated shawls of bright reds and lapis with woven threads of gold proclaimed their status.

Rahmor shifted again. While proud of this latest victory in which he, as well as his brothers took their places as armed warriors of the king, his attention wandered, scarcely noticing the long line of people and animals. He tried to find a comfortable position, but because he stood several hands above his brothers, even sitting he drew attention.

Amenemhat frowned. Since his appointment as regent, the first-born took his title seriously and felt it his duty to keep his siblings in line. While Rahmor understood the importance of his position, he regretted the loss of his favorite hunting and game-playing cohort.

He stiffed a yawn, silently counting the bows from the latest petitioner. How could his father endure sitting so still and regal hour after hour? Would this day never end?

Then she appeared, pushed forward by the other women captives.

And everything changed.

Even though she was bounty of the conquered and forced into a strange land, she stood, shoulders back, head up. Hair the color of flame, slim as the Nile reeds, she moved with the grace of a queen. A knotted girdle gathered her simple garment under her breasts, and the ragged dress fell in heavy folds to the floor.

Then he caught it—the slightest quiver in that proud chin. No one else saw it, he was sure. But his heart warmed.

She stepped forward, her bare feet showing beneath her dress. She faced forward, but Rahmor could see her eyes darting frantically from sight to sight, never lingering—until her gaze met his.

His breath caught.

Eyes the color of the deepest green malachite used to honor Osiris, her gaze was steady, holding his for the longest moment. Heat spread through his body. Still he couldn't break the connection between them.

The woman behind her jabbed her forward with an elbow. Rahmor had to restrain himself from leaping off the dais to throttle the woman.

Several women scurried forward to join the copper-haired woman, and they all bowed deeply before the throne. Words were exchanged between Pharaoh, the pharaoh's viceroy, the woman, and the woman's interpreter. Rahmor heard nothing but a loud buzz. He felt inflamed, captured by the intensity of her gaze. When Pharaoh nodded and whispered to his viceroy, both turned their attention upon the woman. She turned her head the slightest again to Rahmor, a flicker of panic flashing in her eyes.

Rahmor tried to read the expression in his father's eyes. What were the king's intentions toward this woman?

At Pharaoh's nod, the women were separated. All but one—the copper-haired beauty—were shuttled outside. To be held as concubines or servants, Rahmor knew. A guard led the redhead to a side hallway, which meant she was to be added to the king's harem. Obviously he wasn't the only one captivated by her beauty.

Could he prevent that from happening? His father was a generous man who'd shown little interest in his harem in the past few years, hadn't even visited the chambers since he'd sustained an abdominal injury during a military skirmish in the North. Pharaoh had occasionally granted his son access when one of the women caught his eye. Would his father allow him to add the red-haired one to his own harem?

But when he saw his father's gaze follow the woman, he knew.

He had no chance.

FOUR

A steady chirping woke Krista, definitely not her alarm clock. Prying open her eyes, she caught a flash of bouncing red. She concentrated on the reddish blur, trying to make sense of what she was seeing. Finally a red bird came into focus. A cardinal.

Around her, the underbrush came alive in the sun's golden rays. Morning! Stiff with cold, she sat up, vigorously rubbing her arms for some warmth. She hadn't meant to sleep so long, but thankfully, she had survived the night.

The whoosh an eighteen-wheeler sounded from nearby. She must be closer to the highway than she'd realized.

She brushed twigs and bits of pinecone from her hair and stood, tromping in circles to get her cramped legs moving. She pulled her jacket tight, then crunching through the blanket of dead leaves, she found her way to the blacktop road. Rounding a curve, she spotted the highway just ahead. She'd made it!

A diesel had just passed, but a car, a sedan, was approaching.

Frantically waving her arms, she ran toward the car, but the sedan swerved around her and kept going. Two more cars passed before a faded blue pickup stopped.

The slim elderly driver rolled down his window. "What's the matter, little lady? Car trouble?"

"I need your help! Can I use your phone?"

"Let's take a look-see. Maybe I can fix it."

"It's not car trouble. My friend and I were a attacked last night!"

"You were attacked? Who did it? Is your friend all right?"

Now that help had arrived, Krista found it difficult to speak. What she'd been through was too overwhelming—and unbelievable. She shook her head and gestured toward the park's tree-lined entrance a few feet away. "He-he's still in there. Please, I have to call the sheriff." She shivered and ran her hands briskly up and down her arms.

"Let's get you into the warm truck." After she was settled in the passenger seat, the man grabbed a jacket from underneath, covered her, and flipped the heater to high. "There. Now you'll feel better." He thumbed back his hat and pulled out an older cell phone from his glove compartment. "Tell me what happened."

The truck's heater spread warmth to Krista's hands and feet. Safe at last, she wanted only to curl up and sleep. But she couldn't let Todd lie out there all alone, and she had to alert the authorities about that monster.

"We were in the campsite and a huge black monster attacked us. I got away, but it killed him."

"It killed him? Sorry, little lady. I'll let the sheriff know." He flipped the top of his phone. "Must've been a black bear. They're common in these woods, although they're not usually that violent."

"It wasn't a bear. This thing was huge, with big fangs and claws like in the horror movies. And it had red eyes."

He paused and studied her for a long moment. "Lady, did you have a few too many last night?"

"Do I look drunk?" Realizing she probably looked and sounded like a lunatic, she tried to speak in a calm voice. "Please, we're wasting time. Whatever it was, my friend is dead. Still in the campground."

After another long moment, the man punched some numbers into his phone and handed it to her.

"Boone County Sheriff's Office. How can I help you?"

Krista took a deep breath and willed herself to speak clearly. "I need to report some kind of monster in the state park. It attacked my date last night and killed him." Despite her efforts, her voice rose.

"Ma'am, slow down please. You saw a monster in the park?"

"Yes!" She didn't want to sound hysterical. She needed him to believe her.

"O-kay. What kind of monster?"

She detected a difference in his tone, as if he were humoring her. She gritted her teeth and forced a level tone. "Look. I know how this sounds, but my date was attacked by a huge monster with black fur. It killed him then came after me."

The cop sighed. Heavily. "Where did this take place?"

"Near . . ." She gestured to the woods.

"Planter's Grove," the old man supplied. "The state campground outside the city."

"I heard him," the cop said. "Hold on a moment."

Krista heard paper-shuffling noises.

"It'll be a few moments, ma'am. I'm checking with the park ranger."

Krista almost screamed. What was taking so long? Didn't he realize everyone's lives were in danger? Something from out of a horror movie was alive. And killing people.

"The park's closed for the season, ma'am."

"I know that! I'm new to the area, so my date took me there to see the river." She paused, curbed her impulse to scream, and tried to sound rational. "Look, that's not important. What is important is that he's dead. That monster killed him. Can't you understand?" Frustration made her voice rise a couple more notches. She had to gain control and make herself understood. "You have to send someone right now. A search party to track it down. With large guns."

"We'll check it out, ma'am. Thanks for calling."

She heard a click, then the line went silent. She

stared unbelievingly at the dead phone. It was too much. After watching a murderous creature slaughter her friend, running for her own life, then spending the night freezing in the wilderness, she didn't deserve a brush-off. Especially not from the sheriff. Outrage tightened her stomach and rose to her throat, nearly choking her.

"You okay?" The old man's face held concern.

"He hung up," she managed through tightened lips. "That cop actually hung up on me." She clamped her teeth together so she wouldn't lash out at the old man. After all, he'd stopped for her, and even if he didn't quite believe her story, he was trying to help.

"I'm sure they get a lot of crank calls," he said, his voice sympathetic, "especially since it's Halloween weekend." The old man studied her a moment, then took the phone from her clenched hand. "I don't know what happened, but I'm believing you saw something. If there's a rogue bear or a pack of wolves in the campground, they should know. I'm Harlan, and I'll tote you to the station. Maybe they'll listen if you tell them face-to-face."

A one-story brick building on the outskirts of Marsh Springs housed the Sheriff's Office. Tall pines shaded the front door and threw shadows on the two vehicles parked in the gravel side lot—a dark state patrol SUV with the West Virginia seal on the front door, and a larger black SUV with splashes of dried mud on the side.

"It figures. Looks like they pay as much attention to their property as they do to citizens needing help." Krista jumped out of Harlan's truck before he shut off the engine and stormed through the building's glass door, wishing it were one of the old-fashioned wood ones that slam with a loud bang.

A thin cop in his mid-to-late-twenties looked up from the front desk. Behind him, three desks were unoccupied as was the entryway bench.

"Can I help—"

"Are you the asshole who hung up on me?"

"Uh . . ." He flushed, the pale pink clashing with his forest-green uniform.

"I called from the state park about fifteen minutes ago," she raged on, her voice not quite as sharp, "and I needed help. Why didn't you help me instead of hanging up? Is that what cops do in this town?"

The discomfited deputy spun his swivel chair around to face a back doorway.

"Uh, Sheriff? You're needed up front." His wide-eyed gaze swung back to Krista. "Now, please?"

A giant of a man in jeans and a disheveled white shirt strolled in from the doorway, a coffee mug in his hand.

Krista hadn't socialized since her move, hadn't heard anything about the sheriff, but the man before her was far from what she might have expected. He had to be at least six-four, mid-to-late thirties. Dark wavy hair brushed the top of his open-collar shirt.

Eyes a deep hazel, more gold than green. Shoulders broad enough to match his height.

"I'm the asshole who hung up on you. Sorry. Thought it was the usual prank call for Halloween." He offered his hand to Krista. "I'm Sheriff Rawlins. What can I do for you?" He yawned and tried to cover it. "Sorry."

"Am I keeping you up?"

"I patrolled until dawn, cleaning up after the teenagers' Halloween pranks. This is supposed to be my day off, but I had paperwork to do."

She'd been all set with a sharp retort, but his reasonable explanation cut through her rage. She took a ragged breath.

"I called a few minutes ago and told you some kind of monster killed my friend last night and came after me. You didn't pay attention." Frustrated tears moistened her eyes and she swiped at them. "God . . ." She glanced up to cool greenish eyes assessing her.

"Sorry, ma'am. I'm paying attention now. Tell me about last night."

Krista hesitated.

Rawlins frowned. "Are you all right? Do you need medical attention?"

"I need that thing destroyed before it kills again." She took a step and stumbled. The sheriff caught her and gently led her to the back desk.

"Please, both of you, have a seat." Nodding at Harlan, he pulled out chairs, then picked up his desk receiver.

Krista slid into a chair. "My friend is still out there."

"I'll notify the EMS team."

"And the National Guard, the military, and anyone else with large guns." Krista's voice dropped to a whisper. "That thing tore off the truck door as if it were paper." Fingers of ice crept up her spine. She gripped the chair arms.

Without completing the call, Rawlins replaced the phone and gave her his full attention. "Maybe you'd better tell me exactly what happened."

She had to keep calm. If she rambled or got hysterical, she doubted he would believe her. She cleared her throat and tried to speak in even tones.

"My friend and I were in the state park last night, and some kind of nightmarish monster, huge, covered in fur, attacked and killed him. Nearly tore off his head. It came after me too, but I got away."

"Probably a black bear. Most of them stay higher in the mountains, but they occasionally wander down when campers get careless about food."

"We weren't camping, and it wasn't a bear. I don't know what it was, but . . ." In her struggle to stay alive in the forest, and during her ride to the sheriff's office, Krista had managed to put the horror aside. But now, safe in his office, her tight restraint lessened and images flashed through her mind — the monstrous claws slicing through Todd, the terror in his eyes, his severed head dangling on his shoulders. Her breathing quickened. She felt encased in ice. She shivered.

"Are you all right?"

"Sorry. I'm . . . so cold." Her hands shook, then

her entire body trembled.

The sheriff rushed to her. Without a word, he pulled her into his arms.

Krista wanted to protest, but her teeth clattered and she couldn't speak.

Without breaking his hold, Rawlins spoke over her head to his deputy. "Delzo! Get a blanket!" He vigorously ran his hands over her back and down her arms, then held her close to him, lowering his chin to the top of her head.

Heat from his body flowed into her. Oh, it felt so good. She rested her head against his warmth and let the steady rhythm of his heart comfort her. She was safe. The violent images faded, and the trembling slowed. Her stomach settled. She closed her eyes.

"She all right?" Harlan asked.

"She will be." Still holding her, Rawlins took a blanket from Delzo and wrapped it around her. Krista felt secure in a snug cocoon.

Lost in the sheriff's warm embrace, she became aware of his clean masculine scent, just soap and perhaps a lightly-scented aftershave. She didn't know how long they stood locked together, but as conscious thought returned, she realized how content she felt in this stranger's arms. Embarrassed, she squirmed until he released his hold.

He crouched down to look into her eyes. "Better now?"

She nodded and sank into the chair, too embarrassed to look at him, grateful he'd acted so quickly to help her.

"Thank you," she murmured.

"My pleasure."

Something in his tone caused her to raise her gaze to his. She saw compassion perhaps, and something she couldn't identify. She became aware of a fleeting familiarity, a slight memory in the back of her consciousness, but it was gone before she could name it. Had she seen this man before?

Rawlins' gaze held hers. "Can you talk now?"

She had to get a grip. She'd never seen him before; with his features, she would have remembered.

"You should get checked at Urgent Care," Rawlins said. "I'll take you there as soon as I get the basics."

Krista shook her head. "I just want to get home." And out of the mountains and the state, as soon as possible. She wanted to put as many miles between that monster and her as she could.

"I'll call it in, but you've suffered a shock. Even if you refuse medical care, I highly recommend you consider therapy." He punched numbers on the phone.

"I won't be here long enough."

"Not here? What do you—" His gaze still on Krista, Rawlins spoke into the phone. "Hank, we have a possible bear attack at Planter's Grove. Survivor says the male victim is deceased." He paused, then, "Hang on, I'll ask." He punched a button and turned to Krista. "Park Service is asking which campsite and a description of the victim."

"I don't know the campsite. It was my first time

there, but we sat on a bench by the river."

"I bet it was forty-three," Delzo interjected. "Last time I checked the grounds, the bench was still by the river. I called it in, but . . ."

Rawlins relayed the information into the phone. To her, he said, "And the victim?"

"He is — was, maybe forty-ish. Stocky, just under six feet. Todd Mitchell."

"From the newspaper?" The sheriff's eyes narrowed. "You know him?"

"This is a small town. You're the new reporter?"

She gave a brief nod. "That thing attacked on the road about a quarter-mile above the campsite. They can't miss it. The truck, Todd's Tacoma, is still there, and his body . . . all mangled." She swallowed several times.

The sheriff's gaze never left her as he relayed the information. "Storm's due after midnight," he added, "so we need to get rolling. I'll be out shortly. Thanks." He disconnected, then turned to his deputy. "Delzo, alert the team and check it out."

The young officer rose from his desk and crossed to a gun cabinet standing against the far wall.

"The .270 should do it," Rawlins told him.

"I don't know." Delzo's wide-eyed gaze swung to Krista, then back to the sheriff. "I'll feel better with the .375." He took a rifle that appeared two feet long.

"Your call. Check back with me once you find something."

The deputy zipped up his jacket, slipped the gun into a leather sheath and made his exit.

Krista stared after him. "That was a mistake," she said quietly. "If he's the only one with a gun, he'll die. Just like Todd."

"The Rangers will be armed."

The desk phone's shrill ring jarred Krista. Rawlins answered, listened, and scowled. "I can't officially stop you from going to the site, but you know the routine: keep your distance so you won't contaminate the evidence." Then, "The survivor is with me. I promise I'll get back to you."

Krista didn't know who he was talking to, but she assumed it was about the attack.

He finished the call. "That was Carla at the paper. She heard the buzz on her scanner. I didn't tell her you were the survivor — figured you'd need a break before more interviews."

"I appreciate that. Thanks."

"Could've been a cougar," Harlan said.

"It had to have been a bear." Rawlins turned to the computer and clicked the keyboard. "They're almost in a feeding frenzy before winter."

"I told you," Krista said through gritted teeth, "but I'll say it again. It wasn't a bear. I know what bears look like. This thing wasn't even the same shape."

"Describe what you saw."

"It was covered in hair, or fur, and it had fangs and huge claws. No snout like a bear. It stood upright, like a man, only taller. Much taller." She didn't mention the clothing. He'd certainly lock her away at that bit of information. "It wasn't a bear."

"It was night, and you were frightened. You're mistaken."

"Believe what you like. I know what I saw."

"Let's put that aside for the moment. Before we go further, would you two like some coffee?"

"I don't want—" She caught the aroma of freshly-brewed coffee. Her mouth watered, and she realized she hadn't had anything to eat or drink since her light dinner the night before—before all the horrible events unfolded.

"I sure could use a cup," Harlan said.

Rawlins disappeared into a back room and when he returned with two mugs, he moved with a grace Krista had seldom seen in a man his size.

She took a sip and sat quietly, her hands wrapped around the mug, enjoying the warmth that spread throughout her body, fighting the sudden exhaustion that threatened to melt her bones into liquid. "How much longer will this take?"

"I need more information. Just talk to me. Start at the beginning, and don't leave anything out."

"I already told you."

"Humor me."

She studied him a moment, looking for a sign he was patronizing her, but she found nothing other than a calm, studied interest. After a deep sigh, she started talking, beginning with her move and new job at the local newspaper, meeting Todd and their time at the campground, his rudeness, and hearing the terrible howl.

"Todd thought it was a coyote. I wanted to believe

him." She paused, bit her lip and turned her head away.

"Krista, I know it's difficult, but please continue. If we're going to catch this animal, I need every detail you can remember. Why were you and Todd at a closed campsite? Was it for privacy?"

"Privacy?" It took her a moment before she realized his meaning. "Good God no. It wasn't even a date. He'd been nice at work, so I finally agreed to dinner." She didn't want to admit it was loneliness, a deep, soul-wrenching emptiness that had led to the outing.

"What happened after you heard the growl? Did Todd try to get you to safety?"

"I don't know how well you know or like him, but that's not what happened." Even though she wanted to respect the dead, her voice took a flat tone. Bitter. "He left me out there. With whatever it was."

"What? He left you?"

"I don't want to think about it."

"I know it's difficult, but please continue."

She recalled her terror when trying and failing to open Todd's truck door, his laughter when he left her. She haltingly described the creature's attack and her escape.

Harlan, who'd been quietly listening, grunted and shook his head.

"What an ass," Rawlins said. "Most of the men in this town are gentlemen. Sorry you met one who wasn't. It was criminal to leave you out there all alone at night, especially at this time of year."

"At least he stopped at the end. He was coming back for me."

Rawlins frowned. "Was he? You said you heard a roar, then his brakes. I wonder if the animal stopped him. Maybe he wasn't coming back for you at all."

That hadn't occurred to her. "I hope he was. I'd like to think better of him, especially now. What a horrible way to die." She shuddered.

"Tell me more about this creature you saw. Describe it again for me in as much detail as you can remember."

It was all Krista could do to sit upright. She didn't know if it was the exhaustion or that she knew how preposterous her description would sound. And it was ridiculous. Her shoulders slumped.

"You won't believe me."

"Let me be the judge of that."

Harlan took her hand and squeezed, as if passing some of his energy to her. When she looked up, he smiled and nodded as if to encourage her. When her eyes flicked to Rawlins, he nodded as well.

Still she hesitated. How could she adequately describe the monster she'd seen? How could she make them believe her? Now, in the bright lights of the sheriff's office, it seemed even more outlandish.

But she had to try. As much as she wanted to get home and pack, she wouldn't be able to live with herself if she didn't try to stop that creature from killing anyone else.

She began talking again, hands clenching and unclenching, pausing often to gulp air. This time she described the humanoid face and the clothing. Rawlins had been entering the information into the computer, but at that point he went still. His eyes narrowed. Harlan's mouth fell open. The room was so quiet Krista could hear her heart beat.

Finally, the sheriff exhaled a long, drawn breath. "Mind taking a drug test?"

A drug test? How much more could she take? What little patience she had left completely dissolved.

She had to get out of there. If he refused to believe a monster was roaming the hills, why should she care? It was their town, not hers. She'd leave as soon as she could. Now. Today.

She stood. "Would you please call a cab for me?"

"We're not finished with—"

"I've just spent the worst night of my life and I'm worn out mentally, physically, and every other way. I'd expected help from local law enforcement. Instead, I'm treated as if I should be in a mental ward. So yes, I'd say we're finished."

Harlan rose from his seat. "I'll drop you off." Taking great care, he placed his mug on the sheriff's desk. "I don't know what kind of critter she saw," he said to Rawlins, "and I admit what she says sounds like something off'n TV, but I been around a long time and I'm a pretty good judge of people. I wouldn't be so quick to write her off, iffin' I was you. Just saying."

Krista gave him a hug. How could she put into words how much he'd helped her? "Thanks, Harlan, for everything. You saved my life."

Rawlins stood. "Now wait just a moment. I'll take her home. I have more questions."

"Oh, no—" Krista began.

"It's better to go along with him," Harlan cut in. "Give him all the information you can." When Krista didn't answer, he nodded. "Good luck, young lady." Without another word, he headed for the exit.

With Harlan gone, Krista felt abandoned, left with someone who considered her demented. Or drugged out. She, who always paid her bills before the due date, she, who never had more than two drinks at a time because she didn't want to lose control. She was so straightlaced and focused that her friends had called her Saint Krista.

"You don't believe what I saw," she said, "so why would I want to answer more of your questions?"

"Once a bear attacks a human, it's a threat to the community, and we have to find it. But a monster such as you described? You were upset, your date had just abandoned you. You saw a terrifying bear attack, and you imagined the rest. But I need more details."

"Thanks for nothing. Look, I no longer care what you believe, but I need to get home, and if you're the only way, then let's go." She turned to leave, then paused. "Damn!"

"What now?"

"Would you please call my apartment manager to meet us?" She spoke evenly, overly-politely, trying desperately to keep her tone and emotions under control. If she let go, she'd start screaming and wouldn't quit until they locked her in a padded room. "I can't get into my apartment. My keys are in my handbag, and that's in Todd's truck." She hesitated. "Look, I'm truly sorry he's dead, but I need my things. How soon can I get them?"

"I'll take a run up there after I drop you off, but it'll be a few hours before you can claim your property. We'll need to inventory everything we find."

"A few hours? Can't you speed it up?"

"I'll get you into your apartment, so what's the rush? It's Sunday. The paper's closed today.

"I'm getting out of this state as soon as I can get packed."

"Out of the state? Sorry, but a man is dead, and there'll be an investigation. You can't leave the area—at least not yet."

FIVE

Krista stared incredulously at the sheriff. "I can't leave? Why?"

"An investigation into a fatal animal attack takes time."

"I told you everything that happened, and it'll be obvious I didn't kill Todd. What else do you want?"

"The DNR will have questions."

"Unless you find that creature today and kill it, I'm not staying around."

"I'm afraid I have to insist."

"Oh, no . . ." She slowly backed away. "You don't believe me, that's your problem. I feel sorry for the town because that monster could easily be on the hunt for new victims. But you can't hold me. I know my rights. If I'm not under arrest, I can leave, which I'm doing right now."

Rawlins moved toward her slowly, cautiously. "Miss Hawthorne, Krista, wait." His desk phone rang. He paused and muttered something she couldn't quite hear.

Krista took advantage of the distraction and ran

for the door, hoping the call would delay him long enough for her to get home. If she caught a ride, she could make it in no time.

The sheriff's brick building sat in a secluded lot on the west end of Marsh Springs, separated from the edge of town by a field of oak, birch, and maple trees. Krista ducked through the foliage, her shoes crunching on a carpet of gold and orange leaves.

Once on the other side of the field, she hurried along the graveled shoulder of the two-lane highway into town. Traffic ran intermittently, even though it cut through two mountain peaks and descended east to Charleston, the state capital, or west to Huntington, a major port on the Ohio River. Krista hurried along the shoulder, torn between her instinct to keep hidden and her need for a ride.

Across the road on her left, a grassy area sloped upward until melding into a dense forest. Was that monster out there, waiting for the perfect opportunity to attack? She scanned the brush for signs of movement, but saw nothing.

Feeling like a fugitive, she shot furtive glances around her — not only for the creature, but for the sheriff. Unbelievable. In her entire life, her most serious offense had been a parking ticket. Could the sheriff legally hold her? God, she hoped not. No way did she want to stay here.

A cool breeze blew locks of hair into her face. She brushed them back and pulled her jacket tighter. Pewter clouds were crowding out the sun, and she increased her pace, hoping to get home, packed, and out of the mountains before the storm broke. The last thing she wanted was to be stranded on the side of an impassable mountain highway, defenseless against that creature. She'd only take what she could throw into the car. Anything she left behind wasn't important enough to risk her life.

Everyone in the area was at risk. If that monster had entered the campground from the mountains, it could just as easily enter the town. How many would it kill before law enforcement took action? She wasn't going to stay and find out. She wouldn't be the next one caught in its claws.

If the sheriff weren't so thick-headed and unbelieving, he'd gather everyone in town old enough to shoot, and they'd track that thing down. But no. He'd rather think it was a bear and she was on drugs.

She tromped toward town, determined to get home if she had to walk all the way. And she'd get inside her apartment if she had to break a window. Once she was a safe distance away, she'd mail payment to the manager. Thank God she had an extra pair of car keys.

Just as she reached a furniture store on the edge of town, she heard a car approach. And it was slowing. If it stopped for her, she'd gladly pay the driver to take her the rest of the way. The car pulled to the shoulder behind her.

Krista took a deep breath, and with a smile to show she was friendly, she turned. And nearly cried.

The sheriff's dark SUV idled behind her. She

wondered briefly if she could outrun him, but her aching legs signaled she was too exhausted to try. Utterly defeated, she squeezed her eyes shut and waited.

Rawlins strolled toward her, his long legs covering the distance in an instant, his eyes unreadable behind amber shades.

"What, you're not going to run again?"

She shrugged. "I'm too tired. Besides, you'd probably alert everyone in shouting distance that a deranged stoner is on the loose."

He sighed. "Just get into the truck. I'll take you home."

"Home? You're not going to take me to a drug-testing facility?"

He made some kind of sound and raised his face to the sky. Was he counting?

"Home," he said, exasperation in his voice, "where I hope you'll stay. There'll be an official inquiry, and I need you available to answer questions. That's all." He opened the passenger door, stared at her, and waited.

She hesitated, wondering what to do. Best to go willingly, then as soon as he left, she'd pack. Silently, her cheeks burning, she trudged toward the vehicle and slid in. Just as silently, the sheriff drove into town.

Krista stared out the window and noted the new awning over the drug store, the exact green of the other awnings popping up over storefronts. Krista applauded the old coal- mining town's efforts to revitalize. With the awnings, new paint, and tree saplings cut into brick sidewalks, the town was beginning to look inviting.

When they cruised past the newspaper office on Main Street, she fought pangs of guilt. The crew, among others, had been so welcoming to her, and now she was abandoning them as fast as she could. But what else could she do? The sheriff didn't believe her, refused to protect his town against a deadly monster, so how could she be responsible for their safety?

Two elderly ladies strolling down the sidewalk waved to Hugh. He nodded.

"This is a nice town," he said, breaking into Krista's thoughts, "Nice people here. You get to know your neighbors. It almost died when underground coal mining closed down. But the area's great for water sports and fishing, so we're sprucing it up for the tourists."

Her nerves shattered, Krista wasn't in the mood for the town's history. "I appreciate the tour, Sheriff, but—"

"Hugh."

"You said you'd take me home."

"How about some breakfast first? I haven't had anything to eat, and I bet after the night you had, you're hungry too."

"I don't want breakfast. I want to go home. Maybe you didn't hear me earlier, so I'll repeat it—for the tenth or twelfth time this morning. There's a monster with huge fangs loose in your national park, and it's killing people. You don't seem to be in any hurry to do anything about that, so I'll just get out here and get home on my own." She pulled the passenger door latch several times, but it wouldn't open.

Rawlins veered to the curb.

Krista turned to him, tears of frustration forming. "What's wrong with you? Why won't you let me out?"

"Look. I'm sorry to upset you further, but I assure you, the DNR wardens, that's the Division of Natural Resources—"

"I know what DNR is, for God's sake. Will you please just stop with everything and get me home?"

"The city fire department," he continued calmly, as if she hadn't interrupted, "the medical team, and my deputy are all converging on the site. I'll join them shortly." He slipped on his glasses. "I just wanted to make sure you were okay, perhaps have something to eat. Since you were stranded all night and refuse medical care, a little warm food should help."

She stared at him, at a loss for words, but something about his soothing tone, or perhaps it was the way he looked at her, made her hesitate. His eyes seemed to see into her soul, and his steady gaze had a strange effect on her. Her pulse slowed, and she felt less angst. But once her adrenaline calmed, the strain from everything that had happened last night slammed her with exhaustion. She sighed and leaned her head against the headrest.

"I don't see why you care," she said, her voice low. It took enormous effort to even talk. "You think

I'm a drugged-out whacko."

He pulled back into the sparse traffic. "You have to admit, a werewolf in Boone County is a bit hard to swallow."

"Werewolf?"

"I grew up watching the old monster movies, and that's what your description sounds like to me."

Krista hadn't put a name to the creature, but now . . . "You're not serious, are you? Werewolves are just a myth. Something to scare people at the movies. They don't exist in real life. It's just not possible."

"That's what *I* said. Remember?"

"I mean, if it were possible, how could one survive without being detected before now?"

"Do you honestly think a werewolf is running loose in the mountains?"

"I'd say of course not—if I hadn't seen it."

"It was a black bear, a large one. They're native to the area."

Krista wanted to scream, but too tired to argue, she said nothing.

"Besides, it was too dark to see much," he added. "Close to midnight, wasn't it?" He checked his watch. "The Drop In Cafe is still serving breakfast. Let's grab something, and I'll check back with you after I've been to the site."

"I can't eat anything."

"Trust me. After what you've been through, you need something nourishing."

Krista gave up. Maybe some food would give her

enough energy to pack and leave. Where she'd go, she had no idea. Just as far away from Marsh Springs and the werewolf as she could get. A large city on the other side of the globe, perhaps — with a lot of cops and lots of firepower. She'd call the newspaper from a safe distance and resign. To ease her conscience, she'd send an article about the attack. Whether or not they published it would be up to them.

The Drop In Cafe sat on the opposite end of town, shaved from the encroaching forest with just enough concrete to accommodate tree-shaded parking. Picnic benches overlooked Coal River. In other circumstances, Krista would have loved to enjoy a leisurely breakfast on the riverbank.

Before ordering, Rawlins turned to her. "How about some eggs and toast, and maybe some oatmeal?"

"My stomach's too upset for all that. I'll take toast. No butter."

"You need more than that. At least have some orange juice with your toast."

"Why are you doing this? What do you want?"

"Can't a person do something for someone else?"

"No one does anything without a reason."

"Sounds like you haven't met the right person."

She had no response to that one.

He pulled some bills from his wallet. "We're a small town and we look out for each other."

"Do you have children? Pets?"

"Not even a gold fish. Why?"

"You need someone else to boss around."

He grinned and ordered.

Krista turned to gaze at the river, listening to the water splashing over rocks, watching the tiny whitecaps form and dissolve. On the opposite shore, the grassy hill sloped upward into the forested mountain, the autumn reds and golds sparkling in the morning sun.

This part of the country had such beauty. She almost wished she didn't have to leave. "It's only been a month, but I'd grown to love it here. Too bad it's harboring a monstrous creature."

"Believe me, if it's a rogue bear or a cougar, we'll find it."

Krista sighed. What use would it be to argue with him? Hard to believe such an obstinate man was capable of showing such kindness.

Look out for each other? What a concept. She wished it were true, wished she could find someone who truly cared for others, but she'd learned long ago that everyone had their own motives for the things they did.

What was Rawlins' motive? She didn't know, but at least she was in the company of an armed official. While his gun might not kill the beast, it might make it hesitate.

"You said earlier you recently moved here," Rawlins said, while waiting for his order. "Why a remote mountain town in West Virginia?"

"To get away. I wanted to start a new life, and when I saw the newspaper's ad, I thought it was perfect—a chance to experience something different."

"When you entered the station, I assumed you were a visitor."

"Why?"

"If I'd seen you around town, I would've remembered."

"Oh." Krista met his gaze, her voice soft. How beautiful his eyes were—one minute a greenish brown, the next golden. Flustered, she was glad when their order was ready. Surprisingly, the egg and cheese biscuit was delicious, and she finished it before they reached her apartment.

The two-story building sat across from the library in a block of tree-shaded older homes. Once parked, Rawlins dug in the glove compartment and pulled out a black case holding a few slim metal tools. At her door, he used the tools on the lock and had her inside in just a couple of minutes.

The L-shaped living room held a warm cinnamon-paisley sofa, a wing chair, a small flat screen TV, and a straight-leg dinette in the alcove next to the kitchen. Krista shivered at the chill in the air and turned up the thermostat.

"I'll check on you as soon as I can," Rawlins said.

"I hope to be gone by then."

"You're determined to leave?"

"I'm heading back home to nice safe things like Gila monsters, scorpions, and rattlesnakes."

"That's a pretty selfish attitude."

She bristled. "That's not fair."

"Life seldom is. Look. DNR will want to speak with you, and I need you to stick around so we can discuss the next step."

"What's to discuss? There's nothing more I can do."

"We'll scout the area for animal DNA and have the lab run a complete check on Mitchell's body. They may need more information."

"I watch the TV shows. DNA takes a while. How long are you talking about?"

"Can't say exactly. We'll put in a rush at the lab, but it'll still take some time."

"How long is some time?"

"A week, maybe longer. If it's one of the tagged bears, no problem. DNR can track it. Since it's now a killer, they'll do a search and destroy."

"And if it's not tagged? If it's something unknown?"

"Then they'll call in reinforcements. I'm sure they'll have questions for you."

"I don't see how I can help. I've already told you everything I know."

"You may remember more than you realize. Markings, perhaps, to help identify it. It's worth a shot."

"It's worth a shot to believe me when I tell you it wasn't a bear."

"For now, let's just consider you were under extreme duress and your mind played tricks on you. Figure three weeks, max."

Three weeks? Three weeks of living in an area with that monster on the loose? She'd read stories where the heroines felt the blood drain from their faces, but this was the first time she experienced it. She grabbed the back of the chair.

Rawlins moved faster than she would've thought possible, supporting her, swinging her up into his arms. Before she could protest, they were next to the sofa. He gently set her down.

"Please, Krista, think carefully before deciding anything. If you must go, get some rest first. You're exhausted. I'd hate to find your car in a ditch somewhere." He pulled the blue afghan from the back of the sofa and covered her.

She lay back, studying his face, searching for clues. This complex man perplexed her. One minute he accused her of being stoned, the next he was feeding her and tucking her in for a nap.

After he left, Krista's depleted body cried for rest, but her emotions were in a turmoil. Or was it her conscience?

Was Rawlins right? She was the only eyewitness, so should she stay and try to help with the investigation? That would mean trying to live her life, going to work each day knowing a hideous creature was loose in the mountains.

She pushed herself up and padded to the kitchen and zapped yesterday's coffee. Why was she even considering staying? Every survival instinct she had urged her to run and not look back. If Rawlins didn't believe her, why should she risk her life to try and help? And it would be a risk—as a citizen of the town, and, more importantly, because the monster had seen her.

But didn't she owe something to the good people

in the town? Not only to those at the newspaper, but to the apartment manager who offered a lease simply on a phone call? And to Mrs. Reardon, the elderly lady in the end apartment who'd appeared during move-in day with a hot casserole? And who'd supplied her with homemade cookies for the past month. And the others: the cashier at the market, the gas station attendees—all people who'd made her feel welcome. As the only eye-witness, didn't she owe them her cooperation with authorities? Even though no one would believe her?

It was almost worth staying until Rawlins heard from the lab about the creature's DNA. He'd have to apologize after the results proved it wasn't a black bear, a brown one, or any other known animal. Oh, how she'd relish that moment.

Back on the sofa, the mug in her hands, she still couldn't come to a decision. Even if she wanted to help, was she brave enough to stay, to live each moment wondering if that creature was out there, watching her, waiting to attack again?

What if it took longer than three weeks? What if it turned into a month? Or more?

Could she live each day in fear? Was she willing to try?

SIX

Egypt
The Past

Finally, after what seemed an eternity, the ceremonial hall emptied of the ambassadors and petitioners. Prince Rahmor waited for his father to give the nod to file off the dais, but he was still talking to his vizier. While Rahmor admired his father's sense of protocol, he wished Pharaoh's strict discipline would lessen just one time. The longer he was trapped on the dais, the less time he had to discover where the servants had taken the copper-haired woman.

"Well done, Your Majesty," Neferweben, vizier of the north, praised. Along with Hekhrahn, vizier of the south, he kept close to the king's ear. "You brought enough spoils to keep our coffers filled for years." He bowed deeply. Sweat from the increased numbers of burning incense glistened on his bald head. Perfumed oils of frankincense and myrrh filled the air, barely masking the lingering odors of unwashed bodies and animals that had appeared before the king. White and pink lotus blossoms floated in bowls of scented water.

Pharaoh accepted the praise with a nod. "The land will prosper." Finally, he rose, his fine linen robes cascading to the floor, the crook and flail held regally across his chest. He nodded to Amenemhat who rose, followed by Amenhotep, and on down the line of succession. Rahmor ground his teeth and had to restrain himself from jumping off the dais.

What was it about that woman? As a prince, he had his choice of the land's most alluring women, and his masculine physique plus his military skills added to his appeal. But this woman . . . her beauty captured his senses. It wasn't like him to be so captivated by one slight woman, even if her eyes held his like a soft embrace. Perhaps it was the pride with which she held herself, a captive in Pharaoh's court who, with a slight raise of an eyebrow, could order her immediate demise. Still, she had held her head high. And he'd wondered at her arrogance—until he saw the quivering chin. His heart had melted.

Where were her escorts taking her?

Finally it was his turn to exit, and he sent a silent plea for help from Hatshepsut, his father's stepmother and co-regent for nearly twenty years. Even though Anubis had long since ushered her soul into the afterlife, Rahmor felt his father was always conscious of her regal memory. And, he suspected Pharaoh still felt a sense of competition.

He had reason.

Hatshepsut's reign had been a strong one. Not only had she opened various trade routes, but she had returned from the land of Punt with tree roots of myrrh and frankincense which she'd ground into kohl eyeliner. Both men and women throughout the land copied her use of the charred resin.

Rahmor understood his father's adherence to her rules of court. Since he'd become heir to the throne as a child and Hetshepsut was appointed co-ruler, he'd had to watch her accomplishments — not only in trade, but as a builder. She couldn't be equaled. Her temple of many columns on the Nile's west bank stood as testament to her ability. She'd ruled with great power, and Rahmor appealed to that power now.

Pharaoh led the procession out of the great hall and into the adjoining antechamber. In the atrium, gilded chairs and ottomans covered with animal skins provided comfort, while sheer curtains afforded a degree of privacy. In this room, they could talk and relax out of sight of the curious.

An evening breeze from the causeway billowed the curtains, and Rahmor breathed deeply of the fresh desert air. Refreshing, he thought, after the suffocating incense in the ceremonial hall. He shifted, praying his father would cut short his evaluation of the day's procession.

"Well done," Pharaoh praised his sons and daughters. "I know this day was a long one, but I'm proud of all of you and proud of what we've accomplished. Because of the amount of tribute, our people will flourish for years to come. I must rest now. Go, and we'll convene tomorrow."

Once Thutmose left for his chambers, Amenemhat turned to his siblings. As firstborn and supreme general under his father's strong command, his gleaming golden collar was nearly as large as his father's. He'd been commissioned to carry out Pharaoh's orders and act as advisor.

"I wish to discuss our naval transportation into Byblos, and how we can perfect the maneuver we tried on the tenth day. Let's take some refreshment and perhaps we can construct a better strategy, one which our father will approve."

"Amenhotep," he addressed the second-born, "your prowess with the bow and arrow was second to none, and I'll like you to train . . ."

Rahmor gave the impression of taking part in the conversation; as a minor leader, he had little say in strategy, but he always upheld his duty to his father. Yet this evening his mind was elsewhere.

Where had the servants taken the woman? Was she even now being groomed as a concubine? Or worse, as a minor wife? From the way his father's gaze followed her from the ceremonial hall, he suspected she would be of more importance than a casual addition to his harem.

Which would mean he, Rahmor, would be denied access to her.

He had to learn her destination. What was it his father had instructed? He wished he'd paid more attention during the ceremonies. Did he dare ask Satiah, Great Royal Wife and Amenemhat's mother? Since he was heir, she was held in honor, and as so, supervised the harem. She would know who occupied the chambers and who was destined to be a minor wife.

But to ask her might be considered offensive. Perhaps he'd question Hatiah, the harem's guard who had looked the other way when Rahmor demanded entrance. After all, it wasn't as if the women were love matches; most were taken in treaties with the various provinces — or as bounty in a conquest.

He made his excuses to his brothers and escaped as quickly as he could. He needed to find out where the woman had been taken. That would indicate her future role.

If she'd been taken to the harem in Mer Wer, the great canal city, she was to be a minor wife or a concubine, but if she remained in the palace, then she would be of more importance to Pharaoh. To make sure he didn't miss any, he prayed to all the old gods:

Please, let her be a concubine.

SEVEN

WV
Present Day

A noise, a thundering sound, jarred Krista out of sleep. Someone was pounding on the door.

"Krista!" A male voice.

Blinking, trying to focus in the dark room, Krista sat up on the sofa. Her shirt and pant leg felt wet and sticky, and she found her empty coffee cup in her lap. She must have fallen asleep while holding it.

"Perfect," she murmured. She should get up and change clothes, but her body felt too heavy to move.

"If you're in there, open up!" Sheriff Rawlins' booming voice.

Krista rubbed the sleep from her eyes, and the past two days came back to her in a rush. She switched on the lamp by the sofa and flinched at the sudden glare.

The pounding continued.

Good heavens! He was going to splinter the door. "All right already! I'm coming!" She rose, and using the furniture for balance, stumbled to the door. She felt sluggish, as if she'd had either too much sleep or not enough. Her mouth tasted as if she hadn't brushed in days, and she was sure her hair spiked in several directions. The last thing she wanted was company.

Yet she wanted answers. Had he been to the campsite? If so, what had he found? And did he have her handbag?

Reluctantly, she flipped on the outside light and opened the door, hoping he was alone. "Why all the noise? You scared me to death." She stepped back to let him enter.

Rawlins removed his Western hat to clear the doorway and tossed it onto the wing chair. "Sorry about that. I didn't see a light, so I didn't know if you were still here." He held a paper sack from the local grocery store.

"You're alone?" She checked outside before closing the door.

"DNR wanted to question you tonight, but I convinced Kyle Bowman, the black bear project leader, to wait until morning." In jeans and a bomber jacket, he looked devastatingly handsome. She adjusted her clothes and tried to smooth down her hair.

"They're going to question me tomorrow?"

"In the morning. I'll be here too, so it won't be bad. We just have to figure out what to tell them."

"You mean I shouldn't tell them a werewolf is loose in their hills? Oh, right. I'm a delusional drug addict, so not only will they not believe me, but they'll lock me up."

Rawlins made an exasperated sigh and offered the sack. "Look, I wanted to give you—"

"My handbag?" She grabbed it, then hesitated. She'd left it in the front seat—where that creature had attacked. Could Todd's blood have splattered to the passenger side? If it had reached her handbag, would she be able to touch it?

"It's your purse. So what the problem?"

At a loss, she stood holding the sack. How could she explain it to him? If she said she dreaded finding blood on her handbag, it would make her sound as if she cared about the condition of her handbag. And that wasn't the problem. So she stood mute, holding the sack as if it contained a rattler. After the fuss she'd made in his office, she felt like an idiot.

They stood in silence. He finally spoke, his voice gentle. "It's okay, Krista. I checked. It's clean."

How did he know? Relieved, she smiled. "Thank you." She pulled out her bag and dumped the contents onto the table. Rummaging through the mess, she found her phone. "Everything's here," she said, breathing a sigh of relief. "Now I can call Mom."

"You going to tell her what happened?"

"No reason to worry her. I just want to hear her voice." Embarrassed by her admission, she kept her face hidden while connecting the phone to the charger cord. "I know it's childish, but . . ." She glanced at Rawlins, who was gazing at her with an unreadable expression. Compassion? Couldn't be.

"Not childish at all. I often wish I could talk to my parents."

She was surprised at his pensive tone. He sounded wistful, even. "Have they passed?"

"A long time ago." After a silent moment, he spoke again. "I thought we might go for coffee, but this doesn't seem to be a good time."

"Let's have something here. I have a hundred questions."

He nodded. "I just came from notifying Mitchell's family, so that'll give me a chance to wind down. If you want to freshen up, go ahead. I'll make the coffee."

She caught the tightness around his eyes and mouth and agreed. Notifying the next of kin in any death must be the worst part of his job, and even this powerful man could have his vulnerable moments.

Krista escaped to the bathroom, and after freshening up, she changed into a fresh knit pullover and felt more human. She wished her eyes weren't so swollen and she looked prettier. Did she have time to wash her hair?

No, she didn't want to keep the sheriff waiting. She was only interested in finding out what he'd discovered. Of course it was only that.

Back at the table, he gestured for her to sit, and she watched him, so comfortable in her galley kitchen while searching for cups, saucers, milk, and napkins. In spite of his size, he seemed so at ease with himself, a quality she had lacked since childhood.

She had always been at odds, growing up in a small family of Mediterranean lineage, fighting for control of her unruly locks—the russet of maple leaves in autumn, her fiancé had said, and eyes like new grass. He'd had a way with words, which she later realized was a big reason she fell for him. After all the teasing she'd endured as a child, he was the first man to make her proud of her appearance.

Rawlins found her stash of macadamia nut cookies and set a few on a plate.

"There's some fruit in the lower cupboard." She directed him to the right cabinet, and he halved a banana and added grapes to the plate.

When he took the chair beside her, she caught the scent of soap and a light aftershave. He must have taken a few moments to shower before stopping by her place. For some reason, she felt pleased.

While they ate, he kept up an impersonal conversation about the town and its population. "Most are out-of-work coal miners or their descendants. They're proud, self-reliant, and they watch out for each other."

"I haven't met that many people yet. Except for Todd, everyone else has been so kind—at work, the grocery . . . and Mrs. Reardon, my neighbor who must be eighty at least, but she brought a casserole during my move-in day. And cookies the next. Thought I'd be tired, she said. Nobody does that anymore."

"I'm not surprised. We have some great people here."

"Almost reminds me of Mayberry on the old TV series."

"So why leave? You don't have to."

She gaped at him. After everything she'd told him about the creature, she couldn't believe he still questioned her urgency to leave. Was he a moron? Or simply so stubborn he couldn't admit he might be wrong? Surely Todd's mauled body and the bloody site were enough to convince him something extraordinary had happened. To find out what he'd learned at the site, she ignored his question.

"So what did you find out there?"

Rawlins wiped his mouth with a paper napkin, and with a heavy sigh, sat back, his shoulders drooping as if finally relaxing.

"As County Sheriff, I've assisted with wild animal attacks, watched films about the dangers, but never, in all my years, have I ever seen anything like this."

"What do you think I've been trying to tell you?" Before he could reply, she jumped up from the table. "Want some something stronger? I think there's a bottle of whiskey left from my office party in Arizona."

"I could use some in my coffee about now."

Krista retrieved the bottle from a lower cabinet and set it on the table for him to help himself. She declined when he offered to pour for her.

"The strength that beast had," he said, almost as if talking to himself, "how it literally tore off the pickup door. And the condition of Todd's body." He shook his head. "Most bears eat their kills. This one didn't—or at least there wasn't any sign the body was meant as food."

Krista knew the creature's strength; she had witnessed it. Even though it ripped out Todd's throat, it hadn't attempted to feed. She believed then and believed now it killed purely to kill, as was a werewolf's nature—or at least that was what she'd read about them.

"Do you believe me now?" It was a softly asked question, not an accusation.

"Whatever did this was exceptionally vicious. I'm sorry you had to experience something that terrible."

"Yeah, well, I'm sorry too. You still insist it was a bear?"

"From the viciousness of the kill, the strength involved in ripping off Todd's truck door, yeah. I'm thinking it's a grizzly."

"A grizzly."

"They're not native to his part of the country, but if that's what it is, it could've been raised from a cub by an untrained owner. Someone buys an illegal pet on the black market, raises it to a certain point, then realizes it's more than they can handle. They dump it in the mountains. Happens more often than we'd like to think."

"Good theory, but it wasn't a grizzly. Or a mountain lion, or a tiger, or any other so-called exotic pet."

"We'll find out. The park rangers readied Todd's body for an autopsy and DNA analysis at the state lab, and they made plaster casts of whatever prints we could find."

"Can they really determine what animal did this?"

"Similar to crime scenes you see on TV, samples of saliva, hair, blood are collected, analyzed, and matched to their records. DNR will search for the culprit and destroy it."

"What if it can't be matched? What if the samples come from an unknown species?"

"That's not likely. Their records are too accurate."

"For everyone's sake, I hope they do identify the creature, but I'm betting this thing won't be in anyone's records."

"You're right. Werewolves aren't in the system."

Caught by surprise, she stared at him. Damn him! Foolishly, she'd begun to let down her guard and believe in him. She didn't expect sarcasm when she was desperately trying to hold her world together. Would she never learn?

"Screw you," she finally said, her voice tightly controlled. The urge to slap him was so strong she rose from the table and grabbed the dishes to keep her hands occupied.

"Krista," he said.

Ignoring him, she took the dishes to the sink and slammed them down, the clatter making a satisfying sound. She was so angry her hands shook. She crossed her arms, folding her hands under to keep them still.

Rawlins rushed to her rigid form. She kept her back to him, so he slid his arms around her. She stiffened and pushed his arms off her. "Get away from me."

He instantly dropped his arms and stepped back. "I'm sorry. I intended to lighten the mood, but I realize how it must've sounded. Forgive me?"

She turned to face him. "Until you start to believe there's something huge and monstrous out there and take precautions, everyone in this town is in danger."

"I'll concur one thing: whatever attacked you two is strong. And vicious." Before she could reply, he continued. "Kyle will drop by tomorrow. He's a super nice guy and very patient."

"Fine—as long as he's here in the morning, because I'm not staying. I'll help the town by writing the story, then I'm getting out of here."

"For God's sake, don't describe the animal as a werewolf. I don't want people to think this is a joke."

"Do you think I'm an idiot? I've been a reporter for several years, so I know how to slant the article. Better yet, I'll send it in—from a nice, safe distance."

"What if I got you the best pepper spray on the market? They make some that's especially effective with bears."

"Pepper spray? For that monster? No thank you."

"How about a gun? I'll get you one and teach you to shoot."

"That's not necessary. My fiancé taught me to target shoot in the desert."

"Good. I'll also escort you to wherever you need to go."

"I need to go to Florida. Or California. Far enough away from here to feel safe."

"Think of your health. You've been through a traumatic experience, and you need time. Maybe even talk to a therapist. We have an excellent one, old Doc Henley. He retired from Charleston."

"I don't want to talk to a therapist or anyone else until this thing is found." She sighed. "No one would believe me anyway, and it would be even more frustrating." The anger dissolved, and she felt nothing but hopelessness—for herself and for the town. What would it take for Rawlins to believe her?

"Krista," he murmured.

She glanced up to see the softness in his eyes, and her body went liquid. She flushed. What was happening? He couldn't feel anything other than sympathy for her, especially after thinking she was a drugged-out stoner. Could he? And she certainly felt nothing but exasperation for him. So why was she reacting to his closeness? Was she that needy?

She pushed her wayward thoughts aside and stepped around him to the table. He followed, and she realized he was talking. She had to concentrate.

" —escort you to work each day. Or, perhaps you could do something other than reporting, something you could do from home. How about editing? I'll clear it with Junior Hudson. I'll say you're under law enforcement protection."

"Junior didn't hire me. Carla, the editor, did."

"Okay. I'll talk to her. She'll go along with it."

"If, for some insane reason I decide to stay a few more days, which I'm not inclined to do, I don't need you to talk to her. I'll do it myself."

"If it'll help my cause, I'll get my silver bullets."

That was too much. After all she'd said, after her experience in the woods, the exhaustion and trying to work with him when he didn't believe a word she'd said . . . that was it.

"Get out," she said quietly, so furious her voice shook. "And don't come back." She stormed out of the kitchen and headed for her bedroom to pack. She was pulling her suitcase from the closet when he entered.

"Krista, I'm sor—"

"I told you to leave." She grabbed an armful of her things from the dresser, dropped them into the suitcase, and turned to get more.

He positioned himself between her and the dresser. She silently walked around him, a difficult task since he was so large. He touched her arm.

She instantly stopped and glared at him until he dropped his hand.

"I wasn't kidding. I actually do have silver bullets."

"You have a sick sense of humor, and I've had it with you. Are you getting out or do I have to call . . ." He was the sheriff, so who would she call? Delzo, his deputy?

He continued in a conversational tone as if he weren't aware of how livid she was. "Just so happens, I had them made a while ago for a pageant."

"I don't believe you."

"Go to the newspaper office and do a search. I

know it's closed now, but you must have a key. I'll take you and give you the dates."

Could she believe him? Why would she even want to believe him? He doubted her, mocked her, and yet . . . and yet he'd taken special care of her, making sure she got safely home to rest. He'd fed her and checked up on her. And his eyes held such depths she felt she could fall into them and never want to find her way out.

"If you're serious and you really do have silver bullets, I want to see them. And the only way I'd even consider staying is if you have them with you at all times."

"You really are spooked, aren't you?"

"Good God, what's wrong with you? Haven't you been listening? I'm more than spooked. I'm terrified."

"But didn't you say that thing could have killed you but didn't? How do you explain that?"

She sat on the bed. "I can't."

"Well, try to have some faith. My .44 magnum is a powerful weapon."

"It would be if you'd load it with silver bullets."

"If I keep it loaded with the bullets, will you stay? At least until we get a handle on this?"

"You're asking for more than I can manage. I've seen what's out there, so why should I put my life in danger for people who don't believe me?"

"Because you care," he said, his voice soft.

Damn. The image of Mrs. Reardon with her white hair and unsteady gait came to mind. "I'll stay long enough to write the article and send it in. I'll talk to the DNR guy. That's all I can promise."

"Good enough for now."

She nodded and headed back to the kitchen.

He followed her. "You should know Carla picked up the basics from the scanner this morning, and I allowed her to get some shots of the scene. She'll understand your need for an escort—if you stay and insist on going to work."

"If I do stay a few more days, I can't just sit around and do nothing."

"How can I influence you to stay?"

"Prove to me you weren't lying about the bullets. Show them to me. Now. Tonight."

"Not tonight. You need rest. I need rest. I'll bring them in the morning."

She eyed him, noting his haggard, drawn face, the slight droop of his shoulders. "All right, morning. But don't forget."

He nodded. "Bowman will arrive around nine. I'll be here a little earlier." At the doorway, Rawlins paused and turned back to her. "To avoid a panic— at least until we get the lab results back—write that it was too dark to see anything but an outline of the creature. You can even speculate it might be a grizzly. Just, for God's sake, don't describe what you think you saw."

"Don't you think I'll use some discretion? At least until we have more information?"

He paused. "If you truly believe what you think you saw, remember this: you have nothing to lose by staying at least a month. According to legend, werewolves are only active during the night of the full moon."

"I thought you didn't believe in werewolves."

"I don't, but you do."

After a shower an hour later, Krista crawled into bed. She tried to sleep, but Hugh's words ran through her head. Did she truly believe that monster was a werewolf?

The thought was preposterous. She was a rational woman educated to disregard everything but facts. When she'd scanned the headlines in those silly papers at the check-out stands about aliens mating with human women or a child born with animal features, she'd scoffed.

Yet she knew what she saw. It wasn't human, and it wasn't totally animal, more a combination of both. A savage combination. A monster. A werewolf.

And it saw her.

EIGHT

Krista peered through her bedroom window to the moonlit woods behind her apartment building, searching, yet hoping not to find, signs of movement. Was the creature out there right now, using the cover of night to hunt for prey? For her?

After Hugh left, she'd tried to sleep, but the window drew her. She felt an obsessive need to keep checking, to make sure that creature wasn't stalking her apartment.

How ridiculous that seemed — an animal stalking her. But it wasn't an ordinary animal, and she knew what it was capable of doing.

Clouds drifted across the moon, and in the partial light, black trees slashed the snow-dotted landscape. She shivered. When she had leased the apartment, the forest was something she'd loved, and each day after work, she looked forward to relaxing on her back patio, watching the autumn's cooler climate paint the leaves with glorious colors — reds of the maples and oaks, the yellows from the hickories and birches, and beyond to the bluish-white of snow-capped mountain peaks. She'd breathe deeply of the clean fresh air and feel a sense of peace while listening to the sound of the wind rustling the branches and leaves. She thought she'd live the rest of her life in these comforting surroundings.

Now, the woods seemed sinister, a hiding place for a hideous creature.

If she had left town as she'd intended, she'd be safely in the capital city of Charleston by now, instead of worrying about the dark and the proximity of her apartment building to the forest and untamed mountains.

Because you care.

She didn't want to care. It wasn't in her best interest to care. While in the woods after the attack, she'd vowed not to let anything or anyone put her in a vulnerable position again. Yet here she was, staring out the window, watching for a powerful beast that could crash through her window or door at any time.

Why?

Because you care.

Damn, she hated that phrase, but Hugh was right. She cared about the town, the people, especially those at the newspaper who'd been so welcoming to her: Carla Sanchez the editor and Junior Hudson the publisher. Even though he was in his late sixties, he was still known as Junior. His father founded the newspaper, and although he was still living, he retired years ago.

But were they the only reasons she was even considering the ridiculous notion to stay?

Hugh. She had never met such an infuriating man. Yet he'd shown such tenderness when caring for her. As unplanned and unwanted as it was, she had to admit she felt drawn to him, something she hadn't wanted to feel toward any man ever again.

In moving to Marsh Springs, she had hoped for a gentle place to live and work, a pretty, harmonious town completely different from the desert where she'd grown up and learned to mistrust. A town where she could bring her mother and learn to live in a peaceful serenity, free of the anger and resentment that had darkened her days and nights back home. And one day perhaps, after she'd healed, she would find the love she'd been denied for most of her life.

For one glorious month, she had found that peace. Then everything—her plans, her entire life, shattered in the fangs of a hideous monster.

Her eyes felt grainy and tender. She checked the illuminated numbers of her bedside clock. Three-twenty-three a.m. This was madness. She needed to rest for the interview in the morning. She couldn't be jumping up to look out the window every few moments.

Hugh had reminded her that if it were truly a werewolf and the legends were true, it wouldn't hunt again until the next full moon.

Had she seen a spark of mischief in his eyes when he'd said it? She hadn't noticed, probably because she was too desperate to believe that thing wouldn't be out again for at least a month. But hadn't some movies shown a werewolf shifting during other days and evenings? She needed to do some research.

Unbelievable. Never would it have occurred to her that she, a reporter who dealt with facts, would even consider something so farcical. This wasn't the Middle Ages, yet she had seen the beast, seen the tattered clothing hugging the furry body and recognized the intelligence in its eyes.

No matter what anyone else thought, she knew she had seen a werewolf. She checked the clock again: four-ten. Would this night never end? She might as well get a head start on that story. She'd rest after the DNR guy left.

In the kitchen, she brewed coffee and opened her laptop on the table. She started a new file and entered her byline. How should she begin? She finally jotted something down: *Grizzly Attack Kills Local Resident.* She stared at the sentence and changed it: *Local Man Mauled by Rogue Bear.* That didn't seem right either, but it was a start. She stared at the sentence again. One minute passed. Two.

What would the internet say about werewolves?

Another twenty minutes passed and still she sat, staring at that first sentence.

Would search engines list anything other than disparaging articles about such a nonsensical subject?

Almost checking over her shoulder for her practical college professor, she entered the word *werewolf* and sat, eyes wide, as page after page appeared. Fascinated, she read a number of entries before stopping long enough to take notes.

An hour later, her coffee forgotten, she read over her notes. Myths. Shapeshifters. Lycanthrope—a werewolf or someone who suffers from lycanthropy, a belief he/she's a werewolf or can transform into a wolf. Folklore from Early Middle Ages, yet Herodotus in 5th century BC, wrote about a tribe of shapeshifters. In the 2nd century BC, Pausanias, another Greek, told the story of Lycaon, who was transformed into a wolf after sacrificing a child. The term werewolf, she read, originated from two Saxon words: "wer" for man and "wulf" for wolf. Incredible.

Krista sat back and sipped her cold coffee. She had always heard old legends and myths often had a fragment of truth, and this one seemed true. But she couldn't find any information about the effects of a full moon. Did that mean they could shift at will? And how could such bloodthirsty creatures survive through time? Where could they hide and hunt without being seen?

Forests. Swamps. Mountains.

It was entirely possible for them to remain unseen, especially since they transformed back into human form after the full moon—if the moon myth was true. So that meant the creature could now appear in human form, and that was even more chilling. It could be anyone, someone in her town or any other populated area along the foothills. Since it had intelligence, it could even have built a home in the mountains to totally avoid human contact—except when it was time to search for prey.

Was the creature like other wild beasts that tasted human flesh? It was said that once a lion, a bear, or other creatures consumed human flesh, they purposely hunted them. Some said it was because of the taste, yet others said it was because humans were easier to kill.

Whatever the reason, she knew it was out there. And would be back.

If she decided to remain in the area long enough to identify the beast, the sheriff was her best protector. If anyone had a chance against such a creature, it was Hugh Rawlins—and his silver bullets.

Rawlins. She realized she was looking forward to seeing him that morning. How could that be possible? When she had moved to a different state, she'd hoped to get so involved in her new job, her new life, that the bitterness and distrust she'd felt after the betrayals she'd suffered would fade. She no longer dwelt on them, too much had happened. But bitterness? Distrust? Yeah. Those were things she still lived with, although perhaps not as strongly as before.

Because of a pair of hazel eyes and the tenderness in the way they gazed at her?

No, she couldn't let that happen. Yet here she was, remaining in a town where her very life was in danger simply because Hugh wanted her to stay.

What was wrong with her? She'd just met him, and it wasn't going all that great so far. With his urging her to stay even though he knew how frightened she was, even throwing in some coercion over the townspeople's welfare, he wasn't considering her or her feelings. How was he any different from the other men who had betrayed her?

Could she trust him? If he produced those so-called silver bullets, she might be able to feel some trust in him. At least she'd know he hadn't been lying—and that he thought enough of her to bring them. She'd know in the morning.

Morning. The DNR interview. What in Heaven's name was she going to say? Since Hugh wanted her to give some sort of vague description until after the DNA results, she needed something to offer the man. She'd bake some cinnamon rolls to go with his coffee. Most people liked cinnamon rolls, especially home-baked ones. They may help to soften his disappointment.

That was why she was baking the rolls. Not because she looked forward to Rawlins' smile.

Two hours later, the spicy sweet aroma of cinnamon and sugar filling her small apartment, Krista clicked the print option on her laptop, her fingers trembling so violently she could barely hit the right button. Even though she had followed Rawlins' instructions of suggesting the beast could be a grizzly, just going back over that night had brought it all back to bloody, terrifying, life. She kept seeing the creature's red eyes staring at her with such intelligence—right before it ripped open Todd's throat.

She broke out in a cold sweat, but she couldn't

give in. She was a professional, so she shoved her personal feelings aside long enough to send the article to Carla. What would the editor think? Krista was sure losing Todd was devastating to everyone at the office, but to find out another reporter, even one new to the area, was involved, would be a shock to everyone.

She hadn't heard anything about Todd's funeral, but it was only natural his family would plan for one as soon as his body was released. He'd mentioned his parents who were living in town, and she thought he'd had a brother. Or maybe it was a sister. They'd all expect her to attend. And most likely, they'd want to talk to her about Todd's last night. As much as she would like to ease their pain, she hoped to avoid the entire thing. She wasn't in the habit of lying, but no way would she tell his grieving family he'd abandoned her to save himself.

Time for a break. She took the rolls out of the oven to cool, poured a fizzy diet soda, made dry toast, and took her meager breakfast to the sofa.

She was glad she'd taken her shower last night, so other than getting out of her worn, comfy robe and a quick makeup job, she was ready to face the authorities.

Once again, the sound of light knocking on her door woke her. The dawn's first light streamed in through the slatted blinds. She'd fallen asleep again. A doze, actually, but any sleep would help her through the day ahead.

Tightening her robe around her, she hurried to the door. Rawlins would probably think she did nothing but sleep. Silently she opened the door — and, struck by his appearance, stared at him.

He stood immaculate and imposing in full uniform, his shoulders straining the seams of his pressed forest-green wool jacket. Resting snugly on his lean hips, his leather utility belt held the usual law enforcement equipment: handcuffs, baton, flashlight, ammunition, and his handgun. He looked dangerous — and devastatingly handsome.

And there she was, again, hair disheveled, no makeup, and dressed in her old ratty robe. Eyes downcast, she stood aside for him to enter, her hands moving to straighten her robe and brush her hair out of her eyes. She wished she could disappear through the floor.

He didn't seem to notice. "This place smells delicious. Cinnamon toast?" He headed straight for the kitchen and found the pan. "Cinnamon rolls! And here I thought this was going to be a hellish day." He smiled at her, causing her heart to flutter, then he rummaged through the cupboards for two plates and coffee cups.

"You go ahead," she murmured, turning to escape to the bedroom. "I must look a mess."

In two strides, he crossed the small space to her. "Don't go yet." He touched her hair and gently fingered a wayward curl. "You look fresh from sleep. And beautiful."

He was so close she felt the warmth from his body. Her gaze swept his lips, wondering how they would feel pressed to hers. They had thinned that first day in his office when he was annoyed with her, but now they were soft and full. She raised her gaze to his eyes, drawn in by the green depths, lured by the promise of . . . what? She felt giddy, slightly woozy, as if she hadn't slept—which she hadn't. Much. But this was different.

"I—I must . . . have to . . ." What was wrong with her?

He took her hand. "You need coffee. Have a roll with me. We should have time before Kyle gets here."

She dashed to the bathroom for a quick repair, brushing her teeth and hair and dressing in slacks and an emerald cashmere cardigan. As a finishing touch, she added her Black Hills tricolor gold earrings. She wanted to look professional so the DNR agent wouldn't immediately dismiss her as a kook.

When she returned to the kitchen, Hugh had poured coffee for them both, set plates and silverware at each place, and had the rolls and butter in the center of the table. She could grow to love that kind of attention.

He glanced at her, then took another long, electric look. "You're beautiful."

"Thanks." Her cheeks flushed, and she chided herself for feeling so pleased. Wasn't she going to avoid romantic entanglements?

He pulled out a chair for her, then, after seating

himself, he turned his gaze to the pages next to her printer. "I see you've been busy."

She sat quietly, still basking in his compliment.

'Sorry. This is rude, but I don't have much time." He pushed her laptop aside to make room for the pages, once again making himself at home.

Strangely, even though she'd always guarded her privacy, she wasn't offended. What was this man's hold on her? She had met handsome men before, but never before had she felt so completely mesmerized.

Her gaze moved over him as he read, taking in his strong jawline, his shoulders, then dropped to his imposing utility belt. The gun. Oh yes, bullets! First things first. Did he bring the silver bullets? She had to quit feeling like a schoolgirl with a crush on the football captain. She took several gulps of her coffee not only for an adrenaline rush, but to break out of her dreamy state. She needed to know: could his word be trusted?

"Do you have the bullets?" Her tone was confrontational, as if making up for romanticizing the sheriff, as if she didn't expect him to have remembered.

"I have them, but I'll show you after the interview."

"But—"

"Not enough time right now." He read the article while he ate.

Even though she wanted to demand he show her the bullets now, she knew the article was important. She could wait.

She nibbled on her roll, watching his expression

as he read, hoping for his approval, something she hadn't sought since her cub reporter days. The title she'd chosen was, *Rogue Grizzly Suspected in Local Reporter's Death*, and described the creature as a fuzzy outline, just as Rawlins had requested.

She omitted details about Todd's gruesome death or the fact that he'd left her. For the benefit of his family, she had stated he'd been heroic in trying to save her. To salvage her conscience, she ended with a strong warning to stay out of the mountains until the animal was caught.

Rawlins finished reading.

She searched his face, but it was unreadable. Well? What did he think?

"I like it, Krista. You're alerting the civilians of what may be a serious threat without enough specifics to cause a panic. Good job."

She beamed. God, she was pathetic.

He took a swallow of coffee. "What now? Since you're still here, you must've decided to stay another day. I'm happy about that. What are your plans after the interview?"

"I don't know. I didn't think I'd even be here this long."

He checked his watch. "Well, Kyle should be here in another few minutes. We can discuss your next step after he leaves. For now, let's go over your testimony so you can relate smoothly and without hesitation what happened. We don't want him to get suspicious."

"Suspicious?"

"Oh, you know how guilty — "

"Guilty? I'm not guilty of anything except lying for you. Don't forget I'm the victim here."

He sighed, a long drawn-out expulsion of air. He didn't need to examine the ceiling for her to get the message. She reigned in her impulse to slug him.

"I'm simply asking you to do so to avoid a panic in town. At least until we're further along in the investigation. That's not too much to ask, is it?"

He spoke with an exaggerated slow cadence of a reasonable person dealing with someone unreasonable, and that irritated her even more. If he wasn't the most obnoxious person she'd ever encountered, she —

"And we don't want curious people converging on the scene and destroying evidence."

Even though she still wanted to slap him, he had a point. She didn't want people heading for the mountains and putting themselves in danger, so she needed to go along with him. For now. Besides, she couldn't afford any hang-ups, not if she wanted to leave town as soon as possible.

"I'm not sure I can leave out certain details and still sound convincing. He'll know I'm lying. He just won't know why."

A soft knock sounded at the door.

Rawlins rose from his chair. "That must be Kyle."

Krista stared at the door, then at Rawlins. "I'm not ready!"

"Just try to relax, and stick to the description you wrote in the article. You'll be fine."

NINE

Egypt
The Past

Instead of Hatiah, the usual guard, a man of enormous size stood in battle gear with breastplate and sword at the ready. His full mask honoring the god Horus covered not only his head but his massive shoulders, nearly as large as Rahmor's. At the prince's approach, he snapped to attention and bowed.

"A good day to you, your highness."

Taken aback, Rahmor halted. "Who are you, and where's Hatiah?"

"I am Chikere, expressly-appointed by Pharaoh himself to stand guard." At his statement, he lifted his head and swelled even larger.

"Stand aside, Chikere, and let me pass." Although he had supposed his father would post extra guards to protect the copper-haired woman, he was shocked at the extraordinary measures of the mask, normally worn by the high priest in special rites of protection for Pharaoh.

The golden hawk's head warned of the guard's special fighting mastery. Made of glued linen or papyrus then painted, the features were hand-woven to highlight the sharp golden beak and bronze-colored ruffled head feathers. On the right side of the head, a fan of standing feathers added height. Even to Rahmor, it was impressive.

"I'm sorry, My Lord, but you may not enter."

"You dare to deny entrance to Pharaoh's son? Step aside at once."

"Everyone, except our mighty king himself, is denied entrance."

Rahmor had to maintain a balance with his father's overseer. He must exercise his authority, yet he needed cooperation from this man.

"I'm seeking information about a servant girl taken from the Syrian land during the last military campaign. I believe she was brought to Pharaoh's harem this afternoon. Is she in the palace?"

The guard hesitated. Rahmor could imagine the dilemma running through his mind. To not answer a question posed by a member of the royal family could be considered insubordination, for which the penalty was death.

Chikere finally spoke, his voice not quite as firm. "Which girl, your majesty? Several were brought to the harem."

"You couldn't mistake her. Her hair matches the color of your necklace, and her eyes . . . think the green of a fresh papyrus plant on the delta . . ." He trailed off, realizing he sounded like a lovesick pup. He drew himself up and spoke in a commanding voice. "She would have been brought here this afternoon."

Still the overseer hesitated.

"Come on, man! You must have seen her." Rahmor curbed the impulse to thrash him. "Is she here, or was she taken to Mer Wer to reside in the mass harem?"

Chikere fell prostrate to the floor, his arms spread in supplication.

"I beg for your forgiveness, but I'm not allowed to answer questions."

"Then I'll see for myself. I won't stay, but I must know if she's here." Rahmor had never begged anyone for anything, much less a servant. Dark humiliation sent hot blood cursing through his veins.

"My Lord, I can't allow anyone to enter except the Chief Royal Wife or Pharaoh himself."

Then Rahmor knew. His hands and feet went cold, as if he were pelted by the rain of upper Nubia. The girl was to be groomed as Pharaoh's favorite.

In his frustrated rage, Rahmor struck Chikere with his crop again and again until bloody stripes crisscrossed the guard's back. Then, rage spent, he threw it down and stormed out of the room.

At the turn of the corridor, shamed by his actions, he ducked behind a pillar and wiped his forehead. Never before had he lost control of his emotions. As Pharaoh's son, he'd always conducted himself with dignity and treated others the same. While it would be beneath his station to apologize, he'd do something to help the man, even if it was nothing more than a word of praise to his superior.

His thoughts turned to Satiah. If she sympathized with him, she might possibly intercede for him. As the heir's mother, Pharaoh might listen to her. He had in the past. After all, he had hundreds of women in the harem, and it couldn't possibly be a love match. Pharaoh had only seen the girl once.

But then, so had he.

He had to try. In all his years, he had never felt this way about any woman.

She couldn't be forever lost to him.

By the time Rahmor was granted an audience with Satiah a few days later, he was frantic. He'd not seen the copper-haired woman and no one had any information — or any they could reveal.

"No one may see the red-haired concubine," Satiah told Rahmor, her painted lips thinning, "except Pharaoh himself and the few appointed directly from him." Clearly agitated, she changed position in her ebony chair, her white linen sheath falling softly beneath her breasts. Surrounding her, her handmaidens lounged in dresses similar to their mistress', although some wore their sheaths gathered beneath bare breasts. Perfumed air from a lighted brazier floated through the chamber, and a fragrant cone of myrrh rode upon Satiah's black wig.

"What's your interest in the woman?" Her kohl-lined eyes fixed on him. "It hasn't escaped my attention that you've wandered the palace irritating everyone with your questions. A twelve-year-old would show more discretion."

Deflated, Rahmor felt sick. "Does my father know?"

"Nothing that concerns him escapes his attention. If he doesn't see, his priests inform him. So I'll ask again, what's your interest?"

How could he explain? How could he convey the feelings he had for this woman, the intense longing that burned from the first time he saw her? The image of her standing helpless, yet defiant before Pharaoh, wouldn't allow him to rest. Was it pure lust? Of course the physical hunger was there; she was a beautiful woman. But that desire could be satisfied with any of the multitude of concubines available to him as prince. It was something more, a need to find her, to comfort and protect her from any possible harm, something he'd never experienced before, not even with his first crush at twelve.

Unable to explain, he stood in silence before the irate woman. And as a son of the king, even a minor son, he wouldn't humiliate himself by trying to do so. "I have an interest."

"It's an interest shared by Pharaoh, and you lose. She's installed in special quarters off his chambers, and he sends advisors daily to groom her. Even though she's a commoner, she seems to be his chosen one."

Rahmor couldn't hide his dismay. "Will he crown her queen?"

Satiah's black eyes narrowed. "From the way Pharaoh favors her, I'm sure it will happen—if she lives."

"What do you mean? Is she in danger?"

"The rest of his harem can't hide their displeasure. I, as mother of the heir, also feel threatened for my son."

During the next several weeks, Rahmor seldom left the palace, his spirits lightened by occasional glimpses of the woman moving swiftly through the vast hallways, head lowered, never acknowledging him, always surrounded by her entourage of advisors.

His love was hopeless, and while he was content to just be near her, he longed for a smile or even a quick glance, anything to show she was aware of him.

"Honestly, Rahmor, this childish infatuation has to stop," Nefertiri, his sister, counseled. "Amenemhat is getting quite annoyed with you. He says you're useless in games of strategy, that your concentration flies with the swallows."

"I know. I'm trying."

"I'm sure Father will speak to you."

Even though he was sure everyone knew of his sickness— for that's how Rahmor felt—he'd die of disgrace if his father chastised him like a child.

He had to stop this madness. He'd never before

known failure; instead, his great size and determination made him a formidable opponent in anything he attempted.

So what would assist him in overcoming this malady? Perhaps if the woman, whom Pharaoh bestowed the name Neferaneksi, which meant, "Her beauty belongs to me," would simply acknowledge him with the meeting of eyes or even a small smile, he could recover. He could rest knowing she was aware of him, so he devised a plan.

Over the next few days, by darting from the cover of one pillar and then to another like a treasure thief, he dared entry into the pillared halls by her chambers. He noted the times she left and returned from the bathing quarters, never alone, always accompanied by her advisors and handmaidens. When he finally decided to risk exposure, he listened carefully, and when he heard them approach, he stepped in front of the pillar, counting the seconds, praying she'd see him before her entourage whisked her away.

Would she smile? Nod? With a whisper of slippered feet, she, with her handmaidens and advisors, passed without a glance at him. But a sliver of pink highlighted her cheeks. His heart warmed.

For six days he stood by the same pillar at the same time. Six times she passed without an acknowledgement. On the seventh day, two handmaidens glanced his way and smiled. Tay, a former maidservant to his sister, even giggled but was hastily hushed by the senior maid.

How many times would Pharaoh allow him to stand by? And why had he been permitted to do so? Surely an advisor had reported him. Anyone who witnessed a crime against Pharaoh and didn't report it was fed to the crocodiles. Rahmor had no answer, but he wasn't ready to give up.

On the eighth day, he stood, eyes fixed on the woman, and finally, she raised her head, ever so slightly. His heart raced. Would she look at him? Her incredible green eyes rested on him for mere seconds before she lowered her head and hurried on.

Oh, praise to the goddess Hathor! She saw him! He should be satisfied, but floating back to his quarters, he realized her glance was like nectar from the poppy plant. He had to have more. One more time, he rationalized. Just to feel the exquisite pleasure when her eyes met his, then he'd stop this dishonor to his father.

He waited by the pillar the next day, and when he heard the familiar sound of sandaled feet approaching, he straightened. Would she look at him today? Would she make this all worthwhile and show him a smile? When they approached in their hurried gait, his gaze rested on her. Breathlessly he sent a silent message: *Please, please look at me.*

There! She raised her head, glanced briefly at him. But instead of a smile, a lone tear appeared and rolled down her cheek. She quickly lowered her head and moved on.

A tear? What did that mean? He stared, stunned, his heart breaking for her. When they passed, he realized no maidens accompanied her this day; instead, men wearing breastplates and carrying shields and long spears of war surrounded her.

To guard her from him? It couldn't be. Pharaoh must know he'd never harm her.

Why the need for heavy guards? Was her life in jeopardy?

What could he do to ensure her safety?

TEN

At the firm knock, Krista's gaze locked on the door as if an evil spirit waited on the other side. Would she be able to lie convincingly enough? Her escape depended on everything going smoothly.

Her alarm must have shown, because Rawlins, after a reassuring nod to her, opened the door.

Tall, slim, hair a deep reddish-copper, the man stood in the doorway clutching a briefcase, his hat tucked under his arm. While not as massive as Hugh, he was impressive in his olive-green uniform.

"Kyle. Nice to see you." Hugh offered his hand. "Come on in."

With both men in her tiny living room, Krista felt smothered, and she leaned back in her chair like a cornered animal. Why was that? What was this nonsensical reaction she was having? *Just stop it!* She hadn't done anything wrong. It was that obstinate sheriff's fault she was reacting this way. If she could simply tell the truth . . . yet if she did, would they pay attention to her story or dismiss her as a flake? If she went along with Hugh, at least they'd investigate a little deeper and maybe catch that thing. And she could get out of there.

She took a deep breath, determined to relax and not feel so apprehensive. After all, if they suspected her of lying, so what? What harm could it cause? None. Even a rookie cop could tell she didn't kill Todd. Something vicious did, something much larger and stronger than she'd ever be.

After Hugh made the introductions. Krista indicated the dining table. "Please have a seat. We can talk over fresh coffee and cinnamon rolls."

"Krista made them and they're delicious." High smiled. "I know; I've already sampled one."

"Now why is that not a surprise?" Kyle placed his hat and briefcase on an empty chair and took a seat.

"You should talk. I've seen you down three burgers in a row." Hugh filled three coffee cups.

"Hey, that was after an all-nighter, but you got me."

After they demolished the rolls, Kyle retrieved a small recorder and a tablet, complete with keyboard, from his worn briefcase.

"You don't mind if I record this, do you? I want accuracy in my report."

It took Krista aback for a moment and she glanced at Hugh. He didn't seem alarmed. "That's fine." Despite her new resolve, she could still hear a slight tremble in her voice. Did Kyle notice? He frowned, so obviously he did. While setting up his equipment, he talked to her in a casual, chatty tone.

"You've experienced a terrible thing, Krista, and I'm so sorry that happened to you. But you're alive. The main thing is, you survived. Most victims need counseling to recover from such a traumatic event, and I'd be happy to recommend someone."

"Thank you, but no. I plan on leaving the area as soon as I can."

"Hugh mentioned your plans, but I hope we can have your full cooperation during the investigation."

"I don't know what I can do—it was too dark to see much."

"You might remember more than you realize."

"I'm not sure I want to remember." At least that much was true. She glanced at Hugh again. He nodded his encouragement.

"That's understandable," Kyle replied, "but if you could help me with as many details as you can recall, it'll help us catch the animal that much faster."

"I'll do what I can."

"First, please know fatalities from black or brown bear attacks are few. Actually, there have only been a couple in the last hundred years, but campers need to know they can be quite aggressive this time of year. They feed extensively before winter and will take advantage of all available food sources—"

At his mention of food sources, Krista saw again the beast tearing out Todd's throat. She shuddered and went white.

Hugh glanced at her. "You okay?"

Unable to speak, she nodded.

"I'm terribly sorry," Kyle said. "Use of that word was thoughtless of me. Do you need a moment?"

"No," Krista managed. "Let's just get this over with."

"From the viciousness of the kill, it could've been a cougar, although cats kill to feed, and there were no signs of —"

An agonized sound escaped Krista.

Hugh spoke up. "Let's move on, shall we?"

"Of course." Kyle turned to Krista, fingers poised over the keyboard. "Why were you and your date —"

"Co-worker," Krista interrupted. "Not a date."

"Why were you and your co-worker at the park that late at night? People don't usually go to a closed campsite this time of year."

"He wanted me to see the moon over the river." That sounded lame, even to her.

Kyle's hands paused over the keyboard, and when he looked up, his eyes were narrowed.

He was suspicious. Of what, Krista couldn't guess. Drugs? Did both he and Hugh suspect she and Todd had been doing drugs?

"Perhaps you'd better start from the beginning of that evening," Kyle's tone had changed slightly, "and keep in mind that every detail you can recall is important."

At first, Krista recounted the evening with Todd in a near sing-song voice, and how dark it was in the campsite. Should she mention the howl? Better not.

"Go on," Kyle said.

She continued, watching his face to see if he believed her. She had to get through this torture. When she got to the attack, she slowed, her voice dropping to a whisper. Kyle had to ask her to speak louder and more clearly. She tried, but by then, images were forming of that night, images she'd managed to push aside. Her voice shook, her hands trembled, and she could barely speak. "Please, no more. I just can't relive it again."

"Just a couple more minutes if you can, Krista. It's important. If you need to take a break, I'll wait."

"What more do you need?"

"To the best of your knowledge, can you confirm it was a bear?"

There it was. The question she'd dreaded. No matter her resolve, she felt flustered and dropped her gaze. *No!* She should have held his gaze. To look away was a sure sign of lying. She hoped he hadn't noticed. When she raised her head, she saw he was regarding her quizzically. And there was that frown again. Her cheeks went hot, but she had to make it right.

"I only know it wasn't a cougar," she said, "or any other form of cat. It was too dark to see anything but an outline, but it was big, shaped like a bear on hind legs. Only bigger." That much was true. That image would haunt her forever.

"Could you see any markings? Anything that would help us identify this animal?"

"I told you, it was too dark."

"Would a sketch artist help you remember?"

At his continued probing, she saw again that creature, holding Todd, ripping out his throat. Her stomach rebelled, and she swallowed bile. She clutched her hands and couldn't speak. She shook her head, praying the interview would end.

"Did you hear any sounds?"

"Sounds? Good heavens yes — that creature's growling, snarling . . . an awful sound. And Todd . . . his screams."

She saw again his terrified gaze latching onto her, pleading for help she couldn't offer, then the creature's maniacal eyes staring at her right before tearing into Todd's throat.

"God . . ." Hot acid rushed to her throat. Moaning, she dashed for the bathroom and lost her meager breakfast. Hugh knocked at the bathroom door.

"You all right?" He waited a few minutes, then asked again, "Can I do anything?"

"Give me a minute." She ran cold water and wiped her face and used mouthwash. Staring at her reflection in the mirror over the sink, she told herself she could handle this. She just had to get through the next few questions. Surely he'd realize she couldn't offer more. Still, her face was nearly as white as the porcelain. When she opened the door, she hesitated. Hugh was talking to Kyle, his voice impatient, demanding.

"She's had enough for today, Kyle, and what you have should add to your investigation. If you need more, let me know."

When Krista quietly stepped into the living room, Hugh was handing Kyle's hat to him. Obviously, the interview was over. Thank God.

Kyle appeared startled at the sudden rush to get him out. "I'm not through, Hugh."

"Yes, you are. At least for today."

"Something's not right. She's holding something back, and I'm not sure what it is."

"She survived a fatal bear attack. Her friend didn't, and she's still traumatized. Even you saw that, so what's your problem?"

Kyle gathered his notes and recorder and stuffed them into his bag. "I'm not sure yet what's wrong, but I've been in this business too long not to know she's hiding something. I'll go now, but I want to talk to her again."

"Don't you think she's had enough?"

"Did they dump a grizzly? Was that why they were in the park on a frigid night? Everything was closed. If they did and it turned on them, there will be a criminal investigation."

"Good God, man. She's only been in the state for a month. How could she know anything about that? If that's what happened."

Krista couldn't believe what she was hearing. She knew he was suspicious, but of that? She grabbed the back of the sofa for support. "I did no such thing," she managed, "and neither did Todd."

Kyle stood and faced her. "At this point I'm not saying you did, but I'm asking that you don't leave the area until the investigation is complete. If either of you did set a grizzly loose, you need to let us know. A fatality occurred as a result, and you must be available for more questioning."

Hugh nearly pushed him out the door.

While relieved Kyle was gone, Krista stood rigid. After everything else that had happened, the DNR thought she did something illegal? Something criminal?

Hugh turned to her. "I'm sorry you had to go through it all again, but at least it's over—for now. All we have to do now is wait for the DNA results." He picked up his hat. "I'll leave you now so you can rest—"

"No! Don't go yet." Krista paced the room.

Hugh hesitated. "I have to talk to Kyle, calm him down. What do you need?"

She halted and faced him. "Right now it's taking all my control not to run to my car and get out of this horrid place."

"Kyle asked that you not leave."

"He expects me to stay here? Well, I won't do it. If DNR wants to talk to me again, they'll have to find me." She paced again.

"You're upset and—"

"Of course I'm upset! Wouldn't you be? Oh never mind, you're the poster boy of logic."

"You need to calm down and think rationally. You can't have the DNR chase you, and I don't want your face on the FBI website."

"Good God, an FBI fugitive?" She paced again. "I can't believe this is happening. How did my life spin so out of control?"

"We'll get this all straightened out, but you have to stay. You'll be all right. I promise."

"How can you promise anything? You're as bad as Kyle. You don't believe me either."

"Trust me. We'll get everything untangled, and it'll be all right."

"Trust you? I'm in this mess because I slipped and trusted you. If I'd left right after this happened, I'd be on the other side of the continent by now."

"You can believe this: I won't let anything happen to you."

Somehow, his soothing tone cut through the haze of anxiety. She halted and searched his eyes, hoping for some kind of miracle, desperately wanting to believe him.

"I know it's early, but let me fix you a drink." Rawlins headed for the kitchen.

"I don't need a drink. I need . . . I need . . ."

"What, Krista? What do you need?"

"I need to feel safe."

"You will be. I'll escort you wherever you need to go."

"You can't be with me twenty-four hours a day, and if I'm going to stay even an hour longer, I have to know I can protect myself. If you really have silver bullets, I want some. A lot of them. Do you really have them? Or were you lying?"

Hugh tossed his hat onto the wing chair and withdrew a small wooden box from his jacket pocket. Inside, four sections were lined with what appeared to be some sort of a cloth material. Nestled in their protective slots were four gleaming silver bullets.

Krista had never seen anything like them. She reached for one.

"Put these on first." He extracted white cotton gloves from his pocket and handed a pair to her. "We don't want to scratch or scuff the metal." He carefully handed a bullet to her.

It looked just like the 9mm ammunition she used when target practicing with her fiancé in Arizona, but it was so glossy she could almost see her face. "Is it real silver?"

"Absolutely. I watched the gunsmith craft them. He's also a silversmith who takes pride in his work."

She turned the bullet upside down, fascinated by the reflected shine and the uniqueness. "Why go to all that trouble just for a pageant? Why not use a fake bullet? No one would know."

"I'd know, and it wouldn't be the same. Besides," his gaze leveled on her, "if I commit to something — or someone, I commit fully."

When she met his gaze, a liquid warmth spread through her body all the way to her toes. Her cheeks flushed. Flustered, she handed him the bullet, which he replaced in the box, then safely back into his pocket.

She cleared her throat and averted her gaze. The last thing she wanted was for him to know his effect on her. "Thanks for showing them to me, but you'll need more for this creature. A lot more."

"You let me worry about that."

"But—" The ring of his cell phone interrupted her.

As he talked, he moved into the kitchen. For privacy, she presumed, not that her tiny apartment afforded much. When he spoke, his tone changed, became brusque, harsh.

"Where?" He listened, then turned to face her as he spoke. "I'm leaving now. Be there shortly."

"What's going on?"

"An accident in a town nearby. I have to go." He took both her arms. "I want you to listen carefully, and please, for once do as I say."

"You're scaring me."

"Good. Maybe you'll listen. I want you to stay right here. Do not, under any circumstances, leave this apartment until I return. Is that clear?"

She knew. All of her instincts knew what happened. Her breath came in short gasps. "It's that creature again, isn't it? It attacked someone else, didn't it?" She searched his face. He couldn't hide the truth. She wrenched out of his arms and dashed into her bedroom. "I'm getting out of here. Now!"

He overtook her and grabbed her arm to stop her. "Think this through. If you leave now, you'll be in the open, exposed—"

"I'll be in my car!" She yanked her arm free.

"You saw what that beast did to a pickup. How easy do you think a car door would be? No. You'll be safer right here."

He was right. That thing could rip open her car door as easily as if it were made of cardboard. "I'll stay on one condition."

"Which is?"

"Do you have more of those bullets?"

"In a safe place."

"Get some and carry them with you. Leave that box with me. And give me a gun. Now. Before you leave."

"No problem. I carry a spare in my car. You'll stay?"

"Just until you get back."

"Listen to me. If that creature is anything like you described, it has intelligence. And even though I don't buy your werewolf theory, we'll say for the moment it is a werewolf. If so, and since it saw you, it could follow you anywhere. You'll be safer here with me until it's caught and destroyed."

Oh my God, he was right. Even though Hugh was the most exasperating man she'd ever known, he calmed her with a sense of comfort, even protection, when he was near—not that she'd admit it to him.

She nodded. "If you have more bullets, a lot more, I'll stay— until that thing is caught."

"Agreed. And don't worry—I have an ample supply."

ELEVEN

About fifteen minutes after Hugh left her apartment, a timid knock sounded on her door.

"It's Mrs. Reardon. Are you all right?"

"Just a moment!" Krista stashed the Beretta M9 Hugh left with her and the box of ammo in her bathroom cabinet, then, letting out a breath, opened the door to her white-haired neighbor. The woman wore an apologetic expression and held a steaming casserole dish. Krista stepped aside.

"If I'm intruding, just let me know, but I baked this for you." Mrs. Reardon handed her the dish nestled in a red-checked kitchen towel. "Be careful, it's hot. It's an egg casserole. With mild sausage. I have trouble with spicy stuff, you know, but I do get hungry for a nice tasty sausage."

Krista stared at the woman. With trying to sort through the terrible morning, yet not reveal the horrific events to her neighbor, she stood at a loss for words.

"I'm rambling. Here, let me." The woman took the casserole from Krista's hands and carried it to the kitchen. "I'm sorry to bother you, and I don't mean to be nosy, but I couldn't help but notice you didn't go to work this morning. And that nice sheriff has been here a couple of times. Are you all right? Is there anything I can do?"

Her gentle concern made Krista homesick for her mother, a longing so intense that it melted all of her reserves. Everything she'd held in since the attack dissolved, and she broke into deep, crushing sobs. Immediately her neighbor was by her side, guiding her to a dining chair, all the while patting her back and crooning to her as if Krista were a baby.

"There, there. Poor thing, all alone in a new place. I understand. Just remember you have friends. You'll be all right, there, there." She went on, her soothing tone comforting Krista.

After a few moments, when her tears dried, Krista felt drained, staring absently at her kind neighbor, wondering how much to tell her.

"How about a nice cup of tea? You stay right there and I'll make it for you." Mrs. Reardon ambled to the small kitchen and rummaged through the cupboards until she found tea bags and a kettle for water. Once it was ready, she poured two cups. Krista offered to help, but her new friend shushed her. "I can do it."

"Thank you." Krista hiccupped a couple of times.

Mrs. Reardon pulled her chair close to Krista. "Oh honey, I'm so sorry you're troubled. Anything I can do? I may not be physically capable of much, but I come from strong stock, and I got good ears. I can listen if you care to talk. Sometimes it helps."

Krista stared at the woman's heavily-lined face, sure she'd seen a lot in her long lifetime, the thin white hair gathered in a little knot on top of her head, and especially at the kindness evident in her blue eyes. She could just imagine this frail woman in that creature's claws. She shuddered. No way. No way could she abandon Mrs. Reardon or any of the town's people to that creature. She would stay until that beast was caught and destroyed, and if she could help in any way, she'd absolutely do so.

"Mrs. Reardon, do you have a place to go to for a while? Any family or friends you can stay with?"

"Something's wrong, isn't it? Might as well tell me. I can find out from Junior Hudson if you don't." She smiled, her tired eyes taking on a youthful, jubilant shine. "No matter how old or big that boy gets, I can still intimidate him. I was his sixth-grade teacher, you know. And while I may look like a useless old lady now, in the old days I didn't put up with any nonsense. And there wasn't a person who didn't know it."

Krista almost gasped. Her sweet neighbor had a sassy side. Suddenly, Krista felt better. She'd made a friend — a friend she could relax with and talk to.

"Might as well fix another cup of tea. And let's have some of that casserole. Suddenly, I'm hungry, and I have a story to tell you."

An hour later, Mrs. Reardon sat stunned. "I can't imagine such a terrible thing, but thank the good Lord you were spared. You do as that nice Sheriff Rawlins told you. He'll make sure that animal is caught."

"Please, please, promise you won't go anywhere until that creature's destroyed. It's vicious and I don't want anything to happen to you. Have your groceries delivered. Medications too."

With a smile, the older woman patted Krista's hand. "I'm not worried. We finally have a capable, dedicated sheriff, and now that he's signed on full-time, I'm sure he'll handle it. He's nearly as big as a grizzly, and such a hunk."

Krista's cheeks pinked. She knew all too well he was a hunk, but right now, she was concerned about her neighbor. "At least have someone take you where you need to go. Can you do that?"

"You know he's single, don't you? You two would make a ne pair — once this is over, of course."

"Mrs. Reardon, please. We're talking about your safety. I can't think of anything but that creature loose in the hills. Who knows what it's liable to do next."

"All right. If it'll make you feel better, I'll be careful." She rose to leave, and Krista walked her to the door.

"There's our new neighbor, Brandon Cole! He's moving in today." The elderly lady turned back to Krista with a mischievous twinkle in her eyes. "He's single, and with his looks, he'll make the girls swoon. You should meet him." Before Krista could stop her, Mrs. Reardon called him over.

"No! I don't want to meet anyone." Krista ducked inside.

"Too late. He's on his way. I swear, I don't know

why our town's so popular now. First you, now this nice young man, but I'm glad he's here. Puts some new blood in this old town."

Ignoring the younger woman's irritation, she greeted the man with a big smile and made the introductions.

In his early-to mid-forties, he stood just over six feet, clean-shaven except for a neatly-trimmed goatee. Krista had to admit he was nice-looking with even features and eyes the exact shade of his sea-green parka. He was sure to set the feminine hearts fluttering.

She was in no mood to be social, yet she didn't want to seem rude. Gritting her teeth, she nodded and muttered something about the weather.

With a smile showing even white teeth, Brandon removed his glove and offered his hand. "I always thought I'd love to live in snow-capped mountains, but it's cold here. Coming from Southern California, I'm not used to it."

"You're moving here from California?"

"Sounds strange, doesn't it? But I'm starting a new job and a new life here."

"He's a doctor, you know." Mrs. Reardon beamed with pride as if he were her son or grandson. "Just what this old town needs."

"Doctor of Chiropractic," he added. "But I'm changing careers, and my new position will help me get started. I'm a bit early, though. I wanted to check homes before my fiancée arrives next month."

Too preoccupied with her own life to encourage

further conversation, Krista welcomed him again, then muttered an excuse to withdraw. When she closed the door, she could hear both her neighbors talking.

Her lack of sleep caught up with her. She stuck the leftovers in the fridge, stacked the dishes, and lay on the bed, wondering what Hugh had found.

But as exhausted as she felt, she couldn't sleep. She kept glancing at the window. How close was that monster? Could it crash through? That beast was strong enough. And intelligent too; she'd seen it in its eyes. Was it out there right now, watching, just waiting for her to be alone?

Finally she shoved her dresser in front of the window. It could probably still get in, but at least the heavy piece of furniture would slow it down. Still, she couldn't sleep, so she settled on the living room sofa across from the front door. The thick wood may not be crash-proof, but it faced the street, and if that beast had the intelligence she thought it did, it would think twice before daring a visible front entrance.

The conversation with Mrs. Reardon ran through her mind. So Hugh was single? She'd assumed so, especially since that first day when he said he had no dependents, but she realized she knew nothing else about him. Maybe another day she'd ask. Her neighbor seemed to know a lot—about him, about the town. And something she'd said struck a strange cord, but what was it? Exhaustion melted the day into a blur and nothing made sense. Finally she slept. Sometime later, the phone rang. It was Hugh.

"Was it that monster?" Krista gripped the phone,

barely breathing. "Did it attack someone else?"

"I don't think so. The victim was mauled, but I think it was a cougar."

"Why? How do you know?"

"Tracks. Look, we're pretty busy here and I don't have much time. I'll fill you in later."

"Is the victim . . . is he . . . she — "

"He's unconscious, but alive so far. Still, I want you to stay in until I get back this evening. We have to decide some things. Make some plans."

As soon as she disconnected, Carla called.

"I got your article. *¡Dios mío!*" She lapsed into her native Spanish. "Krista, I had no idea you were the survivor of that attack. Are you all right? Were you hurt? Need anything?" Her questions came one after another with little room for an answer.

"I'm okay, thanks. I'm even thinking about returning to the office in a day or two. Just as soon as I feel steady enough."

"Well, don't rush it. We'll be powering down anyway for a few days — in observance of Todd's passing, you know, so take as much time as you need. And let me know how you're doing."

She'd be back to work in a day or two? Krista hadn't planned on saying that, but was it true? She was surprised to discover it was. Now that she had decided to stay until the creature was destroyed, she needed something to do, something to occupy her mind so she didn't relive Todd's death again and again.

What to do until Hugh returned this evening? Call Hannah, her mother.

Krista kept her voice as normal as possible. "Things aren't working out here, so don't plan on moving yet."

"Ah honey, why not? You were so hopeful. Did anything happen to change your mind?"

Krista invented some excuses.

Hannah went silent for a few moments. "Honey, I know you. What aren't you telling me? You're not still grieving over Chuck, are you? He and his new wife moved out of state somewhere, so they're gone."

Krista hadn't even thought of Chuck Stillwell, who'd jilted her on the morning of their wedding, and she realized it no longer hurt to think about him. Looking back, she realized his habits were strange, always taking three or four days each month to go hiking in the desert, never allowing her to go. He needed to "commune with nature," he'd said. She hoped his new wife tagged along anyway and made him miserable. She smiled at that impish thought without a trace of regret.

"Krista? Are you all right? Should I come out there?"

"No, mom. I'm okay." She had to assure her mother nothing was wrong, or Hannah was liable to take the next plane to West Virginia to help her daughter through whatever was troubling her. The last thing Krista needed right now was to worry about her mom's safety, so she had to sound convincing. But what could she say? "It's ... just different here. The people are different, and it's getting so cold."

Her mother laughed. "That's just getting used to a different state. I know. Remember me telling you how Dad and I met?"

"Yes, mom. You've told it a hundred times." Krista knew what was coming, so she prepared herself to listen. Again.

"He was stationed at the Great Lake Naval base — Illinois, you know — when we met," her mother went on as if she hadn't heard Krista. "Such a handsome man with that head full of dark hair and brown eyes. When I first saw him at the taco place, sitting on his motorcycle, I knew. He wasn't one of those hoods. Oh no, he was polite. But insistent on a date." She sighed, and Krista smiled, thinking of her parents in love, even if they were her adoptive parents.

"When your dad and I married, I moved from Illinois to Arizona," Hannah went on. "That was quite a change for a girl who'd never been out of her home city. Give yourself another month or two, then decide. I'm not in a hurry to move, so I can wait. I have memories here."

She went silent, and Krista knew her mother's thoughts were drifting into the past, not only to her husband's death, but her son's. She needed to turn the conversation to something lighter, something fun, so she told her mom about Mrs. Reardon, and then mentioned the sheriff. She lied and said they'd met while having lunch at the Main Street Diner.

"Oh? I can tell by your voice you like him. Tell me more." Her mother's voice sounded hopeful.

"Right now there's not much to tell, but I'll let you

know." They ended the conversation on a lighter tone, and Krista resolved to call again soon.

She checked the fridge to see what she could prepare for dinner, showered, and pampered herself with fresh nail polish and all the little things she normally did before a date. She pulled her hair in an upsweep, and while glancing at herself in the mirror, she hesitated. What in heaven's name was she doing?

It wasn't that she wanted to be pretty for Hugh; it was because she needed something to do while waiting for his arrival. She needed to think of things other than this latest attack. That's all it was. Disgusted, she released her hair and purposely dressed in a shapeless, faded rust-colored lounger.

While her meatloaf and baked potato dinner was cooking, she took a glass of iced tea to the living room and turned on the TV. Was there anything on the evening news about the attack? The reporter mentioned it briefly, and while he said the victim was in critical condition, the attack was under investigation. She switched to a sitcom rerun and checked her watch. According to what Hugh had said, he should be there soon. What would the DNR have discovered?

When he arrived later that evening, she observed the dark circles under his eyes, the lines of fatigue around his mouth and felt a stab of guilt for taking all his spare time. Before bombarding him with questions, she offered him a seat at the table.

"You look like you could use a drink."

"Anything you have will be fine." He placed his hat on an empty chair and sat down at his usual place with a sigh.

"Hungry?"

"I haven't stopped moving since I left here."

Krista prepared a whisky shot and checked dinner.

"Smells good." High finished the shot and refused another. He sighed again. "I'm so damned tired of bloody messes and people dying."

She paused after taking dinner out of the oven. "Was it the werewolf?" She held her breath.

"Cougar."

"How can you be sure?"

"The shape and size of the tracks. Looked like an adult and a cub, probably came down to feed. We both know your grizzly's tracks are much larger than three-to-four-inches wide."

"You're certain that's what it was?"

"Absolutely."

"I don't know whether to be relieved or more concerned." Krista prepared plates for them both.

"Don't celebrate yet."

"Why?"

"The victim never regained consciousness. Now DNR will go on the hunt for the cats, and it'll push our grizzly further into the hills."

"But isn't that a good thing? Get it as far away as possible?"

"Not if we want to destroy it. We have to find and eliminate the threat."

He was right. To see that creature destroyed was the only way she'd ever feel safe.

After they finished dinner, he helped her clear the table, and relaxed with another shot in his coffee. "We need to plan your immediate future."

"It's simple. I'll go to work, come home, and go to work again until this thing is found."

"Stay home a few more days and get some rest. You've been under quite a strain. Then I'll escort you to work each day—if you still insist on going in. Maybe by then Kyle will have some results so we'll know what we're dealing with."

"I already know what we're dealing with, and I will not stay home."

"Why won't you listen to me? I'm only taking precautions for your own safety."

"I realize that and appreciate it, but if I stay in this apartment, I'll lose whatever sanity I have left. I have to be at work by nine in the morning. What time will you pick me up?"

Lying on the sofa that night, trying to fall asleep, she thought about this latest attack. Was Hugh being truthful about the cougars? She hoped so, yet if it had been the werewolf and it was attacking more frequently, wouldn't the chances of tracking it be better?

But where did it come from? And what was bringing it out of the shadows now?

TWELVE

Egypt
The Past

Troubled by the woman's tears, Rahmor barely touched his evening meal and retired early. Instead of relaxing, he paced the chamber floor. Why was she tearful? And why guards instead of her maidens? Had someone threatened her life? If so, he'd crush them with his bare hands.

His immediate suspect was Satiah. Could she be involved? He hated to think a woman so highly positioned as his father's chief wife could be behind such a foul deed, but jealousy was a strong motive. Scribes had recorded too many unexplained royal deaths to not be aware of the danger.

His father had to know of a threat to order the guards. Whom did he suspect? Rahmor desperately wanted to talk to him, to get information and to let him know of his own attachment to the woman Pharaoh had brought to his harem. After all, he had always been open to discussing issues. Yet this involved a woman his father favored, and doubts clouded Rahmor's brain.

He sat on the edge of his bed, the woven reeds giving slightly under his weight. He lay back and folded his hands under his head and closed his eyes, but weighed by indecision for the first time in his life, sleep eluded him.

He pulled his game of Senet from a cupboard and placed the bright green board of thirty squares on a table. He rolled a pawn down one row of ten and made corresponding moves on the board, but he could summon no interest in the outcome.

If the possibility existed that Pharaoh wasn't aware of his son's infatuation with his new favorite, he'd surely know after a discussion. And what would happen? While Rahmor knew his father loved and honored him, he also knew of men who had abandoned their family for the love of a woman. Did he dare stand in judgment before Pharaoh and risk his displeasure? What if his father banished him from the kingdom?

Did he dare risk the love of his father for this woman? His land?

Frustrated, he threw the long board against the wall with such force the sliding drawer pulled apart and struck his bronze trinket box. It hit the floor with a loud clatter.

A guard dashed in, fully-attired in a breastplate, his spear held at ready. "Your Highness! Are you all right?" He looked wildly around for the danger.

"False alarm. You may go."

"Yes, sire. I'll be just outside." When the guard turned, he spotted the Senet board and, with a slight grin he tried to hide, retrieved it and placed it on the table.

Having no patience with indecisiveness and certainly not his own, Rahmor stood. He'd find a way to see the woman somehow to talk with her. Then he'd know what to do.

By the time he entered the atrium that separated his apartments from his father's, he had an idea. Tay, his sister's former handmaiden, the one who'd noticed him waiting by the pillar and giggled, would help him.

Whenever he'd visited his sister, the maiden had favored him with shy smiles that had, over the years, grown bolder, and her gaze followed his every movement. It might take some persuasion to get her to agree, as doing so could place her life in danger, but he felt she'd want to please him. That would eliminate one problem, but he still had another. Since it was forbidden to enter the harem, how could he talk to Tay? He'd need an ally. Who in the palace would risk their position and possibly their life for him?

Strolling through the lush gardens, listening to the water cascading down a three-tired fountain, Rahmor spotted colorful rose bushes and immediately his sister came to mind. Meritamen loved the scent and adored the velvet petals. He paused. His sister! Of course! She would help him; she owed him.

At one time Pharaoh had arranged a political marriage for her with a Byblos prince. She'd wept for days. Usually daughters of kings obeyed without question, but in this case, Meritamen couldn't abide the prince's company, so Rahmor risked his father's displeasure and intervened. Finally, after a lengthy deliberation, their father acquiesced. If his sister refused to help him now, he'd remind her of that unpleasant time. As an enticement, he'd present a bouquet of her favorite flowers.

Careful of the thorns, he chose a few roses that varied in shades of red and pink, then plucked several cornflowers and yellow chrysanthemums. He strolled another few feet to the bushes and dwarf trees. Maybe a papyrus stalk or two for greenery. He glanced at the water lilies in the fish pond, but they had closed when the sun disappeared below the hills. He bypassed the figs, pomegranates, and other fruits. The harem's garden grew them and her maidens made sure she had a supply each week.

He entered his sister's apartments and found her lounging on a chaise chair, two maidens attending to her hair while another sat at her feet applying lotion or cream. Her chair was carved from the finest imported woods and adorned with a lotus flower inlaid in gold. Sheer pastel curtains separated the lounging area from the sleeping niche, and on a stone table next to her chair, her black wig sat alongside her wide collar necklace and several rings.

Her maidens smiled and blushed at the sight of him and continued with their mistress's grooming.

Rahmor felt awkward carrying the bouquet, so he presented it quickly. "For you."

With a puzzled smile, Meritamen accepted it. At seventeen, she didn't associate with her brothers as often as when they were children, so she seemed pleased.

"Welcome, my brother. Come, sit, and have some wine." She nodded to a maiden who rose from the floor to fill a golden cup for him.

Too unsettled to recline, he took the cup and drained it. By this time he wanted to smash something. He was a royal prince of Egypt. He didn't ask for favors: people asked them of him. He just hoped his great size masked his mortification.

"Dismiss your maidens. I want to speak of a private matter with you."

After they'd left, he told her of his plan.

"And you want me to help you enter our father's harem? I will not even consider it. He'd certainly be furious and he would have every right. We both know he has plans for her."

"It's no secret she is his favorite, but you know how I feel about her. I must have a moment to speak with her."

"You have been on the great sands too long. If I were discovered, our father would surely banish me to some distant land. No."

"You leave me no choice. Remember how I risked his displeasure when he planned for you to wed the Byblos prince?"

She stared at him in disbelief, but finally, she agreed. "It'll take me a few days to arrange it." She turned her back, clearly dismissing him.

"It must be tonight. No one knows our father's plans. He may whisk her off tomorrow."

"Tonight? Impossible!"

"Nothing's impossible, my sister. You can do this. I'll wait for you in my chambers, and you can send word when Tay is ready to help." With as much dignity as he could summon, he exited her chambers and entered his own.

He waited. He retrieved his game of Senet. He paced. What was taking so long? At the entrance, he peered past the guard, who immediately snapped to attention. Would Meritamen be able to arrange such a complicated meeting? And in secret? He sent a silent prayer to Isis and Hathor to aid him on his quest.

Finally, just before Ra returned from the underworld to bring the morning light, a light tap on his door revealed one of Meritamen maidservants. She bowed.

"Please follow me, Sire."

Had Meritamen succeeded? While he'd demanded her aid, he hadn't been sure she could arrange it, especially so quickly. The maidservant led him past his sleeping guard, a dark liquid spilling out of an overturned cup at his feet. Drugged, Rahmor surmised. Otherwise, sleeping on duty would result in the man's death.

Quickly, her bare feet moving silently over the

tiled floors, she led him through the palace to the harem's entrance. Fire sconces lit the hallways. His heart pounding as if he were a slave escaping his quarters, he followed.

Near the harem's entrance, he spotted Chikere, the special guard, sprawled on the floor, snoring loudly, an act, which if discovered, resulted in a cruel and instantaneous death. To the side, Tay stood plastered against the extra harem guard, passionately kissing him and pressing a cup to his lips. He didn't seem to notice Rahmor or the maidservant.

The maidservant led him into the apartments, silently weaving through the different chambers until arriving at another entrance. Like his own, Neferaneksi's guard lay snoring at the foot of the closed ornate door. The maiden, her gaze on the guard, stepped carefully around him to lead Rahmor through the door.

He caught a glimpse of the apartment, nearly a duplicate of Meritamen's chambers. His heart pounded. His pulse raced. Was it actually going to happen? Would Neferaneksi appear?

He waited.

Finally, his deepest desire came true. Praise to Ra, she entered the room. Wearing a sheer linen dress of white, she stood before him, her head lowered, her gaze on the floor.

His heart swelled and nearly burst.

"Sire," the handmaiden whispered, "the guards will awaken soon. We must hurry."

Knowing he had a limited time made this

moment even more treasured. Rahmor simply stood and gloried in the sight of her, letting his gaze move lovingly over her delicate frame, taking in every detail from her shining copper curls to her rounded hips. Finally, he stood close enough to speak and even touch the woman who had captured his heart.

Softy, so he wouldn't frighten her, he stepped closer. Gently he lifted her chin, adoring her delicate cheekbones and finely-chiseled nose. Her full lips were made for his touch. And when she shyly lifted her eyes to meet his, his breath caught in the emerald depths.

"You're so beautiful I can barely speak. I've waited for this moment for so long." A hint of a smile from her made his heart sing. "Do you have someone in your homeland who loved you? A husband, a father?"

"No, sire. I had no one. I was an orphan."

The sad way she said that tore his senses and aroused all of his protective instincts.

"I will love you. Forever."

A single tear formed. "Oh sire, how I wish it were you who would take me as wife."

Rahmor touched the tear and brought it to his mouth, wishing, for the first time, he were king and could take this woman as his queen. But it was not to be.

From behind him, the whisper of footsteps approached. "Sire, the guards are rousing. We must go."

He touched his cheek to Neferaneksi's in a final

embrace, and before he could endanger her life, he turned and left the room, knowing he'd left his heart with her.

THIRTEEN

WV
Present Day

The morning dawned overcast with a possibility of snow, and Krista searched the low-lying clouds from the passenger window of Hugh's SUV. Under normal circumstances she would have loved the winter experience, but now, on the way to the newspaper office, she simply wanted to get through the days with as few complications as possible. Snow, although she'd originally been excited about the prospect, was another complication in finding the creature.

Hugh drove silently, occasionally throwing her a churlish look. She ignored him. They'd said enough last night, and he wasn't too happy with her. She hid her smile, pleased she'd finally won an argument with him. She sat silently, trying to prepare for the questions she knew she'd be asked.

Even though it was a weekday morning, a *Closed* sign hung on the office door and the blinds were drawn. Between the blinds and the window, an *In Observance* poster with Todd's photo stood in the center. Krista imagined they'd be working on a follow-up about the bear attack.

As soon as Rawlins pulled up, Carla burst through the door, her plump, fortyish body moving faster than Krista had ever seen.

"I just happened to see you guys arrive," Carla gushed through the passenger window. "Shouldn't you be home resting?"

"That's what I told her," Rawlins said. Several pedestrians stopped to listen.

Embarrassed by the attention, Krista mumbled to Rawlins, "Thanks for the ride."

"Call when you're ready to leave. If I'm not available, I'll send Delzo."

"Any news?" Carla asked the sheriff.

"Still under investigation. I'll let you know."

Inside the office, everyone gathered around Krista, offering coffee and bottled water.

"Your article was superb," Junior Hudson, the publisher, told her. "Because you sent it in so quickly, we'll be able to get that special edition out tomorrow." With his bald head and gentle nature, he reminded Krista of an older, chunkier Mr. Clean, and he always treated the staff with courtesy and respect. "It wasn't necessary for you to come in, but now that you're here, we have some questions. If they prove to be too much," he continued, his bass voice lowered to convey sympathy, "we'll understand. But there will be a lot of public interest, so as soon as you feel comfortable, we'll need assistance on a follow-up to your article."

"We're all so sorry about Todd," Sunnie Powell, the office manager, added, "but thank the Good Lord you, at least, were spared."

Working past retirement age, Sunnie was the senior staff member and ran the office with firm, yet gentle persuasion. Her uncle, along with Junior's father, started the weekly paper years ago and moved his family from Louisiana to West Virginia. She still spoke with a slight southern drawl. She could be found after-hours in her office, attending to something the others had forgotten or neglected. Of average height, she wore her gray-streaked dark hair just below shoulder length, and behind her clear-framed glasses, her eyes were warm and kind.

"What a horrendous, tragic night for you." Carla pushed her purple-rimmed glasses in place. "My photos of the scene will be perfect with your article. I just wish I could've gotten closer. I'd like you to take a look at them."

"I'm not ready to see them, and no, you don't wish you were closer." Krista thought of Todd's bloody corpse and shuddered.

Carla didn't pay attention, or perhaps she didn't hear. She rushed to her desk and grabbed a manila envelope.

Sunnie put her arms around Krista in a silent, supportive hug. "Hey y'all, let Krista settle in, perhaps work on something benign, like the upcoming Thanksgiving Day festivities before—"

"Did Todd really, like, try to keep the bear off you?" Wendy Knowles broke in. Her thin multi-ringed fingers wiped sudden tears. At barely eighteen and the office clerk, she had believed his flirtations and had unsuccessfully tried to hide her crush on him. How far he had taken things with the girl, Krista didn't want to know. She just hoped he'd shown good judgment and maturity for once, in dealing with her.

"Let's let Krista relax and have a seat before we all bombard her," Junior suggested. "After what she's been through, she must need some time to gather her thoughts."

"Oh. Of course." Carla clutched the envelope, her crestfallen expression portraying her disappointment.

"I appreciate your sympathy and understanding," Krista told them. "I described what happened as best I could in the article, so if you've read that, you know as much as I do." Maybe not quite everything, she silently added.

"Okay, people," Junior said. "We have work to do. Krista, you could do some proofing, perhaps the entertainment section, or as Sunnie suggested, the upcoming Thanksgiving articles."

Krista nodded, relieved to be assigned something pleasant to edit.

After about an hour, the words blurred. Her eyes watered. Her cumulative lack of sleep was catching up with her.

Junior approached her desk. "I know you've been through hell, and I hate for you to have to do this, but do you feel up to checking Carla's photos? She had to stand behind the crime scene tape and I'd like you to check her captions for accuracy. I wouldn't ask, but I want to get the special edition to the printer asap."

The last thing Krista wanted was look at the scene's photos. How far did her sense of duty extend?

"I-I'm sure they're accurate."

Carla bounced up from her desk, manila envelope in hand. Her expression was sympathetic, but Krista could see how badly she wanted to hand the photos to her.

"It would mean a lot." Carla extended the envelope.

Silently Krista took it and escaped to the back supply room. A stool stood before a long counter attached to a wall filled with various framed snapshots of the community and events over the years. Needing a few moments to gather courage, she scanned the framed photos, all of which she'd seen in her month of employment.

Some of the black and white photos showed the town a few years ago with its vacant buildings, one after another, boards plastered over their windows, some with cracked windows and doors. The city streets were nearly deserted.

Krista had learned about the southwestern part of the state's decline after observing huge trucks and machinery rumbling through town. In their rush to get at the coal faster, mining companies laid off generations of under-ground miners and replaced them with massive machinery and dynamite to strip the earth of vegetation and blow up age-old mountaintops. Once proud men and women were forced into poverty, and the town struggled to survive. But the people's spirits refused to be forever crushed, so they met and decided on a new industry: promoting the local rivers and lakes for fishing and whitewater sports.

Slowly, the town was coming back to life, and any news of a new store or business opening was celebrated with fanfare. Junior was the prominent figure in most of the photos, as he and Mayor Jennings attended shop openings, grocery store promotions, and other chamber events. Underneath the black- and-white photos, recent color shots of the same buildings happily displayed new windows with green awnings, fresh coats of paint, and signs saying, *Welcome! Now Open.*

Her glance settled on a shot of the County Council, County Commissioners and Rawlins. She smiled and leaned forward to read the caption: *Officials Welcome New County Sheriff.* Gazing at his image, she felt a slight comfort, almost as if he were there, encouraging her, letting her know she wasn't alone. She could do this.

She took a deep breath and opened the envelope, but something disturbed her and she took another look at the photograph. Her gaze wandered over the City Council members, then settled on Hugh. What bothered her about it?

She tried to dismiss it knowing she'd seen the

photo many times over the past month, but a nagging feeling of recognition beyond knowing it was him persisted, as if she'd seen a similar shot somewhere, at some other time, but it was fleeting, gone before she could taste it. It wasn't the best shot of Hugh, with his head slightly lowered as if he were ducking the photographer, but it was him, standing nearly a foot taller than the others. Of course she felt recognition — by now she knew every inch of his face. A warmth spread over her chilled senses, and she felt ready to view Carla's shots.

She slid them one by one from the envelope and had to give Carla credit — she had moved fast. The photos had already been blown up to eight by tens.

Krista quickly scanned them, and thank God, Todd's body had already been removed. Only the blood evidence remained on his pickup and the surrounding ground. Carla had at least ten of those. Several officials, including Rawlins, Delzo, Kyle, and others of the DNR, were shown taking samples, measurements, and plaster casts in the various stages of their investigations.

The last ones, close-ups of the pickup's door hanging by a torn piece of metal, highlighted the blood and claw marks. Krista visualized what the photos couldn't show — the creature tearing out Todd's throat. She broke out in a cold sweat.

She must have made a sound. Immediately the door flew open and Sunnie swooped in. Gathering the photos, she put them on the counter before she turned to Krista.

"I'm sorry to invade your privacy, but I was standing by the door. Are you all right?"

"I need some air."

"Oh honey, of course you do." Sunnie helped Krista to her desk chair, gave her a bottle of water, and turned to Junior. "She shouldn't be here, or at least she shouldn't see those photos today. It's too soon."

"You're right," he said. "I apologize."

Carla shoved one last glossy in front of Krista. "This should make you feel better."

Krista stared at an eight by ten of Todd, and the caption read, *Local Hero Gives His Life for Another.* She swallowed the bile that rose in her throat.

"It must be so difficult," Junior said, his voice filled with sympathy, "to be here among Todd's fellow workers knowing he sacrificed himself to save you."

That did it. Krista rushed for the restroom, barely making it before losing her breakfast. She rinsed her face and mouth with cold water and waited for the trembling to stop.

How could she continue to lie to these kind people? Shouldn't they know the truth?

When she opened the door, she overheard Carla talking. "Survivor's guilt," the editor was saying in a whisper. As soon as Krista appeared, she reddened and went silent.

"Okay everyone," Junior announced, eyeing Carla. "No more. I'm assigning the entertainment section to Krista and that's all. Anything else we might need, we'll send by email."

"Or text," Carla added.

"And no photo attachments until further notice. Agreed?" Junior emphasized to Carla.

"Got it."

"Krista, may I speak to you?" Sunnie led her to her cubical and offered a chair. She poured water from a bottle into a small electric hot pot and brewed tea, then handed the cup to Krista. "I ran out of powdered milk, but I have sugar."

"This is fine, thanks." Krista sipped the tea, curious as to why the office manager wanted to speak privately to her, but she wasn't overly concerned. Sunnie had always been thoughtful and kind.

"Honey, we all appreciate your devotion to duty, but you've been through a terrible trauma, and you need time to recover. Today's experience proves that. I think you should take some time off and consider counseling. We may be a small town, but we have some fine doctors, and I happen to know an excellent psychologist." Sunnie smiled. "He lives right here in town, and he's a good man. My grandson."

Krista wasn't sure how to answer, wasn't even sure how she felt. "I appreciate your concern, and I'll think about it." She sighed. "I'm not sure anything would help. When I stay home, I keep replaying that night, kept seeing that beast—bear," she corrected. "I thought work would help me get through the days, but now I don't know. Besides, you lost one reporter.

If I left, you'd be at a serious shortage."

"That's something you shouldn't worry about. Your concern should be to recover, whatever it takes. Please give some serious thought to talking to a professional, even if it's not my grandson. It helps to talk it all out."

Junior popped open the glass door. "Think about what?"

"Krista's future."

"Yes." He cleared his throat. "One thing I must mention," Junior added, his voice holding a note of something odd. Trepidation? "I've been asked by Todd's family to arrange a time they can talk to you."

"Junior . . ." Sunnie's voice held caution.

Not that, Krista thought, and not this soon. Before she could protest, he continued in a rush.

"I understand it may be difficult, and it may be too soon now, but you can understand their need to know about his last night alive."

Krista's face, her entire body felt on fire. She had to get out of there. They all thought she was overcome not only with the horror of that night, but with gratitude to Todd and some guilt thrown in because he'd died and she hadn't. Yes, she was grateful to be alive, but how long could she pretend that louse was a hero?

No way could she face his family. They would expect her to show humility and gratitude, and all she wanted was to scream her frustration and rage that by his selfishness, he'd forced on her the most horrible night of her life. Not only did she witness another human being fatally mauled, but because of that night, all her security was gone. Evaporated. Just like her belief system in what was real and what was not.

Mumbling an apology, she escaped Sunnie's office and hurried for the front door. Carla rushed after her with her jacket and offered to take her home.

On the short drive, both women were quiet. Finally Carla broke the silence. "I'm sorry about the photos."

"You were just doing your job." After a pause, Krista asked, "Have you lived here long?"

"All my life. Well, born in Charleston, but I grew up here. Why?"

"Have there been other . . . bear attacks like this one?"

"Bears are all around since we're a mountain state, but they don't usually hurt anyone. One or two have attacked in the past, but they were not as nasty as this—at least not in my memory. No casualties, and never from a grizzly." She was silent a moment. "You don't regret coming here, do you?"

If she only knew. But Krista had promised Hugh to say nothing more than what they'd prepared, and she'd keep her word. When they pulled up to her apartment complex, Carla shut off the engine.

"I wanted to take you home so I could talk to you privately."

Krista tensed. "About what?"

"You know we're a small town, and we don't

have many heroes, so I have an appointment with Mayor Jennings this afternoon. I want him to appoint a special day for Todd. You know, do it up big in the city park with balloons for the kids, and have our vendors there grilling hot dogs and hamburgers."

A buzzing began in Krista's head.

"And to beat the snowstorm," Carla rambled on, "we have to do it in the next couple of days. I know it'll be a scramble to get it done so quickly, but if we all work together, we can do it. What do you say?"

"Say?"

"I want the City to sponsor a tree in Todd's honor, and I was thinking it'd be fitting if you'd plant it." Carla paused just long enough to gulp a breath. "Just think! His family and the whole town would be there. I'll arrange for a microphone so you can talk about that night, but of course leave out the gory parts."

God. No way would she attend a celebration for that man, much less plant a tree in his honor. And talk to his family about his bravery? She'd never been a good liar. They were sure to suspect she was hiding something, and they may even presume it involved a romance. Even the thought of that made her want to shower.

Then, an even worse picture pushed its way into her thoughts: the city park filled with people — men, women, and children of all ages playing, having fun, the air rich with their laughter along with the scent of hot dogs and hamburgers . . . all noises and mouth-watering scents to attract a monster. How many people could it slaughter before the officials killed it?

She couldn't allow that to happen. She had to convince the sheriff to put a stop to Carla's plans. "No," she whispered.

"It would be your day as well as Todd's."

"I'm sorry, but no." She opened the car door.

"But why? You're not being fair. You should be grateful to Todd and willing to do anything to help us honor him."

Krista wanted to laugh, to scream, *Not fair? Grateful?*

Carla pressed her point. "Look. If it's because you're new in town, just think how this'll help. People will know you after this, and they'll be more willing to talk to you for future articles."

"Thanks for the ride," Krista managed before exiting the car. She ran to her apartment and shut the door on Carla's last words. From the expression on the editor's face, Krista knew their budding friendship was in danger. If Carla fired her, it wouldn't be so bad; she'd be able to leave—once the DNR cleared her. If they did.

Where would she go? Back to Arizona? Perhaps. Especially now that her ex-fiancé and his wife had left. Arizona did provide some advantages—she wouldn't have to move her mother, and she was sure her old newspaper would welcome her back. She just wasn't sure she wanted to live there again, but she couldn't pinpoint a reason why.

She changed into jeans and warm fuzzy slippers. Smoothing down her lavender pullover, she felt the loose material at her hips and waist. Since her disastrous wedding day, she'd lost weight, but it was even more evident since the attack.

Damn, how long before DNR realized they had some kind of monster roaming the hills? That they'd need a militia to track it down and kill it? Then she'd be free to leave. No more terror, no more lies, no more deflecting questions, no more werewolf, no more Rawlins' overbearing tactics and sarcasm . . . no more Rawlins.

No more Rawlins? She blinked, surprised at the loss she suddenly felt.

She couldn't possibly have feelings for him; she had only known him a few days. Yet she couldn't deny a strong attraction to him. It wasn't something she wanted. She didn't want to feel anything for anyone in Marsh Springs.

Her coworkers at the newspaper were good people, and even though Carla might be a bit overly-eager, she was only doing her job. Sunnie, on the other hand, was someone she would like to know better. She felt they could be friends, someone to whom she might confide. Everything. Including her feelings about Hugh?

She thought back to that first day in his office, replaying the details of how he'd held her when she lost control, of how she'd taken comfort from his strong heartbeat and felt the flow of warmth from his body to hers. And after she'd tried to escape, he'd followed, and instead of locking her up, he'd fed her breakfast and tucked her in for a nap. Such a man of contrasts. A man of mystery. She found herself wishing she didn't have to leave.

What? She blinked. What was she doing? While she might acknowledge an attraction to that big bully, she wouldn't allow herself to feel anything more. She'd treat him as an ally until that creature was destroyed, and that was all.

But could Hugh kill it? He might be nearly as big as the werewolf, but unless he caught it in human form or had an ample supply of the silver bullets, he had no chance against it. Question after question ran through her exhausted mind: how long would she have to depend on Hugh to take her to work? To pick her up again? How about grocery shopping, or any of the other errands she attended to in the course of a week? How long would she have to live this abnormal life? How long before the officials realized what they had and killed it? Could they kill it? When would it strike again? And would a celebration in the city park lure it in?

Hugh said he had more ammunition, but did he have enough to defend himself against that creature? To defend her? To arm the town if necessary, and destroy a werewolf? He seemed to feel he could handle the situation, but could he?

Could she rely on his judgment, especially when he didn't believe her?

Settled on the sofa, her exhausted eyes closed but popped open again. Would she ever feel safe again?

For her own peace of mind, she needed to see for herself how many of the silver bullets he had.

FOURTEEN

"Kyle and I spent the day at the state lab." Hugh set Krista's table while she plated the fried chicken he brought from the Main Street Diner. "We wanted to emphasize the urgency of the DNA samples."

Platter of chicken in hand, Krista stared vaguely at him, her thoughts preoccupied with the silver bullets. How could she convince him to show her his extra ones?

"We took photos," Hugh continued, "and I think, by their reactions, they'll cooperate and rush them through."

Krista set the platter on the table and silently regarded him. He was talking, but she had no idea what he said.

"Did you hear me?"

"What?"

He turned to her. "Something happen at the office today?"

"Carla wants the City to sponsor a celebration day for Todd."

"I know. I've tried to discourage her, but she's

144

determined. I talked to County Commission Chair Bradley and Mayor Jennings, and they think the idea is great."

"Hugh, you can't let them do this—at least not until this creature is destroyed. Think of how many people could be killed if that thing comes down into town."

"Let's don't sound an alarm just yet. We should wait until Kyle gets the DNA results to see what exactly we have. I doubt anything will happen before then, so you can ease your mind on that."

"But you don't know, and it's too big a risk to take."

"If it's what you say, it won't want to expose itself to that many people."

"You can't know that for certain; you don't even believe in it." She regarded him silently. "I want to see your supply of silver bullets."

He threw her a surprised glance, then pulled out a chair for her. "I told you I have an ample supply." He passed a bowl of mashed potatoes to her. She ignored them.

"If they have this celebration soon, you'll need to be there with your special bullets. And have enough for your deputy too. Do you have enough for that?"

"I've told you I have."

"I want to see for myself."

"What brought this on? Don't you trust my word?"

How could she answer that? With her history of disappointments, of having her faith ground into dust, how could she trust again? Especially now with her life in danger. "I learned long ago not to trust anyone."

"That's a broad statement — and a sad one. Have I given you reason to not trust me? Or my word?"

"That thing could kill a lot of people on the kind of day Carla is planning. And my own life's at stake." She grew quiet. Thoughtful. "For some reason, I feel it's . . . out there, waiting."

"That's why we're taking the precautions we are."

"Then you must believe there's a horrid monster out there ready to kill me."

"Let's say I'm more open to that belief."

"Thank God we're finally getting somewhere. So show me your bullets."

"Not tonight. I've had a long day and I'm exhausted. You must be too."

"When?"

"I'll pick you up after work tomorrow. Then we'll go."

"Go where? Where is your supply?"

"Not far. Trust me."

"We're back to that again." When frustrated tears threatened to spill, Krista rushed to the bathroom and shut the door.

"Are you all right?" Rawlins followed and asked through the door.

"Give me a few moments."

"You got it." His footsteps withdrew, hesitated at her bedroom door, then resumed to the living room.

Krista wet a towel with cold water and patted her face. She needed to calm down and think rationally — if any part of this entire situation could be considered rational.

Had he given her reason to doubt his word? Other than his initial belief that she was exaggerating her description of the monster, he'd been attentive and protective. Even tender with her, something she'd never experienced before. So why was she so hostile and demanding this evening?

She dried her face and stared at her reflection in the mirror, noting the red streaks of fatigue in her eyes, the dark circles surrounding them, the new lines on her face. She'd aged several years since this horror began, and the only possible way she could see to end it was to cooperate with Hugh — and trust he knew what he was doing. She took a deep breath, straightened her hair and clothes, and felt ready to face him.

He stood waiting in the living room. "You pushed your dresser in front of the window?"

"It's the only way I could sleep."

"Ah, Krista, I'm so sorry you're going through this." He pulled her into his warm embrace and she rested her head on his shoulder, relishing the comfort she felt in his arms. For a brief moment, she felt safe.

He bent to gaze into her eyes. "Get your coat and come with me."

"Where are we going?"

"I'll take you to my home. I keep a supply of bullets there."

His house sat on the edge of town near the Drop In Cafe. They pulled in the driveway and parked in front of a detached garage. Streetlights illuminated the older bungalow home with its large front porch supported by thick square columns. He unlocked a side door and led her to a small room lined with hooks for coats and two benches. He removed his coat and invited her to do the same.

"This is a mud room, isn't it? I've heard of them, but this is the first one I've seen. What a handy place."

"I don't suppose homes in the desert have need of them."

She grinned and followed him through a kitchen with butcher-block counters and tile flooring, then down several steps to the basement. He flipped light switches to reveal a room lined with shelving, le cabinets, and several gun cabinets. He even had a utility sink. A long bench and two chairs, one overstuffed with a matching ottoman, and a straight chair stood in the center.

Once she was seated, he took a metal ammo box from one of the gun cabinets and pulled a bench close to her. He straddled it. When he opened the box, she could see row after row of gleaming silver bullets.

"Are they all silver?" Without waiting for an answer, she went on. "Why so many? Are you hunting the werewolf too?" Even though the question was in jest, she studied his face, hoping to see signs he finally believed her. Even so, how could he already have a supply of the bullets? It had only been a week.

"A mix-up in the order. Instead of one box, the silversmith made a hundred. They're unusual, and he went to a lot of trouble, so I kept them."

"Must have cost you a fortune, but thank God for the mix- up."

"Yes." He put the box away. "If the mayor goes ahead with Carla's plans and if anything monstrous shows up, we'll be ready for it. Feel better?

She nodded, relieved he wasn't exaggerating. He truly did have an ample supply. "Thanks for letting me see."

"My pleasure. Would you like a drink?"

"I could use something tonight, but nothing too strong. I'm not much of a drinker." Since her father had indulged too much too often, Krista had always preferred iced tea or a soft drink.

"I think you might like this wine." He pulled a deep burgundy bottle from a wine cooler she hadn't noticed, and from a cabinet next to the sink, two stemmed crystal glasses.

Krista took a small sip and tasted fruit with just a hint of alcohol. Delighted at the delicate flavor, she took another sip.

"Delicious! The taste is familiar, but I can't place it."

"Plums. From an old family recipe."

"You make your own wine? You are a man of surprises."

"Yes." He turned his back and busied himself at the

sink. "What time shall I pick you up in the morning?"

"I'm not sure. I'm not sure I want to go back to all those questions. And photos. Not to mention everyone thinking Todd was such a hero. I thought I could do it, but . . ."

"You've had enough trauma, and you shouldn't put yourself through more. Carla has what she needs for now, so you should stay out of the public eye. At least for a while."

"You'll probably be surprised, but this time I'll agree. I'll ask her about editing from home."

"Good. I'll be able to do my job better knowing you'll be safe."

She flushed, basking in his approval. What was wrong with her? At times this man treated her as if she belonged in a mental ward, yet she reacted to him like an adoring groupie. He always had that effect on her, and she wondered why.

Her stomach rumbled, and she apologized.

Hugh stood. "We didn't have our dinner. I'll run out and pick up something."

"But—"

"The Drop In's just around the corner. Don't move, I'll be right back." He climbed the stairs and was gone before she could even reply. Leaning back in the chair, she sighed, the first time she'd felt this safe and content since the night of the attack. It had to be the wine. She closed her eyes and let herself drift onto a floating cloud.

A few heartbeats later, she opened to eyes to the spicy scent of something savory and delicious. Hugh carried two white sacks down the stairs and set them on the basement sink, then filled a platter with food. Krista sat up.

"I must've fallen asleep again. I'm sorry, I—"

"Never apologize for sleeping. You need all the rest you can get." He set a small tray between her chair and the bench, then loaded it with the platter, two plates, their refilled glasses, napkins, and cutlery.

She watched him, moving with such ease and treating her, again, with tender consideration. If anyone could melt that frigid heart of hers, he was the one, but it was difficult to start a relationship with a werewolf running wild.

Her empty stomach rumbled at the platter piled with cheeseburgers and tacos. Two hot dogs with chili topped with . . . Cole slaw?

"You must've bought out the place!"

"I didn't know what you liked," Hugh said, taking a seat next to her, "so I picked up a variety." He passed her the plate of hot dogs.

"Cole slaw?" she said. "I've had sauerkraut on a hot dog, but never slaw."

"Try it. You haven't lived until you've had a West Virginia slaw dog." He took one and devoured it in three bites.

She watched him, then tried a small bite. To her surprise, the blended flavors of spicy chili, mustard, crunchy onions, and the sweet creamy slaw was unusual and delicious. She finished hers nearly as fast.

Hugh grinned and picked up a napkin. "Mustard," he said, and dabbed a spot at the corner of her mouth, his gaze holding hers.

Krista caught her breath and couldn't look away. Tonight the golds in his eyes were brighter, and flecks of gray and green mingled with brown.

Her ringing cell phone interrupted her thoughts. Her mom. She took a quick swallow of wine, then answered.

"Hi, Mom. No, it's not that late, but I'm getting ready for bed. Can I call you tomorrow?" After their goodbyes, she raised her eyes and found Hugh' gaze on her. He passed her the plate of food, but her hunger satisfied, she declined.

"Thank you. That was delicious."

He finished the tacos and one cheeseburger, then set the platter aside. "I assume you told your mother you were moving back to Arizona. Was she disappointed in your change of plans?"

"I'm not sure she ever wanted to leave Arizona, but she went along with my decision."

"Sounds like she loves you very much."

"I was her gift in life."

"Babies usually are."

"I was four. My real parents were killed, so was adopted you see, after Mom had given up having a daughter."

"I'm sorry. That explains your trust issues."

"Not that. My adoptive parents were wonderful. At least Mom was. Dad was too—for a while. Then he forgot I was alive."

"Care to tell me about it?"

Could she do so? She had never talked to anyone about her past, always keeping her thoughts private, her feelings tucked securely away. Oh, she knew people overcame more severe traumas than she'd experienced, but her life had left her skeptical of men. Cynical even. But Rawlins was another matter. Was she ready to confide in him? To trust him?

He'd been truthful with her, her inner voice reminded her. He had the bullets. Even though he was stubborn and often obnoxious, he'd never lied to her.

And the way he cared for her, always checking on her, keeping her current on the investigation. He was protective even, about her safety and especially with DNR.

Krista sat back and swirled her glass and watched the reflecting prisms of light, letting her thoughts drift to the past and to the fateful night her life changed. Was that the beginning of her lack of faith?

"I don't mean to intrude," Hugh said. "If it's too difficult—"

"It was night," she began, "and we were in the car. I was standing in the back between my parents trying to talk to my mother. What about, I don't remember. There wasn't much traffic, but we hit something ... or something hit us. Something smashed the windshield, and I heard glass cracking. Then screams ... and other noises."

"What noises?"

Krista shrugged. "I don't quite remember, but it

seems like growls, like a mad dog." She cast a perplexed look at Hugh. "That doesn't make sense. If we'd hit a dog, it wouldn't have caused that much damage."

"Remember anything else?"

"My mother pushed me down to the floor, urging me to stay quiet. I survived, but I don't remember much after that. Shock, the doctor said, then sometime later, can't remember when, going to live in my new parents' home."

"It sounds as if, by pushing you down, your mother saved your life."

"She did." Lost in thought, Krista went silent.

Rawlins was very still. "Do you remember her?"

Krista could see her mother's reddish hair and beautiful green-gray eyes, and how tender she'd always been with her. She touched the silver ankh pendant she'd inherited from her mother, and like her mother, always wore it. In the center, a small royal blue stone shone with golden flecks.

"May I see your necklace?"

Krista leaned forward so he could examine it. "It was my mother's."

"An ankh inlaid with lapis lazuli. Beautiful."

"Most people have no idea what it is. How do you know?"

"I've collected artifacts from that period in history. It was . . . a memorable time."

She straightened. "You have Egyptian artifacts? Where? May I see them?"

"They're . . . not here. One day I'll show them to you."

"Why not now? Or tomorrow? I'd love to see them."

"It's a bit of a drive, and we have other things that must take priority."

"Oh. Of course."

"Do you remember anything else about your mother?"

"I can barely see her now, but I remember the scent she always wore. I've searched for that same perfume, but I've never found it."

"I'm so sorry, Krista. But I understand now."

"There's more, but not tonight." She went silent.

"Would you like another drink?" From somewhere in the house, chimes from a grandfather clock struck ten. "On second thought, it's getting late, and you need your rest. Let's get you home."

"The wine was so good I'd like just a bit more." She sat back, feeling more relaxed than she'd felt since the nightmare began. After he refilled their glasses, Krista finished hers, surprised with each sip at how all of the strain of the past week melted away. "Rest. Yes. I think you'd better take me home or I'm liable to fall asleep right here."

"I wouldn't mind your staying with me." He leaned closer to her, his gaze moving over her eyes and then her mouth. "Actually, I can't think of a greater pleasure than coming home to you in my bed."

She should've been insulted at such a blatant remark; instead, liquid heat flushed her cheeks and spread through her body. She met his gaze, his amber eyes with golden flecks, so warm and watchful, always concerned about her. His mouth, with lips full and slightly parted, so very close. How would they feel pressed on hers? At the thought, she nearly shivered in pleasure, something she had never felt before, not even with her fiancé.

Without breaking his intense gaze, he caressed her cheek, then brushed her lips with his own, so very lightly she wasn't sure they touched. Even so, her treacherous body reacted. Her heartbeat quickened and she longed to feel his arms around her.

"You smell so nice," he murmured, his eyes so warm she felt the heat all the way to her toes. Then he sighed and pulled back. "As much as I would love to take this further, now is not the time, and especially not when you've had too much wine."

She swallowed. "Wouldn't most men love that opportunity?"

"Some men, perhaps."

"And you?" she asked, surprised at how interested she was in his answer.

"I prefer you fully conscious. And aware." He kissed the tip of her nose, then rose and took her hand. "Let's get you home." At her apartment, after checking each room, he stepped outside.

"Thank you for this evening," Krista told him. "It was the nicest I've had since this nightmare began."

"It's not over yet, so get as much rest as you can." He gazed at the waning moon, his expression thoughtful. Before she could speak, he turned to her, and she caught a faint yellowish glow in his eyes. He quickly looked away and when he turned to her again, his eyes were normal.

She glanced at the moon too. The glow in his eyes was nothing. Just a trick of the moonlight.

FIFTEEN

Egypt
The Past

Rahmor stationed himself in front of the usual pillar and waited for Neferaneksi. It had been nearly two weeks since her last appearance, and he listened for sounds of her slippered feet as eagerly as a peasant listened for his secret lover. Each time a slip of air stirred through the halls, he straightened, his breath stopping, thinking, hoping it was her. Each time he wilted.

The sun's rays lengthened on the tiled floors, and he knew in his heart it was useless. Finally, he trudged back to his chambers. Was she ill? Had she been moved to another location? He needed answers. As much as it demeaned him, he had to see Satiah again.

A sentry led him into her chambers. As before, she sat upon her lapis chair and scowled at him. Her gown of sky-blue linen fell in folds to her sandaled feet.

"This has become tiresome, Rahmor. You must

know the woman is lost to you. Find something else to do. Go play your silly chariot games. Go to war. Just give up this futile pursuit of yours and leave me alone. I have my own concerns."

"I must know of her. Why have I not seen her? Is she well?" He sent a silent prayer to Amun-Ra for her health and safety.

"She's well, but that's the least of your difficulties. She's to be Pharaoh's Great Royal Wife, his chief wife, mother to his heir." She spewed the words much like the red cobra spits venom and, Rahmore felt, just as deadly. "As such," she continued, "she will be kept away from palace eyes, to be favored solely by the king. You've lost her. Forever."

Rahmor avoided the pity in his brothers and sisters' eyes by spending the next few days walking the great Nile. As an experienced military officer and brother, his presence was required during Amenemhat's strategic campaign planning, but he offered nothing. When in Pharaoh's presence, he remained subdued, speaking only when addressed. Pharaoh said little, but Rahmor felt his father's thoughtful gaze on him, and finally, he was commissioned as ambassador to the Hittite empire to reinforce their treaties and to increase trade.

Rahmor did his duty greeting the people as well as nobles, but he went through each day as if he were in a trance, not seeing, not hearing. He knew his actions were intolerable, not only to his family and king, but to himself. He hadn't even spent a moment alone with this woman, so what was this hold she had on him? But no matter how he castigated himself, his thoughts returned to the copper-haired woman and her sad, haunted eyes.

One morning while camped outside the city, Rahmor instructed his servant to prepare his meal early. His plans to journey southeast meant all hands had to prepare the caravan soon after daybreak, and though he traveled lighter than his brothers, his tent alone took more time than he preferred.

During his breakfast of dried perch from the Nile and pita bread filled with mashed fava beans, his servant entered his tent with two more jugs of plum and pomegranate wine. Rahmor raised his brow in question, and the servant bowed deeply.

"My Lord, I beg your forgiveness for disturbing your meal, but two emissaries from our great pharaoh have arrived. They demanded to see you. I brought refreshments for them."

Rahmor set his mug aside. "Excellent, Khamet. You may grant them entrance."

Khamet bowed again and withdrew, and when he returned shortly and led two men inside, Rahmor recognized his father's special envoys. All three prostrated before their prince.

"You may rise." The servant discreetly withdrew and let the tent flap close. Rahmor indicated the wine jugs as well as dishes of figs and dates. "You may refresh yourselves."

"Thank you my prince," the older of the two said. "This is most welcome. Our journey was of the utmost importance— and speed."

"You have a message from Pharaoh?"

"Not from Pharaoh, my Lord, but from his Chief High Priest. He sends greetings and a request of the utmost urgency that you return to the palace. He said you would recognize the name, Neferaneksi."

The copper-haired woman. Rahmor shot to his feet. "We must leave immediately. Khamet! Attend me!"

Within minutes, the two emissaries, one still chewing his last bite of food, mounted their horses and accompanied Rahmor in his chariot. All horses charged southward at a full gallop, but once in the full desert sun, Rahmor slowed. While his need to reach the woman was urgent, he was enough of a horseman to care for his animals. They had a long way to travel and he had to protect them from perishing in the heat and great distance.

When they arrived home, he didn't stop at the palace to refresh himself or to cleanse away the sand from his robes. Instead, he headed for Amun's temple at Karnak. Once past the corridor of sphinxes, he found Norihor, the High Lector Priest, Keeper of the Secret Knowledge, waiting for him.

The little man bowed deeply, his linen robes scraping the floor and his strap of office crossing his shoulder and chest. His oiled shaved head reflected light from the five-foot wide burning fire pit in the center of the chamber, and on his feet were papyrus sandals. Golden statues and busts of the gods stood guard, their painted eyes observing the exchange.

"Prince Rahmor, we must waste no time. The Chief Royal Wife, Neferaneksi, nearly lost her life to an intruder, and Pharaoh wants her protected by any means."

"Someone tried to kill her? Thank the gods she was spared. Where is he? He must be fed to the crocodiles!"

"Her guards overpowered him, and in the struggle, one of the men stabbed him through the heart. He died before he could reveal who sent him."

Then it hit Rahmor. *Chief Royal Wife.* "They married while I was away?"

"Yes, my Lord. She's now his royal wife, his chief wife, and if she lives, mother to his future heirs. Pharaoh wants her protected by any means necessary."

"'If she lives? Of course she must live. But why send for me? How can I help?"

"Please do not take offense." Norihor bowed deeply, his eyes to the floor. "It is no secret of your . . . admiration for this woman. Who better to serve her, to guard her life?"

Attending Neferaneksi as a guard, of remaining by her side at all times was a high honor, and Rahmor couldn't have been more pleased. "I'll do anything. Did my father suggest my name?"

"The particulars do not concern Pharaoh. His instructions were to give a loyal subject enough power to subdue any foe that threatens her. You, mighty prince, came to mind as the best source, not only for your devotion to this woman, but also your great size."

"Yes, of course. Anything."

"We dare not waste time." From a hidden recess beneath the golden figure of Amun-Ra, the priest took a silver ankh amulet and handed it to the prince.

Half the size of his palm, it was unlike anything Rahmor had ever seen. Instead of an open loop, the solid silver top portrayed a snarling animal's head similar to a jackal. Eyes of emeralds from local mines, prominent red fangs of carnelian, it felt warm in his hand and the longer he held it, the warmer it became. The eyes took on a glow. What sort of magic was this?

"Keep this with you at all times, my Lord," Norihor told him, watching the prince carefully. "If you agree to submit to the ritual, the amulet will aide in our quest."

"What kind of ritual? What will it involve?"

"It'll take more than a simple ceremony, and it may be dangerous. I'll ask the gods to grant powers to you beyond anything I've before known, enough to subdue any foe. You must be submerged in waters blessed by the gods, and if they accept our offerings, you'll surface bestowed with powers enough to protect the chief wife against anything. But I must warn you—although it's written on the ancient scrolls, handed down from Osiris when he created civilization—I've not performed this ritual before, and I'll call on the ancient keepers of the secret knowledge to assist me. How the gods choose to do so will be revealed only after the ceremony is complete." The priest searched his eyes, sweat dripping from his shiny bald head. "Do you dare take that risk? To insure the magic, I must have your permission."

"Let's not waste another moment. Let the ceremony begin!"

SIXTEEN

Krista woke and lay staring at the ceiling, thinking about the evening with Hugh—and his kiss. Even though it was a light touch of affection rather than passion, she could still feel it. She touched her lips with wonder. Was this love? Had she fallen in love with him?

Never before had she reacted to any man the way she responded to him, not even to her fiancé. She'd never allowed herself to do so, had never met anyone who could tear down her defenses, but Hugh was another matter. Even when she realized what was happening and wanted to deny the attraction, her body betrayed her and wanted more—more touches, more kisses, more.

Last night was exceptional. For the first time she'd felt comfortable talking about her past, and when he responded with such compassion and understanding, she'd relaxed even further and shown him the prized ankh from her biological mother, which she always wore.

She fingered it now, her thoughts on her mother, wishing she'd had more time with her, not only for the love she'd missed, but for the knowledge her mother could have shared with her about her lineage. Why had her mother always worn an ankh? Who were her ancestors?

With the ankh in mind, she suddenly saw again the beast — and the medallion around its neck. Her breath caught: a silver ankh similar to hers. Why did a horrific beast wear an ankh?

And why was the medallion so special to her mother? Could they both have Egyptian connections, and, as implausible as it sounded, could those connections be the reason that beast didn't kill her?

Hundreds of possibilities ran through her mind, each one more whimsical than the last, until finally, she realized how ridiculous it was. Even to her. There couldn't possibly be a connection. Ankhs were popular and available most anywhere. That's all it was. Besides, she couldn't possibly live with the thought of any sort of connection to that beast.

Where was it now? Was it lying in wait to attack again?

As always, she had no answers. She threw back the comforter, and a few moments later, padded to the kitchen to brew coffee. She checked her watch. The office should be open now, so after pouring a cup, she punched in Carla's number. Before hitting the call button, she hesitated.

Would the editor be so willing to assign her jobs after she turned down her request to speak at Todd's celebration? She didn't know Carla that well, so she couldn't judge how she'd react. She'd call Junior instead. While she hated to bypass Carla, she needed the work, not only to escape thinking about the beast, but for the money. Even though she planned to leave, she had to pay bills until then. And she'd need travel money as well. She punched in Junior's number, then, her finger poised over the call button, she hesitated again. No, it wouldn't be right. Carla hired her, so it was Carla she had to call.

The editor, a bit of frost in her voice, agreed to have articles sent for proofing and line-editing.

"You will give more thought to being there for Todd's celebration, won't you?" she asked before disconnecting. She could have used the celebration as a sort of bargaining power, but, Krista acknowledged, she didn't. Her estimation of the editor rose a notch, and she wanted to give something in return.

"I can't promise anything, but I'll give it some thought."

"The mayor loved the idea, so we just need the city council's vote. If they go for it, which I'm sure they will, we can put this thing together in a day or two. With a rush on fliers and banners, we can make it work. I just need to know if you'll help us out after all, so let me know asap."

A day or two? Damn. One thing could be said for

Carla— she didn't waste time. Now what? Even if Krista considered swallowing her repugnance and participating for the town's sake, she could only hope the myths were true, that the creature wouldn't shift until the next full moon. Or, if the worst happened, at least Hugh and Delzo would be armed with silver bullets and could bring it down. Still, if it did show up, how many people could it kill before it was stopped?

She poured fresh coffee, but distracted, she sloshed most of it onto her hand. She jerked and her cup dropped onto the floor, shattering into little pieces. She ran cold water in the sink and thrust her burning hand under the flow. Frustrated tears fell, melding with the water. What was she going to do? Finally, when the sting faded, she cleaned up the mess. It was all too much to think about. She needed a distraction, so after wiping her hands, she decided to do some work.

As she opened her laptop on the table, her phone rang. To her surprise, the display read Sunnie Powell from the office. They chatted a few moments about her health and decision to stay home.

"I'm glad you're taking a few more days off," the manager said. "I admire your dedication to work, but it's obvious you need more time to recover. Anyone would."

"Thank you." Krista went silent, curious as to why she called.

"I hope you won't think I'm too forward, but would you mind if I stop by during lunch? I'd like to talk to you away from the office. Or would it be better for you after work?"

"I'd love a lunch visit, but you sound so mysterious. Is anything wrong?"

"I don't mean to sound that way. It's just a county government thing. They need Junior's and my vote to sponsor a celebration day for Todd, and they need our decision today. If you feel up to it, I'd like to discuss it with you."

"I see." Discussing the proposed celebration was the last thing Krista wanted to do, but out of admiration for the woman, she couldn't refuse to talk to her. "I'm not sure what I can tell you, but of course you may stop by. If you like homemade chicken and rice soup, I'll have lunch ready."

Krista tried to focus on the proofing jobs Carla sent, but the call from Sunnie concerned her. What would the woman ask, and what answers could she give without revealing too much? She didn't want to criticize a dead man, yet did she want to keep lying?

Most of all, she couldn't support a gathering of so many people while that beast was loose. Especially not so soon. But Hugh didn't want her to spread panic about a mythical creature, and especially not until they had the DNA results and knew exactly what was loose in the hills. So what should she do? She honestly didn't know. She only knew it was a mess.

When Sunnie knocked on the door, Krista had the table set, the soup ready to be served, and French bread warming in the oven. It was the first time anyone from the office visited, and she wanted to make a good impression. Besides, she liked the woman and hoped they would be friends.

Sunnie wore a long-sleeved pink blouse over charcoal gray pants, and her only makeup was a light pink gloss. She handed Krista a small box from the bakery. "I couldn't come empty-handed. If I'd had time, I would've baked a sweet-potato pie."

Krista opened it to reveal two frosted brownies, two chocolate donuts, and two slices of pineapple upside-down cake. "They look so good. You didn't need to bring anything, but I'm glad you did. Thank you! And one day, when everything's back to normal, I'd love some of your pie. I've heard of it but have never tasted it."

"I'll be happy to bake one for you."

Krista set the box on the table, feeling frumpy in her jeans and purple knit pullover. She must've done something awkward like smoothing down her top, as Sunnie's keen eyes caught something in her manner. Or perhaps it was Krista's blush and her glance at her fuzzy slippers.

"Honey, I love your jeans. I've always wanted to wear them, but somehow, they never look right on me. Perhaps because I'm so short and not model-slim?" The older woman chuckled.

Krista laughed with her and felt like giving her a big hug. She wished Sunnie were stopping by for a social visit instead of wanting answers to questions Krista preferred not to give.

Maybe if she were vague enough, the older

woman would give up. But from the month she'd been at the office, she knew Sunnie was thorough. And as persistent as Carla, although not nearly as brash.

Soon they were sitting at the table, and after tasting the soup, Sunnie pronounced, "Absolutely delicious, and I must have the recipe. It's so nice of you to provide lunch, especially when I'm the one barging in on you."

"The soup was already made. Besides, I spend a lot of time alone. I'm happy for the company, especially now when I'm confined to this apartment."

"It appears our ne sheriff is taking good care of you. At least you have that."

Krista put down her spoon. "I don't mean to sound rude, but how do you know what the sheriff does for me?"

Sunnie smiled. "You forget. We're a small town."

Krista's cheeks went hot. "Oh."

Sunnie touched her hand. "Oh no, I didn't mean to sound nosy. Or critical. He's such a nice man, and the entire town highly respects him. If he's found someone special, I'm glad. Not that you need my approval, but if it's true, I'm happy for both of you."

"He's been very kind."

"When our previous sheriff announced his retirement before his next election a couple of months ago, we were concerned, but we were lucky Hugh came along when he did. The county commissioners unanimously appointed him to fill out the term. We're all thankful we have a sheriff who takes pride in his work."

"Was Hugh the deputy before the sheriff retired?"

"No. He just suddenly appeared and stepped right into the sheriff's role as if he'd been born for it. We were very fortunate."

Krista couldn't believe what she was hearing. "Two months ago? You mean Hugh hasn't been here for years?"

"Oh no. The buzz is he came from the southwest somewhere, just over a month ago. You seem surprised."

"The Southwest?" Odd. That's where she'd lived. "I guess I am. I assumed he'd been here forever."

"He's taken to the community and the community to him as if he'd been born here. Why? Does it make a difference? I assure you, it doesn't to us, and he's quite capable of protecting this county. And you."

"No difference, I guess." Krista ate her soup in thoughtful silence. She didn't know why the news was so surprising. Did it really matter how long he'd lived in Marsh Springs or where he'd moved from? It shouldn't.

But she was reminded of something she'd heard, a catchphrase about never truly knowing another person. Last night she'd revealed part of her past to him, yet what did she know about him? She only knew he wasn't married and didn't have children. That was all. The next time she saw him, she'd make a point of asking him. After all, trust was built on knowledge, wasn't it?

They finished lunch, cleared the dishes, and Krista braced herself for the questions Sunnie might ask. Now she wished the woman would leave. She'd rather be alone to fully absorb the news about Hugh and figure out why it bothered her.

"I'm sorry to bring up something so unpleasant, especially after such a nice lunch," Sunnie began, "but as I said on the phone, I have some questions about that night, and you're the only one I can ask."

"All you have to do is read the article."

"Maybe it's instinct, but I have a feeling there's more than you revealed."

"You can understand if I'd rather not talk about it."

"Of course I understand and I sympathize, but the City is voting today on sponsoring a celebration day for Todd, which I'm sure will be devoted to honoring his bravery the night he was killed. You, of course, would be crucial to the event, but Carla said you're reluctant to participate. Can you tell me why?"

How could she answer that? She liked Sunnie and hoped to remain friends, but she could see no purpose in revealing Todd's contemptible behavior.

"He was a good reporter."

"That he was." Sunnie finished her tea, then set the cup down. "But honey, I have my doubts about the kind of man he was. While I know that night must have been extremely traumatic and still is, your reluctance seems to go a bit further than I'd think. If my suspicions are correct, I need your help to avoid a possible embarrassing situation if certain facts come to light."

Krista rose, wiped the counter, folded the dishtowel, anything to avoid the truth.

"What could possibly come to light? It was just Todd and me that night, and if I say nothing, nothing can ever be revealed."

Sunnie sat back, her gaze intense. "I see."

Krista avoided looking at her, but she could feel the heat from the woman's knowing eyes. What could she say without revealing the truth? Not about Todd, as that wasn't important to anyone but to her, but about the danger? She knew she couldn't live with herself if she failed to warn the town and the beast attacked and killed more people.

"I'm not sure you do. Todd's behavior is only part of my reluctance. You must remember he was brutally mauled, horribly, to death. Until that animal is found, everyone's lives could be at stake, especially if they gather for any type of occasion."

"I get your concern, but never has a bear, even a vicious one, wandered into town. They usually avoid people and crowds."

"This one certainly didn't."

"My dear, what did happen that night?"

Krista's cell phone interrupted the conversation. The display read *Kyle Bowman, Division of Natural Resources.*

"I'm sorry, but I must take this call."

"You take your call, and I'll let myself out. I

believe I have enough to cast my vote."

Relieved she was leaving, Krista dreaded talking to Kyle. It could only mean another unpleasant conversation, but she knew if she didn't answer, he'd probably show up at her door.

"This is Krista."

"Miss Hawthorne? This is Kyle Bowman, and I have some results I'd like to discuss with you. Would it be convenient to stop by this afternoon? In about an hour?"

He sounded professional, but not brusque. Had he learned she wasn't a criminal? Still, she dreaded the meeting.

After disconnecting the call, she thought of the popular phrase, "From the frying pan to the fire."

SEVENTEEN

Kyle had sounded pleasant enough; but still, Krista wanted Hugh there for support. Even though she was innocent of any crime, as a reporter she knew wrongful convictions happened. Not often, but enough for her to be concerned. With the way things were going in her new life, she had no way of knowing what Kyle might accuse her of or what he might say. She picked up her cell and clicked on Hugh's name. He wasn't available, so she left an urgent message.

God, she hated feeling so dependent on Hugh or on anyone. This new life was supposed to be free of stress and of relationships, without relying on anyone for her peace of mind. Even so, she wanted him there. Needed him there.

While waiting, she brewed hot tea, then paced the living room, finally changing to more professional clothes — woolen slacks and a plaid jacket. In front of her bedroom mirror, she liked the look, but it was too much, as if she were trying too hard. She changed to pressed jeans, black tailored blouse, and a navy cardigan buttoned to the blouse's pointed collar. For the finishing touch, she added gold button earrings and a simple gold chain.

Her cell phone rang, and Hugh said he'd be there in about twenty minutes.

Just then the doorbell rang.

"Please hurry. He's here." She disconnected, then took a quick glance in the mirror. Deciding she looked presentable, she answered the door with confidence — at least on the outside.

Kyle looked imposing in his olive uniform, but he wasn't frowning, nor did he have handcuffs ready to haul her away. At least that was a good starting point. He greeted her cordially. Once in her apartment, he placed his hat on a chair and turned to her. She spoke first.

"Mr. Bowman, before you say anything, please know I'd rather wait for the sheriff. He should be here shortly." She hoped her voice didn't shake. She cleared her throat and indicated a kitchen chair. "Please, have a seat." She rattled on. "Would you care for some hot tea, or would you prefer coffee? I also have orange juice." God, she sounded like a flight attendant. She had to calm down, or he'd certainly think she was guilty.

Before he could answer, his cell rang. "Excuse me." He answered, glanced at Krista, and agreed to whatever was said. He disconnected. "That was Hugh. He asked that I wait to give my report until he arrives."

Her gaze fixed on him, Krista absently nodded

and slid into a chair opposite him.

"Relax, Miss Hawthorne, you should know you're no longer under suspicion."

She stared at him, not quite comprehending. After all the anxiety, the scenarios she'd imagined, she felt a bit numb.

"I'm not? Are you sure?"

He smiled. "I'm sure, but I'll wait for Hugh to explain. And yes, I'd prefer coffee, thank you."

She prepared a cup for him and tea for her, her pulse slowing from a gallop to a canter.

When Hugh arrived a few minutes later, she was so glad to see him she had to restrain herself from throwing her arms around him. She didn't want Kyle to think she and Hugh had anything more than a professional relationship. Hugh's appreciative glance gave her even more confidence, and she led him to the table where the two men greeted each other.

"Because of the severity of the attack," Kyle began, "and Hugh's and my persistence, the lab rushed the analysis. Actually," he said with a grin, "a friend owed me one, and he stayed up all night to complete the report."

Krista waited. Get on with it, she silently urged.

Hugh nodded. "I've been in constant contact with them, but I haven't heard this morning's update."

"Using DNA samples from the victim's wounds and clothing, from his truck, specifically the driver's door, and even soil samples, the lab ruled out a grizzly as well as black and brown bears. What animal it was, we don't know. The results were inconclusive."

Krista shot Hugh an *I-told-you-so* look.

Hugh acknowledged with a raised eyebrow, then turned to Kyle. "What now?"

"We'll send the remaining samples to Quantico and see what they find. But in the meantime, Miss Hawthorne, you should know you're no longer a suspect."

"Thank God." Sudden tears embarrassed her. She excused herself to go to the bathroom. Once she felt composed enough to rejoin the men, she opened the door, and in the hallway, she overheard Hugh, his voice nearly a whisper. Intrigued, she paused to listen.

"—enough experience to take a guess. What do you think it was?"

Krista held her breath. What would Kyle say?

"I'm not sure I even want to voice it aloud—even to you, but the results showed a mixture of wolf and human DNA, which we know is impossible. Even then, neither was pure. It was as if each strain had integrated, merged even, and I don't know what to make of it. It had to have been contaminated."

Krista knew it hadn't been contaminated, and she felt vindicated. Maybe now Hugh would believe her.

They ended the meeting cordially, with Kyle promising to keep them informed of any updates.

"I heard what he said," Krista said to Hugh after she shut the door. "Still think I'm a whacked-out stoner?"

"I never thought that."

"Of course you did, but we won't argue about it. Bring me up to date. Have you talked to Jennings this morning?"

"I did." He took a sip of coffee. "Got any of those cinnamon rolls left? I haven't had lunch."

"Don't change the subject, but no, none left. Tell me about your conversation, and I'll make some scrambled eggs and cinnamon toast with lots of butter."

"Ah, woman, haven't you heard bribery is against the law?"

"Hugh . . ."

"It's not good, I'm afraid. Unfortunately, he still loved the idea of planting a tree in Todd's honor, and he agreed with Carla, who just happened to be there. He thinks you should plant it. I told him you were still too traumatized to do so, and I tried to get him to at least postpone the day, thinking our first snow would force the celebration inside the school auditorium. But Carla argued against that. She'd talked to the vendors, and they all agreed. Jennings finally said if you couldn't be there, he'd plant the tree. All they needed was the vote. I was about to attend the special meeting when you called." He checked his watch. "I'm sure it's over by now, and I can guess how they voted."

"Can you find out?"

"Start my toast, will you?" He picked up his cell phone. After a brief conversation, he clicked off. "The meeting's not over yet, but the secretary said it's looking good — for the celebration."

Krista silently prepared the promised lunch for Hugh, her thoughts running wild, the heavy dread pressing on her chest and back. What should she do? If she declined to join the town, to plant the damn tree, would she be welcomed back at work? And she needed to go back to work, needed her salary to live on until the creature was found and destroyed. And if she quit the paper or they fired her, would anyone else hire her? As Sunnie said, Marsh Springs was a small town, and everyone would know. They might understand, but they might not be as warm as if she'd participated.

But an even bigger reason to attend loomed in front of her. She seemed to have some sort of connection to that creature, and if, by any chance it was lurking nearby, could her presence lure it in? Hugh and Delzo could be ready, and once they destroyed it, all her anxiety would end. No more sleepless nights, no more worrying about Mrs. Reardon or anyone else in the town. It would be over, and not only would everyone be safe again, but she'd have her life back. It was a chance she had to take.

"Damn, damn, damn." She didn't realize she'd spoken until strong arms wound around her and pulled her back against a warm chest. She relaxed for a moment, needing Hugh's strength. He reached around her to turn off the stove, then turned her around to face him.

"Whatever you're up to, and I can guess what it

is, don't. I'm here, and I'll take care of it."

"You can't take care of this. This is something I'll have to do."

"If this event does happen, and if you're thinking you have to attend, which I strongly advise against—"

"I have to," she interrupted. "I have my reasons."

"What reason could you possibly have? It's insane to even think about it, especially after all you've endured."

"I'm not sure I can make you understand."

"Try."

"It's not only you and me," she began, "but the town's safety. Mrs. Reardon." She trailed off , searching for words. Then she explained her reasoning. He frowned, eyebrows drawn as he listened, his face darkening into a scowl.

"You're willing to be bait for a monstrous creature? What if this so-called connection is gone? You don't know the mind of this beast. What if . . . what if something happens and I can't bring it down? What then?" He didn't wait for an answer. "You can't do this. I won't let you. It's worse than insane; it's suicide."

"I have to, Hugh, but I need your support. Promise me you'll have enough of your bullets and you'll supply Delzo with them too."

"I can't talk you out of it?"

"As much as I want to get into my car and make a run for anywhere but here, I'm going to the ceremony. I'll let Carla know. I just hope to heaven your bullets work. My life will depend on it."

EIGHTEEN

Egypt
The Past

After a restless night on the temple's padded lounge, Rahmor's eyes closed just as the sun's morning rays brightened the recessed room. He must be ready at dawn, the priest had insisted. They must perform the ritual at first light.

Someone tapped him on his shoulder. "A thousand apologies for disturbing you, my Lord, but I have your morning meal." The female servant bowed low and backed out of the room.

Instead of breakfast, Rahmor wanted to find the priest and begin the rite, but he knew his body would need strength for the ordeal ahead. Dangerous, the priest had cautioned. Rahmor accepted the warning. He must protect Neferaneksi by any means, and if that meant undergoing a perilous ritual, then that's what he must do.

He sipped the plum wine, downed half the pomegranate and figs, but couldn't manage the mashed beans. He forced down the grainy pita bread, followed by more wine. After setting the tray on the floor, he found a loincloth draped over a chair and quickly slipped it on. He palmed his silver ankh medallion and went in search of the priest.

In the ritual chamber lit by the blazing seven-foot flre-pit, Norihor chanted before the flames. In his finest robes and ceremonial headdress, dominated by the spitting cobra of Wadjet, the goddess of divine authority, he welcomed his prince.

"You have the medallion?"

Rahmor opened his palm. The emerald eyes glowed a greenish-red and seemed to fasten upon his own. Startled, he almost dropped it. He handed it to the priest.

Norihor took the ankh, carefully threaded it on a long silver hammered chain, and handed it back to Rahmor. "You must wear this at all times, sire. It will protect you." The prince slipped it over his head, coming to rest near his heart.

"Now, you must drink this." Norihor handed the prince a golden goblet encrusted with stones of blue lapis lazuli, green emeralds, the lighter peridot, and red jasper. Steam or some kind of froth swirled near the top of the liquid. Rahmor took a tentative sip and made a face.

"It is herbs to aid in the transformation. You must drink it all."

Rahmor closed his eyes and emptied the cup. Sweet raw honey couldn't override the pungent garlic, the frankincense, the fenugreek, and other herbs he couldn't imagine. He swallowed hard to keep it down and returned the cup to the priest.

"Excellent. Now to make your body pure." He led Rahmor to a golden statue of a god standing at least nine feet tall. Instead of a normal head, the likeness of a scarab beetle sat atop of a human body. Norihor bowed.

"O Khepre, we ask that you purify this mortal so he may rise from his bath ready to begin the pain of metamorphosis. Oh god of creation, who moves the sun across the sky as the beetle rolls balls of dung across the sands, we ask for your guidance and we give thanks for your mighty power."

Next to Khepre stood the golden sun god Ra, formed as a man with the head of a hawk. He wore a solar disk as his crown, the sacred serpent to the front. Reborn each morning as the sun, he stood above the other gods in his supreme power.

The priest then led Rahmor to a hidden recess behind the statue. Soft sheer curtains billowed around a bathing tub. Once submerged, a nude maiden wearing a black wig and kohl-lined eyes appeared and stripped off Rahmor's loincloth. She carefully bathed him.

Rahmor observed her attentions, even when she cleansed his entire body, but he felt as if he were watching from afar. He felt light, as if he'd consumed too much wine.

The priest led him back to the central chamber, and Rahmor walked slowly, concentrating on placing each foot in a careful step. The fire blazed higher, sending waves of heat into the room. A hum emanated from the golden statues standing guard around the chamber, their painted eyes watching from lofty heights. An oval bronze tub of water sat next to the re-pit. Norihor poured powder scents and oils into the steaming water, causing a white vapor to rise.

"Step into the tub, my Lord, and if we are successful, you will rise transformed into a mighty warrior blessed by the gods. No man will ever bring you down."

With the aid of a servant, Rahmor entered the water and sat submerged to his chin. He waited in calm serenity, knowing if the priest were skilled enough and the gods favored the rite, he'd soon be near Neferaneksi, his copper-haired beauty, living in her presence, ready to give his life for her if necessary. His life didn't matter; nothing mattered except being near her.

The High Priest moved to his wall library and carefully, lovingly removed a scroll from a concealed cabinet underneath the bandy-legged figure of Bes, guardian god of birth who chased away demons of the night. From a drawer, he selected a faded ivory wand with symbols of fearsome deities of the ancients.

He crossed to the statue of Amun, the hidden one, mysterious of form and creator god who wore two plumes and carried an ankh.

"O god of creation, protector of Thebes, guide your servant, Prince Rahmor, as he journeys to the wave of creation and passes through. Return him as a godly one to fulfill his duties to our earthly god, the pharaoh."

He implored Osiris, god of resurrection; Set for strength, and others that Rahmor's befuddled senses no longer heard. He only wanted to sleep.

Brandishing his wand, the priest spoke over Rahmor, then, with a dash of green powder thrown into the water, pushed the prince's head under the water, then immediately drew him to the surface.

"Rise, O mighty one! Rise in your new form, hailed by the gods to stand with them. Rise!"

His words cleared the mist in Rahmor's brain enough to hear the command, and he rose to stand on legs that failed to hold him. Servants raced to support him.

Nothing had changed. He was still Rahmor, but now with a depleted body lacking in strength enough to stand on his own. But the fog in his brain was beginning to clear.

The ritual had failed.

From beyond the chamber, the whisper of sandaled feet scurried away from the chamber. Someone had been listening. But whom, and more importantly, why? Rahmor was too weak to give chase.

"Priest, you must perform the ritual again."

"Yes." Sweat rolling off his head and face, Norihor staggered to the nearest chair and slipped off the heavy headdress. He clapped his hands, summoning his servant. "Wine," he mumbled to the nude woman. He lapsed into silence, not even glancing Rahmor's way.

"We must begin again immediately," Rahmor persisted. Even a day's delay was dangerous for Neferaneksi. The traitors could succeed in their next attempt on her life.

"I must have time . . . I must recover." Eagerly, the priest took the wine from the servant girl, then, suddenly aware of his breach in propriety, he instructed the servant to serve the prince first.

"Priest, you'll recover in a crocodile's belly if my father discovers your delay. We'll meet again in the morning dawn. This time you must not fail."

NINETEEN

The Present

The morning of the celebration dawned with a gray overcast, the clouds so low they obscured the mountains. Standing at her window sipping coffee, Krista understood Carla's urgency.

Snow was on its way, and from the looks of the clouds, they could expect a major storm instead of the dusting of before. She couldn't help but wish for a heavy wet snow to force a cancellation of the day's events, but if that happened, her plan wouldn't work, and she'd continue to live in terror. No, as much as she dreaded the day ahead, she wanted this nightmare to end.

She glanced at her kitchen table, set with side plates and butter for the cinnamon rolls Hugh loved. She hadn't eaten, and from her clenched stomach, she knew she wouldn't have anything for quite a while. If she only knew what the day would bring. If it didn't snow, would the event attract the monster?

And if it didn't appear, would she be coerced into planting that tree? She didn't know which she dreaded most, although the possibility of facing that monster again was so terrifying she could barely take a breath.

She checked her handbag again just to make sure she'd packed her handgun and silver bullets. Hugh and Delzo would have theirs as well, and the city police would also be there. With everyone on the alert, she'd at least have a chance of survival.

A blue pickup truck pulled up and parked near the last apartment, a pickup like the one Mrs. Reardon's son drove. He usually visited in the evening after work, so his arrival this morning probably meant he was taking her to the ceremony — unless she needed to grocery shop or visit the doctor.

Krista leaned forward to peer in the direction of her neighbor's apartment. The son entered her apartment, and a few moments later, they both exited. Mrs. Reardon looked happy and full of smiles as she climbed into his truck. They were probably going to breakfast, something her neighbor enjoyed when she had errands to do. But, if they did show up at the ceremony, how could Krista keep her safe? She couldn't force the woman to stay near Hugh. She was sure the old woman would want to visit with friends.

Her mind spinning with possible scenarios and none of them good, she finally gave up and checked her watch. Hugh would be there in an hour. She drained her cup, and her stomach rebelled. With one last glance out the window, she moved to down an antacid tablet and get dressed.

Although the cold front moving through the valley dropped the temperatures to near freezing, it didn't snow. Krista planned on wearing her barn jacket and gloves, but when Hugh arrived, he had other plans. Even though he wore his full uniform and matching jacket, he brought an orange quilted winter coat and an even brighter orange knit cap for her.

"Where did you even get these things? I'm not going to wear them. I'll stand out like the proverbial sore thumb."

"That's the idea. And quit complaining." Hugh pulled off her jacket and forced the quilted coat over her arms as if dressing a toddler. "Didn't your mom ever tell you to bundle up on a winter day?"

"A winter day for me meant wearing a sweater. I conceded to the cold when I bought my jacket a couple of weeks ago. It's lined."

Hugh picked up the jacket and inspected it. "Well, what am I worried about? It's lined . . ." He tossed it on a chair. "That jacket won't begin to stop a West Virginia wind. And you need something on your head. Trust me. You'll feel warmer with a hat." He pulled the stretchy knit cap over her head and tugged down the front, nearly covering her eyes.

"Oh, for heaven's sake." Krista reached up to reposition it. "I'm gonna get you a cat to boss around."

"You can't boss cats."

"Exactly." She raised her sleeves. "Why such bright colors?" She headed for the bathroom to check her reflection in the mirror. "I'll stand out like a Mandarin duck."

He followed. "That's the idea. I want to be able to spot you in an instant. Besides, Mandarin ducks are beautiful."

She met his gaze in the mirror. Awareness of his intentions, of his concern, washed over her, and she accepted his gift. "Just one problem." She flexed her arms and didn't like the constriction from the heavy padding. "How am I going to protect myself if I can barely move?"

"By staying next to me at all times. No matter what. Got your weapon?"

"In my handbag."

"Let me see."

She retrieved her gun from her bedroom and brought it to him in the living room, where he inspected it. With a nod, he handed it back to her.

"When we get there, tuck it into your pocket before we get out of the truck. I want to make sure you have immediate access to it, although I don't intend for you to leave my side. But it's better to be sure."

With his words, her mind spun sudden images of the beast, of its fangs and claws, and how easily it tore off a pickup truck door. What insane notion made her think she could possibly stop it? It could turn on her in an instant, and it could kill her. Not some vague time in the future, but now. Today. Was she ready to die? Her resolve suddenly wilted. "I'm not sure I want to do this."

"Great! Let's stay home. Your intention is a noble one, but it's also ludicrous. It's far too dangerous to bait this thing."

She searched his face, her doubts clashing with her determination. She desperately needed courage. He met her gaze, and after a few moments, her anxiety began to melt away, and she felt a tranquil shell of protection surrounding her. An inner knowledge washed over her as if silently assuring her he would be there to protect her with his life.

She straightened. "I have to do this if I want my life back. I'm ready to face this thing."

At the city park, Krista was amazed by the line of cars in the driveway and by the bustling activity taking place an hour before the festivities began. Bundled in coats and jackets, waiting residents strolled the grounds while others took seats in folding chairs facing a raised platform. Carpenters busily added finishing touches, their pounding sounds competing with loud squawks and squeals from someone testing a microphone. Food vendors were setting up grills and popcorn stands while others were tying balloons to strings.

"My God, would you look at this." Krista took it all in. "I can't believe Carla put this together so quickly."

They pulled into the only available parking spot, which happened to be near a small group of people.

She spotted Carla, Junior, and Sunnie from the newspaper, County officials, Mayor Jennings, and a man accompanying two women she didn't recognize. The women joined the mayor's group, and Krista had the feeling the newcomers were Todd's family. Carla glanced her way, smiled, and waved. She said something to the group, and everyone turned toward Hugh's SUV.

"Oh no." Krista wanted to turn the truck around and spin out of there, but too late. She was trapped.

"Krista! Hugh!" Carla's voice rose above the park's clatter. She waved and motioned for them to join her circle.

"Damn," Krista whispered, waving back at the editor.

"Just say the word," Hugh whispered, "and we'll get out of here."

"Might as well get it over with." She did a quick scan of the grounds. No sign of the monster. At least not yet. As soon as she opened the door, Carla's group moved toward her.

Jennings made the introductions. For a short, round man, his voice was surprisingly deep. And boisterous. Krista had never met him, although she'd seen him at different functions during her month in town. He smiled a lot, which was what he was doing now. Krista's nerves screamed.

She was right: the elder man and woman were Todd's parents, and the younger blond woman his sister Marge. Krista had heard he had an ex-wife, but no mention of her was made.

"I'm so sorry for your loss." Krista took each family member's hand, starting with Mrs. Mitchell. That one tiny condolence was all she could manage to say.

"I'm so glad you agreed to talk to us." Marge grabbed Krista's hand. "It means so much to my mother." She indicated the older woman, who, with moistened eyes, nodded. "And of course to dad and to me too."

Krista desperately wanted to avoid talking to any of them, to escape from the sad-eyed family. She glanced from the sister to the parents and back again, searching for more words of comfort, even if they were lies. She failed to find anything.

The savory scent of grilled hamburgers drifted to them along with freshly-popped corn. Even with no appetite, her mouth watered.

"We understand from the article that Todd saved your life," Marge continued. "Please, tell us everything you can about that night. It would mean so much to us—and to the rest of his family. He has a young son, you know, in Oregon. He couldn't be here, but we'll be sure to tell him about his father."

A son! Now she'd really have to choose her words wisely.

More people entered the park, and Mrs. Reardon, her son, and the new neighbor all arrived together.

Hugh frowned. "Who's that?"

"Brandon Cole. He's from California."

"What's he doing here?"

"New job, he said."

195

"You met him?"

"Once. He's a new neighbor. Mrs. Reardon introduced him." He disappeared into the crowd, and Krista shrugged, having no further interest. Mrs. Reardon spotted her and started toward her, then veered the other way. Krista had hoped she would stay close so she and Hugh could protect her, but the older woman knew most everyone in town, and seeing Krista with Todd's family, she probably didn't want to intrude.

Protect Mrs. Reardon? Oh no! With horror, Krista realized she hadn't transferred the gun from her handbag to her coat pocket. She sure couldn't do so now, not in front of everyone. Maybe she'd have a chance a bit later. She must've made some kind of noise, a quick intake of breath. Hugh shot a questioning glance at her, but everyone else was looking at her, so she couldn't send a message.

She glanced at Hugh's utility belt and his bullets. The silver gleamed, even on an overcast day. Feeling reassured, she managed a comment to Marge.

"A son?"

"He lives with his mother, but I know what you say today will be a legacy he'll be proud of."

Oh God . . .

Hugh must've seen her distress. He spoke to Marge, his voice gentle. "It's nearly time to begin, and Krista is scheduled to let the townspeople know what happened. If you have questions, you might ask them at that time."

"Good idea." Marge checked with her parents for

approval. They nodded. "Anything you can tell us would be appreciated," the mother said. She was so polite Krista wondered how she could have raised such a dickhead son.

"Time to take our places." Carla took Marge's hand and led the group to the platform.

Trapped. Krista moved toward the platform as if she were trying to run in deep water, all the time scanning the area for signs of the monster. Would it appear? She realized she hadn't seen Hugh's deputy.

"Isn't Delzo supposed to be here?" She tried to keep the alarm out of her voice.

Before Hugh could speak, Jennings piped up. "I asked him to bring the tree to the platform. I thought it would be more impressive if someone in uniform brought it in. For the crowd, you see."

Hugh frowned. "Neither my deputy nor I answer to you. I instructed him to watch for Krista and me, to stay near us at all times and that's where I expect him to be."

"Let me remind you, young man, I'm mayor of the city, and I wanted — "

"Come on, you two." Junior put an arm around both men, although he had to strain to reach Hugh. "Let's don't get into a pissing match—excuse my language, ladies. No harm done."

Music from a patriotic march began from the podium's recorder.

"That's our cue," Carla said too brightly. "Let's go."

Hugh's mouth tightened, but he nodded. Slipping

a protective arm around Krista, they trailed the group heading for the platform.

After a few hesitant steps, a slight ringing began in Krista's ears. Her heartbeat increased until she felt the pounding in her temples. Nerves, she thought, but she slowed her steps. Silently, Hugh matched her pace.

The air changed, became heavy. Threatening. A prickling sensation chilled her arms and the back of her neck. She scanned the park.

Nothing appeared out of the ordinary, but with increasing horror, she knew. The beast was close. Her brain screamed for her to run, but she tried to reason away her panic. Stick to the plan. Just trust the plan, but she hadn't counted on her body's reaction. Her legs trembled. She stumbled.

Hugh tightened his grip. Concerned, he glanced down at her. "What's wrong?"

A terrifying, bloodcurdling howl sounded from the opposite side of the park.

Krista caught a glimpse of the maddened creature darting through the crowd on two humanoid legs, roaring its rage, red eyes searching, she knew, for her.

She couldn't catch her breath, couldn't speak. She fumbled in her handbag for her gun, but it slipped out of her shaky fingers. Her small group turned to each other, then to Hugh. What was that? In the park, some people stood and looked around, puzzled expressions on their faces.

Before she could draw a ragged breath, Hugh

snatched Krista and ran for his SUV Once she was safely locked inside, he drew his weapon and zeroed in on the creature, but pandemonium had broken out. Sounds of terrified screams and crashing chairs drowned out the music. The crowd scattered in all directions, running in front of Hugh, blocking his way.

"What's happening?" Jennings yelled, wildly swiveling around.

The crowd parted long enough for Krista to catch a glimpse of the creature darting toward Mrs. Reardon, who was standing alone and looking confused. *Oh no, God no!* Someone screamed, followed by that terrible growling and snarling.

Hugh dashed toward the beast, but by the time he'd weaved around the panicked crowd, it had disappeared just as suddenly as it appeared. Discarded food and wrappers littered the now-empty park. Broken chairs and mutilated bodies lay on the ground. .

Hugh knelt beside a woman's bloodied body, and Krista realized it was Mrs. Reardon. Her kindly neighbor was dead and it was her fault. She couldn't draw breath. She felt suffocated and clawed at the door and then the window, but Hugh had locked everything so tightly the SUV was sealed. She could only watch the horrific scene from the passenger window.

Then Hugh did something so strange she couldn't comprehend: slowly turning in all directions, he scented the air as if he were a wolf tracking his prey. *What on Earth . . ..?*

He paused, staring in an easterly direction, then holstered his gun and loped back to Krista. Without a word, he jumped in his vehicle and raced away from the park.

Krista stared at him, then covered her face with her hands and sobbed.

TWENTY

Rawlins sped up the highway heading out of town, then took a cutoff leading higher in the mountains. Krista stared quietly out the window at the thickening forest, her mind replaying the events in the park. She'd frozen just as she'd done the first time she'd seen the creature, and as a result, townspeople had died, including her neighbor and friend, Mrs. Reardon. Tears rolled down her cheeks.

"I know what happened was devastating," Hugh's voice was gentle, "but if you're blaming yourself, don't."

But she did blame herself. She felt empty. Barren, just like the winter forest on either side of the road. She should have done something. Instead, she'd been so frightened she couldn't even hold onto her weapon. Fat lot of good all those silver bullets had done. The image of Mrs. Reardon lying in a pool of blood flashed in her mind again. *God . . .*

They hit a bump and she held on. They'd left the cutoff and were now racing up a rocky path.

"Where on earth are we going? And why so fast?"

It seemed as if they'd been driving for hours.

"I'm getting you to safety. It's not far now."

"What's not far?"

"A place I've prepared. You'll see."

"What about the townspeople and their safety?"

"My first concern is you."

"Why? You're the sheriff, sworn to protect them, not just me. I don't understand."

"You don't need to understand right now. Just trust me."

Krista silently regarded him. He was putting her safety before his duty to the county? While she acknowledged the strong attraction between them and had to admit she felt special because of his concern, what would the town think of his abandoning them? Was he destroying his future with them?

"Hugh, you can't do this. The county needs you. I loved this area . . . before . . ." A muffled sob escaped. She turned to gaze out the window.

"Oh hell." With a look of frustration, Hugh reached across her to open the glove compartment. "Grab my headset, will you?"

She rummaged under some papers and pulled out his Bluetooth headset. He fixed it to his ear, pressed a button on his steering wheel, then firmly spoke a command. "Delzo!" Within a few moments, he was talking to his deputy.

"I had to leave, Delzo." He listened for a few moments. "I don't know. Krista witnessed the beast attack her friend and neighbor, and it was too much for her to handle, especially so soon after Todd's death. I had to get her out of there." He listened again. "Yes. In the meantime, you're in command. I'll let you know when I'm ready to return. Oh, he did?" He paused. "Got it." Without further explanation, he clicked off.

They hit a large enough bump that nearly unseated her, and she hung on even tighter. Where on earth was he taking her? And why so far from town?

He drove on in silence, maneuvering through the brush-covered path winding through high mountain trees. Finally he stopped his SUV before a steep overhang about twenty feet high, got out and went through the strange ritual again of turning in all directions while sniffing the air. What on earth was he doing?

"Wait here. I'll be right back." He pulled a pair of work gloves from underneath his seat and headed for the rocky shelf, nearly concealed by twisting vines.

Krista took a quick look around the icy forest. Patches of crusted snow lay under barren tree limbs. She shivered in the cold.

Hugh pushed aside heavy vine strands, ducked around them, and disappeared. Soon she heard the rustling of dry leaves and the crackling of heavy brush and sticks.

Was it the beast? She scanned the area around her. Had it followed them? As unlikely as it seemed, she knew the creature was capable of many things. No way was she going to sit out here alone, not another minute. She opened her door and ran to the overhang and ducked around the thick curtain of foliage as he had done. She found him pulling and snapping thick twining vine strands to reveal the narrow entrance to a cave.

"You left me alone out here. Wasn't I frightened enough for you?"

"You weren't in danger. I made sure of that. Besides, I was right here, just a few steps away. You just couldn't see me— which is why I chose this spot."

"Chose it? For what?"

He tucked his gloves into his back pocket, then took her arm. "Follow me." He led her through the darkened entrance and guided her through an even more narrow passageway to the left. "You'll need to duck down for a few steps."

Gripping his arm, she followed his example, and they soon straightened. As they moved further into the mountain, the ground smoothed out, and her footing became sure. She soon felt air movement and had a sensation of openness, as if the ceiling had expanded. From somewhere beyond, water owed. Just ahead, a light glimmered.

They took another slight curve, then emerged into a small chamber lit by electric wall sconces. In the corners, fire braziers stood cold and unused. A slight hum could be heard.

He followed her gaze. "Modern technology. I no longer need the braziers."

"But how?"

"Generators."

He led her through another passageway to a vast chamber so unexpected that Krista stopped abruptly and stared. Soft lighting revealed luxury sofas, chairs, and small tables of the finest mahogany. An area rug covered the floor. But what caused her quick intake of breath were the golden busts of pharaohs and their queens placed around the room, along with animal sculptures she recognized from Egyptian movies and photos. Painted ritual masks of molded linen or papyrus hung on the walls. Krista recognized Anubis, the jackal god of death, and Bast, the lion goddess of protection.

Krista turned her astonished gaze to Hugh, who was watching carefully. "This is incredible. Is it all yours?"

"Yes."

Krista moved to take a closer look at the busts and sculptures. She'd seen similar figures in magazine photos and always thought them fascinating. Hugh had mentioned he collected some pieces, but this went beyond anything she could have imagined.

"I've never seen such a collection outside of a museum. How did you get these? Are they reproductions?"

"No." He didn't elaborate.

"But why? Why all of this?"

"As I told you, it was a fascinating time in history." He moved to an ornately-carved armoire. "Would you like a cognac? I'd normally offer tea this time of day, but I think we could both use something a little stronger."

She took her time gazing at the artifacts, then took a seat on one of the cushioned sofas. "What I'd like is an explanation. I don't understand any of this. Why did you build such an elaborate place? It must've taken you years to carve it out of the mountain."

"A lifetime."

"But Sunnie said you'd only been here a few weeks, so how could you say a lifetime? And why would you want to build something like this?"

Instead of answering, he handed her a glass of the caramel-colored liquid.

She wasn't familiar with the different liquors, but she was sure the ornate glass was of the finest crystal. She tasted the faint apricot flavor in the liquor, then emptied the glass.

"You should sip, not gulp, especially not on an empty stomach."

"Why, Hugh? Why so lavish a place, and why so isolated? I need some answers."

He finished his drink, placed the glass on a side table, then slowly turned to face her as if carefully choosing his words.

"Sometimes, in my line of work, I need time alone, so I bargained with the city: I'd be on-call twenty-four hours a day, but for four days each month, I'd be unavailable. On those days, I come here, a place unknown to anyone else."

She studied him. "Why here? What are you hiding?"

"We all have secrets we prefer not to share, don't we? Suffice it to say it's for the greater good."

"How do you expect me to trust you if you keep secrets?"

"One day I'll reveal them to you, and you'll under —"

"One day? Why not now? From the time we left the park, you've been mysterious with half-answers and it scares me."

"You have nothing to fear from me. I'd think you'd know that by now. I've done everything possible to keep you safe."

That was true, and even though she hadn't planned it, she relied on his help. His strength. But he must have a life outside of the sheriff's office.

"Surely you don't spend every day off here. Don't you have a lady friend?

Family? Anyone you want to see on your days off?"

"You're the only one I want to see. That should be evident by now."

"Oh." That one word was all she could say. Not only did his statement warm her, but something was happening with her vision. The room was fading in and out of focus. And her tongue didn't work right. She couldn't seem to form words.

"Are you all right?" Hugh strode toward her.

He sounded as if he were speaking from a great distance. She sank back in the cushioned sofa and tried to keep her eyes from closing.

"Sorry," she managed. "Lack of sleep . . . must be catching up . . ."

"I think you drank the cognac too quickly. We can talk another time. For now, you need rest." He scooped her into his arms and carried her out of the room and down another short passageway.

Only mildly curious, she wrapped her arms around his neck. "Where . . . we going?" A calming peace spread through her senses. The morning's massacre faded in importance, and even though she still had questions, they didn't seem to matter as much. She was alone with this man, the one man who had always cared for her and risked his own life for her. She sighed, content to be held in his protective arms. Her tight control vanished and she rested her head on his shoulder.

"You're going to bed."

She nuzzled his neck. ". . . join me?"

"I'd love to, but I'll wait. I want you completely aware when I make love to you."

Make love to you . . . How she wanted this man, but she couldn't form the words. Only vaguely aware he'd entered another room, she was nearly asleep when he gently placed her on a bed, slipped off her shoes, and covered her with a satiny quilt. After a soft brush of lips on her cheek, he left the room, and Krista fell into a deep contented sleep.

When she woke sometime later, she sat up in the oversized bed and checked her watch. She'd slept four hours, four full hours, the longest uninterrupted rest she'd had since the nightmare began. While her head felt a little heavy and she had only a vague memory of anything after Hugh had given her the cognac, she felt gloriously alive.

She looked around the unfamiliar room, softly illuminated by a floor lamp in the corner, and tried to figure out where she was. The room was masculine with dark woods and a bed larger than a king-size. A cushioned chair stood next to a lamp table in the corner. A plush dark green area rug covered the floor, and tapestries of knights and castles woven with rich warm red, greens, and yellows covered the walls.

Yawning, she stretched, then glanced behind her. A silver ankh, nearly five feet high, hung on the wall. She fingered her ankh, feeling close to Hugh, pleased he too, shared her love for a period in time important to her and her mother.

She listened for sounds of activity, but she heard nothing but that quiet hum. Was Hugh asleep as well? She slipped out of bed and went in search of him.

Outside the room, a passageway led in several directions, and she took the one most familiar. It opened to the main room. Hugh lay sprawled in an armchair, his long legs spread in front of him, his glass of brandy tipped over on the floor.

Krista let her gaze roam over him, admiring his form, loving the tender way he cared for her. Poor man. He deserved to sleep in his own bed.

Her gaze moved to his mouth, the full lips that had once brushed hers in an affectionate kiss, then to his masculine arms. How would they feel locked around her in a passionate embrace?

"Feeling better?" His eyes were still closed, and he hadn't moved, not a muscle.

"How did you know I was here?"

"I felt your presence."

"Oh."

Fully awake, Hugh rose from his chair. "I imagine you'd like to freshen up."

"Oh yes."

He led her through the passageway to another room and opened the door. "You should find everything you need. Meanwhile, I'll prepare breakfast. Take your time, and when you're ready, you'll find the kitchen off the great room." He stepped close and brushed back an errant lock of her hair.

She stared into his eyes, wondering again how he seemed to know everything she was thinking, everything she felt. She reached up and ran her fingers over his lips, wanting desperately to kiss them.

He groaned and pulled her close. Sighing, he rested his chin on the top of her head. "You feel so damn good, but as much as I want to take this further, you need nourishment before anything else."

Burrowing her head against his shoulder, she caught his fresh masculine scent, a bit like the forest after a cleansing rain. Aware that she needed a shower, she drew back and he released her.

He ran his fingers down her cheeks to her lips, then dropped his hand. "I'll check on you in about a half hour. If you haven't found the kitchen by then, call my name. I'll hear you." He turned to leave, and she almost called him back.

Hoping the bathroom had a shower, she entered the room and stopped in shock. Somehow Hugh had built a luxury bathroom in a mountain cave most women would love. An updated claw-foot tub stood in the corner of the large pearl-tiled bathroom, the iridescent light color adding a feeling of spaciousness. Above double sinks, a mirror covered the entire wall. On the side wall, a mirrored vanity held everything a woman could need plus some extras. She should've known Hugh would think of everything, almost as if he'd planned her stay. Around a niche, a slate-tiled walk-in shower held two showerheads, and she let herself imagine a time when she might share a shower with him.

Never before had she felt such desire for a man, such need. Not even for her former fiancé. Their engagement and even their lovemaking had been more of a convenience than an expression of love or affection. Even though she'd yearned for that great romance she'd read about, she'd never believed enough in a man to give of herself, to let go and fully express the love she'd buried deep in her heart. No wonder he chose someone else.

Twenty minutes later, feeling totally refreshed, she wrapped her freshly-washed hair in a towel and opened a closet door. From inside, she took a fluffy white robe and cotton slippers. Of course they all fit. How could she think otherwise?

More than ready for breakfast, she followed the scent of bacon and found Hugh in a dream kitchen she'd love to have. Stainless steel appliances set in rich cherry wood cabinets. Countertops of a rich reddish granite. He was flipping pancakes on a grill set in an island at least seven-feet long lined with chairs. He glanced up with a smile when she entered the room.

"Ah, just in time. Hungry?"

"Starved." She took a chair in front of him. A platter of bacon sat next to the grill, and she couldn't resist. After devouring two pieces, she washed them down with the glass of orange juice he'd set next to her plate, then poured coffee from the carafe.

They shared a companionable, easy breakfast, with no reference to the questions Krista wanted to ask or to what had happened outside the cave walls. For now, she felt content just knowing she was safe with the man she loved.

Yes, she loved him, she finally admitted, sipping the last of her coffee, watching as Hugh's big hands encircled his mug. No longer would she fight the feelings she'd had since that first day in his office when he'd held her in his strong, protective embrace. Even though she'd been locked in the horror of the night before, she had responded to his arms, his heartbeat, which seemed to meld with hers.

When she raised her eyes to his, she found his gaze on her, his eyes warm, as if he knew what she was thinking. She could barely breathe.

"Krista." He spoke her name softly, reverently, as if she were someone he adored.

She responded as if he were making love to her. Her heart beat wildly. Her mouth went dry. Never before had she felt so wanted, so beloved.

He rose, stepped toward her, and pulled her trembling body into his arms. He covered her mouth with his, and she kissed him back with a passion she didn't know she possessed. When they parted, he pulled off the belt on her robe and she stood unmoving, allowing it to drop to the floor. She waited quietly, naked and unashamed for the first time in her life.

His eyes devoured her, and he whispered, "You're perfect, the most beautiful woman I've ever seen." He kissed her cheeks, her mouth ever so gently, and she wrapped her arms around him and pressed her body close to his. He cupped her head and pressed his lips to hers in a kiss so searing her trembling legs went weak.

"I've waited so long . . ." He lifted her into his arms, then they were moving toward the passageway and into his bedroom. He laid her gently on the bed and caressed her mouth with his, outlining her lips with his tongue. When he gently sucked her lower lip into his mouth, liquid fire spread through her body. He pulled away from her to rise. She felt empty, abandoned.

"No . . . don't leave me."

"I'll never leave you." He shed his shirt and jeans and stood before her, his dark hair brushing his broad shoulders, his arms strong enough to support her, tuffs of curly dark hair running from his chest to his hips and below. She had never seen such a magnificent male body.

She rose on her knees and pulled him down until she could feel his entire body covering hers. His weight felt glorious, but he lifted himself onto his elbows and began kissing her, burning her lips with his heat. She wound her hands around his neck, running her fingers through his hair, over the powerful muscles in his back, and down to his lean hips. He nuzzled the soft spot on her earlobe, his tongue sending shivers of pleasure though her body.

She gasped, her need for him growing with every delicate touch. "Tell me again you won't leave me."

"I've always been there, sweet Krista. I've loved you since the day you were born." He trailed kisses down to her breast, then took one swollen nipple into his mouth, his hands moving lower, caressing every inch of her body.

"How can . . . oh!" Pure sensation shot to her loins, and nothing mattered except the throbbing heat building inside of her.

He leisurely caressed every part of her body until she was nearly panting with desire. She arched against him, desperate to draw him deep inside. When he entered her, she cried out in surprise, the pleasure more intense than anything she'd ever known. When they were spent, they lay side by side wrapped in each other's arms.

Sometime later, Krista woke to find Hugh snuggled against her, his warm breath tickling her ear, one arm hugging her belly, a leg slung over her knees. She felt safe, wrapped in his loving embrace. She turned her head slightly, not wanting to wake him, but just enough to gaze at this man who'd loved her so completely, who'd brought her such pleasure. She'd never known sex could be like that. That making love could feel so much like . . . love.

Her adoring gaze swept over his face and she smiled at the silken lock of dark hair that had fallen over his forehead, giving him the boyish look of a mischievous child, his closed eyes that when open, held hers with such love, and down to his straight Grecian nose and over full lips that had brushed hers with such exquisite tenderness.

She felt a slight change in his breathing and raised her gaze to find him watching her. He smiled.

"What do you see?"

She returned his smile. "I see a beautiful man I adore, and one I trust with my life." She gave him a quick kiss on the tip of his nose.

"Ah, I love that, and I love you."

"You should. I've never said those words before."

He propped his head on his hand. "You never told anyone you love them, or that you trust them?"

"I loved my parents, and I thought I loved my fiancé, but I never completely trusted anyone."

"Why? What caused such mistrust? Was it because your natural parents died and you were adopted?"

"I don't know. It's not important."

"It is important."

"I don't want to delve into my past. Not now, not when I'm all snuggled with you and feeling wonderful."

"I'd say this was a perfect time."

She regarded him, his warm gaze on her, waiting, as if he wanted to hear about her life. As if it were important to him. Maybe it was. She'd heard that a person couldn't move forward until they'd faced and dealt with their past, and now she felt ready to deal with hers and move on.

"I'm not really sure when it began." Krista thought back over the years to her childhood, trying to remember when the first threads of mistrust wove into her life.

"Maybe it started then. I remember how I felt when, even as young as I was, I realized I'd never see my mother again. Oh, I loved my father, but there had been a special bond between my mother and me. I couldn't stand not seeing her, not being with her ever again." She lapsed into silence. Hugh pulled her closer and she snuggled as close to him as she could get.

"I think I tried to forget the early days right after the accident, but I vaguely remember strangers taking me to a dorm-like institution and living there with other girls around my age. I have no idea how long I was there, but then I was living with my adoptive parents. At first I think I merely existed, eating when told, sleeping when led to a bed in what I was told was 'my room.' I don't remember much, but I eventually grew to accept and love my new parents. My new mother, especially, made the effort to get to know me, to help me."

"And your new father?"

"He was nice, but I remember waking in the middle of the night to harsh, angry words coming from their bedroom. He moved out about a year later, and he told me the usual: he loved me and wanted to spend time with me." Her voice trailed off, remembering a past she'd tried to forget.

"And did he?"

"For years I waited at the appointed time, dressed and excited, ready for him to pick me up and take me to the museum, to a movie, wherever it was he'd promised. He never showed. Not once. I kept waiting, though, until I finally realized in my late teens he didn't mean a word of what he said. I never saw him again."

"Ah, baby, I'm so sorry. No wonder you had such a difficult time with men."

"Then, of course, my fiancé. With only a phone call, he ran the morning of our wedding. I had no idea he was seeing someone else. Looking back, I still can't believe that happened." She looked at Hugh. "Why didn't I know? Was I so blind? To him, to his needs? If he loved someone else that much and I didn't know, didn't even suspect, then I must not have paid enough attention to him, to our relationship. God, I can almost understand."

"It wasn't your fault, at least it wasn't all your doing. Sometime things happen for the best. After all, if he hadn't left you, I might not have the honor of holding you, of making love to you." He began kissing her again, and needing to be held, she kissed him back with a fervor that surprised her. She pulled him to her and threw her legs over his hips, drawing him even closer. He groaned, then covered her body with his.

When she woke again, Hugh was sleeping soundly beside her. She lay completely still a few moments, not wanting to wake the gorgeous man beside her. In all her life, she'd never dreamed she'd be so completely in love with such a wonderful, caring man, that she'd ever feel so happy and content as she was now, safe with him, secure in the unique home he'd built.

She'd have to ask more about his mountain cave later — how he'd built it, how long it took — when they were having dinner, or even afterwards, although she knew they should return soon to Marsh Springs and to their jobs — if they still had them. She was sure the townspeople wouldn't be too happy with their sheriff abandoning them after the creature's attack.

But she was too happy in her new life with Hugh to consider all that now. She wanted to find the bathroom, then the kitchen. She envisioned surprising him with plates of bacon and eggs, and maybe some toast, or even soft fluffy biscuits with melted butter topped with apricot or orange marmalade.

She made her way to the passageway and headed for the kitchen. A few feet from his room she passed a slightly ajar door. When she peeked in, she understood Hugh's confidence in having enough sliver bullets. Immediately she recognized the stacks of boxes filling shelves that lined three walls. The fourth held racks of handguns and rifles. Curious, she opened one box, and rows of gleaming silver bullets shone back at her. She'd entered a weapons room. It must've taken him years to stockpile that much repower and ammunition, but why he'd do such a thing, she had no clue.

Further down the passageway, a soft hum from a closed door caught her attention, and she hesitated, wondering what other hidden wonders he'd built. Hugh had mentioned generators supplying the power to the home. Was that what she was hearing? She put her hand on the knob, ready to turn it, but she paused. As close as she felt to Hugh, this was still his home, and he was entitled to his privacy. Yet, she didn't draw back. The first door stood partially open, so she didn't feel guilty investigating. But this one was closed. Firmly. She stood at the door, her hand on the knob.

"Krista," Hugh spoke from behind her, "please, don't open that door." His voice was soft, yet commanding, but she detected a different note, something she couldn't identify.

Her hand still on the knob, she glanced back at him, at the plea in his eyes.

"Don't. Please don't, not until I've had time to explain."

Explain? What on earth could possibly be on the other side of the door that would cause him such distress? With her?

Without making a conscious decision, she turned the knob and opened the door. Inside the room four dehumidifiers ran with quiet hums. Wall sconces softly illuminated standing shelves of photos—of her. Shocked, Krista took a closer look.

The shelves and three walls were lined with photos of her, small snapshots to large portraits of her entire life, from the time before her natural parents were killed, running as a toddler to her mother's arms, to shots of her at dance recitals, her first day of school to her graduation ceremony. How did he get those? And why? She moved closer to a shot of the audience, and she gasped. It was unmistakable—there, sitting in the row of seats was Hugh, his head lowered slightly as if he were trying to avoid the camera, much like the photo at the newspaper office. No wonder he'd looked familiar.

She whirled around to him, but she couldn't even form the words for the hundreds of questions running through her mind.

His look was one of resignation. "Let me explain."

"I don't want to hear you right now." She turned back to examine the walls. Snapshots of her fiancé and her on different outings, of her entering college . . . then she nearly cried out— several large pictures of her mother, again, from the time her mother was a baby to a blurred one of her in their family car.

A strangled cry escaped Krista. The snapshot brought back the night her parents were killed so clearly it was as if it were a movie happening right then in her mind: she recognized the dress in the photo as the one her mother wore that night. Again she turned to Hugh, her eyes full of tears, questioning the impossible. "How . . ." Without waiting for an answer, she kept moving, kept examining the photos, stopping beside black and white snaps of another woman with features similar to her mother, and again, from the time the woman was a baby.

"Your grandmother," Hugh told her.

More photos of women she didn't know, then copies of census reports with women's names circled, dating back a few hundred years.

Then, on the wall behind a row of shelves, several silver ankhs hung, all different sizes from small medallions to as large as the one over the bed. But her gaze found one, and her entire world crashed to an end.

Hanging on a chain was a silver medallion, one she thought she'd seen before. She stepped closer for a better look, then backed away in horror, recognizing the exact one the creature wore the night it attacked Todd and chased her.

TWENTY ONE

Egypt
The Past

Just before dawn the next morning, Rahmor hurried to the ritual chamber and found Norihor, the high priest, in his ceremonial robes, chanting and waving his ivory wand before the blazing fire pit. Orange-red flames spiked with each wave, nearly licking the ceiling. His male servant, clad in a loincloth, stood next to him holding an open scroll, his bald head shiny with sweat. Both bowed low when Rahmor entered.

"I'm ready to begin, Priest. We must not waste time."

In their recessed niches surrounding the chamber, ancient gods of gold stood watch, their painted eyes silently observing the proceedings. Rahmor heard again the quiet hum that emanated from nowhere and everywhere. The bronze oval tub of water sat near the fire. As if to reinforce his command, the prince clasped the silver medallion around his neck and stepped to the tub. He took the servant's arm to assist him.

"Wait!" the priest yelled. "Do not enter the water!"

Rahmor threw Norihor such a look of outrage that the servant ran behind the golden Ra, and the priest cringed, nearly doubling over.

Head down, he implored the prince, "I beg your mercy, my Lord. I must first sanctify the water with offerings to the gods." Rahmor nodded.

Norihor straightened, clapped his hands for the servant to bring the scents and oils, and when he poured them into the water, the familiar white vapor rose to cloud the tub. He turned to his prince.

"Just one more step, my Lord. You must drink again of the elixir." He nodded to his servant, who hurried to a niche and returned with the golden goblet encrusted with jewels.

Rahmor scowled and turned to the oval tub. "I'll enter the water without the aid of the herbs."

"But my Lord—"

"Get on with it!" With the assistance of a servant, Rahmor entered the water and sat submerged to his chin. The rite could not fail this time. Neferaneksi needed his protection. He had not seen her for two days, and he feared she was bound inside her chamber walls.

Norihor took the ancient scroll, and with a nod of acknowledgment to each surrounding god, began to read the transformation rite. Once again, he implored the mighty god Amun to guide Rahmor through the wave of creation and to return him as a fierce warrior and protector. Waving his wand, he begged Osiris, Set, and the other gods to aid in the prince's transformation. He chanted over Rahmor, then, after throwing a dash of green powder into the water, he pushed the prince's head under and pulled him to the surface.

"Rise, O mighty one! Rise in your new form, hailed by the gods to stand with them. Rise!"

With the aid of a servant, Rahmor rose to his feet and waited for a surge of power or some kind of transformation. Since he'd not partaken of the offered wine, his thoughts were clear. His gaze fell on the priest, who was eagerly watching and clasping his wand in front of him as if for protection.

Nothing had changed. Rahmor had not changed. He felt nothing except disappointment. And a growing fury.

"You failed, Priest! Your magic is nothing!" Rahmor didn't wait for assistance; he stepped out of the tub. "I'll inform my father and find another priest!"

Norihor fell to his knees and bowed low, his forehead touching the floor. "Oh mighty prince, please forgive me, I beg of you. Have I not served your father and his household well all these years? Please, my Lord, give me another chance. I'm the keeper of the ancient knowledge, and I will not fail."

From the chamber entrance, a female Nubian servant with only a golden cloth girdle around her hips, took a step into the room. "I beg of you, Norihor. May I enter?"

Rahmor recognized her as one of Satiah's servants.

Her gaze fell on the prince then returned to Norihor. "Please, I must speak to you."

The priest rose in indignation. "Why do you dare intrude upon us this morning? Do you not realize you're in the presence of the prince?"

The young girl bowed to the prince, then addressed Norihor. "As you instructed, I've been keeping watch on . . ."She paused and glanced once again at the prince.

"Yes, go on! You've been keeping watch, and what? What do you have to report?"

"Her priests are performing the ceremonies this morning, Norihor. She demanded a ferocious warrior to stop Prince Rahmor from protecting Pharaoh's chief wife." She glanced once again at the prince and bowed her head.

"Yes, yes, go on. And did her priest fail?"

Rahmor frowned, glancing from one to another. "What's this? What's happening here?"

The servant girl, after another glance at the prince, continued. "From their reactions, her priest is succeeding with two males, although Satiah keeps demanding more. What they're creating is so monstrous they're locking the poor souls into the pit. She wants to select the worst for more rituals, hoping they'll obey her instructions and transform at will."

Norihor frowned and began searching in his cabinet. "You may go."

"Who's the 'she'?" Rahmor demanded, using the drying cloth. "Who wants to stop me, although I have my suspicions. What's going on?"

"You must not leave the chamber, my prince. Your life is in danger. Certainly Neferaneksi's if they succeed in stopping you."

"I demand to know what's going on."

Taking a packet of herbs from the cabinet, the priest gave his attention to the prince.

"At the end of yesterday's ritual, I heard footsteps leaving the chamber, slippered feet as if a female had been listening. Watching too, I presume."

"Who would do such a thing? And why?"

"As the servant said, someone wants to stop you from aiding Pharaoh's wife. That someone wants her eliminated, and I'm sure you know who is behind it."

"Satiah. And if her priest performed an identical ritual and created a monster, we must do the same. I must be more powerful than anything Satiah's priest can create. We must begin again."

"Yes, my Lord. In the morning—"

"Now, priest! I won't wait for morning!"

Norihor fell to his knees again, his hands clasped together in supplication.

"I need rest and strength to carry on. Just one more day, please, my Lord."

"You'll either perform again this instant, or I'll kill you myself. Now rise, and do your duty!"

Two more times Rahmor sank beneath the steaming water only to rise without a transformation into power. The sun's rays lengthened on the tiles with each ritual, nearly touching the priest's chamber. Rahmor's disappointment built to a burning rage, until finally, he'd had enough. He stepped out of the tub and rained water on the tiled floor before the unnerved priest, too angry to accept a drying cloth.

"And you call yourself favored of the gods? Bah! Any of my servants could do more." He yanked the medallion from his neck, threw it with such force that it clinked against the golden Amun, then pointed to the chamber entrance. "Begone! Take yourself out of my father's household! Take nothing with you except the useless robes you're wearing, and live out your life in disgrace. Go!"

Norihor dropped to the floor and bowed low, his forehead to the tiles, his arms stretched in front of him in supplication. "Please, my Lord. One more time. I beg of you."

"It's late, and if I know Satiah, she'll have that thing they created, trained, and ready to go by now. I need a priest as powerful as hers. Not you. You've lost your power. You've had several tries and you've failed every time. You're no good to me or to my father."

"Allow me one more time, my Lord. I promise I'll succeed. I promise on my life."

Perhaps it was exhaustion, but Rahmor's fury dissolved into frustration. He sank onto a chaise lounge.

The priest clapped his hands for his servant. "Wine! And bring refreshments."

To give him strength, Rahmor nibbled at the

mashed beans and pita bread and drank the wine. Should he spend the necessary time to find another High Lector Priest? Such keepers of the ancient's knowledge were rare, and he knew of only one other than Norihor. If his sources were correct, that priest was traveling on a mission sanctioned by Pharaoh and out of reach until early next week.

Did Rahmor want to wait? Each hour, each moment lost presented a risk to Neferaneksi's life. He'd then have to recruit the priest and make sure he knew the ceremony. More time lost. Neferaneksi . . . her beauty may belong to his father, but her safety was in his hands.

His decision made, he stood.

"One more time, priest, but my patience is at an end. If you fail, you die." He stepped back into water cooled by the late hour.

"Yes, my Lord. This time I'll not fail." Norihor beseeched all the gods of knowledge, of the ancient magic handed down from one Lector priest to the succeeding one. He then whispered to his servant, who moved to the colossal green figure of Osiris, standing regally with his crook and flail, his painted white robes flowing nearly to his feet. After a quick bow to the god, the servant ducked behind the massive statue only to return a few seconds later with another scroll. When he stood next to Norihor and received the priest's nod, the servant carefully unrolled it. Norihor began to read.

"Osiris, great god of death and rebirth, grant your special powers to Rahmor, faithful servant to your people, grant him the power of rebirth." He then called upon Isis.

"O wife of Osiris, mother of Horus, giver of the life force, protector of the kingdom, bestow your magical powers upon the prince before you, so he might protect Pharaoh's chosen wife, the giver of life for the future gods on earth." In a low voice, he chanted another passage from the ancient scroll his servant held before him.

The quiet hum radiating in the room centered in Rahmor's pulse and charged through his veins, spreading ice and fire. How dare anyone threaten Neferaneksi! The traitor must die! He'd tear him limb by limb and rip out the throat of anyone who dared threaten his beloved in any way. Each muscle and sinew tingled, elongating, stretching skin and creating new, his mouth ached, and even his teeth hurt. New dark hair sprouted over his face and hands and down his body.

Norihor's servant threw a fearful glance his way, then, after a stern command from the priest, darted low to grab Rahmor's medallion from the chamber floor. Norihor threaded the chain on a long flail and carefully slipped it over Rahmor's head.

What audacity! Rahmor stood, growling with rage, water cascading from his expanding body. His hands grew, his fingers curled into claws. He flexed them, glorying in their sharp power. He was at one with the gods. He heard a fierce howl and realized it came from him. The priest hastily backed away.

The servant fled the chamber.

Through a veil of red, Rahmor burst from the bronze tub taller, stronger, his body more powerful than he could have imagined. Words failed him. Instead, he growled and snarled, and finally, from deep in his belly came a howl so fierce the priest ran in terror.

TWENTY TWO

WV
The Present

Krista's stunned gaze darted from the silver medallion to Hugh, then back to the medallion, trying to make sense of what she was seeing. Hanging on the chain in front of her was the same ankh that had been seared into her brain, the exact one the creature wore the night it attacked Todd and chased her through the forest.

Why would Hugh have that medallion? Why would he have photos spanning her lifetime, and of her mother's lifetime, including her grandmother and her grandmother's mother, and of her ancestral women dating back to hand-written notes of a time before records were kept?

Unable to grasp what was before her, she spun around to the photos, then back to the medallion, and finally to Hugh, a hundred questions behind her eyes.

"I don't understand . . ." She forced down the

heavy dread squeezing her body and nearly choking her. "You've got the creature's medallion? Why would you . . .?"

She stared at him, her breathless voice trailing off as images of the Egyptian artifacts she'd seen in his home raced through her mind, then of Hugh that night on her doorstep, the night he'd brought her home after showing her his supply of silver bullets, the night she'd opened to him and shared her treasured memories of her mother. She saw him again, standing outside her door gazing at the moon, the yellow glow in his eyes, and it hit her.

Hugh, the man she'd learned to trust with her life, the man with whom she was in love, was the creature!

She backed away from him. "No, not you, not you . . ."

"Please Krista, don't be afraid. I'd never harm you. Let me—"

She stopped. "Wait . . . you can't be. You were with me at the park . . . when the beast appeared and attacked the crowd." Her gaze swept the medallion again and back to Hugh, her eyes begging for a reasonable explanation, anything to dispel the unbearable conclusion she'd reached. "You can't be in two places at once."

"No. I wasn't the beast that day."

"*That day*?" She regarded him, trying desperately to understand, her world falling apart as she read the sorrow and truth in his eyes. The terrible realization nearly brought her to her knees. "Two of you? There are two beasts?" She couldn't swallow. "Oh, my God . . ."

"Krista, please let me explain."

Hearing nothing over the pounding blood rushing in her ears, her panicked gaze fixed on him, and she backed away until she bumped into one of the free-standing shelves. Hugh grabbed her to steady her. She screamed, and when he dropped his arms, she ran for the exit, but he was too quick. He pushed a button on the wall and the heavy door sealed shut, locking them both in the climate-controlled room.

Krista searched for a knob, a handle, anything that would open the metal door. But there was nothing. Frantically, irrationally, she pounded on the door, checking over her shoulder to see if the beast was heading toward her.

"Krista, you're all right; you're in no danger from me." Without moving toward her, Hugh spoke in a soft loving tone. "Nothing here will harm you. I would never harm you. I live to protect you. I brought you here, to this cave, to protect you." His voice was soothing, calming.

She barely heard him. She'd blocked everything except her frantic attempts to get out of that room. He didn't try to approach her, didn't try to restrain her.

"Let me out!"

"Please calm down and listen to me. If you leave the cave now, your life might be in danger. The beast might be out there, waiting. Oh my beautiful Krista, you have nothing to fear from me. I'm so sorry you found out this way. Please let me talk to you, to explain."

She pounded on the door until her strength gave out. She was trapped. Breaking down in quiet sobs, she collapsed on floor and waited for Hugh to turn into the raging, snarling beast. But she heard nothing except his reassuring voice as he kept talking to her. Then he too, went quiet. When her sobs finally died and she sat, spent, on the wooden floor, he spoke again.

"I want to tell you a story, a story of the distant past, of a love so strong it's endured several millenniums."

She didn't look at him. She didn't know what would entice the man to turn into a beast, so she sat quietly, not daring to move, hoping, praying, he'd open the door. After a minute, an hour, an eternity, some of his words found their way through the wall of terror and helplessness she felt. Love? Millennium? Thousands of years? Nothing made sense. It was too much to bear and she was exhausted, so she sat with her head against the door, not moving, her eyes closed, waiting for death.

Slowly, he moved toward her, his steps merely a whisper. She braced herself. She covered her face with her hands.

Hugh dropped to the floor near her. He sat without moving closer and he didn't touch her. After a few moments, he began to talk, his soft voice nearly a whisper, beginning with a story about Prince Rahmor, an ancient prince of Egypt, sitting on a dais with Pharaoh the day he first saw a copper-haired woman, part of the bounty from a successful military campaign in the northeast. Her beauty drew his attention, but it was her bravery in face of her vulnerability that had captivated him.

Hugh spoke so lovingly of the prince's adoration for this woman that his words pierced the terror in Krista's heart, and she listened, fascinated by the story of an Egyptian prince and his tortured love for a slave who became queen.

"—and when Rahmor emerged from the water the last time," Hugh continued, "the transformation was complete. He was a beast of terror."

In spite of her fear, Krista wanted to hear more. "Did the beast lose all reasoning and kill the copper-haired woman?"

"No, Krista. Even as a beast, the prince loved the woman and vowed to protect her against her enemies for all time."

"'For all time?' I don't understand."

"During that last ritual, the priest, knowing his life was at stake if he failed again, invoked a secret passage that was so powerful even the previous High Lector Priests kept the scroll hidden away. It not only changed Prince Rahmor into a beast at will, but it granted him a long life to protect Pharaoh's chief wife and their future female heirs to the throne. The gods granted that wish. Literally."

"What does that mean?" She was trying to follow the story, as implausible as it sounded. It seemed important to Hugh— and in some way, to her.

"It means Rahmor is still alive, sworn to protect not only Neferaneksi, but her bloodline of women following her. Your line, baby, your heritage."

Still not comprehending, she stared at him. "My heritage? How could that be? And Rahmor? He's still alive? After these thousands of years?"

He nodded. His face, his entire demeanor, spoke of sadness. Resignation.

Krista, still trying to understand, held his gaze. "This Prince Rahmor ... he's the beast? And this elaborate cave is his?"

"Yes. He's one of the two beasts — one created to protect the slave who became queen and all of her female descendents, and Satiah created the other to stop him."

"God . . . two of those horrible creatures . . ." She glanced up in time to see pain at her words ash across Hugh's face. She leaned her back against the door and stretched her cramped legs in front of her. A headache was forming behind her eyes, but she ignored it. She needed to concentrate, to understand. "I'm sorry, but none of this makes sense. And what do you mean, 'my heritage?'"

"You are a direct descendent of Queen Neferaneksi. That's why your mother wore the ankh, why her mother wore it, and her mother's mother and so on, back to the time of the pharaohs."

Trying to keep up with Hugh's revelations, Krista's thoughts were spinning from one fantastical disclosure to the other, each one too mind-boggling to believe. How could she possibly comprehend them all? And how could he expect her to believe him?

Yet, wasn't she the one who was convinced she saw a werewolf, a creature of myth?

Hugh remained silent, giving her a chance to sort through it all.

What he was saying was too fantastical to comprehend. Could she possibly believe him? Yet if he was truthful, that meant she, her mother, and all her female ancestors were descendents of an Egyptian queen. She fingered her ankh, thinking of her mother, remembering back to the evening she was sitting on her mother's lap and her mother slipped the silver chain over her head.

"Always wear this, sweetheart, in honor of your sacred heritage."

Tears moistened her eyes. Through all of the things Hugh had revealed to her, it was her love and curiosity about her mother that prompted an explanation.

"You knew my mother?"

"Yes, I did. Toward the end, she knew the beast was closing in, so she asked that if it succeeded in killing her, I protect you any way I could."

Suddenly, memories that had been buried in Krista's mind surfaced, and she saw again the crash that took her parents' lives, felt her mother's hand pushing her to the floor.

"Stay quiet and don't move!"

She heard again that terrible sound from outside the car. Eyes wide, she realized it was a howling. "It was that beast that night. It hit our car and killed my parents." By pushing her down, her mother protected her.

Hugh met her knowing gaze. He spoke quietly, sadness in his voice. "I knew the beast was closing in, so I needed to get both your mother and you to safety. I was here that night, making final preparations to bring both of you to the cave. By doing so, I failed to protect her when she needed me the most."

Krista heard the regret in Hugh's voice, and she longed to hold him, to offer comfort in the way he'd comforted her.

But she still needed to fully understand. "But why is Prince Rahmor after my bloodline? After me?"

"It's not Prince Rahmor; he's doing everything possible to protect you from that beast. Remember in the story when the first wife, Satiah, created another beast to destroy the queen and her bloodline? That beast killed your parents, and now that you're the remaining survivor, it's after you. That's why I brought you to a remote mountain town in West Virginia and to the cave I'd prepared."

"You didn't bring me here. I answered an ad. Hugh, even if I believed what you've said so far, how could you possibly do such a thing?"

"By arranging for that ad in the Marsh Spring's newspaper to appear. By getting you out of Arizona."

"You did this? You arranged for me to be here? Why?"

"Because it was decreed in the ritual that I live to protect not only the queen, but also her female bloodline. I'm Prince Rahmor."

TWENTY THREE

Krista sat back, her incredulous gaze on the man she thought she knew. Accepting him as a shape-shifting beast was incredulous enough, but what he was saying now was truly beyond belief. Did such magical powers truly exist?

"You're Rahmor, son of Thutmose the Third? The 'Napoleon of Egypt' pharaoh?"

"I am."

As a journalist she'd been trained to seek out the truth, to accept nothing but the facts. What Hugh expected her to believe sounded preposterous. Yet, as unbelievable as it all seemed, the werewolf truly existed. She'd seen it. If she could accept one implausible fact, why not the other?

"Let's say I could believe all of this, and you're Prince Rahmor . . ." She broke off and massaged her temples. "Oh, my head's splitting. I can't deal with all of this right now; it's too much."

"I understand you need some time." Hugh leaned close and tenderly brushed a lock of hair away from her face, his gaze full of compassion. "Your beautiful green eyes are swollen from crying." He pulled her to him and held her. "I have a suggestion. You go freshen up, and while you're doing that, I'll prepare breakfast. Or would you prefer dinner? It's been hours since we've eaten, and after all that's happened, you must feel depleted."

Krista wiped the last teardrop from her face. "I don't know what I prefer. I don't even know what I feel. I just want to lie down and forget any of this ever happened."

"You need nourishment. Have something to eat first, then lie down. Will you do that for me?"

Raising her gaze to him, she searched his eyes for the man she'd known, for the man she'd trusted. Was he still there? Did she dare trust this strange man/beast before her? She needed to think, but her eyes felt raw and swollen, and now it felt as if hammers were slamming the base of her skull. She just wanted relief from the pressure, from the pounding in her head, the heaviness in her soul.

Hugh rose, lifted her to her feet, and pressed another button. The heavy door slid open with a soft whoosh.

"I'll meet you in the kitchen. When you feel better, we have some decisions to make." Just as she shuffled through the doorway, he softly added, "And please don't try the entrance. It's sealed against intruders."

Krista hadn't even thought of trying to escape; she knew all too well what could be waiting outside for her. Making her way to the bathroom, she thought of what Hugh/Prince Rahmor had said. Decisions to make? Right now she couldn't even decide what to call him.

When she entered the kitchen about twenty minutes later, a shrimp salad lay waiting, accompanied by hot crusty French bread. Krista realized she was ravenous, despite all that had happened. Keeping her eyes on her lunch, dinner, whatever time it was, she ate in near silence, aware of the strain between them. She could feel Hugh's gaze on her, but she wasn't ready to talk.

He finished his meal, shoved his plate aside, and poured another glass of wine. He offered to fill her empty glass, but needing a clear head, she declined and sipped from her water glass.

"I don't know who you are or what to say to you." She tried to keep the desperation from her voice. "I only know Hugh, the man I loved with all my heart. Hugh, who made love to me and made me feel alive. I was ready to share my life with him, and now I don't even know what to call you. Are you Hugh or Prince Rahmor?"

"I'm both. But please, Krista, think of me as Hugh, the man who did in fact, make love to you. The man who has loved you all your life. The man who is willing to die to protect you."

A tear spilled down her cheek. "I loved that man, but I'm afraid he's gone. Forever."

"I haven't gone anywhere. I'm right here." Hugh stepped from his chair and lifted Krista to hold her close. At first she struggled, and he instantly released her, but when she didn't move away, he drew her to him again. "All the great poets have said love is in the heart. Listen to mine. Hear my heart beat with love for you."

Curious, she allowed the embrace. He felt warm and wonderful, just like the man she'd known. She lay her head on his shoulder and listened to his heartbeat, the same strong rhythm as that first day in his office. She breathed deeply and recognized the familiar clean masculine scent with just a hint of soap and aftershave. Her own heart answered with joy. Whatever else this man was, he was still the man she loved.

She gazed into his eyes. "Oh, thank God, it is you. I haven't lost you after all."

"You'll never lose me." He held her tenderly until finally, she stepped back and sat down.

"Help me to understand. I need to make sense of all this."

"Ask whatever you need to know."

"You're saying the other beast attacked the town's citizens because it's tracking me?"

"Yes." He took his seat and waited, his eyes holding hers.

"That means I'm responsible for the slaughter — and for Mrs. Reardon."

"No, Krista. You're not responsible. If anything, you're the true innocent in all of this."

"But people have died because of me. And Todd. Tell me about him."

"What about him?"

"Was it the other beast who killed him so

viciously? If so, why didn't it kill me when it had the chance?"

Hugh didn't speak for a few moments. Head down, he fidgeted with his wine glass, ran his finger around the rim, then picked up the bottle and set it down again. Krista watched with amazement. If she didn't know better, she'd think he was embarrassed.

"There must be no secrets between us," he began, "so if I'm going to be completely honest with you, I have to admit I was the beast that night. I killed Todd."

"You? But why?" She didn't know how she felt about that revelation. In one way it made sense — even though the beast viciously ripped Todd apart, it didn't kill her. It didn't even touch her.

"I tracked him from the moment he picked you up, and when he took you to the river, the man in me suspected his intentions. As the beast, I could've scared the hell out of him, which was what I'd intended, but when he made that grab for you and talked to you the way he did, I decided to teach him a lesson. I made a few noises to scare him. That could have been all that happened, but when he left you alone with such little regard for your life, I knew he could decide to eliminate you so you wouldn't turn him in. I eliminated him instead."

"You lost all reason?"

"No, Krista. Even as a beast I have control. To my shame, I allowed rage to consume me eons ago with an overseer in Egypt. Since then, I've never again allowed that to happen."

"I'm deeply sorry for that night. I wouldn't want anyone killed, not even Todd."

He shrugged, as if Todd were nothing more than a nuisance he'd disposed of. "I will say I was surprised when you showed up; I fully expected you to stay hidden in the forest. I'd never want you to witness a kill, especially by me."

Krista had no idea how to respond to that, so she silently regarded him. He covered her hand with his, and she looked down, noting his strong human hand that had held her so gently and had caressed her so tenderly.

Would she know before he turned into a beast? She swallowed, still at a loss. She didn't want a strain in their relationship, so, as something to do, she made coffee and planned her words.

"You said even as a beast you have control. But what about the full moon? Do you need a full moon to, to transform?" She frowned, remembering. "No, that can't be right. The other beast appeared at the city park during the morning hours." Uncomfortable, she couldn't look at him. "I don't know how to ask this."

"You want to know when I turn into the beast?"

She nodded, relieved he understood. "I guess what I'm asking is, do you have control over the transformation?"

"Total control. I love the moon, its cool beauty, the mystical influence it has on earth, and it may have an effect I'm not aware of. But truly, the priest intoned that I change 'at will.' That I've done. Countless times over the years."

Coffee pot in hand, Krista met his gaze, then sat down and filled two cups. "I just don't know what to think. On one hand, I'm appalled at this entire situation, and I'm surprised I'm not screaming." She paused.

"And? On the other?"

"I've never felt this kind of love from anyone in my entire life, so if I don't want to lose it, I'll have to accept . . . everything."

"I'm so sorry to cause you stress. That's something I never wanted to do. I wish . . . I wish . . ." His words trailed off and his eyes lost their focus, as if he were gazing at a place far away.

She had never seen him so reflective. Wanting to offer comfort, she placed her hand on his. "You wish what, Hugh?"

He brought her hand to his mouth and kissed her fingertips, then held it in front of him. "Such a small hand for such a large heart. So trusting." He sighed. "I wish I could've met you in another time, a time when I was totally human, and you were a woman I could've loved and married."

She felt his warm breath on her fingertips, and her entire body responded with love for him. "Would you have married me?" she asked softly.

"I would have adored you then as I do now. We would've had many children with eyes the color of malachite and hair of carnelian like their mother. We would grow old together, and when it was time, we'd take wing and fly to the heavens."

Every nerve in her body responded to his words,

to his warm gaze, and she needed to feel him next to her. She moved to his lap, pressing close to him, cupping the back of his neck to draw his mouth to hers. He moaned and pulled her even closer, kissing her until she was breathless. She twirled her fingers in his long dark curls, and when the kiss ended, she nuzzled her cheek next to his.

"Marry me," she whispered. "Now, in this lifetime."

He tensed and said nothing. She waited, her cheek against his, not even breathing. She drew back. Did she say the wrong thing? She waited a few minutes more for his reply, and when it didn't come, she felt as if he'd plunged a knife into her heart. She searched his face for an explanation, anything, but it was as if he'd suddenly turned to stone.

Her entire world shattered. Fighting tears, she mumbled an apology, stumbled off his lap, and ran out of the room, berating herself with each step. She shouldn't have mentioned marriage. She must've gotten carried away in the moment. What was wrong with her? Of course he wouldn't want to marry her — he was a prince and an immortal, and an immortal wouldn't want to marry a mortal. And on and on, one fleeting thought after another.

He caught up with her and pulled her to him, holding her against her struggles.

"Listen to me. I'd love to marry you, Krista, I've waited a lifetime for you. But there are . . . complications."

"Well of course there are complications. This entire thing is complicated. Don't you think I know that?"

"Come with me." His arm around her waist, he urged her forward, out of the hallway.

She dug in her heels, too upset to go anywhere with him. She'd finally trusted a man enough to let him know what was in her heart only to have him reject her. Again. Would she never learn? She wanted to retreat to a private room to hide her humiliation and heartbreak.

"Krista, it's not what you think. Come with me to the great room where we can talk. Let me explain. Please."

Avoiding his eyes, she relented and allowed him to escort her to the room. Her cheeks still flushed, she sat quietly on the sofa and waited while he paced the room in front of her.

"What you don't know is, I may not survive much longer. I don't want you to marry me believing we could build a life together."

"What do you mean? You've lived hundreds of years. Thousands. Why do you think your life may be ending?"

"A feeling I have that my life is changing. A strong feeling."

"Couldn't it be changing for something wonderful? Changing because you fell in love? With me?"

His glance was as warm as a caress. "I've known more happiness with you in this short time than I've had in my lifetime. Please know that. But it's more than my love for you." He quickly turned to the armoire, but she was puzzled by the look of restraint he'd tried to hide. He kept his back to her as he leisurely filled two crystal glasses with cognac. When he finally turned around to offer her a glass, his face was void of expression, and it frightened her.

She accepted the drink and took a sip, her gaze fixed on him. She knew him well enough to realize he was trying to spare her, silently debating whether to tell her something she wouldn't want to hear. Whatever he had to say must be horrendous, more so than what she'd already had to face, for him to be so distressed. She tensed, feeling as if someone were pushing her chest into her backbone.

"What aren't you telling me?"

He said nothing, simply took a seat on the wing chair.

She waited for him to continue, and when he delayed speaking, she gulped her wine and forced air into her tight lungs.

"Look. I'm a reporter, which means I've been trained to sort fact from feeling, and I can do so with whatever problems we may have. I said 'we' because we're now a team. So tell me everything so we can face it and deal with it. I've already dealt with more than I would have thought possible, and I can face this. With you."

He swirled his wine, seemingly concentrating on the amber liquid splashing against the crystal. He must have come to a decision, as he took a swallow and placed his glass on an end table.

"You're absolutely correct in wanting to know my — our future, and why we may not have one. It's decreed that one day, when the time is right, the beast and I will fight to the death. I feel that time is now."

She couldn't seem to breathe. "Whose death? Which one will die?"

"That's for the gods to decide."

"No," she whispered, "that can't happen. Not now. Not after I fell in love with you." She searched his face, a hundred different thoughts racing through her mind. "But why now? Because the other beast found me? Because of its rampage in the city park?"

"Not in the way you may think."

"What, then? That you two came close to seeing each other and fighting?"

"He and I have tangled many times in the past, but neither could kill the other. We've learned—at least I've learned over the centuries—to disengage when it became obvious neither was going to die. So it's not simply that, but it's a sign. If what I'm feeling is correct, the fact that he found you is strong evidence that my entire life and purpose is coming to a conclusion."

Krista was near tears. "But I don't understand. Obviously he found me when he killed my mother."

"Not necessarily. For some reason, you survived that attack. I'm sure that if he'd known you were there, he would've killed you as well. Why he didn't know is beyond me, and the only answer I get from the Lector priest is something about predestination, that I will eventually learn everything when it is the proper time. That time is now.

"The Lector priest is still alive too?"

"Only the other beast and I have lived since the pharaohs, but the secret priesthood has survived."

Krista's mind was spinning with incredulous images of ancient Egypt, of pharaohs, the other beast, a secret priesthood, but she had to set them aside. If she'd ever needed to think rationally, it was now.

"Let's try to figure out as much as we can and decide where we go from here." At his nod, she continued. "Why, exactly, do you feel this is all coming to a conclusion now?"

"According to the ritual I undertook, I was to live long enough to protect Neferaneksi and her female descendants, possible heirs to the throne. I've done so.

"However, in return for this power, I was to give up a life of my own, which meant for all those years, I was to have no home, no wife or family."

Krista listened carefully, totally captivated by his story. He must've endured hundreds of lonely years.

"But if I were faithful to the decree, one day I'd know great joy, which I believe is now. With you. The priest also warned that with that happiness comes great risk—the battle with the other beast, in which I may not survive."

"But that's a punishment. Why bestow that kind of power only to yank it away when you need it the most? It doesn't make sense." She moaned and messaged the back of her neck. "God, this is giving me another headache."

"I confess at the time I didn't think it through. As a young man, I only thought of protecting the woman I loved."

Krista thought of the shock she'd felt when he recounted his story about the dead queen. He underwent so much for her. She couldn't help but wonder if he still wanted her. She drained her glass before she asked, her voice a whisper, "Is it possible you're still in love—"

"No, Krista. I'm not still in love with her. It was a long time ago, and since you came into my life, I've realized I never was truly in love with Neferaneksi. It was infatuation. And admiration."

"What happened to her? Did she live a long life?"

"She did. She was a gentle queen, kind to everyone, and a loyal wife to my father. We never again met privately, but I stayed near her until the end—a natural end to a human life." He said nothing more, and Krista's heart went out to him.

"I'm so sorry."

"It was all in the past and it doesn't matter now. I'm in love with you. My mission was to protect you, but I've loved you for years."

"How was that possible?"

"I knew you were to be important to me when your mother was carrying you. She had a special glow about her that I recognized, but I knew you were special when you were a teen."

Captivated, she listened carefully, willing him to continue. "And?"

"This is my perspective of the story you told me. You were a beautiful young woman of about sixteen, sitting on your porch steps, your suitcase next to you. Obviously you were waiting for your father as you'd done several times after your parents divorced. After waiting several hours, you must have realized he wasn't going to show. Always before, when he failed to honor his word, you'd get these big tears, and my heart would bleed for you. This time your lips trembled, but you lifted your chin, and I saw that same determination to survive I'd seen on the face of the copper-haired woman all those years ago."

"Neferaneksi?" Krista barely breathed the name. "You're comparing me to the queen?"

"You must remember she wasn't a queen when I first saw her. She was simply a slave held by my father, determined to face whatever the gods had in store for her. As you did then. As you're doing right now. And I love you even more for it."

"You love me as you loved that copper-haired slave?"

He dropped to his knees before her and took her hands. "Krista, I've never loved another woman as much as I've loved you. Not even Neferaneksi held such a place in my heart. Your love for me has made me want to be a better man."

His words brought her to silence, and she felt overwhelmed by her love for him. She pulled him close and held him tenderly, silently, as if drinking in his touch. He nuzzled into the soft spot just below her chin and let her hold him.

When she released him, she sat back. "We must have a life together, Hugh. This can't be the end of the story. The gods couldn't allow us to meet only to let you die. They can't be that cruel."

"I don't know how to answer that. I only know we have this moment together, right now. I can't ask about tomorrow."

"No. I won't accept that. There must be something we can do. We must go to Egypt."

TWENTY FOUR

"You want to go to Egypt? What do you think that will accomplish?"

An old nagging doubt crept into her mind, and Krista dropped her gaze. Did she have enough faith to travel with Hugh to a foreign country? The country of his birth? What if he had a change of heart and left her there, or, what if he reverted to the beast and didn't, or couldn't, change back? Could she survive alone in a Muslim country?

She didn't know, but now was the time to decide whether she trusted him or not. Could she open her heart and put total faith in someone again?

"Krista?" With his forefinger, he lifted her chin to gaze into her eyes.

When his eyes met hers, all her doubts disappeared. "Maybe the priest can perform another ritual to make sure you survive, or maybe he can abolish the decree. Anything! If we don't at least try, we may not have a life together. I want a life with you, so we'll go. And that's final."

As Hugh regarded her with another of his scowls,

she ignored his displeasure and fanaticized a life with him, imagining their home, their children. Could he have children? And if so, would they be normal? No, she didn't want to consider children at this time, not with so many other things to think about and resolve.

Hugh took a deep breath, and when he spoke, his voice was calm. "Even if I'd agree to go, there's no guarantee the priest will talk to you. He'd be so horrified that I'd shared the story with you, he might cast a harmful spell on you. He might even have us both killed."

"He'd do such a thing? After supporting and counseling you all those years?"

"It's possible, Krista. Keep in mind the few Lector Priests who've continued the brotherhood down through the ages have done so in secret, a private sector unknown to the rest of the priesthood. With highly-secret ceremonies. No, Krista. I'm not willing to risk your life."

"It's my life and I'm willing. We have to try." She stared at him defiantly, waiting for his response, but there was none. At least no verbal response, although she could almost hear the silent words behind his fierce scowl. The minutes dragged on until they seemed like hours, but she wouldn't back down. Her future with the man she loved was at stake. Their very lives were at stake.

Finally, Hugh shook his head. "All right. You win. I should've known you'd have that streak of willfulness. Even obstinacy in the face of danger."

The plane circled over the Nile River and landed twenty- three hours after they boarded the first leg of the flight in Charleston. They emerged from the Luxor airport to a dry sunny day of about eighty degrees, which felt more like Krista's native Arizona climate. Still, it seemed exotic after a month in the moist mountain climate.

She was truly in Egypt, a place she had dreamed of seeing since she was a child, but a country she didn't think she'd be able to visit on her salary for many years. She touched her ankh and thought of her natural mother, wishing she could have joined them. What fun to see all the ancient sights together, especially with Hugh, who could tell them everything they wanted to know about their history.

But of course this venture wasn't for pleasure. She hoped one day to return with Hugh and enjoy leisurely tours of the temples at Karnak, Luxor, and the pyramids and sphinx outside of Cairo.

Outside the airport, Krista was delighted to see single horse-drawn carriages standing among the taxis, buses, and mini-vans. She pointed to one, and Hugh helped her up the step.

On the drive to the ferry to cross the Nile, Krista marveled at the ruins of sand-colored columns standing next to neighborhood homes. This was truly a land of old and new. Her fatigue from the long flight disappeared at the sight of the ancient city, and she breathed air filled the scents of spices, flowers, exhaust, and dust, all mixed together.

During the boat ride across the river to their West

Bank hotel, Krista savored the hot dry wind ruffling her hair and eagerly peered over the side to wave to the smaller boats alongside the ferry. She was actually crossing the famed Nile River.

At the hotel, Hugh checked them in and they took their complimentary sugar cane drinks to their room's spacious balcony. City lights brightened the twilight sky over Luxor's East Bank, and as the orange sun dropped below the hills behind them, the glowing red-gold sky faded to violet.

Over the normal sounds of a populated village, a man's song rang out, his slightly tinny voice drawing out the syllables in a long chant.

"Oh listen!" Krista turned her head to hear the haunting cry more closely.

"The Islamic call to prayer."

She listened quietly, and when it was over, she sighed. "What a city. I can hardly believe I'm here. Bet you're happy to see everything again."

"I loved Thebes, the beautiful city I knew as a child and young man. Today's Luxor holds little interest for me."

"I'm sorry. You must miss your home."

"Ah, remember that old adage, 'Home is where the heart is.' I'm home whenever I'm with you."

"Oh, Hugh . . ." She gazed at him, thanking God she'd found him no matter the circumstances.

He stood and stepped to the edge of the balcony. "I have many wonderful memories, of events and of a people long gone, erased as if they'd never happened."

"How can you say that with all the temples and tombs still standing?"

"The builders were geniuses, and the people worked together to contribute to the gods. Still, the monuments are shells of what once was, of a life that's passed away along with our traditions and values."

"What's so different now?"

"Many things. Egypt has a magnificent history, and during the pharaoh's rule, the lower classes worked hard, and they had their own way of life. We recognized that and rewarded those with talents. Women had power and were as respected as men."

"I've read about Hatshepsut and other women of stature. Too bad that's changed."

"When the pharaohs lost power centuries ago and foreign invaders conquered the land, customs changed. Today, the people are friendly and kind, but they're poor, which is why tourism is so welcomed." He nodded to the east. "See the lights?"

"They're so brilliant they light up the sky, even from this far. What are they?"

"From the temples at Luxor and Karnak. I think you'll enjoy seeing one of them, and to the north, on this side of the Nile, are the pharaohs' burial sites. The modern era calls it the Valley of the Kings."

"I'd love to see it. Will we add that to our list?"

"No."

"Isn't your father there?"

"He was buried there as was his right as king. But his tomb was looted, emptied of the things he needed on his trip to the Underworld. Later, the so-called professionals removed his body and unwrapped it. It's now on display in Cairo as are many others."

"I guess I never thought of it that way." She touched his hand. "I'm so sorry.

"I've learned to live with the desecration." He stared silently into the distance.

"Want to talk about it?"

"Like my father and our way of life, it's all in the past."

Not wanting to intrude, Krista kept a companionable silence and enjoyed the Egyptian evening. "Such a beautiful city. So mysterious in its beauty."

"What's so mysterious about it?"

"Everything! Egyptologists have discovered many things, but there are still hundreds of unanswered questions. And to think you lived through those times. It's so unreal I can hardly believe it."

"The scientists will never discover everything."

"Do you know the answers? For instance, who built the pyramids?"

Hugh smiled. "Your eyes light up like an excited child's, but to answer your question, I don't know. They were ancient even when I was born."

"Did you hear anything about them? Myths or stories handed down?"

"It was said that the gods descended from the sky to build them."

"Oh. Do you believe that?"

"It was also said that in those days, the gods walked among us. The universe holds many mysteries, so who knows?"

Krista was silent, letting her imagination soar to ancient days upon the earth, of gods in their glory, helping, instructing ancient Egyptians. Could she believe they lived among the people? And built pyramids and other great monuments? Since she was standing next to a mythological shapeshifter, she knew anything was possible.

She gazed at the stars. Where did the gods come from, and were they still out there? She doubted she'd ever know, but it was a fascinating theory, one she'd like to explore when her life felt a bit more settled.

"What about Ramses the Great?"

"What about him?"

"Was he really that great?"

"He did many good things, but he also stretched the truth somewhat."

"He was supposed to be a great warrior."

"Bah! He had his moments, but my father was greater."

"I have a question, one that's been debated between many scholars."

Hugh turned to her, eyebrows raised.

"Was he the pharaoh of the Exodus?"

"No."

Before she could ask him more, his cell rang. "Delzo. I have to take this call."

She knew he needed to keep in touch with his

deputy, no matter the outcome of this trip, but she couldn't help but feel disappointed. She'd ask him later. Or maybe the interruption was the gods' way of telling her this wasn't the time to ask.

With another glance at the sky, she shivered, surprised the night temperature had dropped so quickly. She went inside.

A few moments later, a thoughtful Hugh joined her.

"Everything okay at home?"

He was slow to answer; instead, he took the chair next to her and poured a glass of complimentary wine. "It will be."

"You're not saying much. Has the beast attacked the town again?"

"No."

She drew in a breath. He was being too secretive for her comfort. "When we were in the cave, you said we shouldn't have secrets, but you're holding something back now. Is it the beast? Do you think it's tracked us here?"

"You're right. The call was about law enforcement business, and no, I haven't detected him so far. Most likely he's transformed back into human form."

"You can detect him? Like tracking an animal?"

"I have that ability as does he."

Astonished, Krista gazed at him. So that's what that strange ritual meant. He was testing the air for the scent of the beast. "You can't detect him when he's human?"

"No."

"And you don't know who he is?"

"That's never been revealed to me. I don't know why, except to possibly keep me alert. I wish I did know."

"Then we're always vulnerable."

"Only when he's a beast. Then I sense when he's near." He sighed. "I'll order dinner, then you can get some rest. After Hatshepsut's temple closes to the public, I'll visit the priest."

"Why her temple? I thought the priesthood would meet at Karnak."

"We did for decades, but when it became such a tourist draw, we moved it to my father's temple next to Hatshepsut's."

"Oh, that's why you booked on the West Bank."

"He had it cut from the cliffs, and the terrace sits a little above Hatshepsut's. One corner collapsed. Then, due to rockslides, most of the actual building has been destroyed. It's of little interest to the tourist, so we meet behind it in an intact undiscovered chamber carved into the mountain."

"Sounds deliciously mysterious, and I can't wait to see it."

"I never said you could accompany me to the temple. You'll stay here."

"Now wait a minute. This trip was my idea, and I'm going to see the priest with you."

"The hell you are. You convinced me to make this trip, but you can't accompany me. I've already explained the consequences, and I won't allow you to risk your life."

"But you just said —"

"You're safe from the beast for now, but not from the temple guards."

"They can't stop me. What if I refuse to leave?"

"You don't understand. The priesthood dates back to my father's time, and the protocol hasn't changed. Today the sentries guard the secret chambers with rifles, and they won't hesitate to use them."

"But you're a prince, the son of a pharaoh —"

"The priests have kept me alive with their magic for two-thousand years. I'm not about to challenge that source when they could direct it to you. You'll either stay here or we'll return to the States right now. What's it going to be?"

Krista observed the set of his jaw. "Good God, I haven't seen this bullish side of you since, since . . ." Unable to think of anything, she stomped to a side chair, dropped down, folded her arms across her chest, and refused to look at him.

Ignoring her displeasure, Hugh picked up the menu and in a conversational tone, read from the menu. "What would you like for dinner?"

"I'm not hungry."

"Of course you are. Now I'm going to order, and I hope you won't let it go to waste. It's a long time until breakfast, and if you want to see the sights tomorrow, you'll need your strength."

"This is just like the day we met. No matter what I said, you were so determined to, to . . ."

"To what? Protect you? Love you?"

"I wouldn't call the morning we met as a day of love. You pretended you didn't believe a word I said."

"Would you have preferred I told you I was the beast?"

"That would've been a lot better than making me feel like I was a crazed druggie."

"Would it? What do you think would've happened if I'd done so? Delzo would have grabbed a high-powered rifle and shot me. I'd be helpless until I shifted."

"You honestly think he'd pull a gun on you?"

"If I shifted into the beast, he most certainly would. That's what he's trained to do. At the very least, he'd call the governor or the National Guard, and someone in that frenzy would certainly have shot me. Then where would you be? I'll tell you—you'd have been an easy target for the other one."

"I didn't think a regular bullet would kill a werewolf."

"It wouldn't, but it could drop me, and I'd be helpless until my body healed itself. That may take time, time when you'd be vulnerable."

Krista hadn't thought of it in that light. If that had happened, not only would she have been without protection, but she would never have known the love she felt for this man—nor had it returned.

He picked up the phone. "Now let's forget this silly argument and have dinner." Before punching the room service button, he glanced back at her, a question in his eyes.

What a dilemma. She didn't want to tell the big lug he was right, but she was hungry. "I've never had a tandoori chicken kabob, but it sounds fantastic. And doesn't it come with Basmati rice and roasted veggies?"

Just after midnight, Hugh rose, fully dressed, from the settee where he'd been dozing. Krista, pretending to be asleep, listened as he slipped out the door. As soon as it closed behind him, she threw off the covers, straightened her pullover sweater and jeans, and slipped into her jacket. Just as she reached the door, her cell phone rang. Damn. It was her mother. She answered, but in reply to her mother's concern over not hearing from her daughter in a couple of weeks, whispered she'd call her later.

"Why later? What's wrong? Why are you whispering?"

Krista didn't want to tell her she was in Egypt. She cut her off as best she could and hurried to find Hugh.

She didn't wait for the elevator; instead, she flew down the stairs, thankful it was a late hour and not many guests were moving through the hotel. Just as she reached the lobby, she spotted Hugh pushing through the outside entrance. Outside, he nodded to a man guarding a rack holding several bikes, picked one, and sped off.

Great. Now what? It had been years since she'd been on a bicycle and she didn't know if she could still ride. But she couldn't stand there undecided for long; Hugh was disappearing fast.

She hurried through the door and approached the same man.

"How much for a bicycle?"

He frowned, and in broken English tried to dissuade her. "No! Not safe for woman without husband. Must wait!"

She ran to the rack. "I must go! How much?" She selected a blue bike that looked in decent shape. "This one!"

The man still stood as if undecided.

"Hurry! I'll pay!" She pulled Egyptian pounds from her bag with no idea how much she was giving him. At that point, she didn't care, but it must've been more than enough. He grabbed them, smiled, and unlocked the bike.

Pedaling furiously, she weaved through the narrow street, lit only by widely-spaced streetlights and lights from the few bars still open. Male pedestrians walked by the hotel, noticed her and yelled something, perhaps thinking she was out for another reason. Hugh had cautioned her on the plane about Muslim countries and their views of women—especially lone women on the streets after dark.

She never dreamed she'd be in that situation so she hadn't paid attention. Now she wished she'd remembered before leaving her room; she would've had a heavier jacket ready, and a scarf to cover her head.

Ignoring the men, she hurried along, searching for Hugh's bike, passing the hotel's gardens of palms and red vines. She felt conspicuous and totally out of place. If she didn't spot Hugh soon, what would she do? Keep riding and head for Hatshepsut's temple and hope to find him there?

At the edge of the village, the patches of green ended and the sand began so abruptly it was as if someone had drawn a line dividing the two. Following the road to the temple, the streetlamps provided little light.

Darkness closed in around her. She couldn't turn back now, but with each turn of the wheel, she checked behind her to see if anyone was following her. She watched the road around her feet. Were cobras out at night?

She shivered.

Hugh had mentioned she'd be vulnerable if anything happened to him. She didn't think she could be more at risk than she felt now as a lone woman out at that late hour in a Muslim country.

TWENTY FIVE

About a quarter-mile from town, a decrepit motorized bike pulled in behind her and gave chase, the small engine sputtering as if ready to die at any moment.

"Hey lady!" male voices yelled. "Stop! Let's party!"

Ignoring the men, Krista pedaled faster. What was she thinking when she left her room without proper clothing? Or went out alone so late at night?

"Hey lady! We have good time!" Their engine missed and slowed.

She scanned the road ahead for Hugh, hoping she could catch up with him before the riders caught her. She pedaled furiously, the deserted, winding road through rolling sandy hills offering little protection.

Behind her, the engine missed again, then died. Male voices yelled for her to stop, but she didn't dare. After several misses, the engine cranked up again.

A fork in the road appeared in front of her. A sign said something, but she didn't dare slow down to read. She pedaled left toward a cluster of low stone structures, which, in the shadows, resembled some sort of waist-high barricades. Beyond them, she could see the cliffs, and just below, the faint outline of Hatshepsut's Temple.

Thank God!

The rickety engine and the catcalls grew louder, closer. She raced toward the building, hoping someone would be there to help her.

The motorbike caught her. It sped ahead and whipped around to cut her off. She swerved to the left, and when her bike hit the sand, it wobbled crazily and went down, throwing her to her knees. Three guys, appearing to be in their late teens, jumped off their bike and fanned out around her. Wearing jackets over loose pants and flowing shirts, they moved easily, laughing and sauntering toward her.

With a strangled sob, she sprang toward her bike, but they were faster. She made it past one of them, but the other two closed around her. A rancid beer smell clung to them.

"Hey lady, don't run! We have a good time!"

Why hadn't she listened to Hugh? Instead of trying to outsmart him, she should've tried harder to talk him into taking her to the priest. She'd made a stupid mistake, one that might cost her dearly. Could she reason with these young men, or were they too drunk to listen?

"I have money! Take it! Just let me go."

An inhuman howl swept through the valley, the pitch low, lingering, and threatening. Krista's breath caught. She hadn't heard that heart-stopping sound since that night in the West Virginia mountains. Who knew what hunted in the Egyptian hills, or what else had survived the ages. Was it Hugh? Or, had the other werewolf trailed them to Egypt?

The men froze. "What?" They looked at each other, then in the direction of the sound. All three talked at once. "Jackal?" "Naa, man, no jackal sounds like that." "What is it?"

Just then Hugh appeared and jumped off his bike — at least Krista thought it was Hugh. While the waning moon threw little light, she recognized the clothing, but the figure appeared larger, in height and bulk. He headed toward the men, his gait slow and easy, as if he knew they couldn't escape.

"You want to play games? Play them with me." His voice sounded different — low and rumbling. He glared at the men and no one moved. All their bravado disappeared as the stranger spoke, his eyes taking on a glow like a cat's in low light. "Come on, I thought you wanted to play . . ."

His voice, mocking, threatening, ended in a growl. Even Krista, who'd convinced herself it was Hugh, stared as his eyes turned into the red horror she'd seen the night the beast tore out Todd's throat. A soft cry escaped from her, and Hugh threw a startled glance at her, his eyes cooling back to gold. The men took that split-second chance to run for their bike, but Hugh, or the creature, was faster. He dashed for the bike, picked it up as if it were a toy, and threw it into the hills where it landed with a crash. His eyes glowing re, he turned to the men.

"Run." With his rumbling voice low and quietly threatening, he spoke again. "If you want to live, run/"

All three took off and didn't look back.

Slowly, Hugh headed toward Krista, his appearance reshaping into his human form, his eyes losing their glow. Even though she knew Hugh as a man and loved him dearly, she had to fight the impulse to run. Now was the biggest test of her life: had she learned to trust? And did she truly trust him? She willed herself to stand her ground, and when Hugh approached her, totally human and his eyes the hazel she loved and wrapped his arms around her, she melted into his warmth.

"Are you all right?" He ran his hands down her body. "They didn't hurt you?"

His familiar earthy scent calmed her. "I'm fine. Shaken, but all right. I should've listened to you."

"Maybe now you'll realize I have reasons for my actions." Gently he led her to the road and to his bike. He stood a moment studying her, his face reflective. "I'd intended to see you back to our room, but now . . . I'm not so sure."

"Hugh, please. I'm just as involved, maybe not quite as much as you, but still. My life's deeply affected by all of this. I think I have the right."

"I tend to agree. Can you ride?"

On her bike, she followed him down the road, and soon the outline of Hatshepsut's Temple appeared in the distance. Hugh led her around the barricaded entrance and dark ticket office to the parking lot. She caught her breath at the magnificence of the famous temple and came to a stop. Just the causeway leading to the pillared three-terraced monument was large enough to hold a multitude of pedestrians, much larger than she'd imagined from the various photos she'd seen.

Hugh pulled up beside her. "Djeser-Djeseru," he whispered, "the Holiest of Holies, dedicated to Amun. She had it cut from the cliffs behind it, as did my father when he built his temple alongside hers."

"What was it like?"

He breathed deeply. "Today, only the smell of dust is in the air, but during her reign, the scent of myrrh from the plants and trees she brought from the land of Punt was heavy, the entire area alive with lush gardens and fountains. The monkeys she brought swung from the trees, and to the delight of the people, performed tricks on command. She loved the people, and in many ways, she was a great ruler."

Krista closed her eyes and visualized the pictures he painted from long ago. She could feel moisture from the fountains and detect the scent of myrrh in the air. She smiled at the image of chattering monkeys swinging from the trees.

"By trading with the people of Punt," Hugh continued, "she brought to our people many wonderful things which we used lavishly. Ebony was highly valued, and just as important, our perfumes and oils from the trees and plants she provided. They're still favored by the people today."

"Did you know her well?" She stared at him in awe, realizing once again he actually lived during the ancient times. "No. I was too young. My father treated her with respect. I don't think he felt love for her, but when he came of age, she appointed him commander of her armies. He may have held some resentment over the way she took control when he inherited the throne. I really don't know. Years later, I realized someone had to since he was too young to rule. From what I understand, she enjoyed her position, and didn't want to surrender the throne to him." He climbed back on the bike. "Let's move on. It's getting late."

She followed him across the sand to a massive stone foundation so deteriorated that huge blocks, nearly crumbled to dust, lay in disarray.

"This was your father's temple? What happened to it?"

"Land- and rockslides, lack of care, then later it was ransacked for the blocks." Bypassing the building, Hugh walked his bike to the base of the cliffs behind the structure. Krista followed with her bike. She saw nothing in the rock face that would suggest a room or even a cave, but she followed close behind.

At one point, he lay down his bike and took her hand to lead her over fallen stones. "Careful now. It's hazardous."

She carefully watched his feet, trying to place hers exactly where he had stepped, weaving around the irregular vertical walls, not realizing anything had changed until he stopped.

They stood in a darkened cavern entrance, much like the one he'd carved in West Virginia, but this one was much larger. A faint sliver of light flickered in the distance, so she knew the cave must be substantial. Taking her hand, Hugh led her about a hundred feet through the twisting cavern until they approached an expanded area with smooth walls and a paved floor. Fire sconces mounted on the walls provided light. Soon the pathway widened, the light brighter.

Hugh turned to her. "Ready?"

Krista drew a breath. Now that she was actually going to meet a Lector priest of the ancient world, she wasn't so sure. But it was something she had to do.

"I think so." She lifted her chin, which caused Hugh's eyes to soften. She met his gaze. "Yes, I'm ready. Let's change our lives."

TWENTY SIX

They rounded the curve of a widened, well-lit passage.

"Halt!" Two male guards in camouflage and facial masks stepped in front of them. Only their narrowed eyes were visible, and they stood with the barrels of their rifles pointed downward. But the tense way they carried them alerted Krista that they were ready to use them at any second.

One man stood a step in front of the other, his gaze sweeping Krista. "In the name of Amun-Ra, do not move forward."

"Stand aside." Hugh didn't yell, but his voice held total confidence and authority

"Yes sir. I beg your pardon, but the lady . . ."

Hugh's voice took on the lower, growling timbre he'd used with the teenagers. "She will enter the chamber with me."

The guard seemed to shrivel. "Yes, Your Highness, I apologize. You both may pass." Both men stepped back, lowered their weapons, and snapped to parade rest, eyes forward.

Although her legs were trembling, Krista lifted her chin, and as she'd seen in movies, placed her hand lightly on Hugh's forearm. Regally, she moved forward, stepping carefully so she wouldn't stumble in front of the guards. She didn't take a breath until they'd rounded the bend. As soon as they were out of the guards' sight, she staggered to the cave wall and gasped for air.

Hugh threw her an astonished look. "You weren't actually worried, were you?"

"You have to admit, they were pretty intimidating."

"More so than I?"

"Of course not, but they had guns."

Hugh shrugged. "So what? If need be, I could've torn them from limb to limb, and folded their guns in half."

Krista paled at the image of the beast tearing into the guards, reminded once again that Hugh could transform into a terrifying creature. When human, he'd always shown such gentle love toward her that she sometimes failed to remember — or perhaps she didn't want to remember.

Hugh led her further into the cavern, and soon they entered a massive chamber highly decorated with colorful paintings and hieroglyphics. Krista felt as if they'd entered a newly-carved painted tomb in ancient Egypt. At least thirty feet by thirty, it was a complete rectangle, the rock so expertly carved the walls could have been smooth plaster.

"Oh! Look at this," Krista whispered in awe. In the center, two life-sized golden statues of a king and his queen stood in royal splendor, the reds and oranges from the fire scones dancing on the gleaming figures. She circled them, her reverent gaze absorbing every detail. "Who are they?"

"Supposedly it's my father and a figure representing a queen. He had several. They were carved to flatter, long before the fourth Amenhotep, or as he's more commonly known, Akhenaten, requested true portraits. An early priest had the figures brought here many centuries ago, hoping they would please me."

"And did they?"

"It was a thoughtful gesture, nothing more."

Krista examined the king first, then moved to stand before the queen, noting the rearing cobra jutting from the crown, the smooth facial features with eyes gazing ahead, to the flowing dress draping her slender figure. Placed around them, as if the figures would someday make use of them, chairs and lounging couches created from ebony and mahogany woods sat waiting, their arms and legs carved to resemble lions' paws.

Krista could have stood before the figures indefinitely, but there was so much to see. She moved around the room, her astonished gaze sweeping the walls and ceiling.

"It's as if we're in ancient Egypt." She scanned painted scenes of kings and their queens, some small, others so large that one or two figures covered the entire wall. Some were featured with children playing next to them while others showed pharaohs in their chariots charging into battle. Blues, reds, and golden yellows appeared as bright as if they'd recently been painted. With one finger, she tentatively touched one section to make sure it wasn't wet. As ridiculous as it sounded, she was surprised to discover dry paint.

"Incredible."

Scenes of feasts, animals, and scarabs, and scribes sitting cross-legged writing on papyrus, appeared between vertical lines of their unique form of writing. The ankh in different sizes was prominent, and on some of the figures, the king grasped a large ankh by the top circle. She touched her pendant and felt a kinship with the long-dead king.

Hugh interrupted her musing. "Let's move on. Even though the entrance is well-hidden, I'd rather we not be here in the morning light. A curious tourist might explore and find more than he'd expected."

"Okay." Reluctant to leave the intriguing room, Krista followed Hugh through a concealed doorway cut into the rock and into another chamber. In the center, a bald man in flowing robes and a headpiece with a rearing cobra stood before a steaming circular pool, a younger man at his side. Both men bowed low, but her attention focused on the pool of water about eight feet in diameter enclosed by a two-foot mosaic wall. It resembled an indoor hot tub with rising steam. She couldn't see the source of the steam. Multi-colored cushions surrounded the vessel.

"Welcome, Your Highness. And the lady is, I

presume, the last female descendant of the queen?"

Hugh nodded. "We wish to seek knowledge."

The priest stood quietly. "I'm at your service, My Lord." He turned to Krista, silently waiting.

She lifted her chin. "I am Krista Hawthorne, descendant of Queen Neferaneksi."

Folding his hands as if he were in prayer, the priest bowed. "Indeed you are. Welcome, Your Highness. I am Lutamun, High Lector Priest, and I am honored by your presence."

Krista glanced at Hugh and caught his look of astonishment. She quickly masked her triumph and turned back to the priest, her expression as solemn as his.

When he turned to Hugh, she took the opportunity to gaze around the room. While not as elaborate as the outer chamber, the room was impressive in its own way with figures of the gods painted on the walls: the kneeling figure of Nun with sharp up-and-down lines representing water beside him; Amun-Ra, the patron god of Thebes; Bastet, with her cat's head and woman's body, plus Isis, Osiris, Horus, and several more she didn't recognize. The golden busts of several gods stood on carved platforms above drawers with golden or polished brass pulls. The scent of myrrh filled the room, which was already humid from the bubbling water. She wiped beads of sweat from her forehead and slipped out of her jacket.

"My life has changed, Lutamun," Hugh told the priest, "just as you predicted. This time I want answers to questions you've previously declined to answer."

"Yes, My Lord, it is time. But before we speak of such matters, you must be weary from your travels. Please allow me to offer refreshment. Some jasmine tea, perhaps?" Without waiting for a response, he nodded to the other man, who scurried through a hidden door in the back of the room, only to return in record time holding a tray with a kettle and two steaming cups.

"The princess and I would enjoy tea."

Krista's eyes widened at Hugh's use of the title for her, but not wanting to appear gauche in front of the priest, she said nothing.

"Please, both of you, be seated." The priest led them to a side niche with two chairs and a small round table, nearly identical to the elaborately-carved ones in the outer chamber. The young man set the tray on the table and stepped back.

"Thank you." She took a chair. Once they were seated, Lutamun, still standing, turned his gaze back to Hugh.

"After you've finished your tea, we will talk."

Hugh poured, and Krista politely sipped her tea as if she were seated at a contemporary State dinner.

A girl servant in loose-fitting pants and a long-sleeved shirt of linen pushed a decorated tea cart holding a variety of small cakes, cookies, a tray of fresh fruit, and another tea pot to the table.

"May I refresh your tea?" Eyes down, she stood before Krista and waited. Finally, Krista realized what she was supposed to do, so she dipped her head in a gesture she'd seen on TV.

At Krista's nod, the girl refilled both Krista's and Hugh's cups, then set appetizer plates and silverware in the center of the table. She cut the cakes, then peeled and cut two oranges and set them in the middle. She then expertly cut a pomegranate into sections, peeling and removing the inner membrane to display the juicy red seeds. She stepped back and glanced at Krista with an unmistakable look of adulation, then bowed low.

Krista caught the look. So this is how royalty lived. She had to admit she'd love the service, especially after a long tiring day, but she wasn't sure she could ever grow accustomed to maintaining a regal demeanor. Even now she wanted to relax her shoulders and sit comfortably, but didn't dare in front of the priest—or his servants, who were all standing by. Hugh took it all in stride, ignoring their audience and helping himself to the cakes and fruit.

She delicately bit into a cake, not sure what to expect, but a moist sweetness flooded her mouth. "It's delicious! I'm tasting orange, lemon, and other flavors I can't identify."

Hugh smiled. "A honey cake with bits of fruit and nuts. Several of our desserts feature oranges since they grow along the Nile."

When Krista had finished, she placed her napkin on the table, just as if she had dined in a first class restaurant, and sat back, her gaze on Hugh.

The priest approached them. "If you'll please step

to the pool, you'll find the answers you seek." He turned to Krista. "Forgive me, Your Highness, but while the ritual may appear strange to your eyes, it's necessary."

Not knowing what else to do, Krista nodded once.

This time she moved slowly toward the center of the room, letting Hugh take the lead. When he sat on one of the cushions, she did as well. The priest remained standing and chanted words Krista didn't understand. Hugh said nothing, so the process must have been familiar.

The male servant passed an urn to the priest, who threw colored crystals into the water. Instantly, the water bubbled rapidly, sending perfumed green, then blue steam into the air. The priest continued his chant and tossed more crystals. Krista caught a vaguely familiar scent. Myrrh? Frankincense?

Fascinated by the process, her gaze swept the priest, then Hugh, who stared into the water, but her eyelids were growing heavy and with each passing moment, it was more difficult to keep them open. She didn't want to fade out now, but the scenery swam before her and she felt lightheaded. Had the tea been drugged? With an effort, she kept her eyes open, but the priest's voice faded until she could barely hear.

After the priest threw more crystals into the water, he leaned forward as did Hugh. Suddenly, the steam parted, and to Krista's amazement, wavy, but colorful images formed beneath the water. People. And they were moving, as if they were alive. What sort of magic was this?

The first image featured a man in sandals and a white kilt hurrying through massive halls decorated with golden images ... a palace? She recognized Hugh. She glanced at him next to her, but he said nothing, just kept his gaze on the water.

Krista turned back to the images, moving almost as if a video were playing. How was this happening? Below the water level, the image of a red-haired woman in a sheer flowing dress appeared, disappeared, then appeared again, moving swiftly through vast halls surrounded by maidens and guards.

Krista drew in a breath. She had no doubt about the woman's identity. The scene shifted to Hugh and a different priest, then Hugh rising from a similar cauldron, growling and snarling, his eyes bloody red, fangs and claws extended. Krista tensed and drew back, but Hugh took her arm.

"You need to see it all."

The priest tossed in more crystals. Steam rose again, then parted. Krista leaned forward. Hugh's image reappeared in the water again, strolling through streets in an Egypt long passed away, then with different women through the ages and dress, until finally, the images stopped during a night scene.

A car on a deserted highway, a man driving, a woman in the passenger seat, and a copper-haired girl child in the back. A terrible howl caused the man to swerve, and the woman, tears in her eyes, turned and pushed the little girl to the floor.

At the sight of her parents that fateful night, Krista gasped and choked back a sob, but she couldn't stop the tears. Even now, she yearned for her mother, but she tensed, knowing what was coming next.

Another snarling howl, and the beast attacked on the driver's side of the car. For the first time, Krista saw a clear path on the passenger side, and she realized her mother could have escaped and run through the woods. But instead of saving her own life, she'd stayed very still with her hand covering her daughter, sacrificing her own life for her daughter's. Krista wept openly now, and Hugh leaned over to take her in his arms.

"I know it's difficult, but there's more. We must not miss anything if we're to find answers."

"You're right." Krista could barely speak, but she wiped her eyes with a cloth the servant provided.

The scene now showed Marsh Spring's city park, the beast attacking, and Hugh's and Krista's escape to the cave. The priest intoned more chants, and a sudden blood-red mist rose and parted to reveal two monstrous figures locked in battle, both growling and snarling, tearing into each other with vicious intensity.

Even though each wore remnants of clothing, Krista realized they weren't human. Two sets of fangs and claws ripped and tore so fast they blurred together, one indistinguishable from the other. Chunks of hair flew, blood spattered.

Krista closed her eyes, knowing one of the savage

figures was Hugh. After what seemed an eternity, one of the creatures threw the other down, and with a savage howl, ripped open its throat. Before Krista could discover which one survived, mist closed over the images.

"No! Don't stop now! Please . . ." Krista stared at the water and willed the images to appear again, but without the priest's crystals, the vapor died and the water was still.

Lutamun faced Hugh, his face void of expression. "I am now ready for questions."

Even though Krista knew the protocol was to let Hugh ask, she had to know. "Which one of the beasts survived? Was it Hugh?"

The priest calmly regarded her, but kept silent.

"Well?" Hugh said. "Answer the lady, Lutamun."

"I regret to inform you that I cannot."

"And why not? Doesn't your magic reveal everything?"

"Not the answer you seek."

Krista gripped the edge of her cushion. "We came all this way for nothing?"

"While I cannot answer your question, My Lady, I can provide explanations and knowledge."

"That would be appreciated." Embarrassed by her outburst, Krista said nothing more.

"If I may, I'd like to tell you a story." His questioning gaze rose to Hugh, who nodded his assent. "But first, let's take but a moment for tea."

Before Krista could protest, the priest clapped his hands for the servant.

"Fresh tea. We'll take it here."

The girl bowed and ran out of the room only to reappear with a tray. She stood behind Hugh and offered a cup first to him, then to Krista, and finally, to the priest, who quickly emptied his cup and had another.

Hugh drank his and gave back the cup.

Krista did the same, and while she hadn't wanted to take the time, she realized she was growing stronger. More alert. This time, the warm liquid spread strength and determination through her veins, and she sat straighter, eager to learn if she had a future with Hugh.

TWENTY SEVEN

"Many years ago," the priest began, "Prince Rahmor's father, Pharaoh Thutmose, known now as Thutmose the Third, captured a slave girl from the upper regions and made her queen. But jealousy from another threatened her life."

Lutamun threw crystals into the water. Once again, a vapor rose and parted to reveal Neferaneksi in a chamber preparing to bathe. Behind her, a maiden quietly removed the top of a container and a hissing cobra slithered to the floor and wound its way to queen.

Someone screamed, and a guard rushed in, and with his sword, sliced the head off the writhing snake. Vapor closed over the scene.

Krista silently cried for more, but again following Hugh's lead, she waited. Finally the priest continued the story.

"The king learned of the treachery and assigned his High Lector Priest, Norihor, to provide protection. If the priest failed, he would be put to death in the most hideous way. Knowing of the prince's adoration for the queen, Norihor chose him. Even with the high priest's magic, it took several rituals—"

"Several frustrating rituals," Hugh interjected.

"And upon discovering that the guilty party was conducting her own rituals to create a monster to stop Rahmor's protection, Norihor took risks. He had no choice but to use the most guarded secret rites from the ancient ones. And after several failures, he finally succeeded far beyond anything that had been decreed. The prince transformed into a horrifying fiend."

He threw red crystals into the water, and as before, the scene showed the snarling beast emerging from the water.

"But even as a beast," Hugh said to Krista, his voice soft, "I kept my intelligence and only used my strength when needed to protect the queen and her line, which includes you—the woman I love in this time."

Krista wished she could take him into her arms to show her support, but she simply covered his hand with hers. His warm glance told her of his appreciation.

The next scene took place with Hugh as a man, speaking with the ancient priest once again, and Lutamun continued with the history.

"Norihor explained to Rahmor the consequences of transforming into the beast, that he would give up a life of his own to spend hundreds, perhaps thousands of lonely years protecting female descendants who could be heirs to the throne. Then one day, when the time was right, the last of the female line would be born." The priest's gaze settled on Krista.

"Me? I'm the last of the line?" She frowned. "I'm not to have children?" Her first thought was of Hugh, that he wouldn't survive and she'd spend the rest of her life in mourning, never to marry or have children of her own.

"If he were faithful to the decree," Lutamun continued, "the gods would favor him with his own special queen. His soul mate, if you will, meant only for him. Even though he would recognize her, he couldn't rest. The other beast had succeeded in killing her mother, so it would be tracking her, biding its time, even more determined to destroy her and fulfill its mission."

"That won't happen," Hugh whispered. "Not as long as I'm alive."

"I know," Krista said, her gaze full of love. "You've always protected me."

"This woman would be the end of the female line of descendants," Lutamun continued, "so after her, there would be no more need for protection. The rite would be fulfilled; therefore, neither beast would have a reason to continue living. They would, at last, fight to the death."

Krista, taking it all in, said nothing.

The story was incredible. She dismissed the possibility of her own death, thinking only of Hugh. She turned to the priest.

"But if I'm the last of the line, why does the other beast want to kill me?"

"It was created to destroy your line. As long as you're alive, it can't rest. It must complete its mission."

"You have powers. Can't you do your own magic to discover which beast will survive?"

"That has not been revealed to me. Only the gods know."

"What about another ritual to ensure his survival? Do you have that kind of power?"

"Krista—" Hugh began.

"My magic is strong, but I will not attempt such a rite."

"Why not?"

"It's in the realm of the gods. I must not question."

Krista couldn't give up. "What about reversing the ritual? Can you remove it so Hugh will become a mortal?"

Lutamun nodded. "That is within my power to do so, but be advised he would most certainly die. If I restored him to mortal, he would lose the power of the gods and instantly age, not a sight you would want to witness. He'd dissolve into nothing but dust before your eyes."

"Oh!" Krista couldn't even imagine such a horrible fate.

"Even the dust would disappear. Think carefully. Is that what you wish? Both of you?"

"Of course I don't want him to die."

The priest turned to Hugh. "You've been silent,

My Lord. What is your desire?"

"I've lived as the beast since my father's time, and I'll continue to do so until the gods decide otherwise." He turned to Krista. "I'd rather spend what time I have left on earth with you and take my chances. I want a life with you, even if it's only for another day, another hour."

Her heart pounding, Krista jerked awake and listened for a sound that might have disturbed her. Hearing nothing but the muffled sounds of a busy late afternoon outside the hotel, she rose on her elbows, her gaze sweeping the room, then settled on Hugh's sleeping form. Nothing seemed amiss or out of place.

Careful not to disturb him, she checked the clock on the bedside table. Four in the afternoon. She'd only been asleep about twenty minutes. Even though the priest had arranged for a ride back to the hotel, their bicycles strapped onto the roof of the taxi, Krista had been so exhausted, she had peeled off her clothes and fallen into bed in her underwear. Hugh joined her, gave her a light kiss, and promptly fell asleep.

But she kept waking every few minutes. She lay quietly, her mind replaying again and again the priest's words, realizing what they'd meant. They both might be at the other beast's mercy at any moment, and Hugh may die. She didn't give much thought to what would happen to her if the other beast won that last battle. If Hugh died, she wouldn't have anything to live for.

She glanced at him, the sound of his soft breathing giving her comfort. What a life he must have led. She couldn't even imagine living through history, actually witnessing the changes in the world and to his homeland. One day, when she knew he'd survived, she'll ask him to tell her about life as he lived it through the ages.

But not now. Not when the beast was out there, threatening their future.

She eased out of bed and paced the room, her steps soft on the plush carpet. Hugh made a sighing sound and turned over. If she were exhausted, she knew he must be more so. He'd had to shoulder so much, not only the years of his past, but during his time with her.

She glanced at him once again, admiring everything about him, from his dark hair that curled slightly against his neck, down to shoulders that had been strong enough to provide comfort and security when she'd needed them. Even now, she could close her eyes and feel the love and strength in those arms, and the thought of losing him was too terrible to even consider.

How could she get through the days and nights knowing the other beast was out there, not only wanting to slaughter her, but to destroy Hugh as well? She had to brace herself to keep her nerves from screaming.

Carefully, she took a bottle of wine from the small fridge and poured a glass, gulped it down, and opened another small bottle.

"You sure you want to drink that much on an empty stomach?" Hugh's sudden words startled her and she nearly dropped the wine.

"Sorry I woke you."

"I'm not. It'll give me another chance to hold you." He held out his arms. "Come here."

Bottle and glass in each hand, she slid onto the bed and crawled to sit beside him. She held out the glass. He sipped, but made a face.

"I'm afraid I've adapted too much to your American ways. I want coffee." He picked up the phone and ordered breakfast for them both, and an extra pot of hot coffee. "We have decisions to make."

"Yeah. We need to plan the rest of our lives." Krista emptied her glass. "Or what's left of them."

An hour later, Hugh slid his and Krista's breakfast trays to the cart next to the bed. "At least you put something in your stomach."

"The grapefruit and marmalade for the toast were delicious."

Hugh pulled Krista close beside him and kissed her forehead. "Do you want to make some decisions now, or do you feel you can sleep?"

"Wish I could sleep, but I keep wondering about the other beast and where it might be. I don't see how we can make decisions with such an uncertain future. I keep thinking about your final battle, and not knowing the outcome hangs over me like a dark shroud, smothering the life out of me. Out of us."

"I know it's difficult for you to live with that kind of threat, which is one reason I didn't want to hear the priest's words. But try to look at it like this: no one knows his or her final hours. We all know our lives will end, but we manage to live anyway."

"I know. It's just ... somehow it seems more certain, maybe because that threat is out there, searching for us."

"But we have a huge advantage: I know when that threat is close."

"Only when it's in creature form. Not when it's human. It could be anyone."

He sighed and affectionately ruffled her hair. "I don't know how to make this easier for you. I just know I don't want to waste whatever time we have left worrying about it."

"You're right. I know you're right, but how do we get through the days?"

"Ah, love. We must not 'get through' anything. We must greet each day with joy, and give thanks for the time we have together. After all, right now we're in each other's arms. What could be better?"

Her gaze meeting his, she felt warmth, as if he were spreading a protective mantle over them. She dearly loved this man. Did she want to spend whatever precious time they had left worrying about what might happen? She had to let the anxiety go and rejoice in their own happiness. Most of all, she didn't want to distract him with concern over her. She had to try harder.

"Let's go sight-seeing! Right now. It's not too late in the day, is it?" She scooted off the bed and headed for the bathroom. She paused, waiting for his answer. When she heard nothing but silence, she stepped back into the bedroom. Even with all of his life experiences, Hugh's face showed the same puzzlement most men wore when totally baffled by their spouse. She retrained from smiling. "Is there a problem?"

He shook his head. "No matter how long I live, I'll never understand women."

She laughed and jumped next to him. "I love you." She pulled his face close and kissed him. "Come on, let's get ready for a glorious evening."

"Both the Luxor Temple and Karnak will be closing soon, but we could make the night show. You'd still see some of the monumental buildings from my father's time and after." He got out of bed, pulled on his jeans, and searched the closet for a shirt. "I have to give Ramses credit. He loved to build."

"He's in the Cairo museum, isn't he? I'd love to see him. I looked it up and was shocked to discover he had red hair like mine, and it wasn't due to the mummification process as they first thought."

"Some were even blonde. I'll take you to see Ramses on a later trip. No way can we see everything this time."

Just as Krista stepped into the shower, she heard Hugh's cell phone. She quickly showered, then wrapped the towel around her and stood still, trying to determine if Hugh was still talking. She heard his voice and realized he was talking to his deputy. Whatever it was, it had to be urgent for Hugh to talk that long. Holding onto the towel, she stepped back into the bedroom.

"What did he want?"

Hugh set the phone on the nightstand. "Oh, nothing important. Just catching me up on law enforcement business." He pulled on his shirt, grabbed his shoes and moved to a side chair.

She waited, but he said nothing more. Wouldn't even look at her as he pulled on his socks.

"He must've wanted something. We're not supposed to keep secrets, are we?"

He dropped his shoe and looked up at her. "He wanted to know if I still wanted my job, and if so, when I planned to return."

"Well, do you?"

"I hadn't planned on it. I thought we could decide our future together. What would you like to do?"

She hadn't fully considered where they'd live, so she felt taken aback by his question. "I don't know." As much as she wanted to see everything Egypt had to offer, the call from Delzo stirred feelings she'd shoved aside. She felt a curious longing, and thought about Marsh Springs.

She had grown to love the town before that night with Todd. The landscape was right out of a master's painting with the pristine snow-capped mountains riding above the treeline, the bubbling streams that washed away her problems, the wind whispering through the tree leaves. And the people. She'd never encountered such giving, friendly people. She thought of Mrs. Reardon and she blinked back tears. Would she ever recover from the guilt she felt over that needless loss of life?

And her apartment. Was it okay? Had the beast broken in to search for her? How about the newspaper? Had all the crew made it safely out of the park? Were they back to work, wondering what had become of her and the sheriff?

"Did Delzo give you any news about what happened after that monster attacked? About who survived and how the town's recovering?" Before he could answer, she added, "I'm truly grateful for this time here, and I'm almost shocked by what I'm about to say."

His eyebrows rose, all of his attention on her.

Her voice low, she continued. "Let's leave for now and return when we can take our time and see everything. Hugh, I want to go home."

"To Arizona? I understand wanting to see your mom. You've been through a lot."

"No. Home to Marsh Springs."

"Why would you want to return there? You know the other beast might be lying in wait."

"You liked it there, didn't you? Everyone respected you and you made friends."

"You're more important to me than any of that."

"I've given it a lot of thought, and I only hope it lost my scent when we came here and is searching for us elsewhere. That would give us a little time to have a life together in a home we both like—until it picks up my scent again and finds me."

TWENTY EIGHT

After a stop at Frankfurt then Washington Dulles International, they finally landed at JFK about twenty-four hours after boarding in Luxor. They still had to catch the flight to Charleston, WV, but they had a three-hour wait.

They lingered over sub sandwiches at the airport cafe, and afterward, strolling past the different gates, she happened to notice the information about a flight to Arizona. She stopped.

"Oh no. I forgot to call Mom back." At his quizzical glance, she explained about her mom calling and how she'd cut her off. "I feel terrible."

She pulled out her phone and clicked her mother's number. It rang and rang, finally going to voicemail. "That's strange. She's not answering. That's not like her." She tried again, and again it went to voice mail. "Still no answer. I hope nothing's wrong."

"Maybe she's out shopping."

"She always takes her phone when she leaves, even if it's only to check the mailbox at the end of the driveway. One time she fell and had to crawl back to the house. That was before cell phones were popular." She tried again. Again no answer.

"Try not to panic." Hugh took a seat at the gate's waiting section. "I'm sure she's all right. If not, someone—her neighbor, the police, or the hospital would get in touch with you. Wait at least a half hour, then try again."

"If she still doesn't answer then, I'm calling the police."

Krista couldn't relax, so she paced the corridor in front of the line of seats, continually glancing at the clock on the wall, watching the hand move forward for each minute that passed.

Images of her mom in a hospital bed, lying helpless and alone, flew through her mind, the woman whose love and devotion helped Krista live a normal life after her parents were killed that night. Why on earth didn't she think to return her call in Egypt? She had only thought of herself—selfish, selfish, selfish. And now her mom might be paying for it.

Finally, after a torturous half hour, she sat beside a patient Hugh and called again. Still no answer. "Okay, that's it. I'm calling the police."

"I have an idea." Hugh pulled her to the flight board and checked the schedule. "We're in luck. This plane stops in Phoenix."

"That's a wonderful idea, and I appreciate the thought, but it's in a half-hour. We can't possibly make it."

"Leave it to me." Hugh stepped to the check-in desk, and after a few minutes, they boarded the plane for Arizona. The flight attendant directed them to the first-class section.

Krista took her luxury seat in the front of the plane. "You're amazing. Thank you."

He squeezed her hand. "Your wish is my command."

"I'd be careful saying something like that. You just might regret it."

"With you? Never."

She laughed. "I'll remember that."

During the seven-hour flight, she called her mother several

times, but as before, she never received an answer. Hugh called ahead and reserved a car for the drive north to New River. On the ground, they loaded the rental car and headed north. She tried to reach her mother one last time.

"She'd answer by now if she could. I'm calling the police."

"We're almost there. Let's check the house first, then we can call the authorities."

"Thank God I kept my key."

When they pulled up to her mom's tan stucco home, the home in which Krista had been raised, a red SUV with out-of-state plates sat in the driveway.

"Who can that be?" She gave a quick knock, and just as she inserted the key, the door opened. Her mother stood on the other side, fully dressed, her smile fading to shock.

"Krista! What are you doing here? I thought it

was the pizza delivery." She seemed flustered and glanced behind her. "Uh, come on in."

Krista hugged her mom. "Thank God! Are you all right?" Her concerned gaze swept over her mother, noting she wore her usual shade of pale lipstick, and that her hair had been combed. "You don't look sick. Or injured." She stepped through the doorway and pulled Hugh in behind her.

"Whatever gave you the idea I was sick?"

"You didn't answer your phone."

"I've had company," she whispered, again glancing behind her.

"Why are you whispering?" Krista turned to Hugh. "This is Hugh Rawlins, Boone County Sheriff."

"Yes, you told me about him." Her voice dropped even lower.

Krista frowned. Something didn't feel right. "He keeps an eye on me, and, he's the man I'm seeing." While she'd always told her mom everything, today she held back her true feelings for Hugh. Maybe it was the strange vibes from her mom.

Hugh offered his hand. "I'm happy to finally meet you, Mrs. Hawthorne."

Her mom took his hand and glanced, once again, behind her. "First names, please. I'm Hannah."

"I hope to see you more often in the future. Your daughter is very important to me."

Without another word, Hannah led them to the living room sofa.

Krista glanced through the archway to the dining

room. It seemed empty, so why was her mother directing them to the living room? Everyone had always gathered at the large wooden table for coffee, snacks, and conversation, but now her mom avoided the room. And the way she kept looking over her shoulder. What was going on?

"Was that the pizza?" A male voice called from the hallway leading to the bedrooms and bath. "Hope so. I'm starved."

Krista's breath caught at the sound of the familiar voice. Not Chuck, not the louse who'd jilted her the morning of their wedding. What was he doing at her mom's house? No wonder she was acting to strange.

Her mom seemed to shrink into the cushion and wouldn't meet Krista's shocked gaze.

"What's he doing here?"

With a helpless look, Hannah shrugged. "He dropped in and wanted to talk."

"And you let him in? After what he did to me? To all of us?"

"He wanted to apologize. For everything."

Krista stood. "I'm leaving. Come on, Hugh."

"This isn't my home, but if anyone leaves, I'd think it should be your former fiancé—unless of course, your mother wishes otherwise."

Hannah shrank into the chair and looked ready to cry. "I didn't know what to do. I couldn't just turn him away."

Krista sat back down. "You're right, Hugh. He's not going to chase me out of my own home."

"Your mother's home now." Chuck entered the

room and abruptly halted at the sight of Hugh. He scowled. "Who are you?"

"None of your business." Krista took note of Chuck's once dark good looks already fading. He appeared bloated, as if he'd lived the past few weeks on his favorite beer.

"I'm not sure I want to answer your question," Hugh said, his voice calm, "but because I'm in Krista's mother's home, I don't want to be as rude as you."

"My, what formality."

"Oh dear," Hannah said.

"Chuck, stop it right now." Krista's voice was firm. "This is my friend, the sheriff of the town where I'm living."

"You visit your mom with the sheriff?"

"Mom, either you tell him to leave or we're leaving."

Chuck plopped down in a chair as if he owned the place. "I'm sorry, Kris. I didn't mean to cause trouble. I only wanted to talk to you."

"Why would you think I'd be here? You know I had my own apartment for years. You were there often enough."

"I stopped there first, but the people said you'd moved. I thought your mom could tell me where you were. I just wanted to see you, talk to you."

"So talk."

His look was contrite, almost pleading. "Not here, not in front of everyone."

"Obviously you've already talked to Mom, and

anything you want to say to me, you can say it in front of my friend."

"Your friend? I bet."

Hugh rose from his seat, his face dark, the same expression he'd worn when confronting the boys on the bike in Egypt. "Apologize to the lady. Now."

Chuck glanced at Hugh. He went deathly pale. His smirk faded. Without taking his eyes off him, he swallowed. "Okay, okay, I'm sorry."

"Say it like you mean it. And while you're at it, apologize to her mother for causing her stress."

"Uh . . ."

Krista had never seen him so uncomfortable, and she loved it.

Chuck cleared his throat and tried again. "I'm sorry, Hannah, and I'm so sorry, Kris. I made a mistake. I panicked that morning and couldn't face you."

"So you just ran? Knowing I was all dressed and waiting for you?"

"I know. What can I say other than I'm sorry? Forgive me? Please?"

"Sorry doesn't even begin to make up for what I felt. I changed my entire life after that day, although," she glanced at Hugh, "now I'm thankful I did so."

"Give me another chance. That's all I'm asking. Let me prove that I love you."

"What about your wife? Did you ditch her like you did me?"

"There never was anyone else. It was just the first

thing I thought to say. Please, Krista. Let me see you. Alone. Give me the chance to make it up to you."

"No way."

"But—"

"I'm in love with a man who shows his love in every considerate thing he does. Now I finally know what love truly is, and I'm grateful to you for allowing this to happen. I've never been happier, and I wish the same for you. But it won't be with me."

Chuck said nothing, but with his face red, he finally stood, mumbled something to Hannah, then turned to Krista. "You win—for now. I'm leaving, but this isn't the last you'll see of me."

Before Krista could reply, Hugh rose and towered over the smaller man. "You might want to rethink that."

Without another word, Chuck scurried out and slammed the door. Krista and her mother breathed a sigh of relief. Hugh suggested dinner. "How about Mexican?"

After plates of enchiladas and fajitas, they returned home and gathered in Hannah's dining room. She served coffee and shortbread cookies dipped in chocolate.

"I apologize again. Chuck seemed so contrite that I let him in. I felt sorry for him."

"You always did fall for a good sob story. But why didn't you answer your phone?"

"I was so surprised to see him that I put it down and forgot it. The ringer must've been on silent. I'm such a ninnie, and I only found it in the kitchen a minute ago. I'm so sorry I caused you to worry, but I'm happy to see you. And your young man." She gazed at Hugh. "I can tell that you're special to my daughter, and I see how you look at her. She seems very happy, and I thank you for that. Her life hasn't always been easy, especially after her father left."

"Mom, you did the best you could, and I love you for it."

Hugh set down his cup. "Krista told me about her childhood and her father, but you were always there for her. As I hope to be."

"If you two are going to talk about me, I don't want to hear, so I'll just leave you to it." Krista wandered down the hallway leading to her old bedroom.

Along the way, she stopped in front of the framed photos hanging on the walls, photos she'd seen countless times growing up, but feeling a bit nostalgic, she took another look. Photos ranged of her as a toddler to enlarged shots of special events such as her high school and college graduations. She remembered them well, and some had shots of the audience.

Looking them over, she recognized family friends, then, she gasped. Hugh! He was in the audience just as he'd told her. He sat with his head slightly bent, as if he didn't want to be photographed. She checked that photo, then the others, and yes, he was in them all. Not that she'd doubted his word, but still, it was gratifying to know he'd been standing by all of her childhood years. Why hadn't she ever noticed him?

She would have wondered who he was and why he was at her events.

They left for the airport the next morning with the promise of sending for Hannah as soon as Krista's landlord completed the repairs on her apartment. She hoped her mom couldn't tell she was lying, but no way would she invite her mom to Marsh Springs with the threat of the other beast in the area.

On the flight to Charleston, Krista snuggled as close to Hugh as the seat divider would allow.

"Thank you—for the visit, for your thoughtfulness, for your love for me."

"Are you truly all right after seeing Chuck again? Did it stir any residual feelings?"

"As you once said to me, I've never loved anyone as I love you. So no, no feelings for Chuck except I'm sorry he's so unhappy. But he chose his actions, and he has to live his own life now. My life's with you." She searched his eyes and saw the relief. Had he doubted her love? After everything they'd been through? She thought of another time he'd been jealous, that first night with Todd. He couldn't have felt that much animosity toward Chuck, could he? "It was pretty obvious you didn't care for him."

"Not once did he ask if you were happy, nor how you coped when he left. It was all about him. But there was something, other than the obvious, something about him I didn't like."

TWENTY NINE

Arriving in Marsh Springs close to midnight after their day of travel—not only the flight from Arizona, but landing at Charleston's airport and winding up the two-lane mountain highway in snow flurries—Krista just wanted a comfortable place to stretch out and sleep.

"Want to stop at your apartment?" Hugh navigated his SUV over the snow-slicked highway, and when the blinking blue lights of the snow plow headed toward them, he edged close to the curb to let the huge machine pass. When they entered the town's city limits, the yellowish glow from the streetlights spotlighted the thickening flurries.

"Let's go to your place. We can check my apartment and face everyone tomorrow."

After a breakfast of French toast the next morning, they headed for town. Sitting in the passenger's seat, Krista's gaze swept the homes in the outlying residential area. So far the houses didn't appear damaged. On Main Street, the buildings lining the snow-packed business section also appeared intact. Cars and residents were moving around, but instead of people strolling the streets leisurely and stopping to talk with friends, they parked as close to the stores and businesses as they could and hurried inside. It all would have been expected except for one thing: on each corner, uniformed soldiers stood in groups of two and three, their rifles held in ready.

"The army?"

"National Guard. The town needed to recover and feel safe enough to get back to normal. Delzo said the new County Supervisor requested them from the Governor."

"*New?*"

"Bradley was killed that day at the park."

"Oh." Another death because of her. If she hadn't moved here, no one would have died that day. She went silent and stared out the window.

"Don't blame yourself, Krista. It wasn't your fault." It was as if he were reading her mind. "The beast was tracking me as much as you. You're no more to blame than I am."

She gave him a reassuring smile, but she didn't know if she'd ever be free from the guilt of so many deaths. "You talked to the new commissioner? Who is it?"

"Boone County has finally progressed. They've joined the rest of the world with a woman."

"Really? Who?"

"Sunnie Powell."

"Sunnie? She's perfect! I know she'll do a fantastic job. I can't wait to see her and congratulate her." Krista gazed at the soldiers in wonder. "How long will they be here?"

"Until Sunnie feels the county is ready to get back to normal. May take a few more days—if the beast doesn't attack again."

"Do you think it will?"

"Probably—when it senses you again. I don't think we're in immediate danger though; I'm not picking up a fresh scent. He may think you've left the area permanently, but we must always be on the alert."

Krista checked her bag to make sure her handgun was still loaded. If the beast attacked again, she thought she'd be able to face it this time, at least long enough to shoot enough bullets to slow it down. No longer would she run. All she had to do was think of Hugh. And Mrs. Reardon.

She absently stared out the window. Had she been selfish in returning to Marsh Springs? Wasn't she further endangering the town?

"Hugh, I'm not so sure we should've come back here. We're putting the town in danger again, and they've already been through a lot. I don't know if they would ever recover from another traumatic event like that day in the park."

"No matter how far away we went, the beast would eventually track us. No, I think we might as well stay here so that when the time comes for the final battle, I can lead him away from people and into the mountains."

She shuddered. "I can't even think of that, but you're right about the mountains."

When they approached the newspaper office, Hugh slowed enough so Krista could peer through the front window. She detected movement, although she couldn't see who was inside. She wasn't quite ready to face them, so she nodded for Hugh to continue on.

The outside of her apartment building appeared normal with the exception of armed soldiers on each corner of the street. Residents seemed to take comfort in the addition as they went about their daily business with apparent ease.

Her apartment didn't look as if it had been vandalized. Krista checked each room, and nothing had been disturbed. With relief, she made coffee while Hugh rummaged through the fridge.

"Looks like we'll need to get groceries." He made coffee and poured cups for them both.

Krista sat back. "What now?"

"That depends. No matter how logical you try to be regarding the National Guard, I saw your face when you spotted the guards on your street. Can you truly go about your life with the militia in town?"

"I'm glad they're here if they help the people feel safe." She sighed. "But on the other hand . . . well, you know how I feel."

"I hope one day you realize you're not the cause of the problem. You happened to be born into tragic circumstances caused by jealousy and greed. I can't change the past, and neither can you. What we can do is protect the innocent the best we can and use whatever power we may have to overcome and defeat the threat. In the meantime, we must not waste what life the gods have given us, and I want to live that life with you."

Moved by his words, she rose and gathered him

into her arms and rested her chin on his head. He remained seated, his arms around her.

"I love you so much," she whispered, brushing his hair away from his face. She kissed a spot on his forehead, his eyes, then his mouth. How she loved this man, and no matter the circumstances, she wanted to be with Hugh as much as she could.

"No matter what, I want to stay here and build a life with you. It may not happen like I hope, but for now, I'm going to believe in a future with you."

"I want that as well."

"First thing I need to do is talk to Junior and Carla to see if I still have a job, and you need to talk to Sunnie. How about your house? Want to check it?"

"It'll be fine. The beast has never dared to approach me there."

"It would certainly help if you knew him in human form."

"If I ran into him today, I wouldn't know he was the one."

"Strange. But then the entire situation is bizarre. Okay. Just drop me off at the paper, and I'll meet you later at Sunnie's new office."

"I'm not leaving your side until you're out of danger. We'll go together."

"I hope they'll understand why we left."

"Well, look who's risen from the dead." Her voice acid, Carla greeted Krista and Hugh.

Krista knew Carla would be upset by her disappearance, but she was taken aback by the unexpected venom.

"Now, now. Let's don't be hasty." Junior ushered Krista and Hugh to seats in front of his desk.

"But our so-called sheriff ran out when we needed him the most. And her . . . she disappeared with him. Not in town a month, and chasing after him like that."

Hugh rose from his seat, his scowl alarming Krista. She touched his arm.

"Please don't. It's okay." With reluctance, he sat back down, and she glanced at Carla. Why was she so angry?

Junior frowned. "No need for that, Carla. Let's find out what happened. Remember, we're a newspaper, dedicated to discovering facts. That's what we'll do now, especially with one of our own."

"One of our own? Hardly." Carla glared at Krista.

Wendy, the office clerk, watched carefully and listened, but when Krista glanced at the eighteen-year-old, she quickly ducked her head.

At that moment, Sunnie breezed in. "I heard you're both back." She gave Krista a hug and shook Hugh's hand.

"Congratulations on your appointment," he said. "If you have the time, I'd like to stop by your office to talk to you."

She nodded. "I have to get my notes ready for the town meeting, so I'll be there."

Krista smiled. "I'm so happy for you. They

couldn't have chosen a more caring person. I'm sure you'll do a wonderful job."

"Yeah, well, the county needed someone in a hurry, and I was available." She took the chair Hugh offered. "I'm so relieved to see you both alive and well. I was so worried."

"I apologize for causing concern," Krista said, then addressed Carla. "And I'm sorry you feel that way, but I had to leave."

"Why did you have to leave? An unbelievable tragedy by a monster straight out of the movies was happening right in front of us. People were dying. As a reporter, it was your duty to stay and —"

"That's enough." Hugh interrupted, his commanding voice bringing everyone to silence. "I know you might be upset, but I won't have you maligning Krista for something beyond her control."

"Please explain what happened. Most of us would like to hear." Junior glanced pointedly at Carla, who, cheeks blazing, took her seat at her desk.

"That morning, when I saw that beast attack my neighbor . . ."Krista choked up and couldn't continue.

Hugh took Krista's hand "Let me explain."

She nodded.

"You can't have forgotten the gruesome scene Krista experienced with Todd's death —"

"As if anyone could forget."

"Krista was a trouper, returning to work just a couple of days afterward. But when she witnessed the vicious death of her new friend and neighbor,

Mrs. Reardon, it was too much to bear. She went into shock, and I had to get her out of there. The doctor diagnosed it as PTSD and advised time to recover. Surely you can understand that."

"Yes, yes, of course."

"She could've called. Or was her phone out of order too?" Carla's glare was hot enough to singe wood.

Krista stared at her in astonishment. What was behind Carla's animosity? It had to be something more than her absence from the paper.

Sunnie, always the diplomat, addressed Carla. "I'm sure Hugh was busy helping Krista. She's here now, and that's what's important."

"Yeah, I bet he was helping."

"Oh!" At the implication, Krista's face lost its color, then went red.

"That does it." Hugh rose, his expression black as death.

With one glance at Hugh's livid expression, Carla jumped up, and made a dash for the storeroom.

Sunnie stepped in front of him. "Hugh, please. We've had enough drama. I apologize for Carla. She's been a bit snippy lately, but we must make allowances. We've all been under a strain."

"Out of respect for you and this office, I'll let it pass. This time." Scowling, Hugh slowly took his seat again.

Krista knew Carla's attitude had to be more than a strain. But what? "I understand, and I apologize again for my absence." She turned to Junior. "Do I still have a job?"

Junior cleared his throat and coughed a couple of times. Sunnie, obviously frustrated with his delay, spoke up.

"I don't see any reason to punish you for something beyond your control." Her gaze leveled on the publisher. "Do you?"

"Of course not. And we do need her. We're dangerously short-handed."

Sunnie rose to leave. "I must get back to the courthouse, and I hope to see y'all at our special city-county meeting at four this afternoon."

Hugh rose. "We'll be there."

"Good. And Hugh, if you wanted to talk to me regarding your job, I don't mind saying this in front of everyone. Until recently, you led our law enforcement team with grace, intelligence, and high moral principles, and I'd love to give you back your job. But there's a problem, and the County has to decide the outcome. You were an official in an elected position who abandoned his office, and we had to follow appointment procedures."

"Understood. I realize I left without notice—"

Before he could continue, the outer door pushed open and Brandon Cole, whom Krista hadn't seen since that day in the park, entered. Delzo followed close behind.

Sunnie gasped. "Oh dear . . ."

With a frantic expression, Delzo headed for Hugh and whispered, "I tried to warn you."

Krista overheard him. What on earth was going on?

"Can I help you?" Junior asked.

"Sorry to intrude." Brandon brushed snow off his shoulders. "I'm looking for County Supervisor Powell." His gaze swept the staff, smiled in recognition at Krista, paused momentarily on Hugh, then settled on Sunnie. "There you are. The receptionist said you'd be here." He shook her hand. "I know I'm a couple of days early, but I couldn't wait to get started."

"Get started?" Krista asked. "Are you working for the county now?"

Brandon smiled. "I'm the new sheriff."

THIRTY

Everyone in the office went deathly quiet. Krista stared at the man in shock. Hugh was the only one who seemed to take it well. He stood and offered his hand.

"Welcome. I'm Hugh Rawlins, former sheriff. You must have met Delzo, my deputy. Your deputy now."

"This is a surprise. I was told you had left the area."

"I did—for a while."

"Oh dear." Sunnie said again, then regained her composure and shook Brandon's hand. "Your early arrival is quite a surprise, but yes, of course, welcome. Do you have a place to stay?"

"I rented an apartment in Krista's complex until Rosa gets here and we buy a home. We're engaged and plan to be married in a couple of months. We wanted to get settled first."

Everyone in the office voiced their congratulations, then quieted down, all eyes on Brandon and Hugh. No one seemed to know what to say. The silence stretched until the tension was so thick Krista could barely draw breath.

"I've been here a couple of weeks," Brandon said, "and I'm still not used to the cold. I don't know how you guys do it."

"It takes a while, but you'll get used to it. I'm Carla Sanchez." Entering the room again, she extended her hand. She smiled, obviously taken with Brandon.

"Hope so. I see the National Guard is still here. Is the county still under a threat?"

Junior answered. "No one has seen the monster, whatever it was, since the initial attack, so we hope it's gone."

"But we don't want to take chances," Sunnie added. "And we want everyone to feel safe, which is why we offered the position to Brandon. We'd originally hired him to fill another position, but since we hadn't heard from Hugh, and Brandon had trained as an auxiliary officer—"

"Auxiliary officer?" Hugh raised his brows. "You weren't with the police force?"

"It's all in my resume, Sheriff, but as a courtesy to you and to Junior, I'll explain. As a medical professional in California, one of my patients was a police officer, and because I had such interest in his stories about the life, he suggested I join the auxiliary team. I took the intensive training and loved it. I was ready for a change, so I applied for and was hired here. And when Supervisor Powell offered the position of sheriff, I jumped."

Sunnie turned to Hugh. "I'm so sorry this happened, especially before I had a chance to talk to you."

"Delzo told me this might occur, so I was prepared."

He was? Krista frowned. Why didn't he tell her? Then she thought of the call he'd received from Delzo in their Luxor hotel room. Law enforcement business, he'd said. He must not have wanted to influence her decision on what to do after Egypt or where to live.

Brandon's puzzled gaze moved from Hugh back to Sunnie. "What are you sorry about? Is there a problem?"

"When the County offered the job as sheriff, we thought Hugh had left town permanently, and –"

"Are you saying my position may be in question?"

"I'm not saying that. We'll need to discuss –"

"I thought my employment was secure. Expecting the increase in pay, I made an offer on a larger home."

Sunnie slipped on her coat. "We need to discuss this at the meeting, so I'll publicly announce the change in agenda to get that scheduled. But maybe Brandon and Hugh might come to an agreement beforehand?"

"Krista," Hugh said, "I'll be back later to pick you up. If you need me before the town meeting, call me."

"What's this?" Carla's sarcastic voice halted everyone. "She needs a babysitter? What good is she to us if she can't even get to the courthouse by herself?"

Everyone's gaze landed on Krista. Heat flooded her cheeks and she wanted to sink through the floor.

"Carla!" Junior's voice got her attention. "I know you're upset, but we're a business, and I won't have that attitude in this office."

Hugh spoke through lips so thin they barely moved. "I've never in my entire life hit a woman, but you're coming dangerously close."

Krista could tell by his rigid posture the effort he was making to control himself. "It's okay, Hugh. I'll take care of it."

Sunnie stared at Carla with a puzzled expression. "You've always been a bit high-strung, but I've never known you to be vindictive, and I don't understand it now. I hope you and Krista can reach an understanding—if for nothing else, for the good of the town. You're both good reporters, and with the shortage, the newspaper needs you both."

Her face red, Carla ignored the reprimands and took her seat, seemingly absorbed by her computer screen.

"Now, if the drama is over for the moment," Sunnie addressed Hugh and Brandon, "we'll meet at the courthouse."

Once the three left, Junior gathered his coat and hat, then addressed Krista, Carla, and Wendy.

"Ladies, with all the changes, we're seriously short-staffed. Carla, you'll head the office and ready the news for print— with the exception of the new sheriff. We must wait for that outcome. Wendy, you've had enough experience to be able to go through the backlog and decide which stories to give to Carla, and Krista, well, I'm not sure what to assign. Ordinarily, because of your, uh," he paused and coughed a couple of times, "delicate nature, I'd have you stay home on sick leave, but we need you here."

"We can get along without her," Carla broke in. "We've done it for two weeks and we can do it until we can hire someone else."

"Carla, I don't have time for this nonsense right now. I must attend a meeting, but in the meantime I expect you to conduct yourself in a professional manner. Now I don't know the cause of your animosity, but I can't have this sort of behavior in this office. It has to stop now. Do you understand?"

Carla rolled her eyes and answered in an over-obedient sing-song voice. "Yes, Junior. I'll behave."

"Krista, why don't you get yourself up to speed by scrolling through the stories we printed while you were absent, including the militia's arrival and its effect on the town. While you're at it, do some proofing."

"Good idea." Krista took her desk chair and uncovered her computer.

"I'm not sure I'll make it back before the city-county meeting," he continued. "If not, I expect you all to be there, four p.m. sharp. It's an important meeting, and I expect my staff to cover it. Got that?" He directed the last to Carla.

"Don't worry, Junior. I'll do my job. I won't run out on you."

At Carla's words, Krista's patience ended. Time to get things out into the open. As soon as Junior left, shaking his head and muttering, Krista approached Carla's desk. She didn't want to get into a shouting match, especially not in front of impressionable Wendy. Carla ignored her, continuing to concentrate on her computer screen, but Krista noticed shades of pink in her cheeks.

"Carla, it's time we spoke."

"I'd rather not. Now go away and do as Junior said."

"I'm not moving until we talk about this."

With slow deliberation, Carla hit a few computer keys, then turned to Krista, her face totally expressionless. "Talk about what?"

"Let's don't play games. This is too important."

"If you have anything to say, say it now."

"Look. What happened in this town was a total tragedy, and I'm terribly sorry I folded. But I did." The reporter's deadpan face didn't change, so Krista thought she could appeal to her human side. "I don't know if you've ever faced a traumatic loss — "

"Of course I have," Carla interrupted. "Most people have. But most people don't run out on those left behind."

"I'm sorry for whatever loss you've experienced, but I've personally witnessed the loss of several people I've held dear. That night with Todd, then the attack at the city park when Hugh — "

"Yeah, Todd and Hugh. You put on this innocence act, but you've certainly made yourself available for the men in this town. I'd think Hugh, being the sheriff, would see right through it. After all, I'd hoped . . ." Turning red, she broke off and busied herself on the computer again.

Krista's eyes widened. When Carla mentioned Hugh, her eyes softened. And she said she'd tried. Tried what? To get Hugh to notice her as a woman? Could it be possible that the reporter had hoped for a relationship with Hugh? She thought of the morning Hugh brought her to the office after Todd's death. She remembered how Carla ran out to talk to Hugh through the SUV window. Krista had assumed the simpering was for her, but now she realized it was not. She touched Carla's arm but received no response.

"I'm truly sorry."

At those words, Carla shot a startled look at Krista as if she realized what she'd nearly revealed.

Acknowledging the pain of a hopeless love would humiliate the woman, so what could Krista say instead? She thought for a moment. "I've always admired your dedication to duty, your professionalism, and I'd hoped we could be friends. But if we can't, we should at least be able to work together without animosity. Out of respect for Sunnie and Junior, I'm going to try, but I will not tolerate further hateful remarks."

Carla ignored her, but Krista caught the sudden moisture in her eyes. Silently, she went back to her desk, hating the pain she'd caused.

She hoped Hugh's interview was going well and that he'd get his job back. As authoritative as he was, she couldn't picture him in any other position, but would losing his job be a sign they should leave Marsh Springs?

Instead of the commissioners chambers, Sunnie chose to hold the meeting in the larger high school gymnasium. By three-thirty, all the bleachers were occupied, and people were still filling the rows of folding chairs in the center.

Krista, along with the rest of the newspaper staff, took their reserved seats in the front row, and below the stage, seated at the table facing the noisy crowd, were Hugh, Delzo, Brandon, Jennings, the city council, and the other commission members. Krista twisted around in her seat to observe people still entering the crowded room, greeting one another as if they hadn't seen each other in weeks. They probably hadn't, not since the creature struck the town.

Exactly at four p.m., Sunnie entered the room and took her place behind the microphone. When the clatter faded, she thanked the commissioners for appointing her as supervisor pro tem. She went on to add information about the National Guard.

"The monster's gone, but the town still lives with the tragedy. While we pray we'll have no need for extra security, they're here to secure our protection. I'm in constant touch with the governor and keeping him up to date, and he'll determine how long they'll remain in our town.

"So for now, let's continue our lives. I'd like to introduce our new deputy sheriff, Brandon Cole from Redlands, California. With Delzo and Sheriff Rawlins' return to duty, we'll have three armed officials to protect us when the Guard does leave."

A great solution. Relieved, Krista smiled and gave her the thumbs-up sign.

Sunnie acknowledged it with a nod, then continued her speech. "As a former coal-mining town, we've seen each other through difficult times in the past. We rebuilt when the mines closed, and we'll rebuild now. Let's rebuild our future—for us and for our children. We're West Virginians, we're from strong stock, and together, we can do this!" That brought the crowd to its feet with applause and whistles.

Krista made hurried notes on the speech and rose to congratulate Sunnie, but people were milling around her to shake hands. She'd be busy for a while, so stuffing her tablet into her tote, Krista gathered her coat and gloves and waited for Hugh.

"Hello, Krista." A familiar male voice greeted her from behind. Every cell in her body seemed to freeze. It couldn't be. Not him. Gritting her teeth, she turned to her former fiancé.

THIRTY ONE

"Chuck! What in hell are you doing here?" A string of curse words ran through Krista's mind, but she paused, took a deep breath, and remembered she was a lady—and a professional. Her mom had always said that people who used profanity either didn't know the right words or were too lazy to use them.

"I have to talk to you."

"Well, I don't want to talk to you," she hissed, trying to keep her voice at a lower level. "Get this straight—I don't want you in my life. I thought I made that clear."

"At least hear what I have to say. I made a mistake. Give me a chance to make it up to you."

"What is it they say? 'When pigs fly.' Now get out of here before we cause a scene."

With a glower, Hugh approached them. "I didn't expect to see you again."

"Anything wrong?" Delzo joined the trio, his curious glance lighting first on Rawlins, then on the other two.

Chuck straightened. "What makes you think anything's wrong?"

Delzo drew back his shoulders. "Just checking. And you are . . .?"

"None of your business. I haven't done anything wrong, so I'd appreciate it if you'd both butt out. This conversation is between Krista and me, and I'm trying to speak to her in private."

Delzo hitched up his utility belt and spoke to Hugh. "Everything okay?" At Hugh's nod, the deputy, ignoring Chuck, smiled at Krista. "Good to see you, Krista. I'm glad you're better."

"Better? Were you sick?" Chuck turned to Krista. "You looked perfectly fine in Arizona."

"She was in Arizona?" At that moment, Carla joined them. "I thought she was too ill to function."

Krista tensed. This was turning into a nightmare. "There was a problem with my mother." Further explanations weren't necessary — a least not to Carla.

Brandon approached the four of them. "Hello again, Krista. And hello to our lead reporter, Carla."

Carla threw a smug glance at Krista, then back to Brandon. "If I didn't welcome you before, I do now." Smiling, she turned to Chuck. "And you. You're new, too." She offered her hand. "Are you Brandon's friend? Help him move?"

"No need for introductions," Krista told Carla. "He's not staying."

"Yes I am — at least for a while." Chuck took Carla's hand, lingering a moment longer than necessary. "Don't mind Krista. We're old friends and she likes to kid."

"You're old friends with Krista?" Carla shot a murderous glance at her. "*Dios mío*, another one."

Hugh took a step toward her, but Krista touched his hand. "I want to type up my notes, so let's go to the office. Now." She turned to Brandon. "Stop by the office for an interview as soon as you get a chance. I'm sure the people would like to know more about their new deputy."

"You got it."

"And Chuck," Carla interjected quickly, "I'd like to interview you, so come by as soon as you can. The town loves to hear about new residents. Helps them feel we're progressing after the horrible past events." With a self-satisfied expression, she glanced again at Krista as if to say she'd show her.

His expression long-suffering, Hugh turned to Delzo. "It's too dark to show Brandon around, so why don't you two relax the rest of the evening and have some dinner. We'll begin the training sessions in the morning."

As they were leaving, Krista overheard Brandon's whisper to Delzo. "Whew, that was strange. What's going on here?"

At her desk, Krista transfered her notes to her computer. "I'll be just a moment."

"No hurry." Hugh sat patiently, browsing some back-issues.

Carla was the only other one in the office as neither Junior nor Wendy had returned from the meeting. Since it was after six, they probably went home for the evening.

Carla hadn't spoken a word since she'd walked in, just headed straight for her desk and began typing. Krista tried to think of something, anything, to break the silence. If they couldn't be friends, she at least wanted to get along with her co-worker, especially if she and Hugh were going to settle in town.

"It was a good meeting, wasn't it? Sunnie did a fine job helping everyone feel more comfortable."

When nothing but silence followed, Hugh raised his gaze from the newspaper to Carla. She still didn't answer verbally, but keeping her eyes on her computer screen, she gave a quick nod and continued to type.

Krista stared at Carla's profile, her patience at an end. Tired after the tension-filled day, she was through with the woman. She'd be cordial, but that was it.

Having decided, she felt ready for dinner and a relaxing soak in Hugh's hot tub. She finished her notes, then dropped her flash drive into her handbag. When she glanced up, she caught Carla staring at Hugh's profile, the yearning clearly evident on her face. Krista's heart went out to her and wished it involved anyone but Hugh. Then they'd have a chance to be friends. But now, it was a hopeless cause.

In Hugh's kitchen an hour later, Krista wrapped her robe around her and sank into a chair with a glass of wine. He was browning hamburger for spaghetti. He threw the frozen lump into the skillet, added onions, garlic, chopped peppers, some spices, and covered it. It smelled heavenly.

"While it's cooking, let's decide what we're going to do now. Clearly, with Carla so hostile, it'll be uncomfortable for you at the newspaper, and with Brandon's arrival, we don't have to stay. So what do you want to do?"

"I won't allow her to influence my decisions. She can do her job and I'll do mine. And I still feel the same way about living in the mountains, that when the beast returns, you can lead him . . . it, away from people." She paused. "But I just can't think of that time." She met his gaze. "You're frowning. What's wrong?"

Hugh busied himself at the stove, chopping the beef, draining the skillet, and adding tomato sauce.

She knew, by his silence, that something was troubling him. "Is it the new deputy?"

"He's okay. He accepted Sunnie's suggestions that he needed experience. He can learn from Delzo and me."

"I bet he wasn't too thrilled about it after coming all this way. I hope you haven't made an enemy."

"As you can imagine, he didn't seem too pleased, but once the commissioners voted to help pay his moving expenses and to throw in some extra bonuses, he relented."

"Good." She yawned. "Sorry. It's been a trying day, but it sounds like everything's working out. So what's bothering you?"

"I'm not sure yet."

Krista set down her glass, all of her attention on Hugh. "What aren't you telling me?"

"Nothing to get upset about."

"Hugh, please. I know you well enough to recognize when something's wrong. Now what is it? Should I be concerned?"

He faced her. "If you know me, you should know I'd never ignore something that could threaten you. While the situation is not yet dangerous, I want you to take some precautions. Do not, under any circumstances, go anywhere, at any time, without me."

It felt as if someone tightened a band around her chest and she could barely breathe. Not yet, please, not yet. We haven't even had time to se le in together. She finally managed, "Is it him? It? Is it close?"

"Are you all right?" Concerned, he crouched by her side. "I'm so sorry. I shouldn't have mentioned it, but no, I don't think the time for our battle is at hand. I'm feeling a slight unease, something I felt in Arizona."

"Chuck."

"He grates on my nerves and puts me on guard. I'm not sure yet if it's because of his personality, his prior involvement with you, or if there's more."

"More? You mean like he might be the beast?"

"How long have you known him?"

Krista sat back in her chair. "I'm not sure. If I

333

remember right, it was during my junior year at college. He'd just transferred . . . no, it can't be him. I would've seen some sign. Wouldn't I?"

"Just to be on the safe side, I want to take you to the cave."

"No."

"Krista —"

"I'm not going to run again. That creature has already disrupted our lives, and we're just now settling back into the community. If I run now, I'll never be able to live here. Besides, it can't be Chuck. If he'd wanted to kill me, he had a hundred chances while we were dating." She caressed his cheek. "Besides, I won't leave you."

He slid his arm underneath her and lifted her into the air. When she wrapped her arms around him, he carried her into the bedroom.

The next morning over breakfast, Krista buttered her toast.

"I've been thinking about Chuck. I still don't think he's the beast, but I don't like him showing up here. For obvious reasons."

"I know his kind — he's out for trouble."

"Well, I certainly don't want him here. Can't you get rid of him?"

"If he doesn't break the law, I can't touch him, can't even pressure him."

"So I have to put up with him?"

"For now. Just try to avoid him as much as you can."

"That'll be hard to do. What do you want to bet

he'll show up at the office."

"To see you? Junior won't allow him or anyone else to make a pest of himself."

"It won't be Junior; it'll be Carla. I'm sure she'll make excuses to invite him to the office as often as she can."

"Why would she do that?"

"To flaunt him in front of me."

He stared at her. "No matter how long I live, I'll never understand women."

Krista threw her arms around him. "You don't have to. You have me."

"And I want to keep you. For now, I don't want you alone with him. Especially now."

THIRTY TWO

Her blue pen in hand, Krista printed a hard copy of an article Wendy had pulled for review, and while it was an interesting one about how the town was trying to get back to normal, her proofing was atrocious.

On her final run-through, the outer door opened and Chuck walked in.

Every nerve in Krista's body tightened She silently waited, hoping he wasn't going to make trouble. After all, this was her place of employment, and she couldn't afford a nasty scene — especially after disappearing for over two weeks. *Please, Chuck, keep it cool.*

To her surprise, he nodded at her and headed for Carla's desk.

Smiling brightly, the reporter stood. "I'm glad you could make it in. And perfect timing. I have some free time." She threw a self-satisfied smile at Krista.

Good God, as if she cared what Chuck did. But it did concern her that Carla might plan to use Chuck to get back at her for dating Hugh.

"Wow!" Chuck smiled and made a point of looking her over. Carla laughed and offered the chair in front of her desk. Junior glanced up from his paperwork, frowned at the two of them, then went back to work.

Carla did look nice to her in black denims and pink pullover sweater. Krista had never seen that particular sweater before, and it beautifully accented Carla's Rubenesque shape. A sparkly gold chain and large gold hoop earrings completed her outfit.

Krista hoped the woman wasn't going to try to entice Chuck into a relationship. Knowing Chuck, it wouldn't take much, but she doubted the reasons behind either person's intentions. Her desk phone rang, and Brandon said he had a break from training. Would this be a good time to stop in for an interview?

"Perfect timing," Krista told him. "I was just finishing another project."

She completed the proofing, slid the folder into her desk drawer, and opened a new word document on her computer.

The bell on the door jangled, and Brandon walked in. Talk about looking good. She recognized his London Fog Trench coat, and with it, he wore black leather gloves and black boots. When he slipped off his coat, his navy blue sweater matched his tailored slacks.

He took a chair next to her desk and shivered. "How long does it take to get used to this weather?" He smiled. "I think you must have icicles in your blood to be used to it in just over a month."

"Not really. I just like it here. And I have plenty of warm blankets. Would you like some coffee?" A few moments later, she typed in his answers to some routine questions, then asked about his decision to stay in Marsh Springs. "You were here when the events in City Park occurred, and of course you're aware of the National Guard. Doesn't the fact that something unknown attacked the residents discourage you from making Marsh Springs your home?"

Brandon shrugged. "Credible people report Bigfoot, alien abductions, and the Loch Ness monster. Besides, this is my chance to put my law enforcement training into practice, and I'm not going to blow it because of something that may not even be real."

"But too many people saw it. People were killed that day, and there's always the chance it may return—which is why the Guard is here."

"We may crash our cars or be hit by a meteor, but we don't stop living because of it."

Krista sat back in her chair. "That's an admirable attitude, but I'm not sure it's a wise one. However, it's your decision, and personally, I'm glad we have another person to protect us."

After a few more questions and answers, male and female laughter from Carla's desk caught her attention, and when she glanced their way, she found both Carla and Chuck gazing back at her. By their smirks, Krista knew they'd been discussing her, and she could imagine what they must have said—

especially Chuck. Waves of heat flooded her body. Her cheeks burned. She wished she weren't such a lady, but like Edith Bunker on that old sitcom, she stifled the angry words.

Brandon glanced their way, then back to her. "Sounds like they're old friends."

"Not hardly." To avoid blurting something she'd regret, Krista turned to her computer, and when she had finished entering Brandon's information, she typed a children's poem, anything to occupy her irate thoughts. Finally, she calmed.

"I have an idea. If you'll excuse me for a moment . . ." She pulled out her phone and sent a text to Hugh, suggesting she invite Brandon for dinner. Hugh agreed, and he mentioned he'd like to include Delzo, so his deputy wouldn't feel left out.

Brandon didn't hesitate. "I'd be delighted! What kind of wine would you like?"

"Wine?" Chuck's head snapped up. "Did someone mention wine?" He stepped to Krista's desk. "Are you having a party?"

Krista couldn't think of a reasonable answer. But she needn't worry — Chuck didn't wait for her response.

"Am I invited? I can bring Carla."

Oh, hell's bells. Now what? "You're not invited. I'm sorry, Carla. Maybe another time. Without him."

"Now why didn't I know that," Carla muttered, ignoring all of them by turning to her computer.

But Chuck . . . he was something else. He tried to cover his humiliation by keeping his expression blank, but Krista knew she'd embarrassed him — and she was sorry. She never enjoyed making anyone feel uncomfortable, not even him, not even when he'd embarrassed her.

But he refused to abide by her wishes and leave, so what was she supposed to do?

Around three that afternoon, Sunnie entered the office, greeted everyone, and whispered to Junior. Krista tried not to stare, but she was curious.

Junior stood and called for everyone's attention. "Sunnie has an announcement of interest to us all." He turned to her. "You've got the floor."

"Hi y'all. I received a call from the governor, and since there have been no further incidents involving unknown creatures or rogue bears, he's recalling the National Guard. Effective immediately. They are now retiring to the courthouse where the transports will carry them back to Charleston. The fact that the governor feels the danger is over must be a relief to all of us. Any questions?"

Krista wasn't sure how she felt about the withdrawal. Seeing them always sent reminders of her guilt, yet they also provided a sense of protection, although she knew they couldn't kill the beast with regular bullets.

No one seemed to have a question.

"Thanks, Sunnie. I appreciate the update." Junior then addressed Carla, "Let's get a flyer out to the public asap."

"I'll get on it immediately." Carla stood and snapped photos of Sunnie, Junior, and Wendy, totally ignoring Krista.

After Sunnie left, Krista and the others watched as groups of uniformed men and women passed the office, finally able to relax and talk to each other.

"A new era for the town," Junior commented. "The danger is over."

Hugh sent a text around four-fifteen. "I'm running a little late," he wrote, "but I'll be there in about an hour, no later than five-thirty. Do *not* leave the building until I get there."

"Yessir." She added a little red heart to the message.

By five-ten, everyone had left the office except Junior and Krista, and he had donned his coat and gathered his briefcase. "You sure you'll be all right? I hate to leave you alone, especially now that the military has gone, but the missus and I are expecting company for dinner."

"Go ahead and enjoy your evening. Hugh should be here at any moment. I'll be fine."

After a few more assurances, he reluctantly left, and Krista flipped on the outside lights, the front office lights, and locked the door. Back at her desk, she pulled her article about Brandon and began her edits.

A slight clatter sounded in the quiet room. She looked up. Everything was in order. The furnace's blower had kicked on and warm air circulated in the office. Funny, she'd never noticed the slight noise before. She bent her head to her article, trying to concentrate, but now she heard every creak in the old building. And the room's shadows seemed larger. Blacker.

She checked her watch. Five-twenty-five. She glanced at the door. Where was Hugh?

She didn't want to be so edgy, but when she went back to her article, she was breathing a little faster.

From the back of the building came slight clicking sounds. Was someone out there?

"Hello?" She listened, but she heard nothing more. Had to be the building settling. After all, it was an old building.

She tried to concentrate on the next line of the article.

The back door's knob twisted. Her pulse racing, she jumped up and glanced over her computer in the direction of the noise, but the storeroom and back door was down a short hallway and she couldn't see. No one in the office used it. The building backed onto an alley with no parking, so everyone always entered from the front. Besides, that door was kept locked. A few clicks, then the creak of the door opening, then footsteps moving toward the front.

Someone was in the office! She grabbed her handbag and fumbled for her gun, finally pulling it out. Using both hands, she aimed it at the hallway.

"I've got a gun! Don't come any closer!"

A large black shadow appeared. It slowly moved forward. It couldn't be the creature — it would move faster, wouldn't it?

A figure appeared. Chuck! In human form.

"Stop right there or I'll shoot!"

He raised his hands above his head. "What are you doing? What's with the gun?"

"What are you doing here? How did you get in?"

He lowered his arms. "I—"

"Get them back up! Now!"

"What in hell's wrong with you? You think I'm going to do something?"

Just then the front door burst open. Hugh covered the distance from the doorway to her side in three steps.

"You move any closer to her, you'll wish you had been shot."

The malevolent look Chuck leveled on Hugh was enough to set an ordinary man running. "You threatening to use your big sheriff's .45?"

"I don't need my weapon to take care of you."

The two men quietly stared each other down. Krista's pulse hammered with the tension. *Please, Chuck, back off.* While she wanted nothing to do with him, he didn't want him dead.

Eventually, Chuck's expression lost its fury and he lowered his gaze. "Okay, okay. You win."

Thank God. Krista took a deep breath and lowered her arms, but she didn't tuck the gun away. Not yet. Just a short time ago, she thought he might be the other beast. Now she wasn't entirely sure. She wanted answers.

"How did you get in?"

"I picked the lock. Wasn't hard. It's a decrepit

building. When you didn't leave with the others, I figured I could catch you alone and finally talk to you."

"You figured wrong." Hugh kept his gaze on Chuck.

"So why sneak in? Why not knock on the front door? Don't you know you scared me to death?"

"You won't meet me or talk to me, so this was the only way I knew to get you alone. Please, Krista, give me just five minutes, five lousy minutes. You owe me."

"I owe you?"

Hugh didn't move from Krista's side. "So what do you want?"

"I want five minutes with Krista. I've gone to a lot of trouble, so go away.

"Not on your life."

"Five minutes, just five freakin' minutes. Is that too much to ask?" He addressed Krista. "After all our time together?"

Against her better judgment, she felt sorry for him. She tucked her gun back into her handbag. "You win. Five minutes."

Hugh checked his watch. "I'm timing it."

Chuck dropped into the nearest chair. "Look. I made a mistake back home. I love you. Please give me another chance. I'll change, I promise. I'm sick over what I did. My life's been shit since I left you and I know I could make it better with you. You always encouraged me, so if you'll give me another chance …"

On and on he went, and the more he talked, the more she realized it was all about him, not what he'd put her through or what his abandonment had meant to her. Just him. Why hadn't she seen how selfish he was? It took Hugh's love to realize what should be between a man and woman.

"Time's up!" Hugh announced.

As if he knew he'd lost, Chuck folded. "Shit."

Krista slipped her arm through Hugh's and faced her former fiancé. "I'm sorry your life's so terrible right now, but I can't help you. No one can help you except you, yourself. I've found the man I want to spend the rest of my life with, and I sincerely hope you can find someone to love. But it's not me. And, I don't believe it's Carla either, so I suggest you go back home. To Arizona or wherever it is you now live. I'd appreciate if you'd leave."

"You heard the lady," Hugh told him. "For your own good, I suggest you leave town."

"Like Hell, I will." At the door, he turned toward them. "You may have won this time, but there's always tomorrow."

THIRTY THREE

After two glasses of wine in Hugh's kitchen that evening, Krista's strange encounter with Chuck faded away. She quietly listened as Hugh and his dinner guests, Delzo and Brandon, bantered back and forth at his wooden table.

He added butter and Parmesan cheese to his seafood fettuccini, and again she admired his grace, his confidence, and his appearance. He was all man, and like a teenage girl, she shivered with delight that he was all hers.

At that moment, while dicing green onions, he glanced at her. Knife in one hand, an onion stalk in the other, he grinned as if he knew what she was thinking. Since others were in the room, she said nothing, but she smiled back, then jumped up to check the loaves of garlic bread in the oven.

Delzo and Brandon sat across from each other at the wooden table, talking and laughing at something Brandon had said. Krista, thumping the top of the loaves for crispness, hadn't caught the source, but she felt pleased they were all getting along so well.

Now, instead of hard feelings at work, Hugh could still enjoy his days.

On the table, a large glass bowl sat in the center, a few remnants of lettuce clinging to the glass sides. One breadstick remained in a mug alongside small bowls of olive oil and butter. Shrimp, crab, and garlic aromas filled the air.

Hugh stirred the pasta. "I hope you're all hungry. It should only be about three more minutes."

"Can't wait." With a grin, Delzo shook his head. "I still can't believe you can cook."

Krista pulled bread from the oven and transferred the loaves to a tray. "You're in for a treat."

"Ha! I'll believe that when I see it. Or taste it. I remember how he always devoured El Fuantes' burritos."

Hugh shrugged. "What can I say? I like Mexican food." He added a cube of butter to the pan. "Besides, I didn't have much incentive to cook. Then."

"Well, if dinner tastes as good as it smells, I'll be over a lot more."

"Me, too," Brandon added. "And when Rosa gets here, we'll have all of you over too. She's a great cook."

"Got a picture?" Delzo asked.

"You kidding? I have tons." Brandon pulled out his cell phone and scrolled through, and evidently finding the best one, turned the phone around so Delzo could see.

At that moment, Krista, carrying a tray holding

the loaves, stepped to the table, and something drew her attention to Delzo. She gasped. Her heart nearly stopped. The tray clattered to the oor. His eyes were glowing, amber, green, green-gold.

She screamed.

Hugh ran to her. "Honey, what is it?" He tried to fold her into his arms. "What happened?"

She wrenched away. "Get your gun! It's Delzo." She ran to the bedroom for her handbag and gun, with Hugh close behind. When she ripped open her bag and felt the gun, Hugh grabbed her hands and forced her to face him.

"Krista, calm down. What about Delzo? What did he do?"

"Let me go! Delzo's the beast!" With the secret out, was he shifting now? Was he this minute jumping over the table to rip them all to shreds?

"You think Delzo's the other beast? I assure you he's not."

"I saw his eyes!"

"Honey, what about his eyes? No matter what you saw, Delzo's not the other beast."

Something about Hugh's assured tone calmed her hysteria. "He's not? He's not shifting right now?"

"No. Come see for yourself." Gently, holding her close, he led her back into the kitchen.

Brandon was filling a glass at the kitchen sink. "Would you like some water?"

Delzo stood with his back plastered to the wall behind the table, his face and entire demeanor one of shock and bewilderment.

He was still human.

"I don't understand," he said. "You know me. What did I do to scare you?"

Her legs still trembling, she sank into a chair. Brandon handed her the water and she gulped it down.

"Thanks. Give me a moment." She took some deep breaths. "It was your eyes," she told Delzo. "I thought, I thought …" She hesitated, not wanting to reveal the monster was a shapeshifter. "Well, it scared me."

"My eyes scared you? God, I'm sorry. Had to be my new contacts. I didn't even think to mention them."

Hugh poured a round of wine for all of them. "Why would you?"

"These contacts are polarized, and every once in a while, I'm told they reflect weird colors like sunglasses sometimes do. Must've been when I looked at Brandon's cell phone."

"The reflection," Hugh said.

Delzo nodded. "I'm so sorry, Krista."

"I feel like such an idiot."

"Don't. From what I'm told, it can be quite unnerving." After dinner, when they were alone again, Krista and Hugh relaxed in his hot tub on the patio. Few clouds covered the night sky, and the full moon shone through a fuzzy halo.

Hugh stared at the moon. "That halo effect means we're in for a cold snap."

"It's already freezing. Last time I checked, it was about thirty-eight degrees."

"Are you cold?" Hugh tightened his arm around her shoulders.

"Sitting next to you in bubbling hot water, wrapped up in your arms, how could I be?" She laid her head on his shoulder and gazed at the moon and stars. "It's so beautiful."

"Especially tonight, here with you and after a nice dinner with good friends."

"I really scared Delzo, didn't I? I'm so ashamed of my reaction. I really thought I'd handle the next encounter better, but now I'm not so sure. I was terrified with Chuck in the office, then tonight with Delzo, I just don't know. Both times I acted like a scared little girl."

He gave a brief kiss on her forehead. "You can't blame yourself, not after all you've been through. As beasts, we're pretty terrifying."

"Well, I hope he forgives me. By the way, what's his last name? All I've ever known or heard was Delzo."

Hugh laughed. "He never tells anyone, but I checked his paperwork. You'd never guess, but it's Archibald. I call him 'Baldy' when I tease him about something. Does he ever get furious. He puffs up like a banty rooster."

Krista chuckled. "Poor guy. No wonder he's always so quiet — "

An angry, wailing howl erupted from the foothills.

Krista stiffened and stared at Hugh. "No . . ."

The wailing continued.

The night air turned to ice and goosebumps covered her body. "Why doesn't it stop? God, please make it stop!"

Still the howl continued on and on until she thought she'd go mad.

Hugh grabbed towels. "It's here."

THIRTY FOUR

At the kitchen table the next morning, Krista propped her head on her hand and tried to keep her eyes open. Coffee would help, but now, when she desperately needed it, it seemed to take forever to fill the carafe.

She'd slept a full seventeen minutes last night. Even though they heard no further evidence of the beast, she kept imagining it bursting through a door or a window. To help her feel safe, Hugh spent the night transforming his home into a fortress. He reinforced the front and back doors with steel plates, and with the press of one button, activated recessed bar gates to close over all of the windows. They slid from the window casings with ease, obviously a mechanism Hugh installed sometime in the past. She shouldn't have been surprised—anyone who could build a luxury home with all the modern conveniences in a remote mountain cave could do most anything.

He entered the kitchen as alert as if he'd had a full eight-hours sleep.

"I hope you'll reconsider and let me take you to the cave until this is over. You'll be safe there."

The coffee finally ready, Krista poured two cups and offered one to him.

"You've made it safe for me right here. Besides, I don't want to spend days, maybe weeks in that place all alone. You'll be here, so this is where I want to be."

"What happened to that terrified woman from last night?"

"Oh, I'm still here, just as frightened as before, but if the beast has found us, and the time for your battle is now, I won't be safe anywhere. If the worst happens . . ." At the unconscionable thought, her eyes filled and she paused, unable to continue.

Hugh lifted her to her feet and folded his arms around her. "Oh my darling, I'm so sorry to put you through this."

Warm and safely snuggled against him, she was able to speak. "You didn't. The beast—and fate did. You've always protected me."

"And I want to do so now. If you won't go to the cave, at least stay here, where it's safe. Call Junior and take a leave of absence."

"I can't do that. You know he'd never put up with another absence. And Carla would have my head."

"Better her than the beast. Why are you so determined to put your life in jeopardy?"

Why was she? She thought of the days before all this started, of spending time on her back patio watching the clouds pass through snow-capped mountains, the sound of the wind rushing through the valley and rustling the leaves on the different trees. She thought of Mrs. Reardon, who'd been so kind to her.

"I love the friends I've made here, and before all this started, I loved the mountains, the rivers . . . It's beautiful here, and I want to raise my children, our children, in these surroundings—not in a smog-choked city."

"Marry me, Krista."

"What?" She gazed into his eyes. "But you didn't want to get married, not with this threat hanging over us."

"Marry me. Now. Today. If you'll consent, I can go into battle without worrying about you. If I lose, you'll inherit all of my holdings and savings and have enough to live in comfort the rest of your life."

"If you lose, not only will I lose the love of my life, but I won't have a life. He'll be free to kill me."

"When I know the battle is imminent, I'll take you to the cave and show you the escape route. It leads to the other side of the mountain, and I have an SUV waiting. You can take it directly to the airport and leave the state, even the country. You can build your own fortress in a crowded city or even on some remote island where you can stay ahead of him at all times. You'll never have to work again or worry about anything."

His eyes met hers with love, compassion, and deep concern.

She could lose herself in those hazel depths. How

she loved this man, and if their lives were fated to end on an Appalachian mountain, then at least she would have known what all the writers had expressed in their prose and sonnets. She could be grateful for that.

And, she inwardly smiled, she had a wonderful secret to share with him, and that would be his surprise and reward when he came for her as the victor.

"Yes, my darling, yes. Let's rejoice in whatever time we have left. Let's get married. Today."

Upstairs in the second bedroom, Krista searched the closet for something special, but she didn't have anything at his home to fit the occasion. She looked again, mentally trying to put something together. By now, she felt his urgency to begin their married lives together, so she couldn't take the time to shop.

Junior hadn't been thrilled about giving her another day off, but even he had to admit she shouldn't postpone a doctor's appointment.

She rummaged through her clothes again, wishing she could find something elegant, but it was hopeless. When she'd hurriedly gathered clothes to bring to Hugh's, she'd only grabbed her jewelry box and an armful of outfits.

From his bedroom, Hugh spoke on the phone, and she heard his muffled voice talking to someone he obviously liked. He sounded relaxed and confident, so some of her anxiety eased, and she began to look forward to her special day.

Her wedding day, the day she'd remember the

rest of her life, the day she doubted would ever happen. She only prayed they could have their magical full day with no further threats challenging them.

She found her sapphire-blue palazzo pants and her off-white silk blouse and put them on. She didn't have pumps, but with snow on the ground, her black boots with low-heels would have to do. From her jewelry box, she took two pairs of pearl earrings and several silver studs. One pair of pearls she put in her ears, and she interwove them and the silver studs to make a swirl design on her right shoulder.

She checked her image. Perfect. The silver added the bit of sparkle she wanted.

Once she completed her hair and makeup, she made sure she had the necessary documents: birth certificate, driver's license and other valid IDs, and descended the stairs. Wearing a dark blue suit, Hugh waited at the foot. He glanced up at her with the most loving and appreciative smile she'd ever seen.

"You're beautiful." He held out a small bouquet of roses.

She took the sweet-smelling flowers. Roses in winter. How did he get them so quickly? He definitely was super-human and could do anything.

He held her coat for her, donned his, and offered his arm. "Got everything? Let's go."

Ten minutes later, Hugh pulled into the driveway of a Craftsman-style home with a wrap-around porch. Layers of packed snow covered mature trees and shrubs, but the walkway was clear.

"Who lives there?" Krista strained to see any movement from the house.

"Someone who wants to be a part of our celebration. Wait here."

The front door opened, and a woman exited. Sunnie! How wonderful! Hugh escorted her to the car, and she slid into the back seat.

"An elopement! Congratulations, you two. How exciting, and thanks for including me. I'm honored."

After obtaining their marriage license at the County Courthouse, Krista glanced around the old building. While it might not be the ceremony of her dreams, getting married in the Neoclassical structure wouldn't be so bad.

"Are we going to be married here? At the courthouse?"

No. I have a surprise for you, about an hour away."

"How mysterious."

"What fun," Sunnie remarked.

On the outside steps, Krista paused and checked all around. Had the beast followed them? Was it watching their every move, waiting for the chance to strike?

Hugh, ever sensitive to her moods, tested the air and shook his head.

Thank God. They were safe—for now.

After an hour on a two-lane mountain road

heading east, the foothills gave way to a scattering of houses, a football field, and an old three-story school.

"That's my old elementary school." Sunnie's voice held a bit of wistfulness. "We're in Whitesville, my home town." They passed several blocks of boarded-up buildings, similar to many old coal-mining towns. "I hear they're trying to revitalize it with some small businesses moving in. I hope they're successful. No matter where I live, my heart will always be here."

A few feet past the outskirts of the town, Hugh slowed, clicked on his turn signal, then stopped. Both women peered out the windows.

On the left side of the road, a plowed path through a parking lot led to a three-story beige Victorian home. *Florentz's Wedding Chapel*, the sign read.

"We're here." Hugh pulled into the lot.

"Oh!" Krista gazed at the home, complete with cupola, tall windows trimmed in white, and a portico covering the entrance. "How beautiful."

"Just like the old romantic movies," Sunnie remarked. "I didn't know that was here."

"They moved it here a few years ago," Hugh told them. "The family had ancestors in Red Dragon, an old coal-mining community near Whitesville, so when they retired from Charleston a few years ago, they had it moved and restored it to its present condition."

"I knew the family well," Sunnie mused. "Their granddaughter was my best friend. I later learned

358

Mr. Florentz was French, a Mason, and Mrs. Florentz belonged to the Eastern Star. He loved cars, and I remember he had a Henry J. He took us for rides."

An older woman answered Hugh's knock and escorted them into the parlor, in which they were served tea and scones. Krista was so excited she could barely swallow. She was actually getting married. Right now.

After about a half-hour, the woman, Mrs. Lanyi, led them to a large room off the parlor in which four rows of white chairs faced an open area in front of tall windows. Small glass tables and wall shelves held swags of roses with baby's breath and flickering candles. A white-haired gentleman entered from a side door.

"This is my husband, Justice Donald Lanyi," Mrs. Lanyi told them. "He'll officiate on this happy occasion."

"Please stand here," he instructed, and Hugh took her arm. Krista barely heard the next few words. She was actually getting married. After a childhood of disappointments, wondering why she wasn't worthy of a father's love, then betrayed by the man she'd thought she'd love the rest of her life, she'd carried bitterness in her soul. But then fate led her to Marsh Springs where some of the kindest people on Earth had befriended her: Sunnie at work, Mrs. Reardon at home, and of course, Hugh. Hugh, her beloved, the man who'd taught her the true meaning of courage and love.

She looked up at him, and he was smiling at her.

Her heart swelled with such love and happiness that her eyes filled with tears. Big drops rolled down her cheeks, and still, she smiled at him. With great tenderness, he wiped them away.

"And I pronounce you man and wife."

Hugh bent to kiss her.

Was the ceremony over? She hadn't even heard the words, but she must have responded. She glanced down at her hand, and on her ring finger, a wide gold filigree ring with a bezel-set marquis diamond sparkled, and on each side of the diamond, swirls of white-gold surrounded small lapis-lazuli stones.

"It's the most beautiful ring I've ever seen." He'd known the exact perfect one for her.

Justice Lanyi pronounced, "I present Mr. and Mrs. Hugh Rawlins. May your lives be long and happy."

Next thing Krista knew, Mrs. Lanyi and then Sunnie hugged her and congratulated Hugh. At the door, Hugh bent down, swept her into his arms, and carried her to the car.

On the way home, Krista could barely talk. She kept holding up her hand and admiring her ring, a tangible symbol of their love.

"When did you get this?"

"I had it made after you moved to Marsh Springs. It's a combination of . . ." He hesitated, glanced back at Sunnie, then continued. "I inherited several rings, and I had the diamond added."

"It's perfect. I'm Mrs. Rawlins. Mrs. Hugh

Rawlins. Mrs. Krista Rawlins. Has a nice ring to it, doesn't it?"

"Yes, dear, it sounds nice," Hugh parroted for the hundredth time. Smiling, he glanced over his shoulder to Sunnie.

Krista caught his look. "Go ahead. Tease all you want, but I'm now a mature married woman, so I can rise above it." Holding up her hand again, she twisted it and turned it in different directions to admire the flashing stones in the waning sunlight. "Isn't it beautiful? Sunnie, you said Whitesville will always hold your heart. Now it holds mine as well."

Just as day faded to dusk, when they were about a block from Sunnie's home, something appeared in front of them in the middle of the road. Hugh slowed, then pulled to the shoulder and stopped. He pulled his gun from the glove compartment.

Krista peered at the figure on the highway. Then she realized what it was. "Oh, God, no!"

Below the rising moon, a giant figure of a man with a golden falcon's head blocked their way. Standing with legs apart, he wore a breastplate, kilt, knee-boots, and held a long spear. But Krista's eyes were drawn to his full head-mask of Horus, the ancient Egyptian god of war.

"What in Heaven's name?" Sunnie murmured.

Hugh stuffed the gun under his jacket, gave Krista a quick kiss, and briefly caressed her cheek. "Stay here. Under no circumstances are you to leave the car."

Her heart pounding in her throat, she nodded.

Hugh opened his door. Bathed in moonlight, he walked to Chikere, the harem's overseer from his father's time.

Chikere snapped to attention. "Greetings, Rahmor. It's time."

THIRTY FIVE

Krista knew exactly what that figure represented. Horus was known as the god of the sky and earth, the protector god, but tonight, with patches of standing feathers around the head and neck, he was on a mission of war. His sharp golden beak pointed downwards, ready to rip his prey into shreds.

No, please, not today. Not on her wedding day. But the two figures faced each other in the moonlight.

"Krista, what's going on?" Sunnie asked, her voice breathless. "Who is that? What is that?"

"Some guy from Hugh's past. He's been following Hugh." Just in case she needed it, she quietly popped open her handbag and removed her handgun.

"I've never seen such a thing. I'll put a stop to this nonsense." Sunnie opened the back door.

"No! You must not get out of the car. He-he's dangerous."

Sunnie picked up her phone. "Well, I'll just call for some help."

"Please, just wait. Hugh will handle it."

"What does he want?"

"All I know is that an old fraternity brother from years ago has hard feelings for Hugh and has been following him, making trouble."

"Bet it's over a girl."

If she only knew. "Probably. Now please, I want to hear." Her gun held discreetly out of sight, Krista climbed over the center console to the driver's seat and lowered the window.

Hugh stopped in front of the figure. "We meet again."

"This time, Rahmor, will be the last."

"That remains to be seen. But not now, and not here. Not with friends in the car."

"I see your friends. No matter. I can dispose of them after I take you down."

"That won't happen."

"Your ego hasn't improved over the millennia."

"I am what I am — the son of a mighty pharaoh."

"Those days have faded as have the paintings in Satiah's tomb."

Krista couldn't hear every word, but she understood enough to follow what was happening. *Please Hugh, don't make him angry.*

"I have a proposal for you to consider, one that's to your advantage."

Chikere laughed. "A proposal? I'm not about to enter into a bargaining position with you. I still carry the stripes from your anger and frustration when I didn't grant your last wish."

"You may not believe me, but I do regret that."

"Regret all you wish, but you will not get a second chance. This time, the odds will be even."

As she watched, Hugh gained inches in height as well as in girth. She glanced at Sunnie, hoping the woman would think the abnormality was a trick of the moonlight.

A low rumbling sound from him became a growl, and when he spoke again, his voice held a threatening timbre. "I can still take you down, and it'll be a pleasure to finally end this."

"That's for Amun-Ra to decide." Chikere silently considered. "What is your proposal?"

"What are they doing?" Sunnie strained to see in the waning light. "What's taking so long?"

"Shhh, I need to hear this."

"In the past," Hugh said, "our battles have ended in an impasse. As we've known from the beginning, our final battle will end in death. If you accept my proposal, you may have the advantage."

"How so?"

"Perhaps I won't fight as desperately."

"And the proposal?"

"I believe you know the location of my mountain cave."

"I do. I enjoyed watching your labors over the years, and the best part is, you never knew I was there."

Hugh brushed that off with a shrug. "We must fight away from town, near my cave."

"I have no location preferences. Done."

"My additional proposal is that—"

"There's more? Rahmor, you try my patience."

"Listen or be prepared to die."

"That's a conclusion not decided. But do speak, oh Prince Rahmor, son of the mighty Pharaoh Thutmose, and on and on ad nauseam."

Hugh ignored the sarcasm. "Give me your word that if you're the victor, you won't harm Krista in any way. And you'll no longer pursue her."

"You ask a lot."

"Accept my offer or take your chances with me."

"But you might win."

"In that case you won't have to worry about keeping your word."

Moments later, Sunnie accepted Hugh's explanation of the encounter, nearly identical to what Krista had said. After dropping her off and testing the air to make sure she wasn't in danger, he headed for his mountain cave.

Krista felt curiously detached as Hugh sped through the rocky hillside. The iridescent moon climbed higher and bathed the snow-covered mountain with glistening silver. Wasn't it ironic that the place Hugh might die would look so beautiful?

"You must listen carefully." His brow furrowed, he glanced at her. "Are you with me?"

At the sound of his voice, she turned to look at him. He'd asked something of her, so she nodded. She couldn't speak, could barely draw breath through the tight band squeezing her chest. She opened her mouth to breathe easier, but it didn't help.

"When we get there, I'll show you the escape route. We won't have time to enter the tunnel, not even for questions, so hear me now."

His words sounded final, as if he knew his last hours on earth were coming to a close. It was here. The final battle. She couldn't lose him, not after waiting her entire life to be loved in the way he had shown her. The gods couldn't be cruel enough to rip him from her, especially not in such a gruesome, hideous way, not someone so good and kind as he.

She listened to his voice, but his words didn't penetrate the airless vacuum in which she found herself. Through the front window, she looked up at the night sky, at the glory of the moon and twinkling stars, and she felt as though her body were floating in time and space along with them. Maybe she could reach out and touch—"

"Krista!"

His strong voice penetrated her protective enclosure, and she snapped back to reality.

He eyed her, then apparently satisfied, he continued. "If I don't come to you within three hours, take that tunnel to the other side of the mountain. You'll find a fully-equipped Humvee ready for you. Take it to the nearest airport in Beckley, leave it there, and don't look back." He went on to explain where he kept all the papers and immediate cash she'd need.

At the cave entrance, he ushered her inside and hurriedly led her to his safe and jotted down the combination. Then he stopped before a wall hanging of an Egyptian warrior standing in a chariot leading a battle charge. He yanked it down to reveal a recessed door that opened to a stairway leading downward. He pointed to a light panel, and when he switched it on, the entire tunnel lit up.

"Just follow it until you reach the end."

Back in the hallway, he turned to her and took her into his arms. She buried her head in his chest and breathed in deeply, capturing his familiar scent to carry her through the next few hours.

He lifted her chin to look into her eyes. "No matter what happens, know I love you, and being with you has been the crown of stars in my life."

"Oh, my darling, you know I feel the same."

"If I don't return, remember me with love, but don't waste your life mourning for me. My sincerest wish is that you lead a beautiful, happy life. Remember, no matter what the future holds, you are descended from a queen. Face each day with strength, pride, and hope, and if the gods are correct, one day we'll meet again."

Overwhelmed with love for this man, she swiped the tears and nuzzled her cheek against his. "Fight with everything you've got, my darling," she whispered. "I have something special waiting for you."

"Something special?"

"To tell you."

His brows furrowed, he searched her eyes, and his own widened. His entire face lit with joy. "Could it be . . .?" He glanced down at her belly. "Tell me now."

"We'll share this miracle when you come for me as the victor. Go now, and go with all the love I can give."

With one final kiss and embrace, he left her.

THIRTY SIX

Inside the cave walls, time stood still for Krista — and flew by as a comet sped through the heavens. Five minutes. An hour. A thousand years. She didn't know.

She paced the great room, stopping before the painted masks of Bast, goddess of protection, and Anubis, god of death.

"Dear Bast, as a woman, know my heart and the faithful heart of Prince Rahmor. Please cover him with your shield of protection in his hour of need. Give him strength in this, his final battle, so that he might live and rejoice in his living child, whom I carry in my womb."

With those words, Krista lovingly caressed her belly, then raised her eyes to the mask of Anubis. "God of the underworld, if the battle doesn't go well and my prince approaches your kingdom, please turn him away. Reward him for his thousands of years of service to the gods and send him back to the living. To me. And to his child."

Head bowed, she waited in silence, hoping,

wishing for some sign that the gods had heard her; instead, she heard nothing but the slight hum from the generators.

With a sigh, she paced again, then headed for the cave entrance. Standing inside the door, she listened intently, hoping to hear some sound, some indication of what was occurring on the other side of the steel door. But again, she heard nothing. Hugh had made the door and walls impenetrable.

Anxious, terrified, yet hopeful, she felt as though a thousand butterflies were winging their way through her body, each fighting for space, for air to breathe. All were urging her on, to keep moving. She paced the hallway, then headed for the escape-tunnel door. To reassure herself, she flipped on the lights, then off again.

No. Don't think negative. She had to think positive. She wouldn't need this tunnel. Hugh was going to return for her. She had to think that way or she'd go mad. She must think of a future with him — and their child.

But the butterflies didn't settle.

Her mouth dry, she went to the kitchen and filled a glass of water. One sip and she set it on the counter, wandered away, and forgot about it.

Again she took the long entrance-way to the cave door and stood listening, and again she heard nothing.

After another half-hour, she could stand it no longer. She caressed her belly. "I've waited long enough. I'm going to find your father."

She hurried to Hugh's weapon's room and selected the box holding a Glock 17 semi-automatic pistol and three magazines. She searched the shelves for the 9mm caliber bullets, praying she'd find silver ones without having to waste time opening all the boxes. She tore open the first box. Thank God, they were silver. She loaded all three magazines, stuffed the pistol into her pants pocket, and headed for the door. She may die in the process, but she had to find out what was happening.

She put all of her strength and weight into pushing open the heavy outer door, and by some miracle, it opened. Once outside, she saw nothing but the black night. Clouds had covered the moon so she could barely discern the hillside around her from the ground.

She heard nothing. The night was deathly quiet, as if all the winter creatures were hiding. Or dead.

Krista took a cautious step then another. She couldn't stumble over a snow-covered rock and risk losing her weapon. Picking her way down the rocky hillside, she heard sounds. A growl. A wolf's growl. Another. Then a snarl. Longer. Louder, as if to declare dominance. A long, drawn-out roar followed. Another, with a lower timbre, matched it. And then the sounds of fighting wolves, snapping, snarling, biting, yelps of pain, more growls.

Krista hurried toward the brawling noise. Ahead were two werewolves locked in battle, claws ripping, fangs biting deep.

One yelped, threw off the other and turned

slightly. The other lunged, tackling him at his knees. They fell, hitting the ground with a thud so hard Krista could feel it several feet away.

Which one was Hugh?

They nipped and bit each other. One rose slightly, the other slammed him to the ground. They rolled. Chunks of fur flew. Animal snarls, howls of pain, blood running. One threw off the other and rose. The other slammed into him and flipped him onto the ground. He held him by the shoulders. Yips and snarls ripped from both beasts.

Krista didn't want to watch, but she couldn't tear her eyes away from the gruesome scene. Please God, please . . . She couldn't form the words.

Glazed red eyes from the beast on the ground rose to her. Pain and defeat dulled the glow. *I'm sorry, my love,* they seemed to say.

"Get up, Hugh. Please get up. Fight him," she urged.

But he lay barely moving. The other ripped another chunk from his shoulder. Hugh's form howled in pain. The dominant beast raised its head and howled in victory.

No, no, no. Why didn't he fight back? Then, as though she were receiving psychic words, she heard his voice:

"Please understand, my darling. This is the only way." Then the words he'd spoken during his meeting on the highway with Chikere flashed through her mind: *Perhaps I won't fight as hard.*

To protect her, he was allowing Chikere to win.

As a beast, Chikere slid a triumph glance at her. He howled in victory. His mouth open, bloody fangs at the ready, he bent to the beast on the ground.

No!

Krista raised the pistol. Please, please God, let her hit the right one. She aimed. She squeezed the trigger. A patch of fur exploded on the dominant creature's left shoulder. Blood gushed. The beast jerked upright and howled. Furious red eyes fixed on her, it took a step toward her. She aimed again and again.

Flying bullets hit the creature, in the shoulder, the chest. the neck. The noise was deafening. Her ears rang, but she kept firing until fur exploded in bloody patches over all its body. With the last bullet, she hit it in its right eye. The beast howled again and crumpled to the ground.

Panting, her pistol still aimed at the creature, Krista waited a few moments. Then, when it didn't move, she took hesitant steps toward the fallen beast. It lay on its side, mouth open, tongue extended, red eyes slowly losing their glow.

The other beast, the one she thought was Hugh, rolled onto its stomach and slowly, painfully, rose to its knees and finally to its feet.

The beast howled, a long wail meaning many different things. It turned to Krista, all seven feet, fangs dripping blood, razor claws extended. Without conscious thought, she gasped and took a step backward.

Above them, the clouds parted and the moon sent

beams of light onto the mountainside and to the furred beast facing Krista. Within minutes, the process began. The extra height and bulk decreased to Hugh's normal six and a half feet. Fangs reformed into normal male teeth. Black fur receded from its face to reveal Hugh's features. Hugh's beautiful features.

Watching the process, Krista couldn't contain the happiness, the relief she felt.

It was over.

Tears of joy rolled down her cheeks. When the process had completely restored Hugh to human, she ran to him and threw her arms around his chest, careful to not cause further injuries.

"Oh my darling, thank God you're alive." Breathing in his familiar scent, one she'd love forever, she thanked the fates he was alive, and she held him as if he were the most precious gift from the gods.

With an exhausted grin, Hugh embraced her. "Thank God for you. When I saw you standing over us in the moonlight with your pistol drawn, you reminded me of Sekhmet, lioness goddess of vengeance and war. What a sight you were, and I'll never forget it. Not only am I grateful, but I'm so very proud of you." He bent and kissed her.

Arms still around her, Hugh turned them to the dead beast, who was still in the process of transforming into a human male. The dark fur disappeared from its arms and torso, revealing a human male's body around six feet. In its mouth, fangs reshaped into human teeth, and the lips formed a natural mouth. Flashing green eyes lost their glow, and on its face, dark fur receded from hairline and cheeks, revealing a handsome, clean-shaven face except for a goatee. Brandon Cole.

"Oh my God." Krista gasped.

Hugh stared down at the man. "I never knew who he was or what he looked like. Now it's truly finished."

"Poor Rosa. Oh!" She looked up at Hugh. "I wonder if any of his stories were true."

"At this point I don't know, nor do I care."

They turned away, and with Krista supporting Hugh, they walked toward his truck.

"Now tell me your secret."

Krista smiled. "You're a smart man. Figure it out."

"We're to be parents?"

She nodded.

"I never dared to hope. The priest said you were the last of the line, so I—"

"I'm the last *female* in the line."

"You mean . . ." He touched her belly with reverence. "It's a boy? I'll have a son?"

Laughing, she nodded. "You have a son."

He stopped stared down at her. "Will it be normal?"

"Normal?"

"As in all human."

"I have no idea, but whatever he is, whatever features he carries, he'll be loved."

With a human yell of delight, Hugh swept her into his arms and, with moonbeams bathing their figures in silver light, he carried her to his SUV.

"Let's go home and celebrate our son."

Thank you for reading *From the Painted Tomb*.

I hope you enjoyed your time in the beautiful state of West Virginia and, along with me, loved the time in Egypt, land of the ancient gods.

If you did like the story, please leave a review on Amazon. Even a one-liner, such as 'I loved the story' makes a difference. Not only does it help others to decide to read it, but it helps me, as an author, with my Amazon ranking. I need your help!

Thank you.

ABOUT ME

Brenda Hill loves things that go bump in the night whether they're serial killers or other strange creatures. She has written about those pesky people who intrude on our lives with deadly force in her suspense novels.

She's still writing about those pesky people/creatures, but with her paranormals, they're in a slightly different form. *The House on Serpent Lake* is a ghost/love story - with a slight twist. And her latest, *From the Painted Tomb*, follows an immortal shape-shifter from ancient Egypt.

Raised in the South, she lives in the Inland Empire of Southern CA, but longs for cool ocean breezes, the forests and clean air of the northern areas of the States, but can do without mosquitoes and horseflies. The bonus? Her son and his family. So here she stays. She enjoys hearing from her readers. You can send an email from her website: **BrendaHill.com**

Follow her on Facebook:
http://www.facebook.com/brenda.hill.33

Bonus Excerpt:

The House on Serpent Lake: A Haunting Story of Timeless Love

THE HOUSE ON SERPENT LAKE:
He Waits For Her to be Reborn

The Intruder

The Past
Crosby, MN

A brief hushed whisper floated up the stairs and disturbed the young woman's dreams.

Frida Peterson woke.

Listening intently, she lay in the feathered bed and wondered what she'd heard. From the window, the normal night sounds from the north woods behind the house were in full concert — chirping crickets, buzzing katydids, and from the marshy area skirting Serpent Lake in front of the house, frogs bellowed, the cacophony of their sawing, hiccupping noise almost drowning out the other sounds.

But nothing out of the ordinary.

She listened a few more minutes, then closed her eyes and tried to go back to sleep.

Then she heard it again. A woman's soft moan, a

sound so out of the ordinary that she caught her breath. She sat up.

Who could be making those sounds in her parents' home? The only other women who lived in the house were her mother, her adopted sister Berina, and Tilly, the maid. Her mother and father were visiting her aunt in St. Cloud over seventy miles away, and Berina had gone to bed early this evening. To finish her library book, she'd said, something about a cattle ranching family in Texas. Tilly was in her fifties, and the sound had come from a much younger woman.

Frida slid out of bed, crept across the hardwood floor, and cracked open the door. After several minutes of silence, she began to think it was her imagination, but just as she turned to go back to bed, she heard a soft thump, then a man's curse.

Someone was in the house.

Her brother? It couldn't be. He'd recently married and he and his wife lived in Deerwood on the other side of the lake. Besides, he wouldn't visit in the middle of the night.

She stood so still she barely breathed. Who was it? What did he want? Crosby had always been a peaceful town, and she had grown up feeling safe. Why would someone want to break into her parent's home?

Maybe he wanted to rob them. Her father was president of the bank in Crosby; maybe the intruder thought he kept money at the house. With her parents away, tonight would be the best time to take it.

What could she do? At eighteen and the oldest, she was in charge. She could call the town policeman, but the phone was downstairs in the parlor. She could scream, but since their house sat on an isolated lakefront clearing a quarter-mile from town, no one would hear her.

A muffled cry shot upstairs.

It sounded like Berina.

Frida hurried down the hallway and threw open the door to her sister's empty bedroom.

He had Berina!

Stumbling on her long nightgown, Frida ran to the gun case on the landing, her unbound hair flying behind her, and yanked open the door with such force that it slammed against the wall. Glass shattered. She froze, listening. He had to have heard the noise.

She didn't have much time. She bypassed her father's rifles and grabbed her six-shot revolver, a handful of .22 bullets, and loaded them as she flew down the oak stairs. She just prayed she wasn't too late.

"I'm coming, Berina!"

Loud whispers and scuffling sounds came from the parlor.

She ran into the room. There, beside the divan, a man with his back to her was adjusting his shirt. Berina sat up, crying and buttoning the top of her nightgown.

Frida pointed the gun and fired three rounds into the man's back.

Everything froze. Even the night creatures went silent.

Berina screamed.

The man stiffened, turned and faced her, his face frozen in shock. Like a fan folding in on itself, he slowly crumpled to the floor. Berina, her face and gown splattered with blood, screamed and fell beside him, gently cradling the man's head in her arms.

Tilly rushed into the room, tying her chenille robe.

"Oh, missy, what have you done?"

Soundlessly, her eyes wide, Frida stared at the bloodied man's face. The gun fell from her hand and hit the oak floor.

A sound, a wailing, keening cry of agony filled the room. She didn't know if it came from Berina or from her.

Galen, the man she loved with all her heart, the man she was to marry in three weeks, was dead.

Chapter One

The Present
Crosby, MN

Something about the abandoned old house struck Lindsay Peterson as familiar.

It sat about a quarter-mile past the modern homes lining Serpent Lake, off a deeply-rutted trail skirting the aspens and pines of the Minnesota north woods.

Eric drove closer, Lindsay shading her eyes against the setting sun's glare on the lake. Beyond low-hanging branches, she could see the two-story house and several outbuildings in a clearing by the water.

"We're here." Her husband guided the rented Blazer along the ruts to a detached garage. "I know it's been a long day, but let's take a quick look before it gets dark." He killed the engine and lowered the windows.

Mosquitoes invaded the car and whined around Lindsay's head. When one lit on her arm, she slapped it and wiped the blood speck with a tissue.

BRENDA HILL

Eric bounded out of the car as if his aunts were still waiting to welcome him, but Lindsay sat frozen, her gaze moving over the house, lingering at the large side window. She knew that house, knew how the rooms were arranged, knew how it felt to wake each morning with her window overlooking the woods in the back of the house. She caught phantom aromas of fresh biscuits from the oven, the huge lilac bushes around the outhouse coupled with the earthy scent of the water.

She nearly wept with longing.

"Come on," Eric said, waiting for her in front of the car. "Aren't you curious?"

At the sound of his voice, the déjà vu dissipated, floating away as if it were a dream she couldn't quite remember.

Frowning, she looked back at the house, which was now simply neglected property her husband had inherited. This was her first trip to Minnesota, so she couldn't know anything about the house and grounds. She must have seen pictures or Eric must have described his childhood home so thoroughly she felt she knew every detail.

That's all it was, wasn't it?

Firmly pushing away her doubts, she emerged from the car. After the long flight from the west coast, followed by another three-hour shuttle from the Minneapolis airport, all she wanted was a hot meal and a comfortable bed at the motel. But Eric was his aunt's only surviving relative and Lindsay wanted to support her husband even if it meant touring the dilapidated property at dusk.

She stepped onto an overgrown lawn littered with twigs and bits of pinecones and followed her husband through thick patches of dandelions gone to seed. Wisps of soft white fuzz floated in the air.

The house hadn't fared any better. Curls of white paint hung over blackened windows, and bare rotting wood spread under chipped paint.

"I don't understand it," Eric said, forging ahead, his long legs cutting through tall grass to the front of the property. "It's such a nice place, at least it used to be. I wonder what happened?"

Following him, Lindsay couldn't venture a guess, especially when she spotted the fully-screened front porch facing the water. True, it might be sagging, but it fronted two-hundred feet of sandy beach and the tree-lined lake. How ideal it all seemed, even with the house in its current state of disrepair.

"Maybe your aunt failed to make arrangements for caretakers after moving to the nursing home," she said.

"Aunt Frida wouldn't forget. Grandpa built this place, even cleared the land himself, and she'd never let it deteriorate. Besides, her attorney was supposed to take care of all that." Hands on his hips, he considered the house. "I just hope the inside is okay. All hardwood floors and a huge rock fireplace. You'll love it. Aunt Frida used to tell stories about Grandpa searching the countryside for just the right stones."

"It doesn't look vandalized," Lindsay said. "Just

neglected. But we'll find out when we pick up the keys in the morning."

Eric headed toward a faded log building about twenty feet from the house. A rusty shovel leaned against the side, its splintered wooden handle enclosed in cobwebs.

"The old storage shed." He jiggled the lock. When it fell open, he disappeared inside. Lindsay smiled, her pride in her husband overriding her fatigue.

He was such a nice-looking man, one of the lucky ones who improved with age. At forty-seven and even with a little thickening at the waist, his bearing was proud and strong.

And he was tall enough so she didn't tower over him, something she'd agonized over since her teenage years. Once again, she thanked the fates for bringing them together two years ago. After a failed three-year marriage in her early youth, she hadn't bothered with much of anything except raising her son — until she met Eric and the world came alive.

She lifted her face to the gentle breeze that whispered across the lake, stirring leaves in the oak trees and gently ruffling her hair.

Suddenly, as though eyes were watching her, little prickles chilled the back of her neck. Whirling around, she stared at the darkened windows in the house, but she saw nothing except the black panes standing as sentries, guarding the house's secrets.

Eric emerged from the shed and closed the squeaky door and joined her on the beach.

She glanced back at the house and it seemed

normal. Old, in need of repair, but normal.

Eric brushed cobwebs from his shoulders. "Pretty well cleaned out except for some old tools. Strange, though. Someone's half-eaten lunch and an old rusted thermos were splattered on the floor. Someone left in a hurry."

Another mosquito lit on her forearm. "Mosquitoes probably got them," she said, slapping it, wishing she'd worn her jacket on the trip instead of the short-sleeved linen pantsuit.

"Don't you like it?"

"Mosquitoes the size of pigeons and a decaying old house. What's not to like?"

"Oh." His disappointment was evident and Lindsay's heart melted.

"I was teasing, honey. Of course I like it. You know I've always wanted to live next to the water. It'll make a great vacation home and I can't wait." She leaned forward to give him a kiss, but before she could touch him, a sudden gust of wind blew off the lake, swirling sand and leaves in the air. Bits of grit peppered Eric's face. The wind rushed over the grounds, moaning as it whooshed through the house.

Just as suddenly, it died.

"What was that?" Lindsay asked, staring at the house.

Eric rubbed his eyes. "Lots of breezes from the lake. Cools things down in summer."

"That wasn't a breeze, that was a gale. You okay?" She brushed his lips with hers, but instead of returning the kiss, he broke contact and backed away.

"I'll check the house," he mumbled, avoiding her eyes. "It's probably locked, but I'll give it a try. Then we can go." He cut away from her and raced across the lawn. She wished she could laugh at his hasty retreat. Instead, she nearly cried.

Was he more upset about losing his aunt than she'd thought? After all, Frida was the last living link to his family. But no, she had noticed his withdrawal months earlier.

Even though she didn't want to admit it, something was wrong in their marriage.

As a computer consultant to large corporations all over Southern California, he traveled two to three days a week, and his homecoming was cause for celebration. During the first few months of their marriage, she'd take time off from the art gallery she owned and they'd loved and played like newlyweds.

But that had gradually changed.

She couldn't say exactly when it had happened, but he began volunteering for every trip that came up. And when he was home, he acted strangely . . . distant. He'd avoid coming to bed until she was asleep.

Was it something she'd done, or did he no longer find her attractive? He had assured her nothing was wrong, that he'd just been working too many hours. They needed the extra income, he'd said, for a down payment on a house large enough for both their children to visit. Their condo was only a one bedroom, so it sounded reasonable. But the distance between them had not improved.

Shrieking gulls caught her attention. She watched them circle over the water and dive for a meal.

The sun dipped behind the tree-lined west shore, and in the growing dusk, the sky burned a fiery red. Clouds picked up the glow, painting long crimson streaks as far as she could see. Below, their mirror images danced on the gentle swells of the water. Lindsay didn't know if she'd ever seen anything so beautiful.

What a haven this could be, miles from the pressures of Eric's work. They could rediscover each other and put the fire back into their marriage.

Lindsay pictured the house freshly painted and the grounds trimmed and neat. Finally, a true home of her own, something she had always wanted but never thought she'd have.

Growing up with a single mother who moved every couple of years, never knowing a home or family except for distant grandparents, her life had always seemed empty. When her first husband came along and professed to love her, she'd hastily married. Then, except for her son, emptiness again. And now this house and grounds. Even neglected it represented love and strong family roots.

They'd paint it white, like it used to be, with black trim around the windows, and . . . *used to be?* Where had that thought come from?

She must have seen photos.

A swing would be perfect, exactly right for those

quiet evenings at home. She was scanning the porch for the perfect spot when suddenly, a curious sadness began, spreading into a grief so strong and heavy that her knees almost buckled under the weight. Tears spilled onto her cheeks.

Bewildered, she brushed them away and stared at the house. What would cause her to feel such sorrow? Was it because it had been a home for a family, and she was afraid she was losing hers?

Eric cut across the lawn to join her.

"Locked pretty tight," he said, his voice breaking the spell.

With one last puzzled glance at the house, Lindsay turned to her husband. His expression somber, he crouched down to the sand, picked up a couple of small brown shells and threw them into the water. She wished he would talk to her, tell her what was troubling him.

"Honey, please talk to me, let me in —"

"I love you, you know," he interrupted. "Just let that be enough." Even crouching, his entire body seemed to sag, and his eyes held none of the roguish twinkle that used to be such a part of him.

Was his anguish due to some problem in their marriage he felt reluctant to discuss with her? But they'd talked openly about everything, including her anxiety-ridden childhood. Or was it something else?

Whatever it was, she'd give him the benefit of the doubt — at least until he recovered from his aunt's passing.

"Okay," she said. "We'll drop it. For now."

His relief was obvious. "Let's check into the motel and get something to eat."

"Eat first. I'm starved."

Just as Eric swung around to head down the dirt road, something in an upstairs window caught her eye. A subtle outline, as if someone were watching them.

"Honey . . ."

He finished the turn.

"What?"

Lindsay twisted in her seat and looked back at the window. Whatever she saw was gone.

"Nothing."

It was only the setting sun reflecting off the glass, creating distorted images that weren't really there.

Chapter Two

Minutes later, they entered Crosby, a former iron mining town spruced up with green awnings and antique stores. Lindsay caught a glimpse of Serpent Lake between Main Street's city blocks and thought how lucky the residents were to have a lake on one side of town and a forest on the other.

But at eight in the evening, the six-block downtown area was dark and deserted except for a convenience store with two gas pumps in front and a video rental place further down the street.

"Hope something is open," Lindsay said, scanning the buildings. A nice dinner and a glass of wine would be heaven after an entire day of traveling.

Lights brightened the inside of one cafe, but according to the sign, it was due to close in ten minutes. Maybe they could order something and take it to the motel.

Inside, the smell of grease and old cigarette smoke hung in the air. Two men in jeans and baseball caps sat at the counter, talking and laughing over slices of pie. A thin, wrinkled woman occupied a booth, her short white hair spiking in all directions, a pink quilted jacket hugging her emaciated body. A radio played country music, and a blackboard listed the day's specials. Most had been crossed out with chalk.

Eric and Lindsay took a booth by a window overlooking Main Street. A waitress about forty, in jeans and a sleeveless blouse, brought them water. *Shirley,* her nametag read. She recommended the hot beef sandwiches.

"Real mashed potatoes," she told them, patting her elaborately fashioned French twist hairstyle. "Peeled them myself. And we have fresh apple pie. Made that, too."

"Do we have time for all that?" Eric asked.

"Sure," Shirley said. "I got to clean up. Besides, I wouldn't throw you out."

One of the men at the counter looked up. "I wouldn't be too sure about that. She's got a mean right hand."

"You should know, George," Shirley said.

Both men laughed.

"You folks passing through?" Shirley asked, scribbling on her order pad.

"We're here about some property I inherited," Eric told her.

"Really?" She arched her penciled eyebrows. "Ain't that nice. Where at?"

"Just out of town. From my aunt, Frida Peterson."

Everything went silent, even the conversation at the counter stopped.

The faint click of the diner's ventilation system

switching on sounded like a bass drum in the sudden silence. Cool air blew on Lindsay from above.

Shirley stopped writing. "The old Peterson place?"

"You know it?" Eric said.

"I've heard of it," the waitress mumbled, glancing at the old woman.

The look they exchanged was strangely intense. The men at the counter dropped some change by their plates and left without speaking.

"Well, your dinner will be right up." No longer smiling, Shirley passed their orders to the kitchen, then became busy wiping the counter. The old woman rose to pay her bill, all the while staring at Eric and Lindsay. She didn't return their smiles.

"What happened?" Lindsay whispered.

Eric shrugged. "Guess it's closing time."

Lindsay was opening her car door when the old woman from the diner rushed over to them and grabbed her hand.

"What is it?" she asked.

The wrinkled eyes bored into her so intently that Lindsay was unable to look away. The old woman finally spoke, her dentures clicking in her thin face.

"Stay away from that house! Evil lives there."

www.ingramcontent.com/pod-product-compliance
Lightning Source LLC
Chambersburg PA
CBHW031416240626
47154CB00001B/67